I0639570

Initiation

By Robert Hugh Benson

Once-and-Future Books

For more fiction by Robert Hugh Benson,visit
www.benson-unabridged.com

Initiation was originally published in 1914

ISBN: 978-1-60210-009-1

Cover by R. L. Brohawn

Table of Contents

Foreword to

Initiation

That the Christian can, precisely by his pain, be in Christ, and in a sense, *be* Christ, and effect Christ's own work, is the ascetical secret beyond which, in reality, none other lies.[1]

Like many sensitive people with vivid imaginations, Robert Hugh Benson could not contemplate the idea of physical suffering with anything other than fear, as he admitted on a number of occasions. Even writing of it in his novels caused similar sensations in his own body — a phenomenon that psychologists call "sympathetic pain." In the process of composing his historical novels he deliberately tried to imagine himself undergoing the same tortures as the martyrs to such effect that "he was 'conscious of very distinct, even slightly painful, sensations in his (own) wrists and ankles.'"[2]

It surprised him more than anyone else, then, when after a serious and painful operation on January 2, 1913, he was able to exclaim to a visitor, "*Have* you ever had a severe operation? No? *Do*! It's such an experience!"[3] Evidently his expressed enthusiasm led to the legend that he underwent the operation without anesthesia. This is untrue, but he did refuse morphia after the operation when he found that the narcotic made him sicker. As he related to another friend, "I was not *in* Pain; Pain and I were looking at each other, and he came nearer and nearer till he was upon me with a blue flash of agony."[4]

His experience with real pain seems to have been something of a release for him, for he was able immediately to say, "Do you know what I said under the anesthetic? Nothing but 'Oh, God.' The nurses thought it was so pious! But *it wasn't pious*. It was a swear!"[5] It was also a revelation. As Martindale related,

---

[1] C. C. Martindale, *The Life of Monsignor Robert Hugh Benson, Vol. II.* London: Longmans, Green and Co., 1917, 357.

[2] *Ibid.*, 355.

[3] *Ibid.*

[4] *Ibid.*, 356.

[5] *Ibid.*

He loved to discuss its details. "The most annoying part of it to me," a friend, who had also been operated upon, said to him soon after it, "is that you'll write a book about yours, and pay all your expenses out of it." "Much more than pay them!" he gleefully retorted; "and *the book's nearly finished.*"[6]

That book, of course, is *Initiation*, the last of Benson's "mainstream" novels to see publication in his lifetime.

Initiation is, first and foremost, an examination of the paradox of the healing effects of pain. Not that this was in any way morbid. All his life Benson was fascinated with pain and the fear he felt for it. As Martindale explained, however, Benson seems to have been able to sublimate this fear and direct it into useful channels:

> . . . his singularly practical tendency always forced him at once to register and *use* it for some outside end, nor suffered him to hug it and live with it interiorly. And his extreme sanity of natural life kept him outside even the dangerous tendencies of religious asceticism. All cruelty he hated, and saw its wrongness, even when he, in some sense, was its victim.

"I hate cruelty more than anything in the whole world," he wrote to Mr. Rolfe,[7] "and find injustice or offensiveness to myself or anyone else the hardest of all things to forgive."[8]

What, however, of the case of a victim of pain who refuses to use it properly, who in fact rejects it utterly? That is the plot of *Initiation*.

The hero — or, rather, victim — of *Initiation* is Sir Neville Fanning. He is a baronet, the lowest rank of English nobility, and a "cradle Catholic," taking both his station in life and his religion very much for granted. He is, as we might expect, a sufferer from the malaise that Benson saw afflicting virtually all upper class English, whether Catholic or Protestant: purposelessness.

---

[6] *Ibid.*, 185.

[7] Evidently from a note written some time before Benson wrote *Initiation*, for he had broken with the notorious Frederick Rolfe ("Baron Corvo") five years previously.

[8] Martindale, Vol. II, 356.

Sir Neville does not even do very much with regard to managing his estates, leaving much of it to his aunt, Anna Fanning (his father's sister-in-law), a widow whose young son, Jim, is Sir Neville's "heir apparent." As the result of a distaste for the obviously plebian origins and behavior of his admittedly cloddish parish priest, Sir Neville does not even set a good example for those of his tenants who are Catholic, holding Father Richardson in open contempt.

While on vacation in Italy, Sir Neville meets a young girl, Enid Bessington, who is accompanying her mother on their annual Grand Tour of the Continent. He is amused — to a degree — by Mrs. Bessington, a woman who never seems to stop talking and yet who never seems to say anything. On a daytrip to Frascati, near Rome, he and Enid exchange confidences, discovering that they seem to have the same attitude towards pain and cruelty.

It seems that Sir Neville has recently become increasingly afflicted with extremely severe headaches. His aunt and his physician have urged him to submit to examination by a specialist. There has, however, been a slight diminution in their frequency and severity. Sir Neville decided that a jaunt to Italy (where he could ignore the headaches) would be much better for his mental and physical health. He declares, "I can't fit that kind of thing into my philosophy. I try to bear them decently, of course; but I don't submit in the slightest. I resent that kind of thing furiously, exactly as I resent cruelty to animals." During a walk they come across a small shrine in the woods.

It was a particularly realistic *Pietà*.

Behind the wire netting that was stretched across its face there was the group of the Mother and Son, painted in crude colors, lately renovated. The Mother, in an indigo cloak, sitting with upraised face, supported the ghastly Body across her knees. The hands and feet ran with crimson; the mouth appeared to grin in a horrible contortion; the limbs were grotesquely elongated and emaciated. Stuck into the meshes of the wiring in front was a small bunch of wilted dandelions. The whole picture was painted in fresco on plaster that had peeled in places; and was half-sheltered by a broken pent-roof of stone.

The two looked at it in silence. They moved on, still in silence. Then the boy broke out.

"There!" he said. "That was exactly what I meant! I think such things are perfectly horrible! What possible good can that do to anyone? It's completely out of harmony too. The very colors are wrong. And, besides, why put it in the woods where things are fresh and clean? And that's exactly why I don't like talking about my headaches."

Ultimately they decide, as Enid declares, that "Pain's a kind of physical sin, don't you think?" As "Part I" of *Initiation* ends, Sir Neville's headaches have become much less severe and have decreased in frequency. He and Enid have returned to England, become engaged to be married, and are facing a very bright future.

There is, however, something of a dark cloud lowering over Sir Neville that (in keeping with his resolute rejection of pain and other unpleasantness) he steadfastly refuses to see. It seems that the almost cruelly honest Jim, with the perspicuity of some children, doesn't like Miss Bessington, of whom he receives a full dose when Enid and her mother pay a visit to Sir Neville's estate. Although she tries to cover it up, Miss Bessington is mean to Jim's collies, Jack and Jill, getting them banished to the stable. She is also artificially "nice" to him, in the way that adults who don't like children often are, and which children are usually quick to detect.

Neither does Aunt Anna, Jim's mother, care very much for her nephew's intended, although she tries very hard to like her. Enid has, however, exhibited a casual cruelty to her own mother, which Neville (although he observed the same thing in Italy) has managed to explain away.

In Part II, as we might expect, Sir Neville's headaches suddenly begin to get worse and (in a move that surprised even Benson, whose original outline for the novel went in a different direction) he is jilted by Enid. It turns out that where Sir Neville's religious indifference is the result of a refusal to acquiesce in God's having given him everything but physical health, Enid's is due to a psychotic selfishness, a condition approaching actual insanity, and which has been responsible for her having destroyed the lives of everyone around her and now, for the second time, of her sabotaging her own chance at happiness by terminating an engagement in a violent temper tantrum over a trivial incident. Sir Neville tries to ignore pain because he refuses to accept the fact of what it is doing to him. Enid ignores pain because she refuses to accept what she is doing to others.

Mrs. Bessington (Enid's mother) is transformed from the ridiculous and rather annoying chatterbox of Part I into one of the most tragic figures in any of Benson's novels. Clearly lacking the mental equipment or spiritual training either to accept or rise above the pain inflicted by her daughter's insane cruelty, she simply bears it and hides behind a constant barrage of nonsensical talk.

Initiation also contains one of Benson's most puzzling creations, Mr. Morpeth, a recent convert from Protestantism who is renting the Dower House on Sir Neville's estate. While obviously of common birth, and a retired businessman with absolutely no pretensions to nobility, Mr. Morpeth is, at the same time, one of Benson's noblest characters. He is quiet, humble, and calm, and has the expressed intent (confided in Anna Fanning) of spending the rest of his life deepening his relationship to God and making up for neglecting his daughter when she was growing up.

Part of Mr. Morpeth's function in the novel, of course, is to offer a contrast to the equally plebian Father Richardson. Father Richardson has an extremely exaggerated opinion of his own importance, far beyond what a good priest should have, and a shocking lack of humility. While chastising Sir Neville for his bad example (which, as Sir Neville's parish priest, is his duty), Father Richardson handles the whole thing very badly, and merely succeeds in increasing Sir Neville's contempt for him:

> "You are very seldom at Benediction," said the priest desperately. (He began to see that he was in a tight corner; but it would never do to acknowledge it, he thought. His dignity might suffer. His motto, as he had confided to his fellow priests more than once, was "Never apologize.")

Things come to such a pass that Sir Neville instructs his servants that he is "not home" when the priest calls, even though the Rectory is on the very edge of the estate, within sight of the manor.

Mr. Morpeth remains something of a puzzle. As chief confi-
dant and informal advisor to Aunt Anna, he assists her in
overcoming a very slight tendency to blame God for her
nephew's sufferings. That, however, could have been handled
by another character, such as her son Jim with the unconscious wisdom of childhood, or even by Aunt Anna herself
with a little un-Bensonlike introspection.

There is a possibility that Benson intended Mr. Morpeth to
be a model for his readers, an example of how to deal with
his own death. As a result of his operation, Benson seems to
have had an intimation of his own mortality, and a sense
that his own life was drawing to a close — as it did, less than
two years later. Just as Sir Neville's sufferings reflected his
own, Benson may have had the idea that Mr. Morpeth's acceptance of his own daughter's sudden death and his calm
reassurances to Aunt Anna as that of Sir Neville seemed
imminent would serve as an example as to how he wanted
his readers to behave.

Mr. Morpeth, however, sets an impossible example. He is a
"full initiate" and is able to accept his daughter's death with
a calm sorrow for the opportunities he will now not have to
make up for his earlier neglect, but also a certain solemn joy
that he was able to do what little he could. He exhibits no
change in demeanor or behavior after his daughter's death,
but takes everything with perfect resignation to God's Will.

Naturally there is much more than this in the novel. Benson did not omit his usual satirical jabs at the English upper
classes. Another one of Benson's delightful characters appears in *Initiation*, Lord Maresfield, who — because he finds
English country house life stupefyingly dull and pointless —
sets out to find a purpose in life and finds it in art (and polo,
what? "But I'm giving up polo.").

Lord Maresfield knows he's not a very good artist ("I splash
about a bit"), but that's not the idea. The fact is that he likes
it, finds it fulfilling . . . and it has enraged his father to the
point where his father and family have apparently cast him
off completely. Lord Maresfield is also, in a small way, a
much more genial version of Mr. Morpeth, offering unexpected comfort and just the right amount of concern at exactly the right times. The reader quickly comes to the conclusion that Lord Maresfield, for all his self-proclaimed "idle-

ness," lives the sort of purpose-driven life that leisure should bestow.

Then there are the Americans, a nation and people for whom it was fashionable to affect a certain disdain . . . unless your daughter happened to snag a rich one. The Heckers, a couple of extremely rich Americans, exhibit this laudable trait of having purpose in life. Being rich (there doesn't appear to be any other kind of American in the English fiction of this period, unless you count the uncouth but good-hearted frontiersman, usually the sidekick of the rich young American) they have come to Europe in search of "culture." Charles Dana Gibson made a career satirizing this phenomenon in his art (the "Gibson Girl" is nearly always caught in the act of spending father's money on some expensive bauble, gown, or social event), but Benson saw in it "American get-up-and-go" applied to the problem of what to do with your life once you had the wealth (gained through honest work instead of inheritance) to enjoy it.

The Heckers clearly do not view participation in social activities as a duty, although Mr. Hecker puts on the expected show of the poor husband being dragged around to plays and museums by "the wife" — and at the same time is obviously enjoying himself. While they would not have characterized it in this fashion, the Heckers are engaged in what Abraham Maslow called "self-realization," that is, getting to work on developing as persons.

In contrast, the English upper classes (in this and other Benson novels) are just as obviously pursuing social and cultural activities as ends in themselves, because they believe it is expected of them; it is their purpose in life. The Heckers put on a good show, but it's clear that it's not because it's expected of them (they are, after all, uncouth *Americans*) — they do it because they want to. Their crudely ostentatious party (which Lord Maresfield enjoys immensely and Enid despises) is a means to an end, not an end in itself.

Ultimately, of course, *Initiation* is not about pain, or death, or even the purposelessness of the English upper classes. It is, again, about *vocation* — about discerning the path God wants us to take to Him. As Martindale observed,

> In this book, then, Benson stated his doctrine that it may be Pain which awakens a man's soul when nothing else can, though of course he did not prove it. Easily it

can be argued that Pain may contract, numb, cripple, or embitter a soul, and drive it into disbelief, cynicism, or despair. He would not deny this; but simply showed you a case in which Pain had proved successful. That is the artist's privilege. Grant me, he demands, the elements I ask; I will mix them, and add another, and I defy you to quarrel with the results. . . . He will agree that not every soul is worthy of Pain. Not indiscriminately will God grant His privilege of suffering. God permit no winds to blow which might quench a flickering wick, and refuses the shock which breaks the enfeebled reed. But, granting a soul of royal quality, Pain, he teaches, all but infallibly must perfect it. The Crucified is there for proof; to Him the true Christian asks but to be assimilated. Convinced of this, he wrote the book at ease and flowingly. And I think he could have pointed to its verification in his own experience. I have felt, and his more intimate friends have largely corroborated this, that his operation marks in him a real stage of spiritual development. At last boyhood was over. Maturity seemed to have arrived or to be swift upon the road. . . . "Pain," I have already quoted from him, "is a vocation like another."

— Michael D. Greaney, editor

Initiation

Part I

Chapter I

Sir Nevill Fanning was doing at least three things at once, in the private dining room of the Hotel Emanuele in the Via Veneto in the City of Rome. He was eating an excellent luncheon, he was observing his fellow guests, and he was giving as much attention to Mrs. Bessington's conversation as that lady required.

It cannot be said that Mrs. Bessington was easy to talk to; in fact, that was an impossible feat. He had tried it in the first days of his acquaintance with her, and even now, when he forgot, tried it still. But he had found that she neither needed his remarks, nor even wished for them; all she required was silence, noddings of the head, and very occasional assents or monosyllabic questions. She did all the rest. It was a little stupefying at first to be pelted with such an interminable torrent of words; he had at first resisted a little, seriously believing that she might possibly wish to hear what he had to say; then he had grown a little impatient; and then the divine gift of humor had saved him; and henceforth — (except, as has been said, when he forgot) — he sat still, now marveling at the spate of talk that flowed forth so sedately, now deliberately thinking about other things, now, occasionally, playing a sort of intellectual solitaire which consisted in counting her full stops — (there had only been five during the whole of the curried-egg course, from the moment she took up her fork to the moment she laid it down again) — and once, with an exquisite joy, switching her on to the Marchioness Daly, his hostess, who sat on his left, and whose horsepower, so to speak, very nearly, but not quite, rivaled Mrs. Bessington's.

He believed that she was talking now about a cousin of hers who lived in Corfu; but he was not sure. If it was not she, it was Selva, the actress, who was in Rome just now. Certainly a female cousin had been mentioned a while ago, and so had Corfu; but an aunt had shot up from the horizon once or twice, and he was not certain therefore as to which occupied the place of honor at present. A Scotch maid of hers too — called MacPherson — (not the Scotch maid she had now, but another one) — had certainly been spoken of; but it surely could not be she who was now curtsying to the late King of Greece and tripping over her train as she did so.

"Most interesting," said Sir Nevill, bringing his eyes back from their excursion. "How very —"

"Ah! But that's not the end," pursued Mrs. Bessington, undismayed. "It was a fortnight after that; no, it couldn't have been that fortnight, because I know she caught influenza from having to wait about for the carriage, and was laid up for three weeks; it must have been. . . ."

She was off again; and once more the young man began to look gingerly about him.

He could not quite make out his hostess. He had a lamentable habit of pigeonholing his new acquaintances; and each pigeonhole had a little label over it, with a sort of inscription. Into these, then, he was accustomed to place people. At first he had been inclined, in view of their common possession of an almost infinite store of words and opinions on every subject, to place the Papal Marchioness and Mrs. Bessington together. They both talked unceasingly: they both wore a glassy expression of inattention when anyone compelled them to listen in return. The encounter between the two had been a glorious experience; he had been stung by the splendor of the prospect; and had wondered which would win. It was the ancient dilemma of striking impenetrable armor with a sword that could pierce everything. He had blinked a little as the two ladies discharged their conversational hoses across him; but he had enjoyed it. Mrs. Bessington had won; the impenetrability of her inattention had prevailed over the shrill and ceaseless arrows of the Marchioness' high voice; and she had been left discoursing on her favorite clergyman at the American Episcopal church, while the Marchioness sulked.

But he was beginning to discern a difference between them. Mrs. Bessington was always amiable; she never, gravely, attacked people's characters; she was harmless and bland, though quite shrewd in her opinions; while the Marchioness had an undercurrent of acidity, and seemed to take a kind of peevish delight in discerning, and thrusting a pin through, little cracks and holes in reputations. He saw that, plainly now. It was evident that they could not be put into the same pigeonhole. Superficially they might have been twins; fundamentally, they were not even sisters.

He scarcely knew how he happened to be here today. He had come out all alone to Rome, three weeks ago, without realizing the potency of his name in the Visitors' List. Then the cards had begun. He had rashly returned some of these calls; and had even accepted an invitation to tea at which two Cardinals were to be present; and there he had found himself a lion in a den of Daniels. The Cardinals had been magnificent, of course, grave princely men, extremely gracious to this young Catholic baronet, and seeming to understand that he, no more than themselves, really liked this screaming parrot house.

One of them had even bidden him use his name with Monsignor Bisletti, if he should wish for a private audience with the Holy Father.

"But, of course, Sir Nevill," he had added, with scarcely a trace of an Italian accent, "you will find no difficulty in any case."

But the rest of the company he did not like so much. It was not that it was different from any other similar company elsewhere; people screamed and gossiped and smelt of furs and eau-de-Cologne, there were meek and trim young men with shining hair, there were tiresome old men who bellowed, there were shy girls, fully as much in London as in Rome. Only he had not expected it in Rome, somehow. He had had a faint idea that things would be primitive and quiet here, that he could moon about and look at Basilicas now and then, that he could poke round in curiosity shops — in a word, that he could be free here, as he could not in London. And he had found the same old parrot house.

It was at this tea party that the Marquis Daly had captured him, and introduced him to his wife; and it was here that she had asked him to choose any day in the following week to come to lunch, so soon as she had first caught him saying that he was going to Frascati, but hadn't settled which day.

"Then you shall lunch with us first, if you will, Sir Nevill; choose your own day. And we will all go out to Frascati together."

Well, here he was. He did not in the least wish to go out to
Frascati with all these people; but there was no escape. Here
he was; and Mrs. Bessington was telling him about her
cousin in Corfu: he was sure now that it could not have been
Miss MacPherson. Meanwhile he was observing the company.

(2)

It had better be said at once that there was a single star in
all this gloom of well-disguised boredom; and the name of the
star was Enid, who sat opposite him. The Bessingtons,
Mother and daughter, had been present when the Marchioness had cornered him four days ago; and the fact that Mrs.
Bessington had added that Enid also wished to see Frascati
again, had been the one consideration that had prevented
him from being rather rude to the Marchioness, and saying,
untruthfully, that, after all, it wasn't Frascati, but Tivoli,
and that he had promised to go with someone else.

He had brought her an ice a few minutes before, and had
sat by her, himself eating another; and she had been to him
for five minutes like a breath of air in a stuffy room.

First she was extremely pretty, but this, honestly, was not
the point. The point was that she had been cool and refreshing and quiet — entirely at her ease, though she could not be
more than nineteen — and had said one or two odd little
things that had been intimate without being familiar. He had
forgotten what they were; they were of no importance; but he
had perceived that she knew what he was feeling, and that
she felt like it too. Then a Princess had wished him to be presented to her, and the thing had ended, until the invitation;
and he had accepted that invitation, aware that he would
have prevaricated himself out of it if he had not talked to
Enid first.

She was nearly opposite him now. She seemed even pret-
tier than he had thought her. She had heavy brown hair, an
extremely clear, pale complexion, big gray eyes and quiet
well-cut lips. She had a large black hat with primroses in it,
and a black lace dress; as she was still in mourning for her
father. He watched her hands once or twice; he had a theory
about hands, and they satisfied him. They were sufficiently
large, quite white and quite strong. Certainly it would be
pleasant to go with her to Frascati.

His eyes wandered along the other faces. Next to Enid, on the Marchioness' left, was an Italian priest, the Lenten preacher at a church in the Corso. Nevill did not make much of him; he was a new type to the young man — of a very rec-ollected and very well-bred air, as of a Guardsman who has become a seminarian. Incidentally, he was a Count in his own right; but Nevill, with truly British superiority, did not think much of Italian counts. The priest had been quite pol-ished, quite detached and rather superior, in the few words he had with him before they sat down. On the other side of Enid sat Mr. Hecker, an extremely wealthy American and the husband of Mrs. Hecker. These were his two discernible points; for Mrs. Hecker, who sat on Nevill's side of the table, at the further end, was one blaze of intelligence, so bright as to obscure all in her immediate circle. She was really aston-ishing, thought the boy — as brilliant, and as hard too, as electric light. He had talked to her a few minutes before lunch and she had summed up her impressions of Rome sim-ply admirably, touching exactly the right points — the small ancient dignity of the less known Basilicas, the flamboyant triumph of St. Peter's, and the "domino houses," as she called them, of the modern municipality. (Certainly these large white flat-faced buildings set with rows of even windows were extraordinarily like dominoes set on end; only it had not struck him before.)

Next to him, beyond Mrs. Bessington, was a sleek-haired young man of about his own age, Mr. Clough, who presented precisely the right front to all calls upon him, and who ap-peared to have nothing whatever behind his front. Nevill had put him away, all right, after three minutes, in a pigeonhole already full to bursting. Last but one opposite Mrs. Hecker was the Princess Mareschi, a small faded lady, rather like a pale Queen Victoria, quite plainly and even shabbily dressed, with an unmistakable dignity, who lived with her imbecile daughter in an enormous palace, the friend of Cardinals, blackest of the black, pious, zealous and resolute — a replica in an Italian disguise of unmarried Evangelical daughters and sisters of ancient English dukes, only she was a Catholic, and talked four languages with equal ease, and they but one. And last came the Marquis Daly himself, the host, whom Nevill had put straight into the pigeonhole that contained persons "not of his sort" (as he would have said), a brisk, anxious man, intensely absorbed in social ambitions and never quite at his ease anywhere — a Papal chamberlain, a Papal marquis, without children or estates, pathetically eager to entertain personages so long as they had any kind of claim to distinction and were not militantly anti-Catholic.

Such was the company. Nevill ran round them mentally once more, wondering when this interminable festivity would be over.

"— How very nice of her!" he said suddenly, perceiving a pause in Mrs. Bessington's conversation, and remembering again the word Corfu.

(3)

What Enid saw, as she made opportunity now and again between the remarks of her Italian priest and the quiet repressed sentences of her American, was a very bright fresh young man, black-haired and black-eyed, with an indefinable look of slight ill-health. She had liked him instantly, as soon as he had sat down beside her with his ice the other day, in the window seat, and had remarked how very odd it was that some ices were so much hotter than others.

"If you will consider it carefully," she had said, "with illustrations, I think you will find that it is entirely a matter of texture. It's the hard ones that are cold."

He had paused to reflect, with excellent gravity.

"That's perfectly true," he had said. "It never occurred to me before — the ones that are like frozen sandstone, aren't they? Now, about colors. Why is Cardinal's scarlet so extraordinarily like flame? Yet it's not the color of any flame I've ever seen."

(That was the kind of thing they said at first.)

He didn't seem at all bored today, either, in spite of his situation between the Marchioness and Enid's own mother. Enid had no illusions at all about her mother's conversation. For herself, she did not find it boring, because she had long ago established an understanding (as she would have called it) that she was to go her own way and not to be talked to like that; but she had watched others under it. This young man, however, seemed to preserve his elasticity well enough. Certainly his eyes roved a good deal, but always came back to attention in time. Twice their eyes had met; and she thought she had read a humorous good-temper into their glance, yet not enough to be offensive to her mother's daughter.

So much for his outward appearance. He seemed natural, breezy, and fresh, in spite of his rather delicate look: he was dressed properly in gray, with a little bunch of violets. She thought he looked *simpatico*.

What she knew about him was very nearly as important. She had learned it from overhearing her mother talking to other people.

First, he was a baronet, the fourth of the line, without brothers or sisters, and unmarried. He was aged twenty-three; he was an hereditary Catholic, and had been educated at Stonyhurst. His father had died four years ago; and his father's sister-in-law, a widow, had kept house ever since at Hartley, and was still doing so. This lady had one boy, called Jim, aged seven. Hartley was a fine place in Sussex; and there went with it another big house in Elizabeth Street. That was about the sum of it. Obviously he was a tolerably wealthy man. There were innumerable other details too, which her mother had spread abroad; but these were unimportant. For instance, it was said that he was rather delicate and suffered from headaches; that though a Catholic, he was not at all bigoted; that his father had been no better than he should be, though he too had died in the Faith; that he was just five feet and eleven and a half inches tall in his stocking feet; that he had broken the Public-school record for the quarter-mile, and that he was one of the six or seven possessors of a tennis court — (the real thing, not the Pretender) — in England; that he had not distinguished himself at present in any other way whatever, but that it was presumed he would stand for Parliament when he had had time to look about him a bit.

Well, these things were not essential. The point was himself, his personality and his general bearing. These, as has been said, Enid found sympathetic. She was quite glad he was going with them to Frascati this afternoon.

She, too, was finding Rome a little trying. It was her third visit; and the least satisfactory. She, too, liked the old better — so far as three years ago could be called "old." She liked the deep courts, with the iron railings before the crumbling church entrances, with the square of blue sky; the old brick-work displaying all the colors of the scale if you looked for

them; the cobbled stones, the broken angles of ancient buildings seen against the blue — : at least she liked these things
so far as she liked anything in a city; and she hated the dom-
ino-faced houses and the bulging carved white-stone pretensions, and the bell-ringing trams and the Vittorio Emanuele
monument. Yet it seemed to be her fate, she told herself ruefully, to live in cities. Her mother and she left England always in October, and came, by stages, out to Rome, where
they remained till Easter; at least they had done so for the
last three years; then, by parallel stages, with intervals at
Cannes and Paris, they returned to England about the beginning of June. They were quite well to do; there was no
anxiety about money; she had an allowance of three hundred
a year of her own; yet they lived only in a small flat in London, which they let furnished from October to June, and took
a country cottage as well. This last was what she most enjoyed, or thought she did; and she would have named as her
Paradise on earth, if she had been asked, to live always in
the English country and to devote herself to Nature. But her
mother always prevailed somehow, in a blank sort of way;
and Paris, Cannes, Rome, Cannes, Paris, was their round for
the winter.

"Yes," she said gravely, in answer to Mr. Hecker's last remark, "I think Italy is just too fascinating, as you say." (She
had decided ten minutes ago that she must play up to the
American. He would merely think her unintelligent if she
didn't agree on such points.) "The . . . the atmosphere is extraordinary. Mrs. Hecker was saying something about it —
about all the strata of Paganism and Primitive Christianity
and the Papacy and cinematographs, all laid one on the top
of the other."

"It's all wonderful to us," said Mr. Hecker with submissive
admiration; "but of course for you Europeans it's part of the
air you breathe all the time."

She assented in precisely the right terms; and caught Sir
Nevill's eye again; and a delightful little thrill went through
her. Obviously he had overheard; and, no less obviously, had
understood her position.

Enid was a lonely soul; and she could not understand why.
She had every possible charm, and no drawbacks so far as
she knew. But it appeared to her that people were disappointing. They took to her violently; they called her by her

Christian name remarkably soon; and she also, she thought, took to them. And then something happened — once especially when an engagement had been broken off — they misunderstood, or they found grave offense where she had intended none; they sheered off. She was not yet cynical; but she wondered sometimes whether she were not in danger of becoming so: people were oddly disappointing and fickle. She was beginning to take refuge in a kind of mystical solitude. Such was the account of herself and the world that she would have given, in all honesty, if there had been anyone she could confide in; but at present there was nobody.

"I must remember that if I ever go to Corfu," she heard the young man opposite say. "It's extremely —"

"No, no, Sir Nevill — not Corfu. She had that experience at Greenwich. I always say —"

Across the flow that once more poured forth, she heard hasty apologies beginning unheard, and, for the life of her, could not help glancing up. He was plainly a little agitated; once more his eyes flickered up and met her own, and there was an amused kind of consternation in them. She permitted herself a delicate little smile. She knew so perfectly what was happening; she had so often witnessed it before under stress of her mother's conversation.

(4)

He was beside her, with an admirable easy art, so soon as he had deposited her mother in the adjoining sitting room. (The Marquis was most particular to follow the Italian custom of sending everyone out in pairs, as they had come in.) And she felt a gentle pleasure in his kind, frank eyes that looked so simply into her own. Round them rose again the noise of the parrot house.

"My word! It's warm!" he said.

They were standing in the window, half-hidden by the heavy damask curtains deemed proper to Roman hotels.

"The motors are ten minutes late already," she said. "Or perhaps it's us! We were to start at two."

"You know Frascati, don't you?"

"Oh, yes!"

"I wish you'd show me round," he said, "when we get there. I . . . I . . . somehow luncheon-parties, however pleasant —"

He stopped, in slight confusion. It was plain that he suddenly remembered that Mrs. Bessington was her mother.
She smiled, with delicious frankness.

"Yes, my mother does talk, doesn't she?"

A very faint look of surprise came into his face.

"But she's simply a dear, isn't she?" she went on without
perceptible pause.

She was quite aware of her desire to please this young
man. Perhaps she had been a shade too precipitate in seeming to criticize her mother to him: so she was relieved to see
his face change again.

"I could hardly say that, could I?" he said. "She . . . she
seems to have traveled a lot. Corfu, you know, and places like
that."

Again she smiled. Really they were getting on very well.
Enid thought herself rather subtle; and it was a pleasure to
perceive how quickly his personality answered hers. The relief from the conventions she had found it necessary to as-
sume with Mr. Hecker was considerable.

"Well, it's Frascati now, anyhow, isn't it? Mother always
forgets whether she means Albano or not."

"It's Tivoli with me," said the boy. "I know there's a waterfall there, and . . . and a villa; but I forget whether it's the
D'Este one or Hadrian's. It's very confusing, don't you think?"

She set him right, deliberately and clearly. He was to keep
firmly in his mind that Frascati had had an English cardinal
as its bishop — two in fact — the Stewart and the other.
Their arms were all over the place. And there was Cicero's
school, too, that he mustn't forget. That was up in the woods.

"Well, you'll give me all the information when we get there,
won't you? I . . . I can't think —" He stopped, as if a little confused.

"I think I know what you were going to say," said Enid.

"You couldn't, possibly!"

"Well, wasn't it that it's the things that matter, and not the
information about them?"

His face showed a pleased bewilderment.

"That's simply extraordinary!" he said. "That's precisely
what I was going to say. How could you tell?"

She looked him fairly in the face for a perceptible pause.

Oh! It's obvious that that's what you feel about things," she
said.

Then the Marquis proclaimed from the door that the motors were round, and Enid dutifully attached herself to her mother again.

(5)

It was the one period of the year at which the Campagna looks hopeful. In summer it is an oven of desolate beauty, thirsty and hot; in winter it is a corpse of magnificent dignity; in autumn it is as tragic as the deathbed of a king. But in early spring it is possible to believe that even the Campagna can hope again, and at least try on garments of rejoicing, as if her brooding memory for once was dormant, and her expectancy awake.

Everywhere today, as they roared and swished over the long roads, there was a thrill in the air. It was impossible to make out details, so fast the motors went; but under the gray flats burned a faint glimmer of young green: the low hills on the horizon wore a haze of living blue.

It had a curious effect upon the young man, as he sat on the back seat, once more the receptacle into which Mrs. Bessington poured the stream of her talk. There had been simply no evading her, if he was to keep anywhere near her daughter; and while he stood irresolute on the pavement, she had simply announced that he was to come in their car. So here he sat, screwed slightly sideways, watching Rome recede into the distance past Mrs. Bessington's bonneted head, and scarcely permitting herself a single glance at her daughter at her side. Beside the chauffeur, he knew, sat Mr. Hecker, attentive and trim.

Motoring immediately after lunch, especially if one sits on a back seat and is unable to smoke — (and it was out of the question here) — produces in certain constitutions a strange receptive kind of coma. After ten minutes from the city gate, Nevill felt entirely stupid. He was whirling backwards; he could not stretch his legs. The pace was so swift that he had to hold his hat in his hand; and Mrs. Bessington was talking about clergymen. Fortunately he had enough humor to keep him polite. He nodded and assented; and said "Just so" and she said "What?" and he said "I only said 'Just so'," and meanwhile he was taking in impressions. He saw, and remembered, the long curves of the Campagna, resembling the long waves of mid-ocean; the strange ruined yellow stucco houses, the sudden signs of little wayside inns, the mon-

strous masses of old Roman brickwork. But a headache was
beginning again, and he longed for repose. Certainly it would
be pleasant to stroll through budding woods presently, as
Mrs. Bessington had promised him. . . . He glanced at Enid.
She was motionless and apparently thoughtful: she had not
spoken at all since they had left the city.

"Aha! There's Frascati at last," observed Mrs. Bessington,
without the faintest pause from her appreciative discussion
of the parish clergyman who had been her pastor at the time
she had been confirmed by the Bishop of Worcester. "It always looks so royal, I think; and, you know, Sir Nevill, that
Stewart Cardinal was bishop here once — the Duke of York
wasn't he — the grandson, I think, of the first Pretender; but
I'm not sure of the relationship; but at any rate George the
Fourth or perhaps it was the Third, always recognized him
and paid him a pension regularly, which I think was very
nice of him; and so he put up his arms here in the Cathedral,
which we must mind to go and see, because so often people
forget to do that, as it's not my idea of a Cathedral at all; so
small you know, and not at all the sort of architecture you'd
think a Cathedral ought to be of, besides having no choir or
anything to sing, except just a few men and boys with voices
like tin kettles; because I remember being out here for Sunday once, and how much disappointed I was, and to see them
misbehaving too, when the canons weren't looking at them;
and the canons too took snuff, you know, which I really don't
think looks very nice, in spite of what people say; but of
course I forgot you were a Roman Catholic, or I wouldn't
have said such things, because you know I always think we
ought to make the best of one another, as I often tell Enid,
don't I, my dear, when she seems to find fault, sometimes —
I don't mean seriously, of course, because I'm sure she
wouldn't do such a thing — (Oh! I wish he wouldn't go so fast
over a bump in the road) — but we're really there at last;
because don't you think it's really wonderful how we cover
the ground nowadays, from the days in which we used to
drive out here with a pair of horses and took two hours over
it too; but there's the Marquis holding up his hand for our
man to stop, so I suppose we'd better get out here, if you
wouldn't mind telling him, Sir Nevill."

She ceased.

(6)

"This is absolutely perfect," said Nevill. "Regard me those curved steps! And the little balcony at the top, and those — those . . . delicious trees."

He spoke rather breathlessly; it had been a long pull.

"I knew you'd like it," she said. "We'll sit down at the top and look at the view."

They really had managed admirably.

The bustle in Frascati had been deafening. First there had assembled round them, at the top of the sort of embanked boulevard where they had left their cars, five or six cabs, all of whose drivers, in rapid Italian, with strange cries interpreted by Enid as English exclamations, had recommended each his own cab, pointing with whirling whip to the erect pheasant's feathers that crowned each horse's head as a guarantee of good faith. Next there had been the guides, one of whom, persuaded that the party was German, had addressed them eloquently and uninterruptedly in that loud and effective tongue; and all these had agreed together with one voice that to visit Frascati without a guide was the merest foolishness. Thirdly there had been the flying squadron of small boys who, imitating the drivers, had chanted in chorus such words as "Yessa . . . ollrighta; goodamorning, sir!" And in the midst the leaders held forth: the Marchioness was the loudest, in a shrill tone insisting that things must be visited in the proper order, and that there was no time for the Capuchin church if Cicero's school was to be seen; and Mrs. Bessington serenely contributed an unceasing flow of experiences there on previous visits, singing a kind of alto (so to speak) to her hostess's soprano, while the Marquis looked nervously from one to the other and attempted to reduce them to a system. This had been the chance of these two. Mr. Clough was already beginning to stroll beside Mrs. Hecker under the clipped trees, his hands clasped behind him about his ebony stick; Mr. Hecker was inspecting the front of a small shop outside of which hung a tattered chasuble. And Enid turned to Nevill.

"Let's walk on," she said; "they can catch us up."

He nodded; and she went forward into the circle and spoke to her mother. Then she came out again.

"I told her, but I don't suppose she heard. . . . Have you ever heard such a noise in all your life?"

A guide ran after them, displaying a badge, as they moved upwards towards the Cathedral square.

"Me very good guide," he said. "Me spik Inglis, not like those others fellas."

"*Avanti,*" said Nevill firmly.

"I tell you —" began the guide.

Enid suddenly laughed, rather sharply.

"*Avanti* means 'Come in'," she said. She turned to the guide and spoke sharply and emphatically. He fell back, suddenly dismayed.

"I thought it was a sort of general dismissal," said Nevill. "How well you do it! What did you say to him?"

"I told him I knew Frascati several years before his grandfather was born," said the girl gravely. "It's the only way. You must exaggerate as much as they do, or they won't take you seriously. I also told him he was badly educated."

"What's the word?"

"*Maleducato,*" said the girl. "Let's see the Cathedral as we come down again. We're all to meet where we left the cars, at half-past five. There'll be lots of time."

The walk up was quite perfectly Italian.

The sort of road — up which, the girl said, carriages really did come — leading upwards from the town from behind the Cathedral, ran between high walls of stained stone and stucco, straight into the heart of the woods. There were queer little houses, with minute terraces in front of them, on the left, for the first couple of hundred yards — built into the wall; the right was unbroken. As they rose higher, the road became even wilder; and all the time Nevill had a deliciously tantalizing sense that the view over the Campagna, at present shut out, must be growing more superb with every step. Then they had come to a high archway, with cypresses beyond it and the beginning of a drive and a kind of lodge, all of gray stone, eloquently ancient.

"That's a villa in there," said the girl. "I forget the name. It's a show-place. Let's leave that too till afterwards."

So they had risen higher and higher; and the woods loomed dark above them. It was so steep that they did not talk much: each said, once or twice, that the carriages would soon catch them up, and Nevill at least, as he turned to see, was conscious of an agreeable disappointment that nothing was in sight, except a somnolent old man, who had eyed them maliciously five minutes ago, as they came up past the steps on which he was lying in the sun.

Then the sweet aromas of the woods began to breathe down on them, sharp and wholesome as the smell of the sea, and the sound of running water reached them. Then they had entered the woods and turned up to the left; and still ascending had seen presently the long stepped slope, with the ancient curved steps at the end, and the terrace of the Capuccini, all under the arch of high trees.

(7)

It was an astoundingly beautiful view, when they had crossed the terrace before the shabby old church and cloister, climbed a convenient heap of stones, and sat down sideways on the stone wall that looked toward Rome.

Again the foreground was incredibly shabby. Immediately beneath them was the wire roof of a very dirty fowl-enclosure, closed on the right by the precipitous wall of the friary. Hens were picking with a spasmodic kind of eagerness, broken by melancholy listlessness, at stripped cabbage stalks, twenty feet below where the two were sitting; and a disheveled cock stepped, lordly, on their outskirts.

But it simply did not matter, as such things do not matter in Italy.

For, below the fowl enclosure, the ground fell away in a considerable cliff of grass and rock, almost straight down, first to a fringe of woods, then to the tumbled roofs of Frascati, all mellow and ancient; and, finally, far below Frascati, to the wide hazy stretch of the Campagna, patched and lined, and washed in, so to say, by great streaks and slopes of color, blue, greenish, gray, brown, infinitely significant, and melancholy or suggestive. There it lay, that tattered carpet of old Roman civilization, crossed by iron roads softened into curves, dotted with sparse shadows, right away to where, a faint wall of pale gray and blue, showed the mighty city herself, closing the horizon, as if Rome were still that place in which all roads, and indeed all wildernesses too must find their end. The warm sunlight lay over all, and a tender blue sky finished the picture.

"Well?" said the girl gently, after a minute or two of silence.

"It's simply gorgeous," said the boy. "But, you know —"

He stopped.

"Yes?"

"It's not the last word — or, perhaps I'd say, it isn't the first word. There's Rome, still, you know."

She nodded two or three times.

"I understand perfectly," she said.

Nevill had a thrill of pleasure.

"I believe you do," he said. "But, Lord! What a prig I must seem! May I smoke? It may relieve matters, because I wish to make some observations!"

A delicious laughter shone all through her face, though her lips scarcely moved. It was as if a flame danced suddenly within her soul. (Really, she was exceedingly pretty, thought Nevill.)

"Please smoke. And please make all the observations you wish. I rather think I shall agree, you know."

He lighted his cigarette, first holding his case towards her with a question in his eyebrows, but in silence. She shook her head.

Then he began.

"It's all too tamed," he said. "There's that Campagna, you know. It looks wild, but it isn't. It's all been trampled down and bedded out, once. You can't forget that. Look at those woods, for instance. They're holding it down all the time. And look at those shadows, which I suppose are houses. They don't even trouble to rebuild them; they're so certain the Campagna can't rise against them. It's beaten; it's dead. And then here are we; and here are those old friars, like lords of the manor, looking down on it all. They've even stuck their old fowl-house down bang in front. Why, in England we should have the drawing room here, to get the view — to be allowed to admire it. Here they don't care a brass farthing. They know it's theirs. . . . Poor old Campagna! . . . And then, you know, there's Rome, planted bang down in the middle — quite happy and content. She knows the Campagna's beaten and done for. She's not afraid of her. Poor old Campagna!"

He paused, astonished at his eloquence. He had no idea he could talk like this. He looked at her; she nodded gravely, twice.

"That's it. Go on, please," she said softly.

He cleared his throat dramatically — and threw a leg over the wall.

"Well, ladies and gentlemen; the next point to notice is that here in these woods" — he waved his hand at them — "the situation's quite different. The mountains aren't beaten yet. They're above the friars and the fowl-house and even old Rome. I know they've stuck their villas here; and Cicero's school, or whatever it is — or is that Tivoli?"

"No: you're quite right. Go on. Tivoli's the waterfall and the Villa D'Este."

"Yes — well — well, those villas and things are only here like a sort of garrison. The woods own them, not they the woods. Look at those slopes up there, and those trees. They're on top, as Mrs. Hecker would say. They're the real thing; they're alive. Look at all those flowers like stars, and the daisies. You don't get flowers like that in the Campagna; or if you do, they don't belong; they aren't characteristic. Isn't that so?"

"Perfectly."

"Well, up here they're all right," went on Nevill, feeling he'd about come to an end of his observations. "Am I talking rot, Miss Bessington?"

For a moment she did not move. He saw her clean profile, very straight-lined and sharp from nose to chin, still looking out over the haze of the Campagna. Then she turned slowly and looked directly at him, with an intent and yet detached sort of interest. He was taken aback a little by her direct-ness.

"I think you've summed it up perfectly," she said. "But there's one thing you haven't said."

"Dear me! I thought I'd been exhaustive."

Her mouth trembled with laughter, and then grew grave again.

"You haven't said on which side you yourself are. I think I know; but. . . but I'd like to hear you say it."

"Why, on the side of the woods of course." (He sighed audi-bly.) "How I do hate luncheon-parties," he added, "even when . . . when I'm sitting by Mrs. Bessington."

"Thank you very much," she said, completely grave.

(8)

"You don't look very well," she said an hour later as they began to find their way downwards again by another path. "You look tired out."

There had been no sign of the rest of the party, though the two had waited within view of a patch of the road which, so far as Enid knew, was the only one into the woods up which a carriage could come; and it was quite certain that the Marchioness would not walk.

They had talked at ease — with those meditative silences that are the highest compliment that each could pay to the other — about Rome, and Life, and Nature, and the Meaning of Things, and indirectly, of course, of themselves all through. Nevill had been pretty frank, and Enid no less — or scarcely less. He had said suddenly, after one of his pauses, that he was a Catholic, and could never possibly be anything else; and had proceeded to say that he was afraid he wasn't a very good one. But he had been brought up to it; and had a chapel and a priest at home, and "all that." And the girl had nodded in her sympathetic way, and said that she supposed that she was Church of England; and had then begun to say that she couldn't ever be a Catholic for several reasons; but had omitted to state what these were; and he had not pressed her.

It was all very satisfactory then; it was evident to both of them that there was something much deeper in life than conventional religion; that "dogmas" did not really solve difficulties, but rather increased them; and that the real secret lay somewhere else.

Neither of them had said anything as to the passage of time; indeed, it was probable that neither understood how very quickly time passes under the charm of such conversations as these. The girl's eyes wandered three or four times rather intently down upon the section of stony road that was in sight a hundred feet below. And at last Nevill stood up.

"We must be going," he had said; and had then wasted five minutes more in crowing like a cock, to the furious agitation of the genuine creature below, in the enclosure. When the cock, after half a dozen vindictive answers, had begun to peck his wives, the two moved off.

Nevill did not seem to like being told he looked unwell.

"I'm not very well," he said shortly. "And I hate and loathe it."

She looked concerned.

"I'm sorry," she said, "I didn't know. What's the matter?"

"Nothing but headaches," he said. "But why should I have them? I simply can't see sometimes, when they're bad. It seems to me unfair."

"You mean —"

"I mean I can't fit that kind of thing into my philosophy. I try to bear them decently, of course; but I don t submit in the slightest. I resent that kind of thing furiously, exactly as I resent cruelty to animals."

She said nothing for a minute.

They were approaching a fork in the path. Overhead the trees, still leafless, yet covered, when looked at *en masse,* with a faint purplish haze that revealed the strong life welling up their fiber, nearly met in an archway. On either side, up on this, down on the other, stretched the tumbled slopes of the mountain, alight with bluebells, and the star-flowers he had spoken of a while ago. The whole place was full of scent and vigor and youth — redolent and suggestive. To their right, and still far beneath, lay the roofs of the little town, extraordinarily golden in the light as the sun sank downwards.

As they came slowly towards the fork in the path, a piece of crumbling wall that stood at the juncture of the ways began to disclose itself as the back of one of those shrines that stand here and there in the Frascati woods. They turned the angle of it; and stopped.

It was a particularly realistic *Pietà.*

Behind the wire netting that was stretched across its face there was the group of the Mother and Son, painted in crude colors, lately renovated. The Mother, in an indigo cloak, sitting with upraised face, supported the ghastly Body across her knees. The hands and feet ran with crimson; the mouth appeared to grin in a horrible contortion; the limbs were grotesquely elongated and emaciated. Stuck into the meshes of the wiring in front was a small bunch of wilted dandelions. The whole picture was painted in fresco on plaster that had peeled in places; and was half-sheltered by a broken pent-roof of stone.

The two looked at it in silence. They moved on, still in silence. Then the boy broke out.

"There!" he said. "That was exactly what I meant! I think such things are perfectly horrible! What possible good can that do to anyone? It's completely out of harmony too. The very colors are wrong. And, besides, why put it in the woods where things are fresh and clean? And that's exactly why I don't like talking about my headaches. Of course the thing's a fact! But isn't it better —?"

He stopped suddenly; and again, for a few yards, the girl did not speak.

"I won't ask about your headaches again," she said, with a tremor in her voice that might be humor or a deeper emotion. "I agree with every word you say, you know."

"And you agree about that . . . that thing up there?"

"Of course I do."

Chapter II

The air was of that peculiar freshness of an Italian spring morning as, three days later, Nevill drove out alone in a little victoria, with his man on the box, for the sensation of a Mass in a Catacomb.

There are just a few things that are inevitable in Rome. He had already done three of them; he had visited St. Peter's; he had trailed after a guide through the Forum, he had visited Frascati. When, therefore, the Marquis Daly assured him that no one could leave Rome without hearing Mass in a Catacomb; that such a Mass had been arranged for by the priest whom he had met at lunch; that the Bessingtons were going because Enid had never had the experience, and that the entire party would be most pleased if he cared to join them there at half-past seven — at the entrance to the Catacomb of Saint Calixtus — there was only one possible answer.

The return from Frascati, three days ago, had been uneventful enough. He and Enid had spied a remnant of the party five minutes after leaving the wayside shrine, and had learned that they had scarcely been missed. Mrs. Bessington, it appeared, had prevailed on a majority to visit the Cathedral; a minority had got as far as the villa whose entrance the two kind passed on their way up into the woods; Mr. Hecker alone had penetrated to Cicero's school, and returned again, damp but triumphant. For the journey back to Rome Nevill had found himself with the Princess and Mr. Clough; and Enid was seen no more.

Nevill was quite aware that something was happening to him. He would, at this period, have thought it ridiculous to say that he was in the least in love with Enid. It was not that at all, he assured himself: it was rather that he began to see that women were not what he had thought them.

He had thought them, hitherto (as most wholesome and well bred young men think them), to be not much otherwise than rather imperfect men; he thought them just a little odd and rather silly, or, if not silly, at least very gravely handicapped by a peculiar constitution of mind. They were emotional in the wrong way, he thought; they could not reason coolly; there was a trace of dishonorableness — or, to put it more mildly, their code of honor was not the same as that of men. Above all, they lacked the quality of comradeship. One could like them rather and be friendly with them, and very courteous: one could even marry them — (he supposed this would have to be done, some day) — but a woman could not be a comrade to a man. She could be almost anything else . . . but not that.

He was thinking gently about all this, as he drove out along the stony-walled way that leads from Rome to Saint Calixtus Cemetery. Overhead the pale sky brightened like a slow smile, and the larks were singing somewhere up in its luminosity. Curious and Italian spectacles presented themselves; now a wine cart coming in from the Campagna, splendidly barbaric with faded paint, hooded on high; now a team of mules straining to drag a load of cut stone blocks; now a group of brown-faced, brown-legged children stared at him from a doorway.

The early air was cold and strong like wine, full of vitality; it produced in him a strange sense of slight intoxication, for he had had nothing but a cup of coffee. He was to breakfast with the rest in the Trappist lodge for tourists.

He was comparing then his former ideas with his new ones. He began to see that Comradeship was quite possible with a woman: indeed, he was beginning to wonder whether it were not possible in a manner impossible with a man.

For he had never before met with such complete understanding. She had even told him what he was going to say — that day at lunch — before he had fully formulated it to himself. She had understood him, and not only understood him, but inspired him to understand as well as to express himself, again and again during the hour's talk in the Frascati woods. He had found himself more subtle than he had thought; she had drawn out his convictions as sunlight draws out the power of the seed. He had held his opinions before, of course, but he had never put them quite so well, even to himself, he thought. Was not that Comradeship?

Then, if this were so, he had been wrong about women. They were not inferior, but just different. And in that difference there lay their power.

Then he reflected, with apparent inconsequence, that it would be pleasant to be at Mass with Enid.

(2)

The group which he found waiting for him just within the gate of the enclosure consisted chiefly of people whom he knew. (Yes, the Bessingtons were there all right, rather in the background.) The Dalys obviously had charge of the party from the official point of view, and Mrs. Hecker from the intellectual.

"And this is all too lovely," she said; "so truly Catholic; and, Sir Nevill, you make it just complete. You stand for . . . for England, you know, and the feudal system. And you've brought your retainer with you, I see?"

Nevill said that it was certainly his manservant, if that would do.

"Yes," pursued Mrs. Hecker, in a kind of ecstasy of intelligence; "and here's the Trappist monk —" (she indicated a meek bearded man in a brown frock who waited patiently a few yards away) — "to take us back to Silence. We're all here — a microcosm, you might say. But what I want to know is, What does all this say to me?" — (she waved an admirably gloved hand round the tangled garden wilderness) — "What is its message to me, right now? What am I to take away with me that I hadn't before?"

(It was all too bright and nickel-plated, thought Nevill. She put so explicitly and adequately the thoughts which other people were content to reflect about.)

"I think the Brother's waiting," said the Marquis a little anxiously. "Father Martinelli will have vested by now."

He led the way, faintly reminiscent in his movements of a dancing master, towards the little arched building that protected the entrance to the Catacomb.

Nevill tried to get near the Bessingtons as the group began to string itself out for the descent, but it was hopeless. He could hear Mrs. Bessington's voice trickling gently on, somewhere in front — he wondered whether it was about clergymen or Corfu, and to whom she believed herself to be talking; but that was all. Mr. Hecker's gray coat and neat trousered legs and trim hair was the only object immediately before him, descending tranquilly and steadily down the long flight of steps into the mysterious darkness beneath, lit by the ruddy light of three or four tapers.

He had never been in a Catacomb before, and he presently found himself quite interested. Floor, roof and walls of the

tunnel seemed all alike, of a curious powdery texture; here
and there he could make out slabs of stone, engraved with
letters; there was also a powdery sort of taste in the air, as of
the last and ultimate essence of dryness. He did not know
much about Catacombs, but he was aware, from fragments of
Mrs. Bessington's conversation on a previous day, that they
were, all told, strung out end to end, about eight hundred
miles long; and that they had been, in the days of persecu-
tion, at once the hiding-holes of Christians, their places of
worship, and their cemeteries. Certainly that was interesting, even if a little stuffy; he did not quite know why he had
got up so early to come to them, though; and the next instant, with a flash of clear-sightedness, he knew very well
why he had come.

When he found himself settled at last in his place, kneeling, since the others knelt too, on the powdery floor, the romance and mysteriousness of it all came on him suddenly.

It was an excavated chapel in which they all knelt, perhaps
fifteen feet high, but with a long funnel coming down from
the upper air far above, shedding an oddly unreal kind of
bluish light which met but did not mix with the yellow light
of the tapers. The walls were dim and dark, but here and
there upon them showed incised slabs, marking, he thought,
the last resting-places of men and women who had lived and
died at least sixteen hundred years ago. There was one
cleared space not far from him — as if the foot of the wall
had been excavated — whence came a soft light as of burning
lamps: he supposed this must be the place where Saint
Cecilia's body had been found lying as if she slept. (So much
he knew from a hurried glance at Baedeker last night, in
bed.)

The little chapel was nearly full of worshipers, but the light
was so odd that he could not identify at first more than three
or four of them. Neither could he see where Enid knelt. A few
faces were brightly and softly illuminated; the rest were
hooded shadows. Above all, however, rose the crimson figure
of the priest in the midst: Nevill could catch his profile now
and again — a fine Italian profile, of a complexion at once
dark and clear — and the glimmer of a silver hair or two
about his ear and temple. The only sound down here was the
steady murmur of his voice. There was a faint aromatic smell
as of crushed box or bay.

The effect of all this was, of course, inevitable. The romance was unmistakable. For here, reproduced before his senses, was a scene that might have been presented sixteen hundred years ago. Here was the same liturgy — most of it verbally the same — repeated by a priest whose descent, both spiritual and physical, was direct. Here were the worshipers; here was the very place; the vestments, the tapers, the altar, the Mystic Bread, the Wine of God; and the Faith that looked on them. The very dresses of the women, in this half-light, the bandaged heads, the loose cloaks — these might have been the common disguise of Christian slaves and freedwomen of nearly two thousand years ago.

Yet the suggestion of all this met, in him, with a real resistance. It was true that he was a Catholic; that he never could be anything else; that there ran in his veins the blood of his Catholic forefathers; that he had a "chapel at home and a priest and all that"; that he went to the Sacraments at least once a year. Yet he was in that mental state, so characteristic of his age, in which his interior interest was not that of Catholicism. He was not consciously insincere; he was not, probably, insincere even unconsciously. If he had been confronted with a crisis, he would have adhered to Catholicism and accepted its dogmas with his will, even if not eminently with his intellect. But to his imagination it meant little or nothing; and it was in his imagination that he lived just now; and with his imagination that he felt that the ultimate secret of things was beneath all dogma; that was a Solution of everything to which Nature corresponded rather than Grace or Revelation. Joy, he felt, was the fundamental emotion of life; not the Passion or the Cross; and Catholicism meant to him the Cross.

He was perfectly correct, of course, in his bearing. He remained passive, on his knees; he even took out a string of beads from his pocket; but he left them idle in his hands. He bowed his head as the bell tinkled; he lifted up his face to see the glimmering Host as it rose between the priest's fingers; he even murmured soundlessly, "My Lord and my God" — (there was an indulgence attached to that, he thought). But his central soul was in another region; in that region for which the mountains above Frascati stood, in the purely material plane; for which Enid was beginning to stand in the realm of humanity — the region of youthfulness and health

and running water and clean joy and star-flowers and golden
sunlight. It was not in the dull, yellow light of tapers, in
crimson vestments, in underground chapels, however romantic, that, for him, Revelation embodied itself.

Then, as the priest drank the last ablution and the
knee-weary worshipers shifted a little into easier attitudes,
he suddenly saw Enid's face against the darkness, as clear as
a flower, and her great dark eyes.

(3)

"Well!" said Mrs. Hecker, with enormous emphasis. "I
think that's all just too wonderful. It's an experience! Isn't
that so, Henry?"

They were out again in the sunshine, and the tangled garden was incredibly fair. On all sides, amongst the monu-
ments and arched tabernacles and mighty stones, blazed the
spring flowers, as glorious as a resurrection. The sun stood
higher, and the morning air glowed warm beneath him, in
vivid contrast to the strange sepulchral atmosphere of the
Catacomb, at once dry and chilly.

"And there's old Rome," she said. "Just as always."

Mrs. Hecker always saw the dramatic element a shade
quicker than anyone else. It had begun to annoy Nevill a little that this was so. Certainly Rome being "there, just as always" was exactly the next point. He had come out of the
Catacomb, from the ghosts of the ages and the homes of the
dead, in the midst of which the Living Sacrifice had been
presented; and there, sure enough, was Rome again, blue
and distant, with the bubble of St. Peter's dome to protect it
— the ancient City that was eternally young. So those long
dead slaves and women must have come out, perhaps with
guards about them, from the house of refreshment and hope,
to see the City of their passion awaiting them in stolid glory.
One might almost forget Rome and the City of Life, down
there in the noiseless gloom; but it would not be forgotten for
long. It was there again, "just as always."

"Well, I guess breakfast is the next engagement," went on
Mrs. Hecker. "It's very carnal and earthly and all that, of
course; and I guess I'm no more carnal than other folks. But I
want my breakfast."

Here again this was precisely the next emotion; and the most *exalté* there could not deny it. There was no more to be said; they must go to breakfast.

The Marquis Daly, who was responsible for the arrangements, had been very particular about breakfast. Fully two-thirds of the worshipers of his party were non-Catholics, and it was necessary to propitiate these by physical as well as spiritual comforts. Yet he dreaded the Trappists' omelets. Eighteen boiled eggs, then, awaited the company, laid in two slop-basins, with nine egg-cups — one for each — set amid saucers of a curious pink-looking preserve, piles of bread and nine tea cups: all ranged on a long table set within the very bare and rather cold restaurant provided at the edge of the cemetery that was nearest Rome. Two large chromo-lithographs of Leo XIII and Pius X respectively, blessed the party from the walls.

Nevill had not a chance at Enid, even now. Mrs. Bessington secured him at her side, and began to describe to him the ways of the hall porter of the flats where she and her daughter had their headquarters in London.

Nevill decided, in the intervals of his assenting to her, that her secret lay in the fact that she said out loud what other people thought. Everyone has foolishly inconsequent trains of thought, selections from which are manifested in speech; but Mrs. Bessington manifested the whole. She gave him, presently, an admirable illustration of his theory.

"He always goes off duty at ten o'clock," she was saying, "when the night porter comes on, and even wears the same cap; because one evening Parkinson — that's the name of the day porter — got impatient, I suppose, when Martin wasn't in time; and as I came in from an early dinner somewhere or other, I saw Parkinson's cap lying there on the table; because I know it was his, as, when I went in to see if any letters had come, I peeped inside the cap, and there was his name in red ink on the white lining; and as I was there Martin came in, late — as I said, and was in a great hurry; so he hung up his coat, just as I was going out, and as I went past the little window I saw him putting on the cap, so I knew it was the one: and it always seemed to me very odd that the people of the flat — in Cadogan Lane, because that's where it is — whoever they are, did not provide a cap for each one of the porters, instead of making them all wear the same one; as I

suppose these poor monks do with their habits, which must
be very unhealthy, I should think; as well as all their living
underground so much, and running up and down all those
steps, and never speaking, except the ones, I suppose, that
look after visitors, because the one this morning talked a
good deal, and told us to mind our heads, I remember, as we
went under that low place in the tunnel; because I think —"

She proceeded to give her views on the Trappist vocation....

Nevill was getting really an adept at doing three or four
things at once. He attended quite adequately to Mrs.
Bessington, and gave an answer now and again to the most
startling opinions which she expressed as to Trappists, and,
indeed, monks in general; and at the same time, greatly daring, set himself to discover what other people were talking
about. Mrs. Hecker was, of course, stating in wonderfully
adequate terms the "message" that the Catacombs had for
her — and not the superficial message either; but quite a
thoughtful one. (Nevill could not catch the whole of it, but its
main purport was that the simple things were the greatest
and most worth coming to terms with.) The Marchioness
Daly was describing a reputed conversation of hers with the
Secretary of State, in which that prelate, it appeared, took
her advice in every particular and begged that he might have
the advantage of it always in future. The Marquis Daly was
discussing, in tolerable Italian, with the priest who had just
said Mass, some recent researches in some newly-discovered
Catacombs. Two more ladies, names unknown, were plan-
ning out the rest of their week. And Enid was silent.

(4)

He saw his chance after breakfast, and took it with marked
promptitude.

She had slipped out alone; he saw that, for he was becoming very conscious of her indeed; and as Mrs. Bessington, still
discoursing, turned to answer a question from one of the unknown ladies, he produced his cigarette case, as a kind of
guarantee of good faith to any who might be observing his
movement, and slipped out also. She was already halfway up
the tiny path; but he was with her before she had reached
the end.

They sat down presently, with their backs to a broken wall,
a little way off from the path. Nevill was aware, with consid-

erable satisfaction, that there would be quite a good time before they need go, as the party, generally speaking, was due
to undertake a small exploration in the Catacomb under the
guidance of the Trappist lay brother. But he thought he
would make sure of his good fortune.

"You don't want to go down again?" he said.

She shook her head.

"No; I think I've seen enough to . . . to get its message," she
said, smiling. "Besides, Mrs. Hecker has interpreted it all for
us, hasn't she?"

There was just a tinge of bitterness in her voice.

"And . . . and I don't like —" She stopped. "What do you
think of it all? It's your first visit, isn't it?"

Nevill drew out a cigarette before answering.

"Yes; it's my first visit. Of course it's very interesting and
romantic. I suppose everybody feels that. But I still feel what
I said the other day."

"Yes?"

"Well, I quite see the drama of it all; the very same service
performed in the very same language, and all that, in the
very same place where the slaves and so on heard it all those
ages ago. And of course, as a Catholic —"

"Go on," she said quietly.

"Well, of course, as a Catholic, I think it very sacred and all
that. But, you know, it seems to me they've missed the point,
somehow. . . . I can't imagine what I should have done if I'd
been a Christian in those days," he added rather irrelevantly.

"Don't you think that it was fresh and new then — in the
same way that . . . that other things are fresh and new now?
We . . . we should both have been Christians — I mean,
really fervent Christians, then, I think."

"By George!" said Nevill. "I believe you've hit it. You mean
that since we don't live in those days, Christianity seems —
well — rather stale; that . . . that it is stale. I don't mean that
it isn't true," he went on rather anxiously; "that's different:
but that the spirit of it is stale and . . . and conventional. And
that the point, just now, lies somewhere else."

She bowed her head in assent.

His delight was deepening into something rather like ecstasy. Never in the whole of his life had he met anyone who
understood, as she did, this particular side of his nature.
More than that, she illuminated it and made it coherent, it

seemed. His deep little convictions, half-formed and inchoate, his views about health and freshness and solitude — even of qualified solitude — those were coming out from him, one by one, drawn by the warmth of her presence, and really they were not so bad after all.

It appeared to him that she must be extraordinarily spiritual and good, to understand like this. He had had no conception that women could be like this, so delicately strong, so resonant, so to speak, instead of flabby. He turned to look at her a little more lowly, excited by his pleasure; and what he saw flushed his intellectual happiness with an even more elementary emotion.

She was leaning back again now, against the old lichened wall, with her head thrown back, and her big gray eyes looking out across the sunlit garden. She had unbound her hat, and the scarf lay in her lap, and the broad soft black straw cast a mystical shadow down to her well-marked eyebrows. Her complexion was perfect of its kind; her face and her slender throat were of an uniform pallor, but without a hint of ill-health. Her long ungloved hands lay half-twisted in the gauze over her knees. Behind her, brightening her as an appropriate frame sets off a good picture, was a sheet of tall lily-heads, and beyond them the garden, and beyond the garden, once more, Rome.

He looked at this for an instant. Then he went on.

"Well, all that fits in, doesn't it, with what we agreed about, the other day? We don't want this sort of thing now. I suppose there are some people who must have it — all the morbid and dark side. But . . . but it isn't the best. After all, the Catacombs are underground, and we aren't — not yet. I'd much sooner be buried at sea, as a matter of fact. Wouldn't you?"

"I know what you mean," she said.

"Of course Death and so on are facts. I'm not a fool or . . . or a Christian Scientist. But why in the world think about them — least of all in anything that resembles religion? I can't help thinking —"

"How are your headaches, by the way? — Oh! I promised not to ask, didn't I?"

He made an impatient movement with his cigarette, flicking off the ash. She had turned abruptly to ask her question, and was still looking at him.

"Oh! They're all right. At least, I take my medicine regularly —"

"You take medicine? They're as bad as that? You've seen a doctor? What did he say?"

She asked sharply and concernedly. It gave him little thrill of delight, in spite of his words.

"Oh! Let's leave all that —"

"No; but tell me, and then I won't ask any more."

"I went a couple of months ago. He told me that . . . that I had headaches. And then he told me to take some medicine. And then I paid him a guinea — no, two, because it was my first visit. And he told me to come again as soon as I got back from Rome."

"Did he . . . did he seem to think it serious?"

"Lord, no! Not nearly so serious as I thought it myself, anyhow. I told him so, too."

"What did he say?"

"He laughed."

"Who was he?"

"Matthieson, the brain man. You see, the local doctor recommended him. He's supposed to know everything that is to be known, about the inside of all our heads."

"He's a surgeon, isn't he?"

"I believe so. He didn't surge me, anyhow, or even hint at it. That would be a bit too much — to make a hole in your head to let out a headache. I hate doctors."

"Yes, I see."

"Well, I hate being reminded of that sort of thing. I believe the way to keep well is not to think about it."

"You went, though."

"Well, I couldn't stand the thing any more. . . . Now, Miss Bessington, for heaven's sake let's leave that, and —"

"But you'll go and see him again, won't you, as soon as you get back, as he told you?"

Her voice trembled, ever so little; and even the heaviest fool could not have helped being flattered by it. And Nevill was not a fool at all.

He turned and looked straight at her. He knew it was unfair, yet the chance of making a tiny advance towards yet further intimacy was too tempting.

"You wish me to?" he said.

She flushed divinely; and then it was her turn to switch back the conversation.

"Of course I wish all my friends to go and see doctors if they're ill. I'm not a Christian Scientist either, you know. Now go on with what you were saying."

So then, they sat and talked in the sunlight.

Voices came and went from beyond the wall, now and again. Once a bearded lay brother went past them in silence as they sat there, not even turning his eyes. It gave Nevill another little text; and when the footsteps had died away, he made his remarks.

"Now there's another illustration. Of course I know they're very holy people and all that; and I've not the slightest doubt that they think all the rest of us very worldly and all that. And yet, you know, I'm as convinced as much as I'm convinced of anything in the world, that that's not the way to do it. If they lived up here in the garden all the time, it would be another matter. But they don't. They have their endless services, out of books, and meditate on death, and deliberately give themselves pain."

"Pain's a kind of physical sin, don't you think?" said Enid suddenly.

"That's exactly it!" he cried in delight. "It's a thing to be resisted. It's hateful and detestable. I'd make acts of contrition for my headaches, if . . . if I thought that was the best way to repent of them. And as for amendment — well, I'm sure I ask nothing better."

(5)

He walked up from his hotel to see the sunset from the Pincian that evening; and his mood was such that, viewing from afar the spruce figures of Mr. Hecker and Mr. Clough advancing towards him, as he came up towards the church of the Trinita, he slipped swiftly into a small curiosity shop, in order to avoid them. Thence, as in the dark interior he examined a plate of rings and charms on the counter, he saw them go briskly past. He still determined to give them two or three minutes to get well out of sight; and then, for very shame, felt himself obliged to buy something. He had almost decided on a small silver crucifix, when something else caught his eye, and he held it up, demanding what it was.

"That is a seal, sir," said the man in broken French.

Nevill said he knew that, but what was the device?

"That is the snake of . . . of Aesculape," said the man, "the god of health."

"I'll take that," said Nevill.

The view was superb, when he reached it.

The crowd on the top of the façade of the Pincian was so dense that he made no attempt to penetrate it; but he moved on to a comparatively empty space beyond, and sat down.

First he looked at the view.

Far beneath him stretched Rome. Roofs, towers, spires, here and there broken by wide spaces and the gulf of narrow streets, lay in one huddled mass, glorious in the evening light. Yet these appeared almost small, so tremendous and dominant was the great dome, which this morning he had seen so tiny, yet even then dominant, from the enclosure of St. Calixtus' Cemetery. There it hung, of an indescribable blue, floating, it seemed, rather than supported from beneath — floating, and transfused in a very sea of splendor, since the western sky not only lay behind it but streamed through it, shining clear through the windows beneath the dome, as if light dwelt within as well as without the tabernacle in which the body of Peter the Fisherman lay enshrined.

It was this, of course, on which his eyes dwelt. They came back and back to it; there seemed no escape. The Jews had done their best; yet the dome of the great Synagogue resembled a vulgar *nouveau riche* beside this kingly dignity. The Government was doing its best; yet the huge Palace of Justice seemed a house of cards. There was no question about it. St. Peter's remained inviolate.

And then the boy's eyes fell on another sight; and he almost sighed with relief. For, out to the right, poised on some tall hill of which he did not know the name, was a line of umbrella-pine's, as fine as lace, incredibly distinct, since every branch, and (it appeared from here) almost every twig, stood against the soft, rosy flush of the heavens. They, at least, were rivals of the dome; and they lived, while the dome enshrined, at the very best, only the dead body of a saint. . . .

He turned presently and looked at the crowd.

They were of every nationality; yet their nationalities did not divide them. One line only cut them sharply into two camps. There were the ecclesiastics, and there were the laity. That, he thought he understood, was the essential difference.

It is true that they were mingled, physically; yet it appeared
to the young man as if an unspanable gulf lay between them.
There went a serpent of black-cassocked seminarians —
younger men even than himself, probably — going swiftly
and steadily back, with flying sleeves, towards their college
before *Ave Maria* should ring: and there played a group of
children, with shrill cries, about a trimmed black poodle who
barked in the midst. There an old priest leaned on the parapet, melancholy and brooding: and, within a yard of him,
came a well-fed townsman, bold-eyed, light-bearded, in a
well-cut suit, twirling a stick. There were the two camps; the
former, with a terrible adequateness, preached and insisted
upon pain and death, as elements of life, as symbolized (it
might be said) by the sign of the Cross; those, however in-
adequately, stood for the joy of life and simplicity and naturalness. It was not that Nevill liked the town-type; he hated
it. Yet it was the nearer to the essential system of things, he
thought, because more unstudied than the precise definitions
of theology.

So he sat; and so he considered; and mingled with all his
considerations was the image of the girl with whom he had
talked as he had never talked with any other.

There was his aunt at home. He was exceedingly fond of
her; and there were certain kinds of things on which he could
talk with her with utter confidence. If people were in trouble,
he could imagine no more soothing comforter than Aunt
Anna: once or twice lately, since he had come into his estate,
he had had cases to deal with; there was a girl who needed
an adviser; there was a mother who had lost her only son.
Well, obviously, Aunt Anna was indicated. Or there were the
Jesuit Fathers at his old school; there was the Jesuit Father
at Farm Street whom he occasionally consulted spiritually —
well, he could say things to those priests he could say to no
one else. But he could not say the kind of things to them he
had said to Enid: they simply would not understand; they
would produce some dogma; they would argue that it was
scarcely likely that the Catholic philosophers — even apart
from dogma — were wrong, and the pagan right. They would
be sympathetic and kindly and understanding, — understanding, that is, down to a certain level, yet utterly incapable of penetrating a hair's breadth below that level. At the

most they would just sum him up as "tainted" by modern agnosticism.

Finally, there were the men he knew, many of whom had
been with him at Stonyhurst. And to those perhaps least of
all could he give his confidences. He could be genial and familiar with them; he could lend them five pounds, or borrow
them. But the relationship was really extraordinarily artifi-
cial; he could not possibly touch on certain things. And, even
if he could, he knew what the response would be. One type
would clap him on the back and tell him to go and take a
blue pill; the other type would be grave, and tell him to go
and talk to Father So-and-so. Whereas with Enid — And he
had scarcely known her more than ten days!

As the sky deepened and glowed above him, and as the
evening chill began to drive home the prudent Roman crowd
— (ten minutes ago the last child had been towed away by a
voluble nurse) — as the lights began to glimmer in the City
beneath, and the flex leaves above him to shiver in the faint
breeze, which, like the sigh of a man as sleep begins to win
upon him, marked the last movement of life before the stillness of the night; he began to see, he thought, the unity of all
this. It was like a silent presence coming into a room which
just now had been filled by conversationalists. All these minute and diverse details, — even the roll of the wheels, from
the great cobbled circus beneath, clearer and sharper than
even ten minutes ago, the tossing rustle of the leaves, the
lights that winked, went out, and then kindled again — those
things seemed to him merged and fused together by the en-
compassing sky that was darkening so swiftly, into one coherent spirit — a spirit of calm and assurance and freshness.
And, as he saw this, he saw too, he thought, that this was
what he had found in Enid. She had silences, like these,
slight yet infinitely significant movements, as when she
turned and said something, looking at him as she spoke; and
then silences again. . . . It was all one; one great and quiet
spirit that penetrated the very depths of his heart; a spiritu-
ality that depended upon no forms, and therefore was limited
by none; a comprehension that needed no words to express
itself in.

Then, as he looked out over the shadowy dome at the sky,
passing itself, even as he watched, from luminousness to
opacity, there came out a single star, that shook for an in-

stant, like a light he had seen just now in the City, and then, again, like that light, settled down into steadiness. The great spirit had gathered itself to a point. . . .

(6)

He went up to his private sitting room, almost immediately after a cup of coffee and a cigarette in the lounge of his hotel. The sight of all these people became a burden. What were they all about? A couple of men talked over cigars in a discreet manner in one corner, eyeing all the while every movement among the rest, following with their eyes a particularly superb-looking lady who wore an orange velvet dress; a very domestic party, with an Anglican clerical father in the midst, laughed and talked with true British reserve over some ridiculous card game. Two old ladies in caps, with ribbons, bent their old heads together and murmured gossip, no doubt, over their crochet-work. They all appeared to him like marionettes, like shadow-figures on a screen, that jerked about with a semblance of life, but had no insides, so to speak. They were not really alive at all. They knew nothing worth knowing. So he went upstairs.

It was an excellent room, so far as hotel rooms can be excellent; and he had done what he could to improve it. A bronze of Antinous he had bought during his second day in Rome stood on a pedestal of carved wood he had bought for it at the same time. A couple of old oil paintings rested on the mantel shelf; a gorgeous piece of antique silk, emblazoned all over with bees and, in the midst with a Cardinal's hat and arms, lay over the corner of the screen. All those would be sent straight back to Hartley when he left.

His writing table, too, looked homely. A couple of big silver frames held photographs — the one of a passionate-looking old man, the other of a middle-aged woman, gray-haired, with a young face, with a boy in a sailor suit. These were, respectively, his father, and his Aunt Anna, with Jim, her son. He stood looking at the second of these for a few seconds.

Then he went through into his bedroom, turning on the light as he did so, and hunted about on his dressing table. But he could not find what he wanted. He came back into the sitting room, and touched the bell; and then before it could be answered, sat down at his writing table, took out a sheet of paper, and prepared to write.

"Yessir," came a discreet voice presently.

"Oh — er — Charleson — did you turn a seal out of my waistcoat pockets — the waistcoat I wore this afternoon?"

"Yessir. Put it into the drawer of the dressing table, Sir Nevill."

"Oh! Get it, will you? I couldn't find it."

"Yes, Sir Nevill."

The man came back presently, and laid it by his elbow.

"Anything more, Sir Nevill?

"No. . . . Oh, yes. I said we'd leave on Easter Monday. I've changed my plans. I'm not sure. I'll let you know when we'll go."

"Yessir."

"And — Charleson —"

"Yessir?"

"I shall leave a note here, with a little box, when I go to bed. See that they're both taken tomorrow morning, early, to the address. That's all. I shan't want you again, Charleson. Goodnight."

"Thank you, Sir Nevill. Goodnight, Sir Nevill."

Chapter III

(1)

The spring sunshine slept peacefully on the wide graveled space in front of Hartley front door; and two collies who had just been out for a run, slept upon the strip of turf, just out of the sunshine, with their long tongues hanging out.

Easter fell late this year, and the trees were, so to speak, just dressed again. The crocuses were out — such at least as had escaped the busy sparrows — and the wallflowers were out, for it was close on Pentecost. To the right and left of the solemn gray house, ran the wide belt of woods, like outstretched arms, between which looked the stone-framed windows, like meditative eyes, right across the flat stretch of meadowland bisected by the straight drive that led up to the great porch from the double lodge gates half a mile away.

The house was of an Elizabethan foundation, though most of the Tudor work had been supplanted by Caroline. Up in the attics were still the criss-cross black beams, the uneven floors and the low ceilings; but the rest of the place wore the stately air that is characteristic of the century after. The porch would have been pretentious if it had not been so genuine. Stone men looked over the parapet, as if further to guard the solemn emblazoned coat that was already guarded, by a couple of ramping beasts. Two long rows of tall windows ran the length of the house, above which peered out the dormer windows of the earlier date. The roofs of stable and laundry showed at one end, and to the north, the high gable of the tennis court above the plantations into which merged the woods. Finally, to the right hand of the house, in a little cleared space there stood, rather to the west of this west front, the domestic chapel of Hartley, in the midst of a rather somber-looking small churchyard, decked with cypresses; and behind it, the roof of the more recently built chaplain's house. As a whole, it was an exceedingly respectable place, not to be reckoned, of course, amongst the greater domestic shrines, yet entirely good of its kind. It appeared to be as much part of the landscape as the woods themselves, or as the solemn lines of the downs discernible away to the south. It seemed that the woods clothed the house, rather than that

the house was built in the woods: the little river that ran as
the boundary of the southeastern gardens on the other side
appeared to have been placed there by design, rather than
that the gardens had been laid out according to its course.

The collies were so deeply asleep that when their mistress
came out at last to see where they were, they never moved.
She stood in the shadow looking at them an instant, with a
faint smile on her face. They were splashed in the black mud
all along their undersides, now brazenly displayed to the
world, and all up their delicate frilled legs. Jack's face was
quiet and solemn, as befitted a male: Jill was still panting in
her sleep as was proper to her hysterical femininity. Their
entire attitude was one of complete and exhausted abandon-
ment.

"Oh! You pigs!" she said suddenly, in quite a low voice.

Jack opened an eye as if to reassure her he was still alive,
and thumped the end of his tail twice. Jill leaped up and began to cry aloud with delight.

"There, that's enough," said the woman. "Come on round to
the gardens; and then you shall go to the stables. *Stables,*
you pigs!. . . . No, Jill; don't be so silly. Not yet; afterwards."

She moved round to the left, and Jack with his middle-aged
and masculine sedateness followed her dutifully. Jill, after
unfitting her tail from between her hind legs, where she had
immediately hidden it upon hearing the fatal place named,
consented to come after, but plainly a little nervous in spite
of the promise.

"Mummy!" said a voice suddenly from overhead. "Where
are you going?"

The woman stopped; and her face twinkled with pleasure
as she looked up to the end window of the first floor: where
the upper half of a boy appeared over the sill, entirely without any clothes on, but brandishing a towel, and with all his
hair on end.

"To the gardens," she said.

"Oh! . . . Are the dogs there?"

"Yes; they're a perfect disgrace. Where in the world did you
find all that mud?"

"Oh! I think it was in the Kestern woods; there was a pond
there; and there was a water-hen there; and Jill, you see —"

"Yes; I quite see, thanks. Well, they can't come into the
house till they're clean."

"Oh . . . Mummy!"

"Yes?"

"It's not their fault, you know; it was mine. You see, I sent in Jack at one end, while Jill went round to the other, and so —"

The woman laughed suddenly.

"Oh! You child!" she said. — "Now get changed quick. I shall be in the pavilion if you want me. Mr. Morpeth's coming to lunch."

"Oh! And is Miss Morpeth —?"

"Go along, Jim, and get changed. Just think if she came along and saw you like that!"

The white apparition vanished.

(2)

The gardens on the eastern side of the house gave a very considerable surprise to anyone who called at the house for the first time. The west side, as has been seen, wore an aspect of a certain severity. There were the solemn front, the cypressed churchyard, the flat lawns cut by the straight drive, and not a flower to be seen except beneath the edges of the plantations on either side. But the eastern side was very different.

First there came a wide stone terrace, flagged underfoot, bounded by a low wall along which stood great stone flowerpots. This was approached from the house (so great was the fall of the ground), by a double flight of stairs leading down in a curve from the door of the hall which ran the whole depth of the building. Beneath the terrace ran a wide gravel path from end to end of the house, and beyond that again, a vast lawn, here broken by a circle of flowerbeds, here by a couple of cedars, here, again, unbroken and as soft as velvet. Then again, further out, came a gravel walk, and again a low wall; and then the river. This river, perhaps twenty feet across, ran swiftly from north to south, as clear as crystal in its chalk bed; two or three steps in the wall, straight opposite the hall door, led down to it; and a punt usually rested here. Forty yards further along, a stone pavilion was built out half over the river, perched in the wall, and was entered by half a dozen steps leading up from the gravel walk.

To this pavilion then, across the wide lawn between the cedars and the flowerbeds, came Mrs. Fanning, as she usually did about the time of the second post. Sometimes she brought her letters with her; sometimes they were taken out to her. If she were not in her own room it was generally understood that she would be here from about twelve to half-past one.

The collies, of course, had made instantly for the water-gate, and were noisily drinking. But even Jack was a little nervous if he were surprised here; for more than once he had been pushed in suddenly from behind by the boy who had conversed out of the window just now. When they had quite done they proceeded to the pavilion, where the sacred dogs' mat lay to the left of the entrance, pushed open the nearly closed door, and resumed their slumbers.

The pavilion was an ideal place for a sunny hour in the morning, even in winter. A wide high window ran in a great semicircle over the river, and was furnished inside with a long deep window seat. Until about four o'clock in summer, and until sunset in winter, all the sunlight that there was streamed in from the south. The chuckling sound of running water, from the current that rushed by beneath, was deli-cious in summer, and not unpleasant in winter. A sensible round table, really firm upon its legs, and furnished with writing materials, stood in the middle of the circular floor. Two well-filled bookcases hung on either side of the door; three or four deep basket chairs stood here and there; the ceiling was a plastered dome within, and a cone without — all of solid gray stone; the floor, adequately tiled, was covered with rugs.

Anna Fanning had sat down upon the window seat as soon as she had made sure that the letters were not waiting for her on the table, and was looking out of the window. By turn-ing her head she could look right up the river for a quarter of a mile, and down it beyond the stone bridge for about a hun-dred yards. At these two extremities the woods came down and hid it. Beyond the woods to the south, however, showed the line of the downs. Even straight out across the river, the view had its charm; for here was the park proper — long roll-ing grasslands, broken by copses, stretching for about two miles and rising gradually towards the foot of the heather hills of Ashdown. Here and there were the cattle, feeding resolutely in the sun; and there, under the shadow of a group of tall trees, she could make out the brown bodies of the deer, resting, just outside the bracken, apart and exclusive like the aristocrats that they were.

Anna Fanning was just forty-one years old, and for the last year had considered herself middle-aged.

She had married, just before she was thirty, old sir Nevill's younger brother Robert; and four years later Jim had been born. They had lived in town for the most part, coming down here again and again, till, when her husband had died a year after Jim's birth, she had come here altogether, six years ago, to keep house for his brother. Then, again, four years ago he too had died, and young Nevill had asked her to stay on.

She was forty-one years old, as has been said; and sometimes she looked a good deal more, and sometimes a good deal less. For, first, her hair was quite gray, though as abundant as ever. It had begun to go gray, as was almost the accepted custom in her family, soon after her twenty-fifth year; and had continued to do so remorselessly ever since. And there were, of course, lines in her face, though still delicate and slight, especially about her eyes, since she would no more have dreamed of massaging her face than of dyeing her hair. Yet, on the other side, she still could flush like a girl; she still kept her figure, and she still carried herself superbly. She was not in the least pretty, but she was quite beautiful. She had very bright gray eyes; she had finely-cut lips that continually smiled a little, but not much; she had a very straight and good profile. Since her husband's death she had been proposed to at least four times, but always by men nearer sixty than fifty; and she had never had even a moment's hesitation in refusing them. It appeared to her that life at Hartley, with a dutiful month or two in London (so long as she was allowed to be at Hartley for the rhododendron season), was an entirely ideal life. Of course it could not continue indefinitely; she had been quite clear to Nevill that when he married it must end; and had laughed frankly at his statement that he would probably never marry at all.

However, here she lived for the present with Jim; and it was all extremely nice. Jim would go to school next year — to the Benedictines, she thought; and she would continue to keep house even more tranquilly during school time — unless, indeed, Nevill married. Here she had her beautiful house, her stone pavilion to sit in, her horse to ride, her church within a stone's throw, her village to visit in; and just a very few neighbors, with whom ordinary courtesies must be exchanged. And then, when Nevill married, she would con-

sider the question as to whether she would take the Dower
House, as he had suggested, at the further end of the park, or
take a flat in town, or a little house near Downside so as to
be close to Jim. She rather thought the last plan would be
best. But there was no hurry. There never was any hurry
with Mrs. Fanning. Things would arrange themselves tranquilly when the time came.

(3)

There approached, as she sat regarding the landscape
through the big curved window, in that almost motionless
attitude that was so completely characteristic of her, the
sound of weighty footsteps.

Anna turned her head as they came up the stairs, and saw
that she had been right, and that it was Masterson himself
who was bringing out her letters. This, she considered to be
very nearly an honor; for there was no one in the whole
world, she believed, quite like Masterson.

He had taken service under old Sir Nevill, as his body servant, at least thirty years ago; and, such was his genius, had
not only remained in it as butler, but had so impressed himself on the place that Hartley without Masterson simply
would not be Hartley. One might as well blow up the porch or
the pavilion at once.

His tact had been infinite when she had first come here to
keep house. He had begged her pardon one morning, soon
after her official arrival, and had requested to know whether
madam wished or did not wish him to give her some kind of
an idea as to how things were done at Hartley. His air of def-
erential detachment from any personal feeling in the matter
had been so superb that the idea of impertinence was simply
not to be entertained for an instant. His manner resembled
that of one general who has been superseded by another in
the conduct of a campaign, but who has vanquished every
pulse of resentment: he merely desired to be of service to his
successor if it were wished; not unless.

Of course she had thanked him very humbly and gravely.
He had proceeded then, still with a magnificent deference, to
point out one or two little matters that were not quite satisfactory, and then, begging pardon again, had departed. He
had renewed his instructions later, on several occasions, had
sketched for her the weaknesses as well as the virtues of

Mrs. Canning, the housekeeper, and had suggested one or two little improvements. Then gradually these instructions had ceased, when Anna had been properly formed; and finally, he had manifested his entire acceptance of her rule by admitting her to the number of his superiors to whom he permitted himself to be brusque in private. This was the last distinction he could confer: he was never, for instance, brusque to the priest; he had never been brusque to her own husband. He never was brusque to anyone except his obvious superiors, and to them only in the strictest privacy.

Well, here he was, coming in at the door, a large figure of a man, gray-haired and rosy, with a fringe of white below his chin, in a swallowtail coat with a V-shaped shirtfront. She wondered why he was here.

"The letters, Masterson?"

"Yes'm. Letter from Sir Nevill, 'm."

He extended a silver tray to her, and there, on the top was the envelope addressed in Nevill's neat upright hand, with the Italian stamp in the corner. (That explained Masterson's ceremonial, then.)

She took it at once, with a certain eagerness. She had not had a line from him since the note in Easter week which announced that he wanted to stay a little longer than he had at first intended. (It was just like Masterson, she thought, to have scrutinized the letters, and to have remarked on it so frankly. But she knew the cause to be sheer loyalty.)

Masterson retired to the door and stood there waiting. Jack, thinking that something was required of him, thumped his tail again three or four times; but his friend regarded him severely. It would be entirely as incorrect for him to recognize Jack in public, as to allow the familiarities, under the same circumstances, to Jim, which he would permit in the pantry. Jack ceased, and closed his eyes with a sigh.

There was a minute of silence in the pavilion after Nevill's letter had been opened; broken only by the chuckle of the river beneath the pavilion window. Anna remembered afterwards the significant little silence.

Then she looked up sharply.

"Yes, Masterson? Is there anything?"

He raised his eyes for a moment, and then dropped them again.

"No'm. . . . No news of when Sir Nevill returns, 'm?"

She seemed dazed a little.

"No. . . . I don't know. I'll tell you when I've read it. . . . He . . . he —"

She broke off again.

Again came the silence, as she turned back once more to the first page. Then Jill sat up and uttered a loud melodious yawn. Masterson still lingered an instant; and then turned and went out.

(4)

So it had come at last — the news of Nevill's engagement — for which she had waited so long. She had told herself again and again that it might come at any time, and that it must come sometime. Yet, now that it had come, it brought to her a greater shock than she had anticipated. It seemed curiously disappointing that it should have come in such a way, without the faintest indication of its approach. She had thought, somehow, that she would have been a witness of the first stages of the affair; that she would know the girl herself; that she would watch Nevill and see how matters developed — perhaps, even, that she would be the confidante of the girl. Two or three names had passed before her mind as possibilities.

For that kind of thing she had been ready enough; she had rehearsed, smiling faintly to herself, little scenes that might have happened; she had even thought that Nevill might come and tell her in this very pavilion. Well, he had told her here, after all; or rather his letter had told her. But it had not been as she had rehearsed it.

She read the name again — Enid Bessington. No; she had never heard of Enid Bessington. It appeared to her curiously disconcerting that anyone called Enid Bessington should be engaged to her nephew Nevill.

A second disappointment lay in the news that she was not a Catholic: and she made haste to take refuge in this. It was quite a sharp little blow that this was so. Of course she had faced the possibility; but a possibility is very different from an assured fact. Of course, too, Nevill said that she was thoroughly broad-minded; that she had definitely made to him the promises as regarded the Catholic upbringing of the children (if there were any), which she afterwards would renew before the marriage was celebrated; he even said that he thought she might very likely become a Catholic herself. But all young men in love thought that kind of thing.

So Anna fixed upon this point as her principal little grievance — as the explanation of her very sharp dismay at the whole news.

For she would not have been human, after all, unless there had always remained in the background of her mind a consciousness that, in spite of probabilities to the contrary, Nevill really might not marry. Never for a moment had she ever permitted herself to wish that he would not: it was entirely right that he should; she had expressly urged it, again and again. Yet she was the mother of Jim, after all; and Jim certainly had been heir-presumptive ever since he had been born; — was, in fact, still the heir-presumptive. Her humanity therefore made its subconscious protest, and experienced its subconscious dismay. But it was wholly subconscious; she would not, even this moment of surprise, allow it to be more. Two points only did she permit to dwell on her mind as disconcerting — one, that Enid Bessington was entirely unknown to her, and the other, that Enid Bessington was not a Catholic.

And then, as she turned the last page of the four she perceived that she must not allow those to be grievances. Nevill was the head of the house; he was perfectly free; he must follow his heart.

"Mummy."

She looked up suddenly; and the heir-presumptive stood in the doorway.

He really was a picture. He had been out riding for a good two hours this morning on a small and very determined little pony, that was, for all that, not so determined as his rider; and he was still flushed from that strenuous exercise and from the cold bath that had followed it. He was close on eight years old; as upright as his mother; he had a singularly fair complexion and straight golden hair, cut like a fourteenth century page's — (it was deplorable to think that by this time next year it would have to be cropped instead) — bright gray eyes like her own, and an exceedingly resolute mouth. He was back in his sailor suit now, barefooted; instead of in the perfectly ridiculous and perfectly charming little riding suit and boots in which he had come to breakfast.

Poor little heir-presumptive!

"Yes, my darling!"

"May I come in?"

He said it like a sort of aside; but it was strictly according to rule that he must ask this always when she was here with her letters. He was beaming on the collies as he asked it.

"Yes, come in."

She watched him first sit down suddenly between the collies and then roll over in a kind of ecstasy, bringing an arm round each shaggy neck and dragging each long nose down into the back of his head. An indescribable sound rose from the entangled group, of scratching claws, loud excited moans from Jill, the steady good-humored growling of Jack, and long whines of pleasure from the boy.

She watched them meditatively.

"Well; be dirty again, if you like," she said, "but remember you'll have to wash and brush your hair all over again."

He sat up, his whole face screwed tight with delight and with the physical ecstasy of having been scratched and nosed all over the back of his neck.

"Oh! Mummy," he began — "No, Jill; go away: I don't want you."

He pushed her violently in the chest.

"Come up here if you want to keep clean — get *down*, Jill!"

He climbed up behind his mother, and threw his arms round her waist.

"Oh! Mummy!" he said, "how jolly it all is!"

At moments like this a kind of joy ran through her that very nearly terrified her. Jim's superabundant vitality continually broke out in violent caresses. He would suddenly embrace his pony's nose before mounting and kiss him between the eyes; or he would roll on the ground, as just now, between the collies; or, again, it was his mother now and then whom he fiercely embraced. He was just one tingling four foot of life that burst out irrepressibly. He had, of course, as such natures do have, long meditative intervals in which he stared, steadily and unseeing, at some entirely familiar thing and when questioned gave what seemed a wholly inadequate subject to occupy his mind so utterly. And then, as abruptly and as inconsequently, he would set his small teeth in a passion of affection and seize his mother — or even Masterson's trousered leg would do — and say how jolly it all was.

But at this moment, breaking upon the news that she had just had, and on her knowledge of the amazing change that it registered in his fortunes, his embrace was like a sword for pain. She felt herself suddenly flush; then she too seized him, pulled him round and kissed him almost savagely between the eyes. Then, ashamed, she recovered herself.

"There, my dear, and now pick up that letter you've just knocked down, and give it me. It's from Cousin Nevill; and he's coming back on Saturday. Quick; or Jill'll get it."

(5)

Mr. Morpeth, who was coming to lunch, as she had reminded Jim half an hour ago, and in whose honor, therefore, he must be even more speckless than usual, was a man she was beginning to like particularly.

At first he had been a name to her, and nothing else. In the long run she managed most of the estate of which Nevill was the official owner; and it was to her, therefore, that the agent had come and reported, six months ago, that an exceedingly desirable tenant had applied for the Dower House, that he was a Catholic with one daughter, that he was a retired businessman of tolerable wealth, that he had made no difficulties at all and that, while he would have preferred a longer lease, he was perfectly willing to sign one for a year only, with a first option of renewing it at the same rent every year for ten years at least. (Nevill had insisted on these terms in case Aunt Anna might want the house herself.)

For the first three months after his arrival she had seen no more of him than absolute courtesy demanded. He and his daughter dined with them once, and no more. Ella, the daughter, was just ordinary, who seemed to make no demands on anyone; and her father had appeared to be exactly what he was — a sensible, quiet sort of man, of almost sixty, who had obviously been in business, and now, no less obviously was glad to be out of it and at peace in the country. Anna could have said no more of him than that. She was just aware that he was paying a good deal of attention to his garden.

Then there had been some trouble about a son of one of the keepers, who had been arrested for poaching. He was a wild hopeless kind of boy, exceedingly independent and irresponsible. She had met Mr. Morpeth one day after Mass and she happened to mention to him her difficulty about the lad; she had talked to him, she said, without the smallest effect; and was in despair as to his future. Then, she scarcely knew how, it had been arranged that Mr. Morpeth was to see him. He had done so; and a day or two later came up to report his success.

That success, it appeared, had been complete. Dick had capitulated; had promised to enter regular employment and was to come up to apologize in person. (This he did next day.) But that was not all; it was the character of a few remarks that Mr. Morpeth had made to herself that had made her for the first time regard him with interest. This whiskered gentleman, it appeared, knew a considerable amount more about human nature than she did; and his manner of speaking of Almighty God, too, had been peculiar. . . . So, little by little, she had begun to understand that Mr. Morpeth was — well — a little beyond her power of understanding. She knew as yet hardly more than that; but she was aware that she would like to know a good deal more. He interested her quite remarkably. Among other things she had come to the conclusion that he was exactly what she meant by a gentleman; and she meant a good deal by that.

Jim had gone in to make himself ready for the second time; and she was still sitting with Nevill's letter in her hand, and the rest unopened, when she saw Mr. Morpeth coming across the lawn. She was conscious of a sudden pleasure at the sight of him. Somehow it was reassuring. She stood up briskly to greet him.

"Come in, Mr. Morpeth," she said. "The bell hasn't rung yet. Good morning."

He looked very ordinary indeed as he came up the steps.

He was in his usual gray tailed suit, and carried his Panama hat in one hand and his handkerchief in the other. His high bald forehead shone with heat, and he was a little flushed with walking. There was nothing whatever noticeable about him except his kindly eyes, and these were not anything extraordinary.

"Good morning," he said. "Yes; it's quite warm, isn't it? I came across the grass. The swifts are beginning to build, by the way."

"You know all about that kind of thing, don't you?" she said. "I love it too; but I don't know anything."

He carefully wiped his forehead once more, and then the inside of his hat; and set hat and handkerchief together on the floor by his chair. Jack rose solemnly and put his nose to them; then he placed that same nose on Mr. Morpeth's knee and regarded him contemplatively. Mr. Morpeth put a hand on the dog's head.

"Yes," he said; "that kind of thing; and Almighty God. Those, I may say, are my business just now." It was just that sort of sentence that had first attracted Anna's attention. At first she had thought it the peculiar kind of thing converts did say; but she had begun to perceive that it was characteristic of this individual rather than of any general type. He said it quite simply and unaffectedly.

She smiled a little, and nodded in assent.

"I've just heard from Nevill," she said. "He's . . . he's coming back on Saturday."

"I hope he's better," said Mr. Morpeth politely.

"Well; he doesn't say anything about his headaches; and he seems to have been doing a good lot. So I should think he was."

"He saw a doctor before he went abroad, you said, I think?"

"Yes, indeed; I made him. And he must see him when he comes back too. But —"

She stopped. Nevill had said nothing about keeping the engagement private; and yet she was not quite sure whether he meant her to speak of it.

"Yes? You were going to say —?"

She suddenly decided she would speak of it. That was the kind of effect that this man's presence did have on her: he seemed to her, in his soul, at least, to be rather like an experienced priest, or a wise doctor. His persuasiveness lay in his eyes, she thought. They were not at all perfect in shape, or exceptionally large, and anything of that kind; but they were narrow and very blue and exceedingly kindly looking.

"Mr. Morpeth," she said, "I may as well tell you. Of course you understand it's confidential until you hear of it from outside. But Nevill's engaged himself to be married."

"Yes?"

"It's what I've always told him to do, of course. But —"

"But naturally it's rather a shock, now it has come; because of your boy."

That pricked her sharply; and she started. For an instant she thought herself offended.

"I quite see that. I cannot imagine its being otherwise," continued Mr. Morpeth tranquilly.

"Oh dear me!" she said. "Yes, of course you're right. That does come in. But that's not all."

"She's probably a Protestant," observed Mr. Morpeth next.

Then indeed she was startled.

"How in the world did you know?" she asked.

"My dear Mrs. Fanning; it's quite simple. First you aren't quite happy about it; and next — well — Sir Nevill was almost sure to marry a Protestant. You haven't met her, I expect; and that's another point."

She laughed outright.

"Well, you'd better give me the news instead," she said, with an air of mock-resignation. "I suppose you can't guess her name?"

"That's quite beyond me —"

"You must tell me," she cried. "How did you guess I hadn't met her? And what in the world do you mean by saying that Nevill would be sure to marry a Protestant?"

"Well; I guessed you hadn't met her; partly because you didn't mention her name, and I think you would have mentioned it first of all if you knew her. And then, I thought from your manner that there was another point you did not quite like; and I could think of nothing else."

"Well; it was a very brilliant shot; and perfectly right. And now about the other."

For a moment Mr. Morpeth did not speak. He dropped his eyes to Jack, and passed his hand over the smooth head two or three times. There was no look in his face as if he were aware he had been at all clever: he was quite natural and quiet. Then he spoke.

"Well," he said, "it's most impertinent of me. But since you ask me, I should say simply that Sir Nevill struck me, on the one or two occasions I met him, as being that kind of young man. He's a little restless, you know; he rather resents being in prison, as he thinks it; and he's very independent, really. Well; that kind of man usually does marry a Protestant; partly because there are a good many more Protestants than Catholics in England; and partly because he would be attracted by their appearance of independence. Sir Nevill is not initiated . . . if I may use the phrase."

Up to the last sentence she understood him perfectly and agreed with him; though never before had she so put it to herself. But she perceived it to be quite true. But the last sentence was beyond her.

"What do you mean by initiated?" she asked gently.

Again he waited an instant before answering. His hand passed rhythmically over the head still passive on his knee, and beneath the ears. His eyes wandered out for a moment through the open door to the lawns and the great house. Then Jill, who had been watching the caresses with liquid pained eyes, whined suddenly.

"There! Go and lie down," he said softly, "your wife's getting jealous. . . . Initiated, Mrs. Fanning? Well; I hardly know what other word to use. Well; the difference between your nephew and yourself, if I may venture to say so."

As his eyes came round to hers she was conscious of a sudden slight flush of pleasure across her bewilderment; and, simultaneously, understood, or thought she understood what he meant. Yet it surely was an odd phrase.

"Please be more explicit," she said, smiling.

"Well, you know," said Mr. Morpeth, "of course I don't profess to say there's a hard and fast line. But it's quite plain, surely, that there is one class of persons on one side and another on the other. The one accepts what happens, so soon as it really has happened; and the other does not. The one knows that the past is inevitable, and the other is not sure. The one is not surprised at things, and therefore does not resent them; he is behind the scenes, so to speak, and understands what it is all about, even if he cannot quite make out the details; and the other looks on from the stalls, and knows nothing except what he sees. I suppose that is more or less what I meant just now."

"But Nevill's a Catholic," said the woman rather inconsequently, as she thought.

"Oh, yes, and I cannot imagine his being anything else. But for all that he struck me as not initiated."

She opened her lips to speak; and then closed them again. Simultaneously the stable bell began to ring.

"Well, shall we go to lunch?" she said.

(6)

It was nearly four o'clock before she found herself alone again in the pavilion; and, somehow or other, the situation wore a very different complexion from that of this morning.

At lunch, of course, they had talked of all the things that did not matter. Ella, it appeared, was not yet back from town; the garden of the Dower House was shaping really excellently. Dick Fottrel, the gamekeeper's turbulent son, was doing well on the railway.

Jim, too, so admirable was his behavior, demanded certain amount of conversation. He did not interrupt once while high and grownup matters were being discussed; but his look of pathetic self-repression made it entirely necessary for the history of the water-hen incident of this morning to be thoroughly reviewed, and for reassurances to be given to the authorities that neither Jack nor Jill had shown any signs of having disturbed a possible nest. Plans, also, had to be sketched with a view to Cousin Nevill's return on Saturday, and the probabilities debated as to whether he might not possibly, seeing that Jim's eighth birthday came in June, forestall that event by giving him his first lesson in tennis, promised so soon as that date should be reached.

Jim, too, had come out with them for coffee into the pavilion afterwards, for the performance of the usual ceremonies with Jack and Jill, who were allowed to lick the inside of the coffee cups clean of sugar, on condition that Jim carefully dirtied them again afterwards. It was Jim's peculiar delight, "because it was so beastly," to smell those cups after the dogs had licked them; and indeed the odor of coffee and dog mixed is as startling as a chord crashed on a piano.

When, at last, Jim was gone away to see if Charleson the footman would consent to come and bowl to him at the net; the two had begun again.

It became more and more astonishing to Anna to find how quickly she was understood by this prosaic old gentleman. Not only did he seem to understand her instantly, but he seemed to be familiar too with the processes and grounds that underlay what she had always thought to be small fancies of her own. For instance, she had spoken of the death of Nevill's father, as being one of the most impressive and terrible scenes she had ever witnessed. It was pretty notorious

that he had lived an exceptionally wild life; and that he had
died comparatively young in consequence; so she was guilty
of no indiscretion in what she said.

"What astonished me most," she said, "was my nephew's
splendid behavior. His father clung to him, you know, very
much at the end — he was simply terrified at the thought of
death. Even the priest — it was old Father Benedict we had
then, you know — even the priest seemed rather taken aback
by some of the . . . the things that happened. But Nevill —
my nephew, I mean — was splendid. He never faltered or
showed the least sign of fear, you know. Now what do you
make of that, Mr. Morpeth? He was the strongest person
there."

The old man nodded quietly, without speaking.

"No; but tell me," she said eagerly. "Doesn't that look as if
he was Initiated, as you call it?"

He looked up at her questioningly.

"Yes, I mean it," she said. "Tell me."

"Well; I should think it was his Paganism that supported
him; not his Christianity."

"Yes; that was exactly true." She perceived it the moment
he had said it. It was certainly not Nevill's grip of what lay
beyond death that had been his strength; he loathed death
and pain, and had said so, again and again. But it was a fine
sort of defiance that had inspired him. Simply, he would not
be beaten. She had fallen silent when Mr. Morpeth had said
that.

She had gone on to describe presently — so extraordinarily
sympathetic did she find this old man — another incident
connected with that deathbed.

"Just before the end," she said, "he was a little quieter. (It
was up in the big room in the front, you know. We haven't
used it at all, since then.) Well, just before the end, he said a
rather dreadful thing. He was holding on to my nephew with
both hands: he kept his strength, you know, extraordinarily.
That was partly what made it all so much more terrible.
Well; he seemed to think that Nevill would suffer for him,
somehow . . . that . . . that it was sure to be so. Well; but
Nevill took him up, and said that he only hoped he would. Of
course, he didn't mean it. I don't think any of us knew what
we were saying. . . . But it was a fine thing to say, wasn't it?"

"It was quite a fine thing to say," repeated Mr. Morpeth tranquilly.

She bit her lip sharply.

"I see what you mean," she said. "You mean that he didn't mean it!"

"You thought so too, though," he said gently.

"Well; I did; and I do still. But do you think that kind of thing really does happen — people offering themselves for others?"

"Why, yes," he said, as gently as ever. "The Old Law even said that it would be so; and the New Law underlined it, surely."

"I don't understand."

"Well; the sins of the fathers are visited upon the children. That is in Nature, as we say. And the New Law says that the children ought to be ready to accept it, willingly. That is the whole idea of Atonement, is it not?"

It seemed very simple, put like that, thought Anna.

"But . . . but you don't think in this case —" she began, suddenly a little afraid.

He spread his hands in a small gesture.

"Who in the world can tell?" he said. "We know the principles of things: but no more. In any case it will be all perfectly well."

Somehow, then, when he left her an hour later she felt reassured all round. This morning, for the few minutes after the opening of Nevill's letter and before the old gentleman's arrival, she had been conscious of a considerable interior disturbance. Now, though he had uttered scarcely a word to reassure her directly, though, even, he had, superficially, corroborated all her fears, she was aware of comfort. It was not that he had taken anything away; rather, he had drawn pointed attention to the facts. But he had seemed to present them in a new sort of setting; and they looked quite different. There remained Enid Bessington; there remained Jim's altered position and prospects; there remained even more than a suspicion that Nevill was not entirely satisfactory. Yet the air had changed. . . .

She sat again in the window seat, staring out at a dancing Mayfly that had rashly left the far bank to adventure himself into the gardens whose scent, perhaps, was drawing him. She was thinking steadily, and with a restored tranquillity, of this new setting of ideas, and simultaneously had her own attention fixed on the Mayfly.

He was dancing up and down in a frenzy of delight; now, for a fleeting instant he tapped the glassy surface of the stream, now he whirled a couple of feet above it.

("It'll be all right," she whispered to herself, thinking of the engagement.)

The Mayfly was nearing safety: one more whirl would land him on the grass. But once more, for the last time, he dipped, close to the bank; and as he dipped, a swirl rose to meet him; a dark nose showed for a moment in the midst of the glass and was gone again: and so was the Mayfly.

She caught her breath for the fraction of a second.

"But it's all part of the scheme," she said aloud.

Chapter IV

(1)

Anna sat in the hall, late on the Saturday night, waiting for the wheels that would bring her nephew home.

It was a great room this, in which she sat, running the whole depth of the house from front to back, from the double doors that opened on the porch on the west, to the double doors that opened upon the curved stairway into the garden on the east. The lower half of the hall was paneled, some twelve feet up; and above hung the long Fanning portraits — a very nearly complete set from the days of the Second Charles — tilted a little forwards, with a shaded electric light at the head of each. On the north side of the hall opened three doors — dining room, servants' staircase, and smoking room; on the south side, two doors; the one nearer to the front led to the drawing rooms; then came the open fireplace, then the door of the big square morning room, and beyond it again, close to the garden entrance, rose up the great staircase that turned twice and ended in a hanging gallery that led right round the square. From this again, opened out the bedrooms and first floor passages. Tall windows, above and below the gallery, four in each wall, lighted the hall, and, in sunshine, showed even the high painted roof that was on a level with the top of the first floor.

It was, then, a room of very great dignity. The furniture was big and splendid; the floor, under the rugs and between, was laid with flagstones: there was some good armor, of Cavalier days, between the portraits: a little copper and silver, and a glass cabinet or two of china, lit up the darker corners. An organ stood between the fireplace and the door of the morning room; and there were high tapestried chairs about the hearth.

In one of these sat Anna. She always looked singularly young in evening dress; her hair seemed as if powdered; her arms and throat were smooth and white. But she had not in the least the air of trying to appear younger than her years. She wore plenty of jewelry and a little fall of black lace, as if to make quite sure of this.

She had dined alone, an hour ago; and had suggested to Masterson to bring the tray in here, so soon as the traveler arrived. Nevill had wired from Folkestone that the boat was late and that he would dine in town. It was, of course, quite dark by now; but she had told the men to leave the windows uncurtained, as it was a still night of stars. Partly she wanted to look at these; and partly she thought it would be pleasant for Nevill, if he cared to look, to see the four windows all aglow with welcome. She had had a wood fire lighted on the hearth, and in Nevill's big bedroom upstairs. She had quite a strong instinct that everything must be very alluring and pleasant for his homecoming, particularly under these circumstances.

She had had plenty of time during these last four days to steady herself for the encounter. Mr. Morpeth had, undoubtedly, set her attitude. She must just take it as done. Nevill was doing nothing that needed protest; he was his own master; he had every possible right to get married; and it was not in the least necessary that his aunt should give her opinion. He must settle such things for himself. There must not therefore be allowed to show even the shadow of a grievance. She must be entirely sympathetic and optimistic. She must congratulate him — really congratulate him and be interested in Enid. She must show that she was really satisfied. And then, when all that had been done, she must begin to make her own arrangements, and ask his advice. But she was feeling quite sure that the Dower House would not do. It was much too near.

She was very pensive, for all her resolution, as she sat quite still and listened for the wheels. She had put down her book, half an hour ago; and had so sat ever since, looking tranquilly into the fire. Jim was asleep long ago, of course. She had looked in immediately after dinner into his room, which was next her own; and he had resembled an angel. Sometimes he stirred in his sleep as she bent over him; tonight he had not.

The house too was as quiet as such a house ever can be. The servants were still at supper; the night was windless, and the fire one noiseless glow. She seemed to herself to be in a kind of parenthesis, in more ways than one. The day of Jim and small duties, and going out to the pavilion and back again — this was all over. And Nevill was not yet come.

Presently, she knew, the bell would ring from the lodge gate half a mile away, as the carriage went by. Then there would break out footsteps and the sound of doors. Masterson would come through and unlock the front door; there would be the sound of skirts overhead as a maid went for a last look at the young man's bedroom fire. Then there would come the sound of trotting; then the roll of wheels; and then . . . and then Nevill would be here again, in this hall — its master come home — and nothing would be the same ever again.

As she thought of these things, the silence suddenly impressed itself on her, as a presence. She became aware, with a sudden movement of her mind, not of the mere negative fact of the absence of sound, but of the positive fact of the presence of silence. The situation, viewed dramatically, as she had just viewed it, seemed to have tightened up her nerves and her intuitions. It appeared to her as if Silence had just spoken; and there ran a little shiver of apprehensiveness through her.

She turned her head, ashamed of herself, to look round the great dusky hall, lit only by hidden lights high up behind the cornice. It was all solemn and dignified and large. Yet even the hall had a kind of significance — she did not know of what. It seemed as if it too waited, like a set scene, for an actor to speak and move.

And then, with a sudden sharp thrill of real fear, she became aware of the great corniced door at the head of the stairs — kept locked now, she knew, ever since Nevill's father had died behind it, in the big bed, gripping the hand of his son. She had passed that door, for a few months after the tragedy of that death, with a distinct sense of discomfort, every time she went upstairs or down, particularly after nightfall. But she had got over that, more than three years ago: she had even gone in one night, alone, with her candle in her hand, and looked round the room and at the great hearse-like bed. Yet here again, was the same sudden thrill of terror, sharp and strong, like the blade of a sword laid against the throat.

This would never do.

She shifted her position in her chair, turned her head deliberately and stared up to where the gallery began. There was the high carved banister, black against the pale wall; the great cornice over the door beyond it. And . . . and of course there was no one there, leaning over the banister, with crossed arms . . . in a certain flowered dressing gown. . . . It was all as empty as . . . as she knew it was.

A swing door banged somewhere out of sight; her heart leaped for an instant and then raced. For footsteps came along the passage from the servants' quarters and the middle door opened. And then there was Masterson, exactly as she had rehearsed, and Charleson behind him.

"The lodge bell's just rung, 'm," said Masterson on his way to the front door.

(2)

The young man looked really extraordinarily well, she thought, as she sat and watched him at his little supper. He had refused to go upstairs and wash his hands: he had said that half the pleasure of coming home lay in doing exactly what he liked, instantly; and what he wanted at that instant were two anchovy sandwiches, such as those he saw before him, and a whisky and soda. Then he wanted a cigarette; and then he desired to talk.

"You must just sit up for once, Aunt Anna," he said; "and that's all about it. After all, it's our house, isn't it? And if we choose to have breakfast with sausages and coffee and marmalade at a quarter past three tomorrow — who's to forbid us?"

Her heart gave her a little painful prick of happiness as he said "our house." Just for the present it was true, more or less; but it would not be so for long.

"Tomorrow's Sunday," she said. "Father Richardson would have a word to say, if we didn't appear before a quarter past three."

"So he would. I forgot. And I bet he'd say it, too."

He spoke with just the faintest touch of bitterness. He did not much like Father Richardson.

It was a curious mingling of pain and pleasure that she felt as she watched him. He looked better, she thought, than when he had gone away three months ago. There was a line or two under his black eyes; but that was to be expected after a journey; and his hair somehow always reassured her; it looked so springy, and curly and so very black; it was not in the least characteristic of an invalid.

Certainly he was in high spirits at getting home. He talked very pleasant nonsense about the crossing from Boulogne, and a sporting Frenchman who had started very spry and chivalrous and had ended very limp. His face was quite green, still, even on Folkestone platform, said Nevill; and he had seen him shudder visibly at the sight of a cup of very strong station tea that was thrust before him by his wife.

"And you've been well?" said Anna.

"Good Lord, yes," said Nevill. "I love the sea."

"I meant generally."

A shadow of annoyance came over his face, but passed again like a shadow.

"Oh, yes," he said indifferently. "Please don't ask me my symptoms. I hate Health."

"You mean —"

"No I don't. I mean Health, Aunt Anna. It ceases to be health if you think about it."

"But really no more headaches?. . . . No, do tell me: and then I won't ask any more."

"They're much better," said Nevill deliberately, lighting his cigarette. "Now, really — Hullo!"

As he turned to throw away his match his eyes caught a small white phantom at the end of the gallery overhead, where the southern bedrooms lay.

"It's only me, Cousin Nevill," said a rather doubtful voice from the gloom. "You see I heard you talking, and . . ."

"Jim! How dare you?" cried his mother. "I told you distinctly you weren't to come downstairs."

"But I haven't, Mummy; I'm upstairs. So I thought —"

"Go straight back to bed this instant."

"But, Mummy —"

"Go straight back to bed."

Nevill raised his eyebrows to her in a question; and his lips just moved in a whisper. She nodded slightly. "Do what you're told, old chap," he said; "and don't argue. I'll come and see you in bed, if your mother says I may."

The small pajamaed figure leaned passionately forward.

"May he, Mummy? Oh! Do tell me; and then I'll —"

"Yes. Now go."

The phantom vanished.

A little silence fell between the two who sat below. To Anna, the apparition of her little son came as a startling

symbol of the matter that still had to be discussed between
Nevill and herself. If Nevill had instantly spoken, it would
have been all natural enough; but he did not. She stole a
glance at him; and he was smoking rather violently, and his
eyelids drooped ever so slightly as they always did when he
was uneasy or anxious or just a shade out of temper.

"By the way," he said, rather abruptly, after that tiny
pause. "Have you told him?"

She did not pretend not to understand. That was not her
way.

"No," she said. "Of course he's always known perfectly well
that this wasn't his home — I mean" (she corrected herself)
— "that it wasn't his own home. I don't suppose he's ever
dreamed of anything else. But I haven't told him about your
letter. I thought —"

"I wonder if you'd like me to," said Nevill.

She smiled.

"He'd love it. Particularly if you told him as a secret. He
loves secrets, you know."

"Have you told anybody?"

She hesitated.

"I've told one person," she said. "I daresay you'll think it
very odd of me. But, you know, you didn't say I wasn't to."

"That's all right. It isn't a secret; though nothing's gone to
the papers yet. Whom did you tell, by the way?"

"Well: you'll think it very odd; but I told Mr. Morpeth."

"What! That old chap at the Dower House, isn't he? Why in
the world did you —"

"Nevill, I like him. I like him very much. I can't think why.
I simply had to tell him. I knew he'd be as discreet as the
grave, anyhow. And he happened to come to lunch just after
I'd got your letter."

"Oh, well. It's all right, anyhow. Aunt Anna!"

"Yes?"

"Look here. Do you mind?"

"Mind? Why, I'm delighted. Haven't I said again and again—"

"Yes; of course: all that. But I mean that it came so suddenly; and that you don't know her; and all that."

She smiled delightfully.

"My dear boy; she's to be your wife; not mine. I'm perfectly
certain that she's everything you think her; and if she isn't,
why, you'll soon make her so."

"She's a Protestant, you know."

"Well, of course, if other things were equal I'd sooner she'd been a Catholic. But one can't have everything. The point is that you care for her, isn't it?"

Then he too smiled; and the very slight look of doubtfulness that had been on his face just now, passed again.

"Yes. That is the point, isn't it? At least it's one-half. And . . . and the other point's all right too, I think. Look here, Aunt Anna: I simply must tell you about her. It's a dreadful thing to do, I know; but I shall burst if I don't. . . ."

"My dear boy, what do you think I'm here for? I'll gladly stay up till four in the morning if you'll talk about her. Don't you see I'm dying to hear?"

He settled himself back in his chair. She thought she had never seen him so radiant; and at that sight the last shred of hope that the thing was not absolutely settled left even the lowest reaches of her subconsciousness.

He first drew a cabinet photograph out of his breast pocket.

"There!" he said, handing it across to her. "That's number one."

She took it eagerly; tilted it a little to catch the light; and looked at it. It presented Enid in evening dress, standing *en silhouette*. The light was exquisitely managed, and every line of her profile told. There was a silence.

"Well?" said Nevill.

Her face rose to his, full of feeling.

"She's extraordinarily beautiful," she said quietly. "Now go on. . . . No; let me hold this. I want to look at it while you talk."

She leaned back, resting the photograph on her knee, to listen.

(3)

"I told you about her people in my letter," he began. "I needn't say that all over again. Her father lost most of his money, as I said, when she was a child, and his place in Norfolk and all that. But her mother's quite well off and there aren't any other children. However, that doesn't matter anyhow.

"The point is Enid."

He lit another cigarette from the stump of the other, and tossed the stump in the fire.

"Well; she's exactly your sort," he began again. "I don't in the least want to flatter you, Aunt Anna; but you know what I mean. She's deep — in the right way. She doesn't care a hang about society and jawing and tea parties; she loathes them as much as I do; and very nearly as much as you do. That was how we made friends at first.

"Then she's religious. She isn't a Catholic, as I said; though of course she may become one. But I shan't press her to, in the least. She's got the real thing — that's underneath all religions. She said one or two extraordinarily good things about that, by the way — when I told her what she would have to promise, and all that. I told her that before I actually put my proposal into words, of course."

"What did she say?" asked Anna without the movement of a muscle.

"She said that she could not conceive that being any difficulty to anyone who understood. I didn't see quite what she meant, at first. Then I saw. She meant that real religion was quite independent of those things — that Catholicism was quite as good, as an . . . an external system, as anything else — if not better. In fact, I know she does think it the best of all. She said once she wished she'd been born a Catholic."

He paused. Anna did not move.

"Well; that's the main thing," he went on. "That kind of thing matters more than anything. If that's all right, everything else will be. Then she's extraordinarily fond of out-of-door things — just like you, Aunt Anna. She told me how she hated the flat in town where she and her mother live sometimes; and about the garden of their country cottage. She'll simply love this place, you know. By the way, I promised to send her all the picture postcards of it there are. Have you got a set to spare?"

"Oh yes," said Aunt Anna.

"Well, she and her mother are coming down at the end of the month — just for a few days. That'll be all right won't it?

"Why, my dear boy — of course. . . ."

"Well, then, that's all right. Where was I? Oh! Yes; about out-of-door things. I told her about the pavilion here; and she said that was exactly what she had always wanted. . . . What's the matter, Aunt Anna?"

"Nothing, my dear, nothing. I was only changing my position. Go on: I love to hear it."

"I told her how much you liked it too. . . . She wants to meet you, dreadfully, you know. She said she only wished you'd stay on here; but that she was perfectly certain you wouldn't; because the really nice people always went away just when you wanted them. That was nice, wasn't it?"

"Very nice," said Aunt Anna.

"I suppose you won't stay, will you?"

She shook her head, smiling straight at him.

"My dear, it's perfectly beautiful of you to want me — and of her too. And I shall remember that always. But it wouldn't do for a single second."

"Why not?"

"Oh! Do go on! We can talk all that out later. I want to hear about . . . about Enid."

Again his face beamed all over with pleasure; and again it came upon her, as it already had three or four times since he had begun to talk, how curiously and deliciously stupid men were sometimes. They were all just large editions of Jim; the meshes of their subtlety would let even camels march through.

"Well," he said, "I really don't know what else to say. You see . . . you see, I'm in love with her."

"You dear boy. You've said quite enough. She's . . . she's just right, I know. And how clever you are to say she's like me. Where did you learn your diplomacy?"

"No; but she really is, you know. . . . I say, Aunt Anna, you do look dog-tired. What a beast I am!"

A clock began to strike — solemn and sonorous strokes from a tall clock under the stairs.

"That's eleven," he said. "And you always go to bed at half-past ten. And I promised to see Jim."

"Well; I think I will go to bed," she said. "I think there's thunder about. You won't wake Jim, will you, if he's asleep?"

He grinned as he rose.

"I think I'd bet ten pounds Jim won't be. He's a determined child. By the way, I'll take my own time to tell him, if you don't mind."

She nodded.

She was standing now, and looking straight at her nephew; at his upright square-shouldered figure and his bronzed face.

"You look a shade tired yourself," she said — "now I look at you. No headache?"

"Just a touch," he said. "But only train-headache."

"Well: I shall tell them not to call you."

She moved across to the bell.

"Nonsense, Aunt Anna — I tell you —"

"And I say 'Nonsense,' too," she said. "You must do as you're told, like Jim. By the way, Masterson was so anxious when you didn't write. He brought me your letter, when you did — and stood over me like a jailer till I could see there was no bad news."

"You mean that letter —"

"Yes: the one I opened in the pavilion, you know."

"And you'll swear you didn't — didn't think it bad news?"

"You silly boy — the best in the world. . . . Here's Masterson. . . . Masterson, Sir Nevill mustn't be disturbed tomorrow till he rings. He'll tell Charleson if he wants breakfast in bed."

"Aunt Anna —"

"You understand, Masterson, don't you?"

"Yes'm."

"And you'll remember too, Charleson?"

"Yes'm."

"Well; goodnight, my dear."

He bent his head to her, and she kissed him lightly on the forehead, as her custom was.

(4)

He stood waiting until he heard her skirts go rustling along the gallery towards her room. Then he kissed his hand to her. (What a darling she was! he thought; and how Enid would love her!) Then he turned to Masterson, who was solemnly removing the tray, not out of the hall, because Charleson must do that; but on to a side table near the entrance to the servants' passage.

"Well, Masterson, I'm glad to be home again."

"Yes, Sir Nevill."

"You don't think much of foreign parts, Charleson told me." Masterson set the tray down emphatically.

"No, I don't," he said, without the faintest deference, as his manner was with the select few who were his idols. "And I don't know whatever you find to stay out there so long."

Nevill smiled delightedly. This was indeed a homecoming.

"Masterson," he said, "I want to tell you something. But you're not to tell anybody else till it's public."

Masterson regarded him stiffly.

"You've put your finger on the spot, Masterson, as usual. I've found a wife — I mean she's going to be. That's what kept me in foreign parts so long."

Masterson grew positively rigid.

"I've told you as an old friend," continued Nevill. "I've told nobody else in England but Mrs. Fanning. Now then, what have you got to say?"

Masterson's grim lips moved; but no sound came from them.

"Shake hands, Masterson; and wish me luck."

Masterson took the hand in a violent grip; his mouth shook with emotion; but he said nothing. He wheeled and went out. Nevill was content. He understood the other well enough.

Upstairs in the passage outside Jim's room and his mother's a single shaded light was still turned on, showing the boy's door to be open.

Nevill pushed upon it with infinite delicacy; and it made a little brushing sound over the carpet inside.

"Cousin Nevill, I'm awake," sounded a small voice from within.

Nevill went in, but still cautiously.

"You little disobedient brute," he said. "I'm sure your mother told you to go to sleep. Where are you?"

"I'm here."

He made his way across towards the voice; and presently found the edge of the bed with his shin, and drew his breath swiftly, with the exquisite pain. But he had no time to recover himself: a pair of arms seized him round the neck and dragged him sideways on to the bed. Then he felt himself violently kissed all over his ear.

"Put your head down on the pillow by me, Cousin Nevill. . . . Oh! How ripping this is!"

He did what he was told; but his headache was certainly a little worse than it had been ten minutes ago. Then in the gloom he began to feel the warm sweet breath of this child on his face. The small hands were again clasped behind his head.

"And tell me everything, Cousin Nevill," whispered the voice.

"My dear, I can't possibly. I can't breathe."

A chuckle of laughter sounded; and the hands slightly relaxed.

"You can. Go on. Did you see the Pope?"

"Yes, of course I did."

"What's he like?"

"He's just an old man in white."

"Did you kiss his toe?"

"No. No one does nowadays."

"Oh! . . . Did you see the wolves?"

"What wolves?"

"The Romulus and Remus wolves. I mean their children."

"No. I didn't know there were any."

"Of course there are. Miss March told me last week. Did you see the King?"

"I . . . Yes . . . I did. In a dogcart."

"Oh! Is he very tall?"

"No: very small."

"Oh! . . . I thought he was big. Are you sure you saw him?"

"Of course I'm sure. . . . Oh! Jim! Don't pinch so. And, you know, I only came to say goodnight."

(His headache was, indeed, in full blast now. It beat intolerably; and every pulse was pain. He allowed to himself that this was not a train-headache after all. It was the real crusted old brand, he told himself.)

"Well; one more thing. Will you teach me tennis tomorrow afternoon?"

"I . . . I should think so. Why shouldn't I?" (He had entirely forgotten the solemn arrangement of waiting till Jim's eighth birthday.)

The entire body of Jim jumped with delight, like a newly caught trout on the grass; and every bounce shook Nevill's tormented head. The headache was growing like a storm.

"Oh! Jim; do let go. I'm . . . I'm not very well."

"Aren't you? Were you seasick?"

Nevill sat up; and in the dark pressed his hands on his temples.

"No; I wasn't seasick at all. But I must go, Jim. See you tomorrow."

"Well; kiss me, can't you?"

Nevill bent and kissed him.

"Goodnight, Cousin Nevill."

"Goodnight, my dear."

At the door once more the voice reached him.

"Goodnight, Cousin Nevill."

"Goodnight, old chap."

"Leave the door open, won't you? Or else the cat can't get in."

"All right, old chap. . . . Goodnight."

"Goodnight."

(5)

He blinked as he came out into the light of the passage again; and still more when he reached the gallery looking over the hall; for the lights were not yet turned out, though he could hear footsteps moving about in one of the rooms that opened out of it — moving about, no doubt, on that mysterious business that always takes servants round a house the last thing at night.

For the moment the light seemed to relieve his eyes — perhaps as a kind of counter irritation; and he waited here, looking down into the hall before going on to his room that was next his father's old room on the other side.

The hall looked very big and majestic from here; and, as earlier in the evening to Anna, it appeared to him to resemble a stage, set for some play. The tall tapestried chairs in which the two had sat a while ago were still in the positions they had left them in, and the little table was between. The red light of the wood fire, now sunk to a steady glow, glimmered on the carving here and there.

And then he suddenly thought of what a perfect setting all this would be for Enid — how perfectly she would fit into the picture. He remembered her long dresses that had seemed to him curiously antique; the thin chain of pearls she wore round her neck; her masses of hair. In these two chairs, perhaps, they would be sitting together, probably, a few months hence. Aunt Anna would be gone, no doubt. That was a pity; and yet, perhaps, just for the first year or two, it might be better.

How exquisitely, too, Enid's slow movements would suit this place. A bustling girl, in a tweed skirt, would be as much out of place as a tourist in a Cathedral. He glanced down at one of the portraits he could see under the gallery to his right. That was Lady Brightington, he remembered, who had married his great-grandfather. He thought there was something of Enid in her pose — not, of course, the least in face or expression; but just in her still manner and dignity.

Then he remembered that Aunt Anna had not given him the photograph back, and clapped his hand to his pocket. He must ask her for it tomorrow.

As he stood upright again from leaning on the banisters, his eyes fell (as again Anna's had done a couple of hours earlier) on the great corniced door that was the entrance to what had been his father's room; and to him too, came a memory of the tragedy that had been played behind it, and a touch of the fear that had been so vivid to him too, at the sight of it, for the first month or two after his father's death. Again the house was quiet. The footsteps below had ceased. The servant had probably gone out at the further end of whatever room he had been in.

Nevill stared a moment or two longer at the door. His pain was coming back now, in swift strides: the pulses that were like stabbing knives in the front and at the top of his head were prevailing more and more swiftly over the pulses that were comparatively painless. Yet, even through that pain, a strange fear made itself felt. To him, too, it seemed for a perceptible space of time, that if he kept his attention fixed on that door for a little longer, it might open, and a figure come out . . . in a flowered dressing gown, with the bandages that held the ice like a terrible crown about the head. Or, . . . or perhaps even now, the door was open; and the figure was there, looking at him: it was only that he could not see it. . . .

And then the pain drove all else away, as physical sensation can eliminate, if it be but sharp enough, the more delicate tremors of the mind or soul; and he went to his room, telling himself that he was a ridiculous ass; and that he must see to it that the room was opened again properly, and inhabited once more. Perhaps he himself had better take it, and have done with it. Meanwhile, here was the headache to be reckoned with.

(6)

Two hours later he still was awake.

The usual program was being carried faithfully through. He had taken his medicine which Charleson had set out, according to custom, on his dressing table; and had then bathed his forehead, first in stinging hot water and then with eau-de-Cologne.

Then he had got ready for bed; and when all was ready had once more soaked his handkerchief and tied it round his forehead. Then he had got into bed, turned out the light, and pretended that he was going to sleep.

Then the interior drama had begun.

It was first a galloping horse that approached from the immeasurable distance to which the hot water and eau-de-Cologne had temporarily banished the agony — that approached, to announce to him that they were all coming back as fast as they could.

This horse galloped slowly and rhythmically, at a steady rate of progress; and the beat of his four hoofs all together marked the blows of pain that he experienced.

The horse came nearer and nearer, growing, as was but natural, in weight as he approached; until he was really there, so to speak. He remained there a few seconds — never longer than about a minute, apparently prancing to the same rhythm, in the same place, without otherwise moving at all. Then he began to recede again on the other side, intolerably slowly, it was true; but yet it was very nearly pleasure that he should recede at all. It was as this movement began that Nevill really resolved to go to sleep before the next. Again and again he reached the point of no longer feeling his limbs in the bedclothes; and once, even, he thought that Aunt Anna was by his bed, looking down on him with an expression he could not make out.

But at that moment two horses began to gallop, again in the immeasurable distance; and the worst of it all was that they would not keep in step.

These two then punctually pursued the course of their forerunner; they approached, they arrived; they remained steadily prancing, the four feet of each rising and falling, not quite together; they began to recede.

Then, three horses came; then four; then five; and then a regiment. He tried to count them sometimes, in a kind of bitter humor; but they were unreckonable. They kept tolerably in step; that was one comfort; but they took longer to arrive, and remained longer, prancing. It was very nearly interesting, when they all pranced together: they looked almost ludicrous — this long line, from horizon to horizon — (the horizons, of course, were his own temples) — rising and falling together like performers in a circus.

Then even these began to recede — very slowly, it is true — yet they receded, further and further, until the thunder of their hoofs was no more than a murmur, and at last silence.

Nevill began to breathe very carefully through his nostrils. He had already arranged his attitude. He turned on his side always, as soon as the troop began to move off; until that he lay on his face with the pillow clasped about his ears: he did so, that is, generally, after the group of three began to approach.

He lay then, softly, afraid to stir, lest a horse should begin to gallop up again to see what he was doing: and sometimes he managed really to go to sleep. But tonight it was useless. In spite of every conceivable precaution, the single horse began to suspect something, as he fed there miles away in the prairies, scarcely stirring the ground as he moved. He began to trot; he began to canter; to gallop . . . and the hunt was up.

It was as the clock struck half-past one in the hall below that Nevill sat up in bed, very nearly delirious with pain.

"This is perfectly ludicrous!" he said aloud to the listening night.

(7)

"Go very quietly past Cousin Nevill's room as you go downstairs," said Aunt Anna to Jim, coming in about eight o'clock, before he was dressed. "Cousin Nevill's only just gone to sleep. He's been awake all night with headache."

"Oh! Has he? Won't he be able to teach me tennis today?"

"No. Now I'm going to Mass, or I shall be late. Mind you say a prayer for Cousin Nevill, when you get up."

"Yes, Mummy."

"And you mustn't bring the dogs upstairs all day."

"Not if I make them walk on tiptoe?"

"No; not even if you make them walk on tiptoe."

Chapter V

(1)

"Come in, old chap," said Nevill.

Jim advanced from the door, by which he had partly entered, with a solemn awe on his face. It had been impressed upon him at last by his mother that Nevill really did not want the dogs to be brought in to cheer him; and when once he had grasped this, he had concluded that Nevill must be very ill indeed. At the same time, it was gratifying to be sent for immediately after lunch in order to see the invalid.

The boy's eyes wandered vaguely round the room as he paused halfway to the bed. The room had the same mysterious splendor that it always had when Cousin Nevill was at home — a splendor it had lacked terribly during these last three months. There was the mysterious row of boots in their little shelf; the silk dressing gown hanging up by the bed, and, above all, the shining array of implements — silver and steel and glass ranged on the white covered dressing table between the windows. There was a funny smell in the room too — very interesting and suggestive. Then his eyes came back to Nevill beneath the canopy.

"Are you going to die, Cousin Nevill?"

"Certainly not," said Nevill. "I shouldn't dream of such a thing. Why do you ask?"

Jim's round eyes roved again, and came back.

"Oh! Then perhaps you'd like the dogs. I've got them chained up in the hall on purpose; and —"

"I don't think we'll have the dogs."

"I could make them jump on the bed," suggested Jim.

"I think not even on the bed. . . . Come round where I can see you, and say good morning."

He was feeling considerably more cheerful after sleep and lunch and, of course, a cigarette. About seven he had rung his bell in despair, and when Charleson had appeared, had asked for tea. Up to that point he had, really, not slept at all. The galloping horses had been far too busy: he had not been aware that there were so many horses in the world, nor that they could be so untiring. They had galloped, with short pauses, for over seven hours: and his head felt bruised all over. After a cup of tea he had fallen asleep; and Charleson, re-entering from the bathroom on tiptoe, had retired still more on tiptoe and informed Mr. Masterson, and Mr. Masterson had informed Mrs. Fanning. Anna herself had peeped in about a quarter to eleven just before taking Jim to Mass, and again at twelve; and still Nevill slept. A little before one he rang his bell again and demanded shaving-water. Hypocritical Charleson had said "Yessir," without comment, and had immediately informed Mrs. Fanning, in person, this time; and a quarter of an hour later Anna herself had come in — just as Nevill was getting impatient.

"You're not going to have any shaving-water," she said. "I have given orders for all shaving-water to be locked up. You're going to lunch here, and go to sleep again afterwards. How do you feel, my dear?

She sat down on the chair by his bedside.

"I am perfectly well," said Nevill. "And I wish to know whether I am or am not the master of the house?"

"Well, if you wish to know, you are not. Masterson is the master and I am the mistress; and we say you're not to get up. . . . Why in the world are the curtains drawn back?"

"I told Charleson to. I can't bear the dark. Look here, Aunt Anna, this is ridiculous. I must get up: this is simply ridiculous."

"Lunch will be up in ten minutes. I ordered it; and Jim and I will eat what's left."

Nevill leaned back.

"Well, all right," he said, "for this once. But I assure you I shall get up afterwards. Don't let's argue any more. I've given in."

So finally it was arranged. Jim was to come and see him at two o'clock, and then, if he really felt all right, he might get up. Here then, Jim sat, with secret instructions to amuse Cousin Nevill as long as possible, until he — Cousin Nevill — looked sleepy. Then Jim was to retire, in good order, and very quietly, and not bang the door behind him.

"How funny you look," said Jim presently, when he had cautiously kissed Cousin Nevill and sat down again with his bare sandaled legs dangling.

"Funny! Why?"

"Well, you're all dirty on the chin — with hair, I mean."

"Oh — no worse than that?"

"And your eyes look funny."

Nevill was silent a moment.

"Jim, old man, is that wardrobe door open or shut?"

Jim regarded the wardrobe.

"Why, open of course."

"That's all right then," said Nevill, "I thought so."

"Are you going blind, Cousin Nevill?"

"No, of course not. Why do you want to know?"

"Oh! Then why did you ask about the wardrobe? Can't you see for yourself?"

"Of course I can," said Nevill a little sharply. "Didn't I say that it was open?"

"Oh!" said Jim. "Yes; so you did."

Nevill felt a prick of compunction. But he really had not been quite sure. He had noticed two or three times since he had awakened that he did not seem to see very well. But it was certainly passing again.

"Sorry, old chap, if I spoke sharply. I didn't mean to."

Jim regarded him anxiously.

"I don't know what you mean," he said.

"That's all right then. How are the dogs?"

Jim did not answer. His meditative look had come on him, and he was gazing earnestly, it appeared, at Nevill's hands that lay clasped on the silk coverlet.

"Anything wrong this time with my hands, old chap? The rest seems pretty wrong, doesn't it?"

"I was thinking," observed Jim, with such gravity that Nevill was a little startled.

"What were you thinking about?"

"I was thinking whether I might get up on the bed."

"Why were you thinking that?"

"Because my legs are cold," said Jim. "But Mummy said I mustn't disturb you."

"That's all right. Jump up."

It was curiously soothing to his nerves to have this child with him. The very frankness of his inquiries as to dying and going blind was pleasant; and still more pleasant was the abrupt change of subjects. He wondered whether this would not be rather a good opportunity to tell Jim about the future. Jim arranged himself with great care. He first sat on the pillow within a foot of Nevill's head; and then he drew up the coverlet over his own knees.

"Oh! Is that over your face, Cousin Nevill?"

A stifled voice answered that it looked rather like it.

Jim earnestly rearranged the coverlet, so that Nevill could breathe.

"That's all right," he said. "Now we're comfortable."

"Jim," said the young man, "I want to talk to you. Are you attending?"

"Yes, of course."

"Well, look here, you're to go to school next year, aren't you?"

"Mummy says so."

"Well, what Mummy says always comes true, you know. How would you like to go a bit sooner?"

"I wouldn't mind," said Jim meditatively.

"Then there's something else. How would you like to live in a house of your own? Just you and your mother?"

"And not you?"

"No, not me, old chap, unless you asked me to come and stay with you sometimes."

"Would it be a nice house?" demanded Jim, prudently.

"Ever so nice. Perhaps it would be the Dower House. That's not far, is it?"

The bed began to jump violently.

"Whatever's the matter?" asked Nevill.

"I'd like that."

"What? The Dower House? Why?"

"There's a well there," said Jim, "without a top to it. I threw a stone down one day."

"And you wouldn't really mind leaving here?"

"I'd come and see you sometimes."

"Of course you would. As often as ever you like."

"I could come, you know," explained Jim carefully, "if you wanted me — if I hadn't anything else to do. You wouldn't mind so much then, would you?"

"Mind what?"

"Why, my not living here any more."

Nevill sighed with relief. That was half his task done. But he must be very careful.

"No, that'd be all right," he said. "Besides, I should have someone else here, you know. I'm going to be married, Jim. What do you think of that?"

"It's not to mother, is it?" asked Jim tranquilly.

"No; nephews can't marry their aunts, you know."

"Oh! And it's not to Miss Morpeth?"

"No. Why Miss Morpeth?"

"I want to marry her myself," said Jim.

"Well, that's all right; I won't stand in your way. How old's Miss Morpeth, by the way?"

"I think she's nearly twenty," said Jim. "But I shall be twenty sometime, too, you know."

"That'll make it all right then. . . . By the way, you're sure you understand what I've been saying — All about your going away, and all that?"

"Oh, yes," said Jim indifferently.

"And you don't really mind not having this as your house any more?"

There was dead silence. Nevill suddenly felt nervous. Was it really possible that he had misunderstood and that Jim did mind? That would be horrible.

"Jim, old chap?"

There was no answer. Nevill couldn't see the boy's face; it was both behind and above him. He tried to screw himself round, but the arranged coverlet beneath his chin gripped him like a strait waistcoat.

"Jim!"

"Oh! Yes?"

"What are you thinking about?"

"I was thinking whether you couldn't get up; and come out and teach me tennis."

(2)

Tea was in the pavilion, Masterson informed him, when he came downstairs at last, a little after four. He had told Jim that he was really very sorry about the tennis, and that a promise was certainly a promise; but then a headache was a headache. The promise should be redeemed this week, however.

He felt remarkably light and cheerful as he came out into the garden; he did not recognize however that it was of the nervous kind of lightness which passes rapidly into irritation. He perceived it was so, however, so soon as he caught sight of a long-coated black figure walking up and down with Anna. He did not much like Father Richardson, his chaplain and parish priest.

The relationship between traditional Catholics and priests is a very peculiar one indeed. On the one hand there is the extraordinary reverence for the priesthood, quite incomprehensible to members of other religions — a reverence sufficiently strong in some countries, though not in England, to have formed the custom of allowing the priest to leave a room before ladies; and in England, strong enough to make a pompous squire of sixty years old and a landowner to stand up instantly when a young priest comes in, and out-of-doors to take his hat off emphatically, when he sees him even in the distance. Every possible reverence, therefore, on the official side is assured and taken for granted: the pompous squire will kneel humbly in the confessional and submit his judgment to that of his newly-ordained chaplain without hesitation; and, in the Catholic Church, it must be remembered, the priest may very easily be the eldest son of the squire's neighbor's gardener.

But the social side is quite another matter. It has even been known in such a traditional Catholic household, when the priest was of humble origin, that he should take his meals in the housekeeper's room without offense being either intended or taken. The two sides are there, emphatically; the man is a priest of the Most High God, and he may also be quite ill-bred; and some very pretty problems therefore sometimes result.

Now Nevill did not like his chaplain at all. He took off his hat to him like a man; he obediently sat in his pew and listened to his pastor's discourses: he even, occasionally, went to confession to him; he sent him game half a dozen times every winter, and fruit and vegetables all the summer: he provided his house for him and kept it in repair; he paid him one hundred and ten pounds a year; he paid all the expenses of the church, and put half a sovereign into the plate each Sunday morning, and five pounds on Easter Day.

And there he drew the line: he did not in the least consider himself bound to consort with him, nor to encourage him to run in and out of the house when he liked. The man was his priest; but not his friend.

An extraordinarily tactful chaplain, or a naturally very well-bred one might perhaps have seen the difficulty. Father Richardson did not. He had large powers — at least he had had them for about eighteen months — but he did not quite see where their limits lay: he was jealous of his dignity as priest; and was rather quick to think that what he considered a rebuff or a negligence was an insult to his priesthood. He had now called this afternoon, to deliver a rebuke that he considered necessary.

He was a small, very dark man, very blue about the chin and lips; he wore a flat hat, and a coat that was neither long nor short: his trousers were well molded to his legs. Nevill, as he approached, regarded him with growing disfavor. He had three or four slight encounters with him on the more or less neutral ground between the clergyman's priesthood and manhood; and had not forgotten them.

Nevill had no hat on, so he could not raise it: but he lifted his hand in airy salutation.

"Good afternoon, Father. Here I am, you see."

The priest gravely inclined his head.

"Good afternoon, Sir Nevill."

"Back again, you see," Nevill went on, as he fell into step with the other two as they turned back towards the pavilion. "And I hope to be here for a month or two at least."

"I'm very glad to hear it," said the priest emphatically. "It makes a great difference when the squire's away."

There appeared to be a shadow of reproach in his voice. Nevill wondered whether the chap expected him to stay at home all the year round, in order to give a good example of churchgoing.

The gambit of conversation was a singularly unhappy one; for it gave the priest precisely the opening he wanted. Father Richardson had a fine working conscience, and a large sense of personal dignity to supply its motive power; and he had come here today expressly in order to rebuke the squire for not being present at Mass that morning.

As they came up the steps into the pavilion, he seized the opportunity. He preceded Nevill and followed Anna, and upon reaching the top step, turned round to relieve that conscience of his. The effect was that Nevill remained on a lower step, as if being lectured from a rostrum.

"I know you'll forgive me saying so, Sir Nevill; but I felt I must tell you what a very bad impression your not being at Mass this morning will have given to your Catholic tenants."

Nevill was completely taken aback. This was a more direct assault than he had ever received. Yet, if he had but known it, it really cost the poor priest a considerable effort to deliver such a rebuke. It was partly because he so feared it, that he had set about it so instantly.

"I beg your pardon, Father. I was ill."

The priest's face worked a little with nervousness. But he was not to be put off like this.

"So Mrs. Fanning was telling me; but I scarcely think —"

Over the priest's shoulder Nevill caught a glimpse of Anna's amazed countenance. But his irritation surged up.

"If you'll have the goodness to let me come in and sit down, Father, instead of keeping me on the steps, perhaps —"

The priest stood aside; and Nevill went by, hot with resentment.

"Sit down, Father."

He himself went across and sat by Anna in the window seat.

"Father," began Anna, with a little tremor in her voice, "I don't think you quite understood what I was —"

"Aunt Anna," interrupted Nevill quite firmly, "please let me deal with this. What are you complaining of, Father?"

The priest's little pointed face was very pale. But he sustained himself by his sense of duty, and dignity.

"I do not think that is quite the way to speak to a priest."

"I beg your pardon, Father," said Nevill, icily polite, "if I was not courteous. I did not mean to be discourteous. Nor do I understand now, what I have said that I should not.

"Your manner, Sir Nevill —"

"We will discuss my manners presently then; but let us first dispose of —"

"Father," cried Anna, utterly miserable, "I must tell you — No, Nevill; I will speak. Father, I was going to tell you that Sir Nevill passed an entirely sleepless night, through pain. He fell asleep about seven and —"

"Aunt Anna, I am sorry to interrupt. But that is not in the least to the point. I want Father Richardson to tell me why he came here to find fault with me, as if I were a schoolboy, before he took the trouble to ask whether or not I was ill. I also wish to know whether he does not think that he exceeds his authority in coming here to scold me, for a matter that in any case is not quite his business."

The priest swallowed in his throat. Then he seized, as such natures will, upon the single point that seemed in his favor.

"I imagine it to be my duty as pastor to speak to anyone of my flock, however exalted his position, who does not do his duty as a Catholic."

The phrase "however exalted his position," jarred like a file across the teeth. Anna perceptibly winced. Nevill drew his breath in with a perceptible sound.

"I am quite unaware," he said, "of not having done my duty as a Catholic. I do not think I have missed Mass on a single occasion, on Sundays or holidays of obligation, for the last five years, without a valid excuse."

"You are very seldom at Benediction," said the priest desperately. (He began to see that he was in a tight corner; but it would never do to acknowledge it, he thought. His dignity might suffer. His motto, as he had confided to his fellow priests more than once, was "Never apologize.")

"I beg your pardon again, Father," said Nevill sweetly. "But I thought you spoke of my duty as a Catholic. I was unaware that attendance at Benediction was an obligation laid down by the Church."

"I meant, of course, as a Catholic landowner," said the priest.

Nevill was thoroughly worked up. He knew he had his pastor penned up. He could not spare him now.

"If you will kindly give me any reputable theologian who lays down as amongst the duties of a Catholic landowner that he should be present at Benediction every Sunday, I will gladly yield, but —"

The priest's dignity was suffering terribly. But he would not withdraw.

"We are quite off the point, Sir Nevill. I began by speaking of your absence from Mass this morning."

"And Mrs. Fanning and myself have had the honor of informing you that I was too ill to be present. Is there anything more you wish to say?"

If, even now, the priest had frankly apologized, or burst out laughing first and apologized after, the thing would have been wholly healed. Nevill's code was punctilious. A frank apology, to him, simply ended the matter. But Father Richardson was quite unable to meet him there; and he said, instead, exactly the wrong thing: his desperation entirely blinded him to its insolence.

"You seem very well and strong now, Sir Nevill, at any rate."

Anna gasped. Nevill leaned back tranquilly and began to play with the curtain tassel.

"Aunt Anna," he said, "we needn't say anything more. Father Richardson does not believe our word. . . . What a charming afternoon it is, Father! It is very nearly as warm as it was in Rome last week. Have you ever been to Rome, Father?"

The priest looked dazed. He was beginning to see what he had said, and he was completely taken aback by his host's extreme composure and the serene change of subject. He tried to follow suit. It seemed the most dignified thing to do.

"I was ordained there, Sir Nevill. I. . . ."

There came a torrent of noises from the lawn, yelps and screams; and the next moment Jack and Jill entered at full speed, with Jim behind, trailing a chain to which were attached two collars.

(3)

"There's no more to be said, Aunt Anna," observed Nevill half an hour later, as their pastor went down the garden towards the church. "He's impossible. Haven't I always said so?"

Jim, too, was gone, and minds could be spoken.

Poor Father Richardson had made matters even worse, if that is conceivable. If he had simply said goodbye when the entrance of Jim and the collies gave him an opening, at any rate that would have shown some faint sense that a breach had opened. Or if, even then, he had said he was sorry for having spoken as he had, and that his last remark, above all others, was quite indefensible (as, in his heart, he knew it to be) — even then the decencies would have been observed. But he stayed on to tea; he talked, as he thought, intelligently and easily; he allowed Nevill, who had war in his heart, to hand him the buttered tea cake, and he had helped himself to a piece of cake; and he had done all this believing that somehow it mended matters, and thinking that if Sir Nevill could talk smoothly about Rome and the weather, he himself could not do better than follow his example. He went away at last then, certainly perturbed by the memory of the previous scene, and quite aware that he had been exceedingly indiscreet; and yet, on the whole, reassured by the naturalness of the other two, and especially glad that he had not been obliged to apologize. It would all blow over, he told himself. Besides, he was a priest, and his rights could not possibly be encroached upon. It might have lowered his dignity to have apologized. He was tolerably content then, as he went back to his house and began to get his sermon ready for the evening.

Anna made no answer to her nephew's remark. Indeed, there was not much answer to make.

"You see," continued Nevill, "it's no kind of good being decent to a man like that. As it is, I shouldn't be in the least surprised if he denounced me from the altar, or preached against insolence and discourtesy to God's priests."

"Nevill! Of course he won't. I'm certain that he's perfectly miserable."

"Not in the very least," said Nevill. "He's congratulating himself, on the contrary, on having been brave enough to beard people of an exalted position. Exalted Position! Ha!"

"Don't, my dear."

Nevill was silent a moment.

"And to think that that man will be chaplain here when Enid comes. It's unthinkable!"

"I'll write to the Bishop," said Anna.

"That's no good. He hasn't done anything to disgrace himself, technically. At least, he thinks he hasn't. When he first came the Bishop wrote to tell me I was very lucky to get such a man! . . . Aunt Anna!"

She lifted her pensive eyes from the floor. She was just about as unhappy as she could be.

"Yes, my dear?"

"Do you see now why I'm not exactly — well — keen on religion? He told us we were liars. Liars, Aunt Anna! Do you realize that?"

"My dear boy, please don't."

"Well, you see now, don't you? I don't want to rub it in. But it's hardly likely that I should be very keen, with a chap like that. Of course I go to Mass, and all that — Oh! I forgot; I don't even do that. I sham illness, don't I; and then lie about it —"

"Nevill! Please!"

"All right. . . . Well, you see now, anyhow?"

"I don't know what to say," said Anna.

"And of course I shall go on sending him game and fruit and paying him every quarter, and settling the candle and oil bill. That's the privilege of us of the Catholic laity, you know. He told us so from the pulpit once, you remember. And he'll wolf it all down, and —"

"Nevill, I can't bear it!"

"Oh, good Lord!" burst out the young man, banging the tassel on the window ledge. "And that's supposed to be religion! Why, there's more religion in . . . in a daisy growing at Frascati, or . . . or a cock that pecks his hens when you crow at him. I haven't told you about the cock, Aunt."

"No, you haven't," said Anna mechanically.

"Well; he pecked his hens when I crowed at him. That's all. At Frascati. That was when I had my first long talk with Enid. My word, that was a day!"

"What did you do?"

"Oh, we went out to Frascati, and Enid and I went up into the woods. And we jawed awed. Heavens! How we jawed! And there was a *Pietà* there —"

"Yes?" said Anna, looking up.

"Oh! It was there. That was all. And we said we didn't like it. And we didn't. It was just a . . . a blot on the landscape; like that little man who's just gone away."

"I don't understand."

"Oh yes, you do, Aunt. You know perfectly well what I think about that kind of thing. It's quite hateful. Why can't they keep those locked up in churches, with . . . with the priests? That little man who's just gone away would think it beautiful. Lord! Fancy a *Pietà* on that lawn!"

He looked out through the still open door beyond the tea things. The evening sunlight was golden here, out of the shadow of the house; and in the shadow the light was growing faintly blue. Through it towered the tall, stately east front, with its solemn windows and its carved balustraded terrace, and its great stones vases dripping with greenery. As he looked, the dignified figure of Masterson came out at the hall and began to descend the steps. He was coming to clear away the tea things. Certainly a *Pietà* would be singularly inharmonious upon this stage of smooth and wealthy peace.

Nevill watched Masterson's approach in silence. The old butler's arms swung stiffly from the shoulders, and he moved with that peculiar air of dignity of which such personages alone have the secret. As he came up the steps, Nevill had a surge of anger again at the memory of the priest, and he took a swift decision.

"Masterson."

"Yes, Sir Nevill."

"If Father Richardson should call again at any future time, please don't show him straight in to either of us. Tell him to wait, and then come and ask if we're at home or not, just as you would with anyone else."

"Yes, Sir Nevill," said Masterson with an immovable countenance, standing like a decrepit statue.

Nevill saw Aunt Anna's agonized countenance; but he was determined to have his way.

"Tell the other servants the same, will you? And if Father Richardson should want to come and see for himself, if we're in the garden, for instance, just tell him what your orders are. Tell him it's the same for everybody who calls. Do you understand?"

Masterson's eyes gleamed a little. He entirely disliked the priest; and indeed all priests. He was not a Catholic.

"Yes, Sir Nevill."

(4)

When the butler was halfway back across the lawn with the tea tray, Anna spoke. Nevill saw that a strong protest was coming, and braced himself to meet it.

"My dear boy," she said, "do you quite realize what you've done? He'll think it fearfully rude."

"I can't help it. I've let him run in and out up to now, because I didn't quite know how to stop it. But if he chooses to ride the high horse and claim the privilege of being a priest — all right, let him be a priest, and have them all, down to the last farthing. But he shan't have any more."

"He'll never forgive you."

"That's a matter for his own conscience then. He can do as he likes about that. So long as he's priest here he shall have his rights. But if he says a word, I shall ask him if the Council of Trent that he's always appealing to, says anything about the Catholic laity — even of exalted position — letting priests run in and out of their houses just as they please. I had him nicely over that landowner business, didn't I?"

"I wish you wouldn't."

Then Nevill blazed a little again.

"My dear Aunt Anna, you forget Enid. I know you'd stand anything: you're a Catholic, you see, and a saint, and a few other things. She's a saint, too; but of another kind. And she certainly wouldn't stand a bounder like that — I beg his pardon, I mean a clergyman like that — coming and going exactly as he pleases. Even if she would stand it, I won't let her. And I may as well settle it, once and for all, and get the row over, before she comes — if there's to be one."

"Oh! I see," said Anna slowly; "that's why, is it?"

"That and other things. But this last business has brought it to a point. I'm rather glad it has. I dare say I'd have let things drift, otherwise. But this has finished it. It's a good job."

"My dear boy!"

"Well, what would you have?" cried the young man dramatically. "What else can you suggest?"

"I . . . I don't know. Can't you give him another chance?"

"No, I can't, Aunt Anna. And I won't. There's a limit, and he's passed it. He told us we were liars. And it isn't the first time —"

"He's never called you a liar before!"

"No, of course he hasn't," said Nevill a trifle peevishly "And I'll bet he won't again. But he's done half a dozen things nearly as bad. Don't you remember when he preached against bridge, just after we'd had the Levesons down here and played till one in the morning? And all the winnings went into the plate the Sunday after, too! I remember that well, because I won nine pounds and had to fork up. Well, he knew perfectly well we'd been playing, and he knew perfectly well it wasn't a sin — or, if he didn't, he ought to go back to school again. That was number one. Then there was —"

"Oh! Don't go on about all that!" protested Anna feebly.

"Well, you know it's all true. But this really is the limit. There's no more to be said."

There was silence again. Then Nevill once more broke out.

"And to think that religion comes down to that sort of thing. . . . Oh! You will love Enid, Aunt Anna. She's so . . . so fresh and big and out-of-doors. And spiritual. She was asking me about stipends for Masses one day, and, upon my word, I didn't know what to say to her."

"Why," began Anna dutifully, "you know perfectly well that you don't pay for the —"

"Oh! I know the stock answer, of course. But stock answers won't do with Enid. She goes right down to things. She hasn't a stock answer in the world. They're only counters, you know. And she uses gold only."

"But, my dear —"

"Oh! Don't go on about that. That's not the point. When you see Enid you'll know what I mean. She's . . . she's like a great wind. And yet she's so still, too. You . . . you . . . What an ass you must think me!"

He was all flushed with enthusiasm, and his eyes shone. There seemed not a trace of illness about him. Anna stood up.

"You're a dear boy," she said softly. "And I hope Enid —"

She could not go on.

"And you're a dear aunt," said Nevill. "Give me a kiss."

She went across and kissed him gently on the forehead, laying her hands on his temples. She kissed him very slowly. She didn't want him to see her brimming eyes.

"There!" said Nevill. "And now it's Pax about Father Richardson If he behaves himself, that's to say."

"And you'll let him come in and out as usual?"

"I will not," said Nevill. "What I have said I have said. I only meant that I wouldn't, after all, go and tell him precisely what I think of him. I had meant to, you know."

"Till when?"

"Till you kissed me."

She turned away to the steps.

"Where are you going?"

"I'm going to get ready for church," she said, with her face still averted.

"You're going to church! After all that!"

"Of course I am. What difference does it make? Come too."

"By George! Shall I. . . .? What a gorgeous slap in the face!"

Nevill lowered his legs from the window seat as if in hesitation.

"Do. But not as a slap in the face."

Nevill replaced his legs.

"No," he said firmly. "I shall not come to church. It would be extremely unchristian to slap him in the face. And, what's

worse, he wouldn't feel it. He'd think he'd brought me to a
better mind. No."

She laughed a little, in spite of herself — a little bubble of
laughter.

"Well, I must go. There are the bells."

"Pray for me," said Nevill, as she went down the steps. And
she turned and nodded to him slowly.

(5)

He sat on a few minutes, listening to the bells. They were
only three in number, but their jangle was very pleasant and
very Sundayish, dimmed, as it was, by the great bulk of the
house and high-roofed tennis court that lay between the
church and the pavilion.

The shadow had crept across by now and lay even on the
pavilion itself; and the river, too, that chuckled so coolly beneath the open window at which he lay, was no longer shot
with lines and planes of golden light. It was soft and liquid
glass into which he looked, faintly tinged here with brown
and there with green, so gently blended that one tint faded
into another without abruptness. He could see two or three
dark shadows, poised at the bottom, motionless, it appeared,
except for the shifting lines that swayed above them.

Far out across the park as he turned to see, the sunlight
still lingered both on the higher slopes and on the motionless
tops of the nearer trees. He could see a couple coming down
from the direction of the Dower House. That would be Mr.
Morpeth, no doubt, and his daughter Ella. They were the
only Catholics, so far as he knew, who lived in that direction.
The village itself was completely on the other side, beyond
the front lodge gates through which he had driven last night.

It was an evening of great silences and spaces, wholly
tranquil; and while the bells, considered in themselves, were
soft and melodious, they signified something, he thought,
completely out of harmony with the evening.

They were, psychologically considered, a kind of interruption. He pictured the interior of the little church, the stations
of the Cross round the walls, the sheaves of burning candles
above the gilded altar; the sparse congregation; Father
Richardson's voice, his personality, his narrow views, and his
lack of breeding. And yet Enid was to come down here — not

only on the visit she was to pay three weeks hence, but as a permanent mistress of it all.

How would she fit in? Well, she would fit in to perfection with the park and the spaces and the stillness and the great house; but scarcely with that for which the church bells stood.

On the whole, now, he did most emphatically *not* think that she would be a Catholic.

It was growing a little chilly, and he shivered once or twice. Then he thought he had better go in. Certainly his headache was all right, and he could see again as well as ever. But it was best to take no risks. He would go and see where Jim was. Perhaps, if he wasn't at church he would like a lesson at billiards.

Chapter VI

By the worst luck in the world it was a day of squalls and rain when Enid and her mother came down for the last week in May. Nevill was raging with annoyance. He had decided that it was to be a perfectly fine day with a few clouds and a gentle wind; but Providence thought otherwise, and an hour before the arrival the sky was overcast; it was rather cold, and the hall windows were spattered with drops.

"Light the fire here," said Nevill heavily to Masterson, as the butler came in to announce that he supposed tea would not be in the pavilion after all. Nevill was sunk in a chair, with his arms dangling down. Aunt Anna was standing up. She had just said she must be going.

"My dear boy!" remonstrated Anna.

Nevill groaned.

"Yes, I'm behaving disgracefully. Aren't I, Masterson? I'm a sulky brute."

"You wish the fire to be lighted, Sir Nevill?" asked Masterson, with dangerous calm.

"Yes."

"Then I will inform Charleson, Sir Nevill," said Masterson yet more icily.

A conscience-stricken silence followed him out into the passage.

"Oh, Lord!" said Nevill. "Now Masterson's offended. You're all in a conspiracy. How am I supposed to know whose business it is to light the beastly fire?"

"You're not fit to have any servants," remarked Aunt Anna.

"Aunt! I shall burst into tears if you speak to me like that. Go away! Leave me to myself! I shall be stronger soon."

Anna was finding it quite hard to keep entirely composed. She could not have conceived that it would be so difficult to behave well, after all the time she had had to get ready. She assured herself that jealousy was absolutely the last of all the emotions that could possibly affect her. It was incredible that she could be jealous. No. It was simple anxiety that Nevill should have chosen well. She cared for nothing else so much as that.

But she found it rather a relief to take him at his word.

"Yes, I shall certainly go away," she said, "after that exhibition. Besides, I've got half a hundred things to see to. You said tulips for tonight at dinner, didn't you?"

"I think tulips," said Nevill. "Oh! I'm so frightened, Aunt Anna. Suppose she thinks it all perfectly beastly? I wish I hadn't bragged so much about the house. And why did I send those picture postcards? Picture postcards idealize so terribly. Suppose she says I've deceived her? Oh! By the way, before you go —"

"Yes?"

"Don't forget about her mother. Engage her in conversation. Just start her on anything. It doesn't matter in the least what. You've never been to Corfu, have you?"

"Corfu! No. Why?"

"That'll do just as well. Tell her you haven't been there, and ask her what it's like. She's great on Corfu."

"Why do you want her to talk about Corfu? I don't understand a word you're saying."

"Oh! You're not clever today, Aunt Anna. Why, I want to talk to Enid, of course! What do you suppose I've asked her here for? But clergymen will do just as well, if you've any objections to Corfu. She's tremendous on clergymen. Do you know any?"

"I once knew an archdeacon," said Anna meditatively.

"He'll do perfectly. Was he an Evangelical archdeacon?"

"I haven't the slightest idea. What difference does that make?"

"Oh! Evangelical ones are her sort. Did he have whiskers?"

"I forget."

"Well, it's very important to remember. Because if he hadn't he's sure to have been High Church, and she can't bear those. For goodness' sake don't go and put your foot in it, Aunt Anna, and mix up High Church and Evangelical. The difference is vital, I understand. Vital! I don't know what would happen if you went and mixed them up. I don't indeed. Oh, dear! I feel so miserable. Where's Jim?"

"Jim's out in the rain with the collies."

"Don't let them jump up on Enid, will you, when they come in? Mrs. Bessington doesn't matter so much. Yes, on second thoughts, I think you might let them jump up on Mrs. Bessington. That would start her all right, by George! I think she was bitten by one, once. Or was it her cousin who lived in Corfu? . . . Anyhow, that's not material. It'll do, anyhow. Yes. Mind you encourage the collies to jump up on Mrs. Bessington's dress with all their muddy paws. Don't forget, will you?"

"Tulips. Corfu. Clergymen. Not High Church. Collies. Cousin. Any more orders?"

"No, that's enough for the present, my dear Aunt. Oh! You are a dear!"

She moved away rather quickly as he turned towards her. Her whole soul seemed knit tight in some strange emotion She simply could not have touched him just then.

"Where are you going?"

"Tulips," she said; and went swiftly through the door that led to the servants' quarters.

(2)

She was behind her window curtains as the carriage drove up; and, utterly ashamed of herself, she watched intently as the door of the brougham opened. Then she saw Nevill's curly head in the rain; and then two female figures emerge. Then all three vanished swiftly into the porch.

She thought she would give them ten minutes. Her rosary took her ten minutes; so she lifted this from her *prie dieu,* and knelt down with it in her hands. Then she found herself after three or four decades contemplating the Agony in the Garden, and stopped. Then she bowed her head on her hands, and clenched those until they grew as white as bone. Then she went to the mirror with her sponge in her hands, looked at her face carefully, passed the sponge over her eyes two or three times, opened the door and went out.

. . . . "It was the guard at Victoria who looked so extraordinarily like my Uncle Henry; not the guard of our train, but the one who was looking after the train labeled 'Crystal Palace,' at the next platform, with his beard cut quite square. You remember, Enid, don't you?. . . ."

Such were the words Aunt Anna heard as she passed round the gallery and began to come downstairs. Then the angle cut off the distinctness of the speaker's words, but the mumble went steadily on. She bit her lower lip fiercely, to keep back her laughter. She felt a little hysterical. She knew, now, that she understood all about Corfu and clergymen.

As she came down the last flight the three looked up all together, and the talking stopped. She felt like a child at her
first party, overwhelmed with shyness.

She heard Nevill saying something, and the next instant
felt her hand grasped, and saw the kindly eyes of a middle-
aged woman looking into her own. Then, still more confused,
she released her hands and turned, and found herself face to
face with Enid.

For a moment she hesitated. Her swift woman's wit took
in, not indeed every detail, but the effect of the whole. It was
a splendid pale face, crowned with masses of hair under a big
hat; and the face was lit by a pair of radiant eyes. A thin silk
mantle hung from the shapely shoulders. Then Aunt Anna
put out her hands, felt the girl's hands in hers, drew the girl
to herself, and, without a word, kissed her slowly on the lips.
(It was what she had decided, upstairs, to do if . . . if it were
at all possible when the moment came.)

"It really is a shame," she heard herself saying presently,
"that the weather should be like this. Nevill had given orders
for a completely different sort of day, and tea in the pavilion.
And it is — oh! Look at that fire!"

Indeed, the fire seemed very feeble indeed. She took down
the pair of bellows and kneeled before it.

"Oh! Aunt Anna —!" she heard Nevill's voice begin.

She was recovering herself finely now. Give her thirty seconds more at the bellows, and she would be all right.

"There!" she said, and stood up again.

"I think it's perfectly glorious," said Enid.

(Oh, yes; indeed she was lovely, thought Aunt Anna. She
was standing and looking slowly round the great hall. There
could be no question at all about her beauty. The photograph
had not lied.)

"Nevill," said the girl. (And, at the name, Aunt Anna set
her teeth like a vice.) "Nevill! You never gave me the slightest idea —"

"That's all right, then," said Nevill. "But the pavilion's the
point, you know. Aunt Anna — Where are you going, Aunt
Anna?"

"Only to ring for tea, my dear. I can't think why they haven't brought it up."

As she came back, Mrs. Bessington moved slowly towards
her.

"I was telling Nevill — you won't mind my calling him that, will you, my dear? You see — well; I was telling him about the guard that was so like my Uncle Henry. It was when we were at Victoria Station. . ."

The hunt was up. Anna recognized it in a moment, and with the deepest relief. She would not be required to say anything. She knew the type. Very tactfully she steered Mrs. Bessington to a tall chair, and maneuvered her into it, and herself into another, close by the tea table.

The Crystal Palace was the subject by the time that tea came in, and Mrs. Bessington was relating the first occasion on which she had taken Enid there — quite twelve years ago — when Enid was only a little dot. And so on.

Aunt Anna ministered the tea admirably. She put in the hot water at the right time; she remembered to put in Nevill's cream before the tea; she even succeeded in learning whether the two guests wanted sugar. Interminably the affair went on. Little by little the two others seemed to disappear from her range of vision. Now and then their voices were heard across the gentle torrent in her own ears; now and again they were silent. Two or three minutes ago the voices sounded quite far off, and she caught Lady Brightington's name. Evidently Nevill was showing her the portraits. Then there followed a long silence. . . .

Mrs. Bessington was talking about coffee now. . . .

"Did you say Corfu?" asked Anna, as she desperately and recklessly turned round away from Mrs. Bessington. The hall was empty; the two others were gone. She had played her part nobly.

"No, my dear. Coffee. But what about Corfu? I was there once, in eighteen eighty-nine, and the spring of eighteen ninety. I was there in the year that. . . ."

(3)

The garden was as exquisite as spring itself, after the rain. By a swift caprice, while Mrs. Bessington was discoursing, and the two lovers were edging slowly round the portraits, the wind had dropped, the sun looked out, and the rain stopped; and, when the two, with infinite and careful discretion, slipped out upon the balustraded platform above the steps, the whole place shone and sparkled like a fairy's dream. . . .

"Oh!" said Enid, and sighed once, deeply.

"Come down quietly," whispered Nevill, "or they'll hear us."

The lawn was wet, so it was obvious that they must pass along the path by the house and right round, so as to get to the pavilion.

"What's that?" asked Enid suddenly, as a bell rang three strokes and was silent again.

"Angelus," said Nevill. "Father Richardson rings it himself at five."

"That's the chaplain, isn't it?"

"Yes."

The girl looked at him, as they turned across towards the terrace.

"You don't like him. I thought so, in Rome," she said. "That won't do a bit. One ought to like people."

"I suppose that is so," said Nevill dispassionately.

"I shall make friends," she said. "I'll manage him. What's he been doing?"

"Oh, well! I suppose one might call it being tiresome."

"Well, if you won't, you won't," said Enid.

"My dear girl, I'm much too angry. Let's talk about something else. There you are! There's the pavilion."

If ever the coast could be clear, Father Richardson had thought, it would surely be for at least an hour after the arrival of guests. He had seen the brougham drive up, from the presbytery window; he had finished his own tea, and rung the Angelus, and it had occurred to him while he was doing so that here was an evident opportunity for him to look in the pavilion for a little pocketbook which he was convinced he must have left there a day or two before, when he had gone across to see Mrs. Fanning about some small matter connected with the chapel flowers. The guests had scarcely come, he thought; the garden was wet; it was obvious that he would interrupt nothing and nobody. He wasted a few minutes searching the presbytery once more for his book; and then, without misgiving, slipped out through the back gate of the presbytery and went across the gardens. He went rather quickly with his head down, straight up the steps of the pavilion, and stood confounded.

"Good evening, Father," said Nevill.

The priest's eyes wandered past him to the beautiful girl who sat in the window seat. Nevill was standing, but it was sufficiently plain that he had also been sitting on the window seat until he heard the steps.

"I beg your pardon, Sir Nevill — I had no idea . . . I came to look for a book I think I must have left here."

Again his eyes moved round, as if searching for his book; and again they rested an instant on the girl's face.

Nevill hesitated a moment.

"May I introduce you to Miss Bessington?" he said. "Father Richardson."

The girl bowed a little.

"I saw your church as I came up," she said. "What a charming place you have here!"

"Er — yes," said Father Richardson.

"I am staying a few days," said the girl. "I wonder if I may come and see the church? I am not a Catholic, Father; but I know Rome very well."

"I shall be delighted," said the priest.

There fell a little pause.

"Well — the book," said Nevill. "We mustn't keep you, Father."

The book was searched for, and was not found. The priest apologized once more, and departed.

"He looks very nice," said Enid. "I wish you'd tell me why you don't like him."

Nevill sat down by her.

He felt entirely annoyed. This perpetual running in and out of the priest "as if the place belonged to him," as Nevill expressed it to himself, was beginning to get on his nerves. What in the world was the use of leaving a scathing message with Masterson if the man simply walked through without question? Yet he hesitated, with the habitual reserve of his class and his religion, to discuss him openly even with Enid.

"He's just rather trying, my dear. He gets on my nerves."

"You mustn't let him. Does he come and go just as he pleases, all over the place?"

"That's exactly the point," burst out Nevill. "At least, it's one of them. He's got his own presbytery and his garden and the whole park. Yet that doesn't seem enough. He doesn't seem to understand —"

Enid smiled a little.

"Poor dear man!" she said. "He simply doesn't know. I'll make friends with him, and then —"

"My darling! That's exactly what I don't want. We've been too good to him already."

Enid's eyes narrowed a little, with gentle laughter.

"Well, you'll see," she said. "By the way — does he know about . . . about —?"

"Not a word. At least, I haven't told him. I've sent nothing to the papers, either, you know, as you told me."

"Well, look here," said Enid. "I foresee all kinds of difficulties if he doesn't know. Tell him this evening, will you? And then I'll go and see the church tomorrow morning, if I may. That'll all be open and straightforward then. You don't know how to manage him, I expect."

She smiled again at her lover.

(4)

An hour later Nevill was ringing the presbytery bell.

He had had a good hour with Enid, till Mrs. Bessington had routed them out. Poor Anna had done her best: she had received a completely exhaustive account of Corfu, she had played her Archdeacon — (views unknown) — and had been answered by a number of little biographies of other clergymen: she had listened, when more personal matters had been approached, to long descriptions of Rome, and the character of the food to be obtained there, with parentheses on Nevill and Enid that had made her wince more than once. And then, with a suddenness to which she had no parry, Mrs. Bessington had informed her that it was time to see what the others were doing, and that Enid must come indoors; and which was the way to the famous pavilion, because she was convinced that they were there. So like a native guide, attached to the attacking general's stirrup, Anna had led her all round by the paths, because the lawn was still wet, and up the steps. It was then that Enid had nodded to Nevill to go, and he had left, hearing as he went the exordium of a discourse upon the porous character of red tiles and the harborage they offered to damp. Mrs. Bessington's capacity for not seeing the wood for the trees, for missing the beauty or the interest of a place and fastening instead upon its least important detail, was abnormal.

One of the very few advantages of the presbytery to Father Richardson's mind lay in the fact that when the bell was rung, the inhabitant could peep swiftly through the sitting

room window and see who was there. Nevill, then, after seeing the priest's head dart, like a bird's, between the lace curtains, next saw him standing within the front door which he
had just opened to his visitor.

"Come inside, Sir Nevill," said the priest. "What can I do
for you?"

Nevill followed him into the sitting room.

To his mind the sitting room was abhorrent. There were religious pictures round the wall of, what appeared to him, exactly the wrong type. A frightful little chipped statue of the
Cure d'Ars stood on the top of the writing desk. A sham
sheepskin mat lay before the hearth. A very small shelf of
theological books hung near the window. A bicycle stood all
along one wall — (Father Richardson had more than once
hinted at the desirability of a proper bicycle shed for the
presbytery) — a white plaster crucifix hung above the fireplace, and a rack of pipes convenient to the hand of one who
sat in the deep basket chair. A rather bright Brussels carpet,
chosen last year by the priest and paid for by Nevill, covered
the floor, except where rather sticky-looking varnished
boards appeared below the wainscotting; a cheerful paper,
with hard-looking bunches of flowers that sprang, so to
speak, to meet the eye, covered the walls. This also, last year,
had been chosen by the priest and paid for by Nevill. The entire aspect of the room ratified and emphasized once more
the opinion so rapidly forming in Nevill's mind that the inhabitant of it was stuffy, second rate and impossible.

He sat down in the basket chair, becoming aware that the
seat of it was unduly depressed in one place, and prepared
himself to begin.

"Found the pocketbook, Father?"

The priest said that he had. It was in the breast pocket of
his coat all the while.

Now Nevill had determined to be rather stiff. Expansive-
ness had not succeeded. So he plunged straight into his subject.

"Now that Miss Bessington has come with her mother, to
stay a few days, I thought I had better come round at once
and tell you how matters stand."

"I think she is the lady you are engaged to, is she not?" said
the priest smoothly.

Nevill glanced up sharply.

"How did you know that?" he said.

Father Richardson smiled a little. He would not have been human if he had not been conscious that he was getting his own back for the defeat he had suffered the other day.

"I heard it two or three days ago," he said. "It seems to be known in the village. Two or three people have asked me whether it were true. I said that I . . . I was not in your confidence, Sir Nevill."

Nevill was conscious of a very sharp and unpleasant pang of compunction. He hastily ran over in his mind the number of people he had told — Masterson, Jim, Aunt Anna: and Aunt Anna had told Mr. Morpeth. Then there were the people in Rome. It might have leaked out in half a dozen ways. And yet he had not told his own chaplain and parish priest. Yet he was conscious of another prick of anger too. Why could not the man have taken it more courteously? What need was there to be so pointed? However, he saw he must eat humble pie.

"I am very sorry, Father, you did not hear it from me direct. I had no idea that anyone knew, beyond my — my very closest friends. I must apologize."

The priest bowed very slightly, with a faint smile.

"Well, it's a fact," went on Nevill. "I was coming to you in any case in a day or two. . . with regard to the dispensation. No dates are settled yet. But I suppose that the preliminaries may as well be set on foot?"

"If you will give me the particulars," said the priest, "I shall be happy to make the application."

Nevill repressed his rising annoyance. He was convinced that the other was delighted with his own magnanimity.

"Thank you, Father. Miss Bessington very much wishes to see the church tomorrow morning. Perhaps you might have the papers ready then?"

"I will do so," said Father Richardson.

"About eleven o'clock then?"

"That will do perfectly."

Nevill stood up. He perceived that he must make yet further amends.

"Miss Bessington and her mother will be staying a few days. I hope you will come and dine with us one evening?"

"Thank you, Sir Nevill."

"I'll let you know then."

His eyes fell on the bicycle.

"I've thought over that bicycle shed scheme, Father. I think perhaps it would be best to build one. It would always be useful."

"Just as you please, Sir Nevill."

Again Nevill had to check his resentment. He understood perfectly that this extraordinary detachment of manner on the part of the priest was intended as a cold and courteous rebuke. Why on earth could not the man be more genial about it?

"Well, if you'll sketch out what you think best, I'll send it to the agent."

"Thank you, Sir Nevill."

"Hopeless!" said the young man ten minutes later as he met Enid in the hall. "I've told him; but he's furious. It seems he heard gossip in the village about it. Lord knows how it got out!"

"Was he rude?"

"No. Too beastly polite by half. Now come round the house. We've loads of time before dressing."

(5)

Aunt Anna felt, towards noon next day, that, with all the goodwill in the world, she could not bear Mrs. Bessington any more at all, just for the present. Mrs. Bessington found her, it appeared, a thoroughly sympathetic listener, and made the most of it. It would be an impossible task to set out in order all the subjects discussed at breakfast; but the effect upon Anna, who had to bear it all, was that it seemed as if she were trying to pour out tea and to see that people helped themselves, and that Jim did not spill the marmalade, as if she were doing these things in a kind of hailstorm.

The conversation seemed to stream and beat upon her brain in an unending clatter, not loud, but universal, so to say. Beneath it, in glimpses of intelligence, she perceived other people doing things — Jim, very polite and awed, watching first one guest and then the other, and then, when observed, devoting himself to his plate again with a demure innocence.

Jim had made his bow, so to say, officially last night when the gong sounded that was the signal for the company to dress and for Jim to go to bed. He had submitted to be kissed with his usual courtesy, looking a little disconcertingly after each caress at the caresser, as if to see how she liked it. Then he had gone gravely upstairs, without turning his head. Mrs. Bessington had improved upon the situation by relating at great length the history of a niece of hers who had suffered from water on the brain some time in the last century.

But Jim had his opportunity since then to observe the visitors. He had sat next Enid at breakfast, and she had paid him the most delicate compliment that can be paid to a child: she treated him as a grownup person, conversing with him without a single meaning glance at anyone else. Mrs. Bessington had, of course, spoken to him as if he were deaf, and never waited for an answer to her remarks. Jim had disappeared after breakfast, and there had been no opportunity of finding out what he thought of the visitors.

About noon then, when Anna, after suitable excuses, had gone off to the pavilion with her letters, and had made unsuccessful attempts to answer them; and as she turned, with the end of her pen in her mouth, had seen Jim, quite alone, with his hands in his pockets, strolling across the lawn, she called to him to come in. Jim, still strolling, came up the steps.

"Yes, Mummy?"

"Come and talk to me. I can't write any more."

Jim sat down politely.

"What shall I talk about?"

He seemed a little depressed, thought his mother. Well, and so was she.

"Where have they all gone?"

"The . . . the old lady," he said, "is very sleepy in the hall. Cousin Nevill's taken the other one to see the church."

"Why didn't you go with them?"

"I think they didn't want me. And, you see, I know the church quite well. Father Richardson's there, too."

Jim's polite self-possession was complete. Anna felt quite sure he was depressed. He crossed one brown leg over the other and contemplated his sandal. Then he began to whistle, very gently.

"Do you like them?" she asked suddenly.

"Oh, yes," said Jim, with a superb indifference. And at that his mother thought it better to probe no further.

(6)

Nevill was not quite as radiant as usual, thought his aunt, as they met for lunch. It was not that he did not talk: he talked readily and easily, and suggested a run in the motor down to the sea. But there seemed to be over him a veil, as thin as a very thin cloud over the sun on a hot summer's day. By the end of lunch it had practically vanished; but Aunt Anna remembered that it had been there. It was not until after tea in the pavilion, when the two guests with Nevill on the back seat and Jim beside the chauffeur had come back from the shore, that she even began to suspect the reason.

Mrs. Bessington had gone back to the house to fetch a book on Phoenician coins — (she was full of surprises like that) — when Enid gave the clue.

"Mrs. Fanning," she said, "we want to appeal to you. Nevill and I had an argument."

Her face shone with pleasantness. The drive had kindled a faint even flush in her face and brightened her eyes. Her beauty certainly grew on one, thought Anna.

"Tell me," said Anna. "You know I shall probably agree with my nephew!"

"Well, if you don't like a person, isn't it the best to make friends with them, instead of trying to look over the top of their head? (Don't interrupt, Nevill, please!) you shall have your side presently."

Nevill subsided.

"That depends," said Aunt Anna judiciously.

"Oh! Don't say that. That sounds prudent. . . . I mean, generally speaking. Supposing you had to live with somebody, for instance, whom you couldn't bear. Wouldn't it be far better to try to understand them and to get at their good points and so on — rather than to be very cold and polite?"

"That sounds reasonable," said Anna.

Enid turned a slow smile to Nevill.

"What did I say?" she said. "Now put your side, if you think I'm not fair."

"Look here," said Nevill. "It's no good beating about the bush. Put it like this. Suppose you hadn't actually got to live with a person — but had a very close neighbor — Say we were talking about Father Richardson" — he said brilliantly — "or . . . or anyone who could make things very unpleasant if he was tiresome. And suppose you had tried being very

pleasant and all that, and . . . and things didn't go well.
Then, I maintain, you'd better try the other thing. I'm speaking quite generally, of course."

Oh! The guileless stupidity of this man, thought Aunt
Anna. Nevill's very device of mentioning the priest's name
put the final touch on her certitude that he was exactly the
person in point. Obviously the visit to the church this morning had been the origin of this puzzle. And yet, what was she
to say? She hated to take Enid's side against Nevill; and yet
Enid's advice had been exactly hers. She hesitated an instant.

"It's no good, my dear boy," she said. "You know exactly
what I think. I think Miss Bessington's theory is perfectly
right."

"Well —" began Nevill — "Why, what's up?"

He was sitting in the window seat facing the door, and
Anna saw his eyes change to a sudden gravity as he looked
past her. She turned quickly, and there, across the lawn,
came Masterson, at an ambling run, with a kind of desperate
consternation in his gait and face. Nevill was up, and at the
door, before Anna could move.

"What is it?" she heard him say.

"Miss Morpeth's . . . an accident . . . want to know if they
can bring her here . . . out riding."

He spoke brusquely and roughly, without a word of respect.
She could only catch a few words; but she caught enough.
Then she too was by Nevill.

"Of course, Masterson. Anything. Tell them I'll come. Is
Mr. Morpeth there?"

(7)

It was a very strange and subdued dinner at which the four
sat that night. The tragedy had come and gone with an
overwhelming swiftness, visiting the house and leaving it
again, all within a couple of hours.

First there had come the tragic burden, borne between four
men — the hurdle torn from the hedge into which the girl's
horse had bolted after an alarm from a motor just outside the
village — the hurdle on which lay a still figure with open
eyes.

Anna had taken command with all the adequateness of
which a sensitive woman alone has the secret. Enid had

come forward, white-faced and excited, as the stretcher was carried in, and lifted one of the hands that hung dangling; and Aunt Anna, scarcely knowing how sharply she spoke, yet with a true commander's instinct, had bidden her leave it alone. Then she had had the hurdle carried into the morning room, and the girl's body shifted with infinite care on to the wide chintz-covered sofa. It looked terribly like death; yet she was not absolutely sure. She had tried to force brandy into the pale lips, and had failed. Then, five minutes later, the little gray-bearded doctor had come.

"It is all over," he said, after two minutes' examination. "The neck was broken. Death must have been instantaneous."

And then Mr. Morpeth had come, fetched across the park by the house motor.

It was perhaps the sharpest agony that Anna had ever experienced — this watching of the curious old man whom she was learning to like and respect so greatly. It was she who had met him in the hall, and told him with a word. Nevill had gone straight off for him himself, a minute before the doctor's arrival.

Then she had followed him into the room where his daughter lay dead, still in her habit and boots — Anna had not dared to remove anything. She watched him go straight across to the sofa, without a tremor, and kneel down there without a word. From the room overhead came the soft sound of footsteps walking to and fro. A starling was twittering sharply, like a child's little musical instrument. . . . Then, after a space of absolute silence, he had risen, kissed his daughter's forehead slowly and lingeringly, and faced round. His complexion was ashy white; but his lips were steady, and his voice perfectly controlled.

"If you will allow me," he had said, "I will take my daughter's body home at once."

She had nodded, but she could not speak. Half an hour later the house was empty of death; but it was strangely still.

Anna could scarcely talk at all at dinner; and, with all the goodwill in the world, there were long silences. Enid was in black. (Anna, somehow, did not like that; and yet thought herself unreasonable for it.) Even Mrs. Bessington fell a-musing, again and again. There rested on them all the shadow of a tragedy and a grief that were not their own.

Nevill had scarcely ever seen the dead girl before, except
once or twice at dinner; and Anna herself hardly more often.
It was wholly of the father that she was thinking. He was
alone now, in that house of theirs across the park, and his
daughter lay dead upstairs.

There was no coherence then in the party. They drank coffee together in the hall, scarcely speaking; and presently
Enid strolled without a word out on to the balustraded terrace that opened on to the gardens. After a minute or two
Nevill joined her; Aunt Anna heard their voices talking together in a low tone; then the voices grew fainter, and she
heard the crunch of gravel.

Outside the night had fallen still, and the sky was full of
stars, against which rose up on one side, as the two paced
along the walk, the great blotting masses of the cedars, and
on the other the façade of the house, with lighted windows
here and there. Neither of them spoke till they had turned
the corner behind the presbytery, had passed down towards
the river, and were standing there, looking out over the low
wall and listening to the rush and sway of the star lit water
beyond. A great fish rose suddenly, and Enid shivered a little.

"It's terrible," she said. "But . . . but how splendid the night
is! Did you know her well?"

"No, my darling. I hardly ever saw her. I think she dined
with us twice."

"And the father? You know him?"

"Hardly at all either. My aunt likes him very much, I believe."

She leaned suddenly against him, and put her hand on his
shoulder. As he turned a little he could see her face and
throat glimmering palely between her dark hair and her
black dress.

"Nevill," she said, "I think your aunt is wonderful. How . . .
how splendidly she took charge of everything this afternoon!"

"She's like that," said Nevill.

"Won't she hate going from here? It must be very hard.
She's been so nice to me, too. I want to ask you something."

"Yes?"

"Do you think I might call her Aunt Anna too?"

Chapter VII

(1)

It had been an extraordinarily happy week for Nevill — though broken abruptly by the girl's death; and when the Thursday dawned that was to take the Bessingtons back to town, he awoke in the mood in which a schoolboy wakes on the last day of the holidays. Yet it was to be a very short term. In a fortnight he was to go up to town and stay there at least three weeks, without Aunt Anna indeed, who had been very resolute about remaining in the country; but with the Bessingtons' flat not further than a couple of streets away. There they would all three spend three weeks at least; there were mysterious legal arrangements to make, and a large number of amusements to be visited. Until the lawyers had been consulted the date of the wedding could not be fixed. October was the month provisionally decided upon.

Immediately after breakfast — again with a schoolboy's determination to make the most of the time — Nevill had unashamedly made his demand, as he followed the three ladies into the hall.

"Enid," he said, "I am going to be quite plain with you. You will kindly go upstairs immediately and make every arrangement that you will have to make before you go. You will be down here again in half an hour's time; and I shall then conduct you to the woods. We shall remain there till it is necessary to return for lunch. And at five minutes past two the motor will be at the door to take you to the station."

"Cousin Nevill —" said a small voice.

"Don't bother me, my dear. . . I'm talking. Well?"

Enid bowed.

"It shall be done," she said.

Aunt Anna saw them go. She was in the housekeeper's room as they crossed the garden. They disappeared: then she heard the distant clash of the gate.

"I beg your pardon," she said. "I wasn't attending. Yes; the mayonnaise will do excellently, Mrs. Templemore."

(2)

The June weather was justifying its name to the full as the two, ten minutes later, reached the place on which Nevill's imagination had fastened, and sat down. The sky really flamed with blue — there was no other word — so far as they could see anything of it, between the high trees here that very nearly met overhead.

They sat on a bench above the ride that curved round here over the crest of the hill that hung over the lower slopes of the park, with their backs against a small marble monument resembling a flat urn, erected in the glorious Georgian days by Nevill's grandfather to the memory of a favorite horse, whose bones lay beneath it. Beneath them, the ground behind the ride fell steeply down to the flats, clothed in bracken and protected by giant beeches. So far as they could see on either side — as well as behind, if they had chosen to turn round — stretched the green scented gloom of the woods. The air was alive with the hum of ten million invisible flies. Between the trees in front, far across the tops of the pines that skirted the edge of the open park, the melting blue line of the Downs faded, like soft penciling, into the steady blue of the sky. In one V-shaped gap showed a patch of indigo sea.

After a minute or two Nevill got off the bench, sat down on the ground, and leaned his head against Enid's knee. (It was exceedingly unlikely that anyone would come this way.) Then he felt, as he had hoped to feel, a hand slipped behind his curly hair. The hand began, very gently, to finger the lobe of his right ear.

"Now," said Enid, "we'll begin. I've got a lot to say too, you know."

"You first, then," said Nevill. "My word! This might very nearly be Frascati again. What a day!"

"Which?"

"Both."

From the farm far across the park beneath them came the shrill crow of a cock.

"I told you so," said Nevill. "There's the cock too. Now he's pecking his hens, I expect. Remember?"

(3)

Half an hour later they were approaching the point.

"I think that's really nice of you," said Nevill. "I love to be told my faults. Let's see, I was a little abrupt with Jim this morning; and I really ought to be able to get up when I mean to. You're perfectly right. I'll go to Mass tomorrow — for a penance; and I'll swear to teach Jim tennis this afternoon as restitution. Will that do?"

The fingers delicately pinched his ear again.

"You don't mind my telling you?" said Enid softly. "I never meant to, you know, when I began."

"Mind it? . . . Go on, tell me some more. I've got lots of faults . . . I know that — I say, look here —"

There was a pause.

"Shall we have a compact?" said Nevill. "You know you've got some faults too. Oh, yes! I can be quite brutal too, if it comes to that."

The finger relinquished his ear for a moment.

"You don't mind my saying that?" said Nevill a little anxiously.

The fingers again reassured him.

"Tell me them this instant," said Enid.

"I won't till you make the compact. Look here, my darling, we're both extraordinarily sensible people, aren't we? — thoroughly wholesome-minded and honest and all the rest. Let's make the compact to be quite plain with one another. But never when either of us is in the least annoyed or upset. We must count ten, so to say, always before speaking. Do you agree?"

"Yes, I think so," said Enid deliberately. "I think that's rather a brilliant idea. You begin."

"Sure?"

"Quite sure. Go on, please."

"Wait. Have you got any more of mine up your sleeve?"

"Two," said the girl, after a moment's reflection.

"What are — No; that's all right then. Because I've only got one against you."

"This instant, please."

"Well. It's about Father Richardson. No; it's not the least what you think."

The soft hand was pulling gently at the short curls now on the back of his neck. It ceased for a moment; then it went on again.

"Well? I'm waiting."

"I think you were rather hard on him yesterday."

"Why! I thought —"

"Yes, I know. You were much too nice to him at first. However, I accepted that. I knew it wouldn't work; but I gave in.

Then he came to dine on Monday, didn't he? And you were
simply delightful to him — all about Rome, and so on. He
loved it. He was quite eloquent about it next day. He congratulated me, really and sincerely, for the first time. . . .
Then, if you remember, we met him in the garden on the
Tuesday, and you insisted on him coming with us. I'm sure
he never meant to. Then, yesterday, you suddenly turned
round on him."

"What did I do?"

"My dear, you withered him! And he really wasn't doing
any harm. He really thought it his duty to come up and say
goodbye on your last evening. He said so to me afterwards.
And you simply turned your back on him!"

The hand was resting motionless now on his collar.

"Well," said Enid. "I really meant to be rather disagreeable.
It was a little too much — our last evening. I thought he
knew better than that! And he stayed an hour!"

"Entirely your own fault, my dear. He simply can't get
away when he once comes. I could have told you that. In fact,
I think I did. . . . Now I'm not in the least objecting — just at
present — to your being nice to him; nor to your being nasty
to him. But I do think you oughtn't to be first very nice and
then, suddenly, very nasty. It's not playing the game."

There was silence.

"I say! You don't mind?"

"My dear boy, I'm very glad you told me. I was only counting ten. I'll remember. I think you're perfectly right. I'll be
more careful. . . . But you know —"

"Yes?"

"I don't think I like Father Richardson much."

Nevill gave a little gurgle of laughter.

"What did I tell you?"

"Yes; I know. You needn't triumph any more. I give in. I'm
afraid he's not quite a gentleman."

Nevill was glowing with delight. He had been a little nervous about halfway through his criticisms. But how perfectly
she had received them! But just a flicker of discomfort came
to him at her last words. But he dismissed it.

"And now for mine," he said. "There are two, you said. Give
us the worst first."

The hand began on his hair again.

"You're sure you won't mind either?"

"I shall positively kiss the rod."

He twisted his head suddenly sideways, and managed just to touch the slender fingers with his lips.

"There!" he said. "Now go on."

"Well, they're neither at all big. The first is about the servants."

"Eh?"

"Well, Masterson."

"But he's perfectly splendid!"

"Wait: you haven't heard. Nevill, my dear, he isn't respectful enough. He really isn't. He's familiar. Do you remember that . . . that time when he came to tell us about the accident?" (Her voice trembled a little.) "Well, I know he was excited then. But that wasn't the only time. You asked him for your cap yesterday, in the hall, if you remember. Well; he was simply rude."

"Oh, Lord!" murmured Nevill.

"Don't say 'Oh, Lord!'; it isn't polite." (The fingers pulled his ear sharply. "Ooh!" said Nevill.) "I mean it. I really do. Of course he's an old servant and all that. But really — Well; that's number one."

"But —"

"Wait. There's number two now. . . . Nevill, you know, I simply love your aunt. I think she's wonderful. She's let me call her Aunt Anna, too, by the way."

"You dear!" murmured Nevill.

"Well; and I know all that she's done for you; and how she manages the house and all that. But, Nevill dear, she really is a little masterful."

"Masterful! Aunt Anna! Help! I want to count ten, please."

"Well — abrupt. Oh! I do hate to say this. But it's your fault, you know; not hers. You've given everything over to her; and . . . and, of course, she takes charge."

"But when do you mean? When was she abrupt? I simply don't know what you mean."

"Well — do you remember when the poor girl —" She stopped. "No; I won't say that. Consider it unsaid, please. Well, I think so, anyhow."

Nevill was silent.

"Nevill, my dear, you mustn't be cross. You're counting much more than ten. You mustn't. That's part of the compact. You don't think it was easy for me to —" Again that round soft voice trembled into silence. And the next instant Nevill was beside her.

"I'm an absolute brute," he said. "And you're an angel to have told me. I really will try to be more — well, dignified, with Masterson. But as for Aunt Anna — well, she's going when we're married, you know. Let's leave her in peace. . . . There! Give me a kiss, please."

(4)

It was with a real physical sensation of constriction in his throat that he watched the motor move off with its dear burden. Enid had flatly refused to allow him to come to the station.

"It's foolish," she said. "And you look so funny going backwards, too. I don't like you at all, then, my dear. You looked so miserable on the way to Frascati, I remember. Besides, we have to say goodbye sometime; and it's so much easier than at the station."

So Nevill had said goodbye to her in the hall, all alone till Masterson came in.

Then, when there was no more than a cloud of dust in the distance he turned to Jim.

"And now, Jim, tennis! Instantly!"

Aunt Anna said nothing. She slipped, without a word, into the morning room behind as he spoke.

Three-quarters of an hour later Nevill lowered his racquet.

"Jim, my dear, it's not the very faintest use till you've got the stroke."

They were standing in the tennis court, Nevill on one side of the net, quite close to it, and Jim under the *dedans,* on the other. Jim was flushed with exercise, and looked a little weary. He had no conception that tennis was like this: he had imagined that they would hit the ball alternately and make a real game of it. But Cousin Nevill would do nothing of the sort. For half an hour, after a quarter of an hour's instruction as to how to hold the racquet horizontally, at a certain angle, Cousin Nevill had bowled balls to him slowly and bidden him (Jim) to hit them back in the proper way, straight at his (Cousin Nevill's) face. This had been rather fun for about five minutes, and then it had become distinctly tiresome. He wanted to slash and bang. Besides, the racquet was dreadfully heavy and his wrist ached.

"I . . . I think if you'd let me do it my way, Cousin Nevill —"
Cousin Nevill jerked his head.

"Look here, old chap; I'm teaching you — not you me. It's not much fun to me, you know. Of course, if you think you can do it better —"

Then he raised his eyes, and there was Aunt Anna in the gallery. He had not heard her come in, and shame and compunction seized him.

"Never mind, old man. You've been learning long enough for today. Now we'll have a proper game for five minutes."

There had followed a proper game, without any rules at all. Jim slashed and banged, and Cousin Nevill had astonishingly the worst of it. Finally he had fallen prostrate in a vain endeavor to reach a ball.

"It's no good, old man. You're too good for me altogether. We'll have another go tomorrow."

"Yes, I liked it, rather," explained Jim to his mother overhead. "But —" (Jim discreetly looked round to see if Cousin Nevill really had gone.) — "But, you know, I don't think Cousin Nevill could have been really trying his hardest, you know. . . . You hold the racquet like this, you see."

He demonstrated to his mother.

It was still very early when Nevill strolled out of the court. But he felt quite certain that he must have solitude; he did not want just now to talk even to Aunt Anna, and next it struck him that it would be very suitable to walk up through the woods again, and — and perhaps go to the seat where he had sat with Enid this morning.

He lit a cigarette as he went.

Again the curious constrained feeling gripped his throat as he stood at last contemplating the seat. The ground was still a little disturbed where he had sat at Enid's feet. He sat there again, leaned back, and closed his eyes.

There came upon him then, in that hour, that amazing sense of the possession of another that comes only to those who love deeply, and still find those depths inexhaustible. It is that one miracle in which none can believe who have not seen and felt: it is the one form of faith that must simultaneously be sight. And it is none the less a miracle that it recurs so often; it is as supernatural as the dawn, as transcendent of law as the beauty of water or the mystery of music; as paradoxical as every final truth.

For the paradox that was burning itself in upon Nevill's heart as he sat here, cheating himself with ecstatic pain into thinking that Enid was still there — only silent — was that he perceived two mutually exclusive facts — his own blinding unworthiness of this girl and his own absolute right to possess her very soul. He had had his first glance into that soul — oh! Months and years ago — at the tiresome little tea party at Rome; and in its tender and beautiful twilight had met eyes that looked into his own with a frankness and a comprehension he had never met before. He perceived now that that had been the moment of recognition between two mates designed for one another from eternity. Then, in the days that had followed — at luncheon in the hotel; at Frascati; in the Catacomb — he had been verifying this — penetrating slowly and reverently into that enchanted realm that was Enid. Then the fire had kindled . . . and he had understood; and misery that was pure joy came down and enveloped him. During those days he had known nothing, understood nothing; he had lived mechanically, driven by a compulsion that was without him as well as within; till he had spoken to her in a fit of despair, and told her what was in his heart. (That was in the Borghese gardens one morning.) And at the memory of that; and of her answer; and of the shattering knowledge that came to him that he had been right, and that the same kind of relation that she bore to him, he too bore to her — at the memory of that he drew a long whistling breath, and opened his eyes wide again and stared up at the rustling canopy of beech leaves overhead. . . .

Then he began to think over again those last days — watching, a couple of yards away, a little line of earth heave and crumble slowly and deliberately, as a mole pushed his way beneath. (He knew he ought to kill the mole, but he quite firmly resolved he would not.)

Their relations had developed marvelously, he thought; and that development had been the last and final ratification of his heart's instinct. She had opened herself to him, he perceived, in every direction; and in all she had shown herself what he had thought her. How perfectly she had understood the house, for instance — that house that had been his home all his life and would be hers too, soon; his house with its own particular personality as individual as that of a human being — its air, its little ways and moods in sun and cloud.

She had seen its three points at once — the hall, the pavilion and the river. He had seen her understanding in her face.

Then there were the people. There was Aunt Anna. Instantly Enid had appreciated her, had noticed her adequateness and her peculiar relation to himself. She had done even more; she had seen and even touched upon, ever so tenderly, the one single little exaggeration in Aunt Anna — her tiny tendency towards masterfulness. He had never noticed that! But he saw it to be perfectly true, now it was pointed out.

Then there was Father Richardson. Well, she had indeed done wonders there; she had gained him over completely by her sympathy with his church, and one or two appreciations she had made. She had been even too successful: she had entirely removed the little soreness that had been between the priest and himself, even too effectively. And then she had seen her lovable mistake, and confessed it. How adorable that was of her!

There was Jim. Well, it was obvious that she had won Jim's heart, thought Nevill. He had been silent always when she was there; yet he had not been able to keep his eyes off her; and Jim was not so easy to please. . . .

Masterson? Well, she was quite right about Masterson, anyhow. Masterson certainly ought not to be quite so abrupt. He would speak to him about it. . . . Well, perhaps he would not speak to him himself. He would just drop a hint to Aunt Anna, and Aunt Anna would drop a hint to Masterson. He did not want to hurt Masterson's feelings. He was a very old servant, and very loyal, really.

Finally, there was the Compact. And the Compact, it appeared, had, so to speak, signed, sealed and delivered the Contract once and forever. It really had been an inspiration.

For what else could be wanting in a perfect understanding between two souls, than such an arrangement as this? What possible chance could there ever be of any drifting apart, when each could speak to each quite plainly and quite tenderly, without the remotest chance of misunderstanding? How admirably and triumphantly successful had been the first experiment! She had told him two faults quite plainly, and he had told her one; and both sides had acknowledged the justice of the other's criticism. That would be their safeguard always in future. How could any shadow between them ever deepen into darkness under such an agreement as

this? Besides, she, at any rate, hadn't any faults. Really that
scarcely had been a fault of which he had spoken; or at any
rate it was all Father Richardson's.

Well, then; here they were. The Understanding was perfect. There was not realm or department where the adjustment was not complete.

And he would see her again in a fortnight. . . . It was all
perfect. Perfect. . . . The mole had ceased his excavations.

He opened his eyes suddenly.

No, he had not been asleep. Only the hum of the insects
and the warmth of this dry heathery soil were very soothing.

Who was that looking at him? Why, it was Mr. Morpeth!
He scrambled to his feet.

"Why, I believe —" he began. And then he remembered. He
had not seen him since the funeral of Ella, three days ago;
and he had done nothing then except shake his hand for a
moment. What should he say to him?

Mr. Morpeth was in his old gray suit with his old gray hat
— the very costume in which Nevill had found him and
rushed him across the park in the motor. There was not a
line different anywhere, even in his face. He still looked entirely as he had always looked — a retired businessman.

Nevill came forward hesitatingly.

"I am so sorry," he said. "I think I must have been asleep. I
m so glad you're out, Mr. Morpeth."

He felt he was doing it very badly, yet he had not an idea
what to say.

The old gentleman smiled naturally and easily.

"I have no kind of business to come waking up my land-
lord," he said. "I'm just taking a stroll round to the church
before tea. It was so hot I thought I would come by the
woods."

He moved on, as if expecting Nevill to come with him.

"I'm going home myself," said Nevill. "You won't mind my
coming with you?"

"But that is most kind of you," said Mr. Morpeth.

Nevill still felt thoroughly uneasy. Sorrow was an unfamil-
iar and rather repellent thing to him. His instinct was to talk
rather feverishly about the woods, and the tunnels of
sun-flecked shadow, through which they were passing
downwards towards the house. Yet his sense of what was due

urged him insistently to make some reference to his own sympathy for the old man.

He was just approaching an attempt, when the difficulty was taken out of his hands.

"I often walked here with Ella," said the other suddenly. "I hope you will let me remain your tenant for a long time."

"Why, certainly," began Nevill. "But —"

"I know you're trying to think of something suitable to say to me, Sir Nevill. But I assure you there's no reason. I am quite content."

Nevill gasped a little. This was indeed plain speaking.

"I can't tell you what I feel," he said. "I — I only wish I could say one-half —"

'There is no sort of need," said the old gentleman tranquilly. "Though I thank you for your kind thoughts. The thing has happened. It was no one's fault. There is no more to be said."

"The motorists —"began the young man.

"I assure you it was not their fault. I have written to tell them so. They were deeply distressed. It was a young horse. But my daughter was an excellent rider."

Nevill wondered whether the man were heartless. But somehow he did not think so.

"Let me be quite plain," said Mr. Morpeth, with the same brisk and intelligent air. "It is far easier, and then we need not speak of it again. I believe very strongly indeed in God's Divine Providence, and I see that sorrow and death are His most usual instruments. It is natural that it should be so in this world, considering all circumstances. Very well, then; I am content. I am not likely to live very long myself, anyhow. I came down here to get ready to die, and this will be a help to me, I think. Let us say no more about it. And may I beg of you to speak quite naturally to me of my daughter, at any time. She was a very good daughter to me indeed, and I love her very dearly. She was very thoughtful for me, always. And I am afraid I was not always so thoughtful for her. I was trying to make amends, when she died. However, she understands all about that now."

(5)

"Yes," said Nevill, a few minutes later, as he met his aunt on the lawn. "That was Mr. Morpeth I was with. He has gone into the church. He wouldn't come to tea."

"Well?" said Anna.

They went up into the pavilion before he answered. He sat down in his old place on the window seat and began to finger the tassel.

"I can't make him out," he said. "He seemed to me quite heartless. And yet I don't think he is. He talked in a most extraordinary way about his daughter. Do you know him very well, Aunt Anna?"

Anna began to minister among the tea things.

"I'm beginning to," she said. "What did he say?"

"Well, you know, I was thinking of what I could say to him, when he began himself. He said he was content, and that I needn't trouble to be sympathetic."

Anna smiled very faintly. (She was looking rather over-done, thought Nevill.)

"Yes, I think that's like him," she said. "He's so very businesslike about it all, isn't he? He was just like that the day after the funeral, too."

Nevill considered a moment.

"Well, he's made that way, I suppose. By the way, Aunt Anna, he wants to stay on as tenant for a good long while, he said. Of course he has got rights, you know, by the agreement. But what about you?"

"My dear, I'm going to settle near Downside."

Again Nevill paused.

"Are you perfectly certain you must go?"

Anna handed him his tea.

"Yes, my dear. Quite certain."

"Oh! . . . I say!"

"Yes?"

"Well? What about *them?* I haven't had a word with you since they went. And we've got those beastly people coming to stay. What time do they get here?"

Aunt Anna said that the new guests were arriving by the six-fifty.

"I can't bear Algy Lennox," said Nevill reflectively.

"And he will think he can play tennis. Well, that doesn't matter. What about Enid? Any remarks to offer? She simply adores you, by the way."

Anna smiled a little, lifting her eyebrows.

"Does she really? Well, I think she's one of the most beautiful people I've ever seen."

"Isn't she! And — and isn't she altogether extraordinary? She's really worthy of the house, isn't she now?"

Anna nodded two or three times.

"Quite," she said.

An hysterical barking sounded from the lawn, and then the sound of adjurations in a boy's voice. Then came a cry of despair.

"Mummy! Are you there? Look out, she's coming."

A whirlwind tore up the steps. Anna hastily leaned forward with protecting arms round the table as Jill burst in, screaming with delight and excitement. Nevill stuck out his leg to save the window seat and his tea.

"Mummy, I'm so sorry," apologized Jim, coming up the steps. (Jill was out again by now, whirling round the lawn.) "I had her on a string, and she broke it."

"Get a stronger string next time, my dear. She's been tied up all day, hasn't she?"

"Yes, as you told me," explained Jim. "Miss Bessington doesn't like dogs really, I think. And then I forgot to let them out till just now."

"What bosh are you talking now?" inquired Nevill. "She simply loves them."

Aunt Anna made haste to explain.

"Jill jumped up on Enid's dress last night," she said, "just before you came down to dinner. That was all. So I thought they'd better be kept out of the way till she'd gone again. And then Jim forgot to let them out."

"But she didn't like it," said Jim. "Because I was there, and heard her say that —"

"That's enough, my dear. Say grace and sit down."

Nevill was silent an instant.

"Did she say she wanted them shut up?" he asked in a low voice.

"No, my dear boy, of course she didn't. And when I suggested it, she said 'Certainly not.' But I thought I'd better."

Nevill's face cleared.

"I thought so. She simply loves dogs and all that. Jim, my boy, you mustn't pass rash judgments. How would you like Jill to jump up all over your clothes?"

"I like it very much," began Jim. "Oh! There's a trout! Cousin Nevill, will you come and catch a trout directly after tea?"

(6)

She sat still, when the two had gone, ten minutes later, Jim speeding across the lawn to get the rod and the brown fly-hook from Charleson, and Nevill down the path westwards towards the bridge.

When at last she heard Jim's footsteps across the lawn, and presently, leaning forward, was rewarded by a nod from him as he staggered along outside, carrying the rod carefully in both hands, with its point carried before him, spearwise, to avoid the branches, and with a landing-net slung over his shoulders; she shifted across to the window seat, whence she might be able to see, perhaps, the beginning of the campaign.

Yes, there was Nevill, just visible at the curve of the river, on the opposite bank, hands on knees, watching the water. Then she heard Jim's steps again on the bridge, and he came into sight. She saw Nevill lift a hand in warning. The figures were clearly visible against the green of the distant woods, and beneath the golden light of the evening sky. It was a perfect evening.

Then she began to think.

Honestly, she had formulated no conclusions which she could really trust, except that Nevill was very deeply and sincerely in love with Enid. That was undeniable. She had seen, again and again, during these last days, a look in his eyes that was unmistakable. He was fond of herself, she knew that well enough; she might even say that he loved her; but the two emotions had really nothing in common but their name. He did not look at her as he looked at Enid. Tiny changes, all but imperceptible except *en masse,* showed in his face as he looked at the other; when he looked at herself it was just the frank, honest, workaday affection of a son for a mother, as, indeed, it ought to be. Well, she had that conclusion fixed and docketed and established. What of the others?

Now Anna long ago had reached the point of self-knowledge in which she could judge of her moods and sentiments as if they belonged to someone else. For instance, she always refused to find fault with anybody, even interiorly, between midnight and ten o'clock next morning; because she knew perfectly well that both sleeplessness and sleep, between those hours, slightly perverted the judgment. Sometimes, even, she would refuse to pass any judgments before lunch, because she had learned how unreliable these might be.

Next, then, she was aware that Jealousy — (there was no other word for it) — had quite distinctly begun to insinuate itself into her soul immediately she heard of the boy's engagement, and that it had considerably increased its influence on her during this last week. She was perfectly furious with herself; but there it was. There had come moments during those last days when she had been forced to go up to her room and lock her door: if she had not done so, she knew that she would have given some sign of what was happening within her. It was this humiliating discovery that had finally decided her that the Dower House would not do. She must not be so near: there was no knowing, not only what misery she herself might fall into, if she lived there, but what a disturbing element she might not be in Hartley itself.

Very well, then; she was jealous. Then how could she possibly trust to any of her own intuitions or judgments in respect to the person of whom she was jealous? All the conceivable efforts she might make after detachment were not enough; she could never know if they were really successful. She might only too easily commit a grave injustice, in entire sincerity.

For her judgments of Enid had been very sharp indeed.

First, she was convinced that the girl was the most dangerous kind of sham — the most dangerous, because in all probability the girl did not know it herself. For instance, there was Enid's statement that she loved the country and outdoor things, and, above all, the whole of that element of which "outdoor things" are the symbol. It was extremely probable that Enid really did think that she liked those things and was of that kind of temperament. Yet what about that very sharp, though quite courteous annoyance of hers when Jill had jumped up on her dress last night? Aunt Anna had been quite truthful just now: the girl had said that she did hope that the poor dogs would not be sent to the stable; and yet Anna saw that that was exactly what she wanted.

Then there had been the religious atmosphere — that general attitude to interior things all round which Nevill had said was the one thing that mattered — that attitude of which breeziness and a love of solitude and quiet and so forth, are significant departments.

Well, Enid had not said much on that, though Nevill had,
upon his first homecoming; but what she had said, once or
twice, when alone with Anna, showed quite plainly either
what Enid thought of herself, or at least wished other people
to think of her. It was a type Anna had met with before — a
kind of Christianized pagan mysticism, a sense of being in
touch with fundamental things, of being beneath dogma, and
yet fully tolerant of it. Nevill had laid great stress on that
element in Enid, she remembered. Well, it was not a bad attitude: it was better than narrowness or dogmatic intoler-
ance! Yet, if that were genuine in the girl, how was it that
Anna had caught in her face a look of unmistakable contempt
on the night that Father Richardson had dined with them,
and had explained very carefully to the company exactly
what was *De Fide* on the doctrine of Eternal Punishment? Of
course he shouldn't have done it; but, if Enid was genuine,
she should not have felt, still less shown, even for that fleeting instant, so sharp a contempt.

Finally there was the element of cruelty — and this was
the worst of all — which she thought she had detected.

She had first noticed it with regard to the girl's mother.
Mrs. Bessington had been talking one evening in her usual
manner, and had flowed on, uninterrupted, for minute after
minute. Then, suddenly, Enid had given a little mirthless
laugh. (Nevill was not in the room.)

"You haven't had one full stop," she said, "for four minutes
by the clock. I've been timing you. Nevill put me up to it."

Mrs. Bessington had stopped dead. Enid had eyed Anna
fleetingly and then laughed naturally enough.

"Poor mother!" she said. "What a beast I am! I didn't mean
it." Then she had taken her mother's hand and kissed it with
a charming and humble contrition, just as Nevill came downstairs.

Now that had quite appalled Anna. She had first thanked
God that Nevill had not been there, and then had wondered
whether it would not have been better if he had. But probably the girl would not have said it, in that case. And, she had
reckoned, if the girl said that kind of thing before other people, what was she like when she was alone with her mother?

That was the worst point. Yet it was not the only instance.
Enid had certainly been a little sharp with Jim one morning
after breakfast. She had laid herself out to be delightful to

him at first; but five minutes after, when Jim came up, as was his way, and slipped his hand into hers, she had turned rather abruptly on to him, and Anna had caught again, she thought, a sudden flare of unloving impatience. (It was partly because of what she had seen in Jim's face, too, that she had questioned him later as to what he thought of the guests.)

Well, here were these intuitions — these observations — and the conclusions that her whole soul drew from them. And yet that distorting passion of jealousy came in and vitiated them all. And could she possibly tell that she was not gravely uncharitable — that she had noticed and counted and exaggerated those little sinister points only, and had ignored the rest? How could she tell? What was she to do? Yet Nevill mattered frightfully. And yet, too, she dared not speak. She must make the best of it — at any rate for the present. That would surely be Mr. Morpeth's advice, if she dared but to consult him.

She sat up suddenly interested.

She had been watching unintelligently the movements of the two, who had moved a few yards away from the river-bank in order to select and affix the appropriate fly. Jim had sat on his heels to watch, jumping up and down, now and again, with impatience. It was too far for her, with the suck and gurgle of the stream in her ears, to hear them talking.

Then, still unintelligently, she had seen Nevill approach the bank, crouching a little, and Jim, like a small replica of him, immediately behind; and then she watched the cautious sinuous movements and the delicate whisk of the rod. She saw it all, even while she thought of those other matters. Nothing had happened, except that the figures had presently moved round the bend of the river and disappeared.

Then they had come back, and there had followed another business with the removal of the fly, she supposed, and the affixing of another. Then once more the casting had begun.

And now she sat up to watch.

For Nevill was upright, and Jim was dancing. Nevill had the rod high, and she thought that, even at that distance, she could make out the curve of it. Then she saw Jim stop dancing, and snatch up the net; and so the two figures stayed, now moving a little, now returning.

And then the group dissolved into laxity again. She saw the rod lowered, and Jim's net drop. Nevill was examining something invisible between his fingers. . . .

"Beastly bad luck," explained Jim a few minutes later. "Cousin Nevill hooked him beautifully, and then the fly broke — I mean the bit of stuff that fastens it. And the trout went away. Beastly bad luck!"

"Beastly bad luck," echoed Aunt Anna.

End of Part I

Part II

Chapter I

(1)

"Come on, old chap," said Nevill, rising and blowing out of the pool. "Straight in. It's just gorgeous this morning."

"Head first?" questioned Jim, a slim shivering figure on the little wooden pier that jutted out over the bathing pool.

"Of course."

"I — I think —" began Jim.

"Don't think. Come on."

So Jim came on, and found himself neatly fielded as he rose, gasping. It really did require a little courage at his age. He could swim a little; but not very much; and the current was considerable here under the little fall that Nevill had designed here a couple of years ago, a hundred yards westward of the bridge where the trout had been so nearly caught a fortnight before.

Overhead the day was perfect. The risen sun, away to the east, shone straight down across the wide meadows that glittered as with diamonds. (Nevill had slipped off his shoes as he had come down with Jim ten minutes ago in his pajamas, for the sheer delight of walking barefooted through the dew-dripping grass.) The tall trees above the bathing place were motionless in the morning calm, but rang unceasingly with the song of birds; blackbirds scudded, scolding, from shrubbery to shrubbery; a thrush, visible against the sky, poured out a torrent of music from the top of a post, in full view of the swimmers, exactly as if he had been engaged to do it. A couple of bullocks, with a kind of rustic stupidity in their long faces, eyed the two splashing figures from over the post and rails that shut off the bathing place from the open park, and swerved suddenly with heads down as Jim screamed with joy and gesticulated.

Nevill found it presently rather hard work battling up against the stream with Jim on his shoulders. He had had another of his headaches three days before, and felt a trifle invalidish still. These headaches made astonishing demands upon his strength.

"Look here, old chap," he gasped. "This is a bit too much. The stream's so . . . so jolly strong this morning I'm going to drift down to the shallow end, and leave you there a bit."

Jim hammered at Cousin Nevill's head.

"No. Go on," he said.

"You little brute! Wait till I get you down."

He swerved in the stream, and with long easy strokes sped downwards. Jim prudently rolled off his shoulders as they neared the tail of the pool, and floundered to the bank. Nevill assured him he should not escape; and then turned once more and began to beat upstream.

The world looked extraordinarily delicious viewed from the surface of the clear-running current. Immediately in front of his eyes the long lines of water came racing down, bubbling crisply from below, bearing a little yellowish foam and blossoms as they came. The fall of the river was small enough: yet it sounded like thunder in his ears. The low green bank on the right, with the bullocks' heads still peering over, was as enchanting as the edge of a new world: the dark shadowed spaces under the beech trees on the left, as mysterious as caverns; and overhead, between the masses of green, he could see that clear haze-veiled sky that promised great heat. It was an exultant, triumphant morning, warm and caressing, yet with just that sting of early coolness that was like the bubbles in champagne.

How frightfully hot London would be! . . . And, for a moment or two, he wished with all his heart that Enid could have managed to come down here instead of making him come to her. Then he remembered the lawyers, and Mrs. Bessington's social delights; and understood that it was impossible.

He was going up in time to lunch with them. (That was why he was bathing here with Jim before breakfast. He would have to leave a little after ten, as he must just go to his house first, in Elizabeth Street, to see that everything was in train for the little dinner this evening. The cook had already gone up to town with a maid or two, Aunt Anna had insisted upon this.) Then this afternoon he remembered, they were all three to go to something or other: he rather thought it was Pictures: but wasn't sure; and this evening to the theater. He had got the tickets all right, by the way.

He was sorry Aunt Anna wouldn't come with him; but she had been quite explicit. She would be entirely in the way, she said. Four was a much pleasanter number than five; and of course Nevill must have a male friend now and again — to entertain Mrs. Bessington, if nothing else. Algy Lennox would do for once or twice: he couldn't be a bore about his tennis, very well, in London at that time. Besides, she simply loathed London. She might perhaps run up for a day or two at the end, and take Jim to the Zoo. But, really, not more, if Nevill didn't mind. So it had been settled; and, although he was sorry she wouldn't come, he felt that there really was something to be said on her side.

Ah! How delicious the water was!

He turned on his back as he came up to the foot of the little eighteen-inch fall, just in that mystical part of a current which, itself very nearly motionless, is quick with a strange thrilling vitality from the plunge of air and water beneath — where the myriad bubbles rise hissing and hushing, and the surface of the water curves and heaves a little. (It is just behind that, by the way, that the trout lie and wait for the food that comes so fresh and enticing down the fall, right down to their level a foot or two above the bed of the stream.)

He shifted slowly from place to place, his head right back in the water, keeping himself afloat by slow paddling with his hands on either side. A film of water washed over his face once or twice; and he closed his eyes. Then with a rush against his limbs, the current caught him, and he whirled down, smiling, still with closed eyes, till all motion ceased. His eyelids glowed before his eyes, red and flaming, against the bright sky. His physical ecstasy was at its height.

(2)

When he had had enough he climbed out, dripping, on to the little pier. Jim was making a great to-do down there at the shallow end. He could see his head, now and again, very agitated, with yet more agitated heels winnowing the water four feet behind. He had meant to duck him; but it was too much trouble: he felt a pleasant languorous ache all over him; and a cigarette seemed absolutely necessary.

He waded through the wet grass to his pajamas and towel, delighting in the brush of the long stems round his feet; dried himself lightly; slipped on his trousers and jacket; got out his case from the pocket, and then, blowing out aromatic clouds, he went back and sat down on the end of the pier, with his bare feet dangling. His head felt a little heavy. He thought he had been in the water too long.

"Cousin Nevill!" cried a shrill voice.

He turned to see; and, as he turned, a dimness, rather like a torn veil, drifted between him and the white little figure that, standing knee-deep in the shallows twenty yards away, was splashing furiously with both hands.

It must be liver, he told himself. Really he ought to be ashamed of it — at his age. He rubbed his eyes quickly with his disengaged hand. Then he looked again. Yes; the dimness had gone. . . . No, it hadn't. It was forming again in shreds and patches.

Jim apparently wanted no answer: he had shouted out of sheer exhilaration. The splashing had ceased, and once more Nevill could make out — but only just make out — the head passing across the sunlit water.

Nevill stood up. He must take a turn or two. Perhaps the sunlit water had affected his eyes a little; perhaps he had caught just a shadow of a chill. As he turned up his trousers, a little tangle of black lines drifted over his hands, and went again. This was ridiculous. No; he wouldn't walk about; he would just lie still on the pier with his eyes shut. That would put him right.

A loud cackle of physical joy made him open them again; and there was Jim in the long grass, entirely unclothed, rolling and tossing to and fro.

"Oh! It does tickle so, Cousin Nevill."

Then as he looked at him, again that veil drifted suddenly across, and for an instant he saw nothing immediately in front. Jim was gone in blankness. He could see the post where the thrush had been singing, away to the left, and the solemn lowered bullocks' heads on the right. There was nothing in between. Again he passed his hand over his eyes, rubbing them hard. Then he turned away again. Jim mustn't notice anything: he might tell his mother, and there would be a fuss.

"You'd better dress, old chap. You'll catch cold."

"Oooh . . !" said Jim, in a long-drawn ecstasy.

"Come on, old man," said Nevill again. "I really mean it. And then we'll go a walk and get warm again."

"Will you come and shoot a rabbit?" demanded Jim.

"Well, we'll go and look for one," evaded Nevill. "Make haste."

He felt perfectly certain that the thing would pass. It had passed before all right. It was simply his liver; he had sat on the lawn all day yesterday instead of going for a ride. It was that; and the sun on the water — no more.

While Jim dressed in the white shirt and knickerbockers in which he had come down, Nevill sat very still with his back to him, keeping his eyes closed; and answering questions now and again.

"Will you take me with you as far as the village after breakfast, Cousin Nevill?"

"We'll see what your mother says," said Nevill with closed eyes. "Don't you ever do any lessons?"

"Oh! Yes!" said Jim indifferently. . . . "Cousin Nevill!"

"Well?"

"Why are you going to London?"

"To see Miss Bessington — Cousin Enid."

"Oh. Why do you want to see Miss Bessington — I mean Cousin Enid?"

"Because I like her very much."

"Oh! Why?"

It had been carefully explained to Jim that Cousin Nevill was going to marry Miss Bessington; and that he (Jim) would, in future, have to call her Cousin Enid. But Jim did not appear to realize that this involved any particular affection on anyone's part — even on Nevill's; it was as if Cousin Nevill was going to engage a new housekeeper — no more than that. He had shown no interest whatever in the event.

"Because she's very nice," said Nevill carefully.

"Oh!" said Jim; as if he had encountered a brick wall.

"Buck up with your dressing, old man."

"I'm ready," said Jim.

The moment had come and Nevill opened his eyes.

For an instant all seemed well. The clear water ran smoothly and swiftly beneath; the cool dark spaces under the beeches opposite looked as they always had: he saw again a blackbird scurry across from one side to the other. Then the veil formed again, as if a hundred spiders were spinning black threads at full speed. Glimpses of light and color showed between the meshes; but no more. Nevill shut his

eyes again; and his heart sickened within him. He still kept
his back turned to the boy.

"Jim, old man."

"Yes?"

"Look here; I've thought of a game. Let's pretend I'm a
blind man."

"Oh! Do you think that would be funny?"

"You wait," said Nevill. "You haven't heard it yet. And
you're my guide; you mustn't touch me; and I mustn't touch
you. But you've got to guide me with your voice; and tell me
where to go." . . . (He was inventing desperately. He was perfectly certain this thing would pass presently, and meantime
Aunt Anna must know nothing. Then he heard the stable
clock strike eight.) "We've lots of time. Every ten yards that I
go without touching anything except the ground is one to
you; and every time I touch anything, like a tree, it's one to
me. I must keep my eyes tight shut all the time."

"Oh! Do you think that's a good game?" asked a doubtful
voice.

"We'll try it, anyhow."

He felt for the edges of the pier with his hands, and carefully got to his feet. Then, a little unsteadily, he walked in
the direction of Jim, until he felt the grass under his feet.

"Now, begin," he said. "You must carry the towels."

He felt it was not much of a success; but it was all that he
could think of. Once when Jim screamed with sudden delight, as the blind man fell heavily over a log, he thought it
might serve a bit longer, but he simply dared not open his
eyes.

"Look here, you mustn't make me fall down on purpose," he
said. "That's not the game. I shall count that three to me."

From that moment the game certainly flagged. Jim did not
seem to find it funny. His voice grew more and more indifferent. Finally Nevill stopped.

"Where are we?" he said.

"What?"

"Where are we?" snapped the other, a little irritably.

"Oh, close to the bridge, Cousin Nevill."

"Very well, we'll stop the game as soon as I touch the
bridge. And then we'll —"

His voice faltered. What in God's name should he do if he
couldn't see? And what, again in God's name, was the mat-

ter? His little headache had quite gone with the exercise. That was one encouragement. But what on earth should he do —?

His hands touched the stonework.

"There," he said, "you've won. Eleven to you and four to me."

Then he opened his eyes and waited.

There was the stonework under his hands; the sunlit water flowing swiftly beneath; the outer edge of the pavilion window just in sight; the gold and green of the park, splendid in sunlight. He still waited: and they remained as before. He rolled his eyes round, and again looked. It was all right.

"Why do you look like that, Cousin Nevill?"

"My dear boy; I've only just got my sight back. Now we'll do any mortal thing you like till a quarter to nine."

(3)

As the clock struck the half-hour they were sitting on the bench with their backs to the Georgian monument. Jim had decided that, as compensation for their extraordinarily stupid game of Blind Man, he would ride on Cousin Nevill's back up into the woods and look for the Holy Grail. This had been done, until the horse had explained that there were limits to everything — even to an unconditional promise — and that if the Holy Grail were not found by the time they reached the seat by the monument, it must remain lost.

Yet, as they sat there at last — Jim with an arm over his late horse's shoulders — Nevill really was not quite sure that he had not found it after all, or, at least, that he was not basking in its rose-red light.

The relief was amazing. His headache was gone; but that was nothing. Rather, there had lifted from him a horror whose weight he had not dared to appraise so long as it was on him. There had not come back to him even one floating shred or film of that fine spun black veil that had dimmed the glory of the stream and the morning; and, with that relief, physical joy had come back at a rush. He was sure, now, that the trouble could not be organic.

The very seat on which he sat seemed transfigured. He was looking out, panting a little, for the Quest had been breathlessly rapid, at the same view — the timbered foreground, the beech-trunks, the pine-tops, the bracken, the far-off line of the Downs — at which he had looked with Enid a fortnight ago, all lit with the morning light. Then he had sat there to say goodbye to her. Now he was sitting here on the morning of the day that was to bring him back to her again. He would see her in a little over four hours. . . .

"Was the Holy Grail real?" asked Jim.

Nevill recalled his attention.

"Real! Oh, I suppose so. No; I should think it wasn't. It was a symbol."

"What's a symbol?"

"A symbol? Oh, well, it's rather hard to describe. It's . . . it's a sign of something that really is true — like a fairy story — at least like some of them."

"Oh," said Jim. He seemed a little disappointed.

"And what is the thing that's really true?" he pursued presently.

Nevill jumped. He was thinking about something entirely different.

"How do you mean! Oh, I see. Well — religion, don't you know. That's what they were after."

"Did they find it?"

Nevill perceived it was necessary to attend. Jim's questions were sometimes most disconcertingly to the point.

Did they find it?

He reflected a moment; and, as he reflected, he heard three strokes from a bell come up from the direction of the house. That would be the Elevation. He stole a glance at Jim, who apparently had not heard it. And, at that instant, Nevill perceived that he really had arrived at a certain quite definite crossroad.

On the one side there was that for which the bell had spoken just now; on the other side, here was the murmur of the woods — like the murmur of the woods above Frascati. And he saw that these were two things, and not one; at least he could not conceive how they could be one. There seemed nothing to unite them, however deep one penetrated. On the one side there was the little Catholic church, where Anna, no doubt, was kneeling at this very moment — with its crucifix over the altar; its stations round the walls — an intellectual-ized and systematized abstraction from one side of life certainly, but not that side in which he himself really lived and breathed. On the other, here were these woods and these myriad flies dancing in the sunlight; this hum of life; these

scents, inexpressibly sweet, of woodland and pine and a puri-
fied breeze from the sea. The two things were two things, not
one. And the girl who had transfigured life to him was on
this side, not that — why, he sat now in the very sanctuary
which she had consecrated by her presence!

Did they find it?

"Jim, you've asked me a hard question. What do you mean,
exactly? Lancelot found it, didn't he? And Sir Galahad?"

Jim sniffed.

"Yes: they found the Holy Grail — in the fairy story."

"But did they find the . . . the thing that it meant? You told
me that it was not real, but that something else was."

Jim was speaking a little drowsily: his head was leaning
against Nevill. Nevill glanced down at him.

"Look round you, Jim. Don't you think we've found it our-
selves, after all?"

Jim raised sleepy eyes obediently, and looked round.

"I don't know what you mean," he said.

"Well; these woods and . . . and the morning, and feeling so
happy and — and the whole thing. What do you think makes
you feel so happy?"

"God," said Jim, as if that settled it.

Nevill felt a touch of impatience.

"Yes, of course," he said. "This is all — all God, in a sort of
way, isn't it? Well then, don't you think we've found the Holy
Grail up here, after all? And if we've found it, then perhaps—"

Jim's head nodded suddenly; and Nevill remembered that
lecturing before breakfast is apt to have that effect, even on
grownup people.

(4)

As they came down to the house again, Jim once more riding on Nevill's shoulders, the physical Pan-given ecstasy was
still triumphing in the young man's heart.

Aunt Anna met them on the lawn: she was just out of
church, and had come round, as usual, through the gardens
on her way back.

"Well, you're a pair!" she said.

It was, indeed, a joyous sight.

Right on Nevill's shoulders, without any compromise at all,
sat her son. His bare brown legs came down over the young
man's blue pajama jacket and were grasped there by a capable sunburned hand. His white silk shirt, with flapping

sleeves, was behind Nevill's black curly head; and just above it his radiant flushed face and golden hair: he was urging his steed on with a towel. And as for Nevill, for all his six feet, he looked as much a boy as his rider; his black eyes were full of laughter; his parted lips showed his white teeth. He was barefooted, too; and his shoes were slung by a string over his neck.

There was a photograph of the Olympia group, of Praxiteles, in the morning room at Hartley. Inevitably she remembered it: for this group was an astonishingly accurate translation of it into completely modern terms. It is true that Hermes wore blue pajamas and had a towel round his waist; and that the infant Bacchus was in white flannel knickerbockers and rode upon the neck of the elder god; yet the spirit was precisely the same. It was a divine gaiety, straight from Olympus itself, prancing on the lawn of an English country house.

"You — you absolute Pagans!" she said.

Hermes' black eyes sparkled even more divinely.

"That's precisely it," he said. "And you're only a poor Christian! How shocking!"

She glanced with a little quick movement of her eyes at the face of the infant Bacchus; but it was occupied with other emotions than that of Pharisaic scandal.

"And we've been to find the Holy Grail," he said irrelevantly. He had no sense of the unities, it seemed.

"And did you find it?"

"Cousin Nevill said so, up in the woods. Go on, Pegasus!"

Bacchus beat with his bare heels, as on a drum, upon Hermes' chest.

"Don't!" gasped Hermes; "or I'll pinch them." (He closed his strong fingers tightly on the little crossed ankles.)

"Oooh!" said Bacchus. And then his feelings overcame him; and he rolled his face passionately in the black curls into which his hands were thrust.

"Oooh! . . . How jolly it all is! Go on, Pegasus, I promise not to kick."

"I think Pegasus had better," said Aunt Anna. "The gong will sound in exactly three minutes. And I'm sure Pegasus hasn't shaved; and . . . and Bacchus must brush his hair."

"Bacchus?" remarked Hermes-Pegasus questioningly.

"He looks like it. Go on."

They were different persons altogether at breakfast and yet the elder of the two children (as she said to herself) was no less radiant. But his radiance was of a different kind; and, indeed, a neat gray suit with a stand-up collar, and thin shoes and clocked socks have a very different effect from the pajamas, and are even less appropriate to Hermes. Jim too was different; his hair had ruthlessly been brushed and resembled a neat aureole. He wore a holland jacket over his silk shirt, and sandals on his feet. Besides, he was entirely engaged in eating an egg according to the proper ceremonial of grownup breakfasts; and had no attention for anything else. He sat in an absorbed silence, scooping out the egg and putting it carefully into his mouth, rolling his eyes once or twice to intercept any possible criticism.

"I don't want to be brutal," said Nevill. "But I feel like a schoolboy going home for the holidays. Why aren't there sausages? We always had sausages on the last morning at Stonyhurst."

"Because it's Friday, my dear boy."

"Lord! So it is! And I'm going out to lunch. And they're dining with me. Will Mrs. Ferguson remember? And if she doesn't — being upset with the journey yesterday, and all that — may I eat meat? I think I shall require it; because we're going to the theater afterwards to see Selva. Ever seen Selva?"

Aunt Anna nodded.

"Once," she said. "She's . . . she's sublime. But I believe she's a most unpleasant person, with a frightful temper. But she can act!"

"Then don't talk scandal, my dear. What does it matter what she's like — so long as she can act? That's what I've paid five guineas for — (or was it ten?) — I don't pay for her temper."

"I expect somebody does, though," observed Aunt Anna.

"Don't be so brilliant, Aunt Anna. It makes my head —"

He stopped short — remembering his little experience this morning.

"— Ache," he added firmly.

When he looked up, she was looking at him.

"Remember about the doctor," she said in a low voice.

"I shall remember to forget," said Nevill. "It's a sound plan."

"No, but —"

"My dear, of course I shall go if there's the very faintest reason. But I really can't go, if I go on feeling as robust as I do now. I'm . . . I'm bursting with health. He'd think I was insulting him."

(5)

The departure was a little melancholy for Aunt Anna.

Nevill's spirits seemed to rise steadily. He vanished after breakfast to see to one or two final things, and she heard him whistling in his bedroom, between snatches of conversation with Charleson. Then an aromatic smell of Turkish tobacco became sensible in the hall.

"I say — Shall I want two white waistcoats? Charleson says so."

She looked up from the *Daily Mail* which she was pretending to read in the hall; and he was leaning over the gallery. Apparently he had been about to come downstairs; for he stood now opposite the tall corniced door of his father's room.

"How can I tell?" she said. "You'd better do precisely what Charleson tells you!" (She wished he wouldn't stand just there.)

"I mean evening ones," said Nevill.

"If you're going to be in town for three weeks, I should think you certainly will. I should take three."

"That's what Charleson says. But I draw the line at two. All right, Charleson, pack two."

A discreet cough and a murmur of assent indicated that Mr. Charleson had been invisibly assisting at the conversation.

"Do you hear, Charleson?" bawled Nevill.

"Yessir," came sharp and clear through the open bedroom door.

"Go back to your room and tell him properly," whispered Aunt Anna. She simply could not bear to see him standing just there. It looked as if it was his own room, somehow.

"I shall issue my orders from exactly where I please," observed the young man. "Is that Masterson below there?"

Masterson came out from the drawing room.

"Masterson; you won't forget about my letters? Oh! I told you that at breakfast. And about sending up that trout if

Dane can — Oh! I told you that too. That's all, Masterson. I forgot. Sorry."

Aunt Anna went presently to see if the motor had come. The clock indicated that it ought to have done so. But there was no motor.

She stood at the porch a moment or two, waiting. This was the rather somber side of the house, it will be remembered. The level flats of turf lay before her, cut by the straight drive, unrelieved by trees. The shrubberies on either side, especially the cypresses about the church, looked like troops of grave guardians of the right of way — like tall men, waiting. Then she heard the motor coming round from the stables, and turned into the house, hearing her name called loudly as she did so.

"My dear! What is the matter?"

"Where's the motor? Why hasn't it come? Give Paul a month's notice!"

He was standing again by the sinister door, whence, through one of the hall windows, he could command a view of the drive. He carried now a light coat over his arm and had his Panama hat on. Charleson, with a couple of suitcases, was waiting meekly for an opportunity to pass.

"It's just coming. Don't fuss, my dear. And let Charleson go by."

"Sorry, Charleson. Is it really coming? Oh, yes, I hear it."

He was more radiant than ever as he kissed her goodbye.

Jim had appeared with the collies, who also, it seemed, must be kissed on their long noses. This was accomplished with some difficulty in the case of Jill, who wanted to do all the kissing herself.

"Cousin Nevill."

"Yes, my dear."

"May I come as far as the village?"

"Well, really, old man —"

"No, Jim," said Aunt Anna firmly. "Remember lessons. Besides Cousin Nevill mustn't stop, he's late."

"Oh! Very well," said Jim superbly.

Her heart was very low as the young man climbed into the driver's seat, and Paul the chauffeur went to wind up the affair in front.

Yet she could not tell what she feared. That miserable passion of jealousy was at her heart again: it seemed an unbearable pain that he should go up like this, without her, in such tempestuous spirits. And he had scarcely said a word to persuade her to come with him! She mistrusted, therefore, every judgment; she told herself that she was wicked and uncharitable; that no one was without fault; that Enid after all, so far as she knew, had as few as anyone else; certainly fewer than this hateful critical being which she called herself. But it was unbearable for all that.

"Don't look so grave, Aunt Anna!" said Nevill with his hands in their long gauntlets, on the wheel.

"I shall go away and cry," she said. "And then I shall probably slap Jim."

Jim regarded her solemnly.

"Fasten those dogs up," she said. "Or they'll run after the motor."

Jim twisted the long leash round one of the pillars; just as Paul climbed up beside his master. (Charleson and the luggage were behind. Charleson wore that peculiar air of humble detachment that quite perfect servants always do wear in such circumstances.) The motor's roar had sunk to a rapid purr.

Yes, the time really was come at last. He would be gone a full three weeks, she knew; and meantime Jim and she must entertain one another as best they could. Jim really could get some lessons done; that was one comfort. He was beside her now, and had taken her hand, as his manner was.

"Don't drive too fast," she said. "There's a lot of traffic near Croydon."

Nevill winked at her solemnly with one eye. Jill was beginning to yelp, spasmodically. Jack had sat down like a monument.

"I shall drive like Jehu," he said.

Then the motor moved off, and Jill's yelps became heartrending. Nevill kissed his gauntlet superbly, as he took the curve round into the straight.

She stood there watching. Jim, silent at last, was stroking very gently the inside of her hand which he still held. Masterson was behind her somewhere, also silent. The principal noise — since it drowned all the others — was the piercing wail of Jill who, with nose pointed westwards, lamented the departure of the one kind of vehicle at which she always barked. Jack, still sitting, regarded the empty drive philosophically, growling now and again, in the very lowest stratum of his throat.

Far away now, down the dwindling road, was the dwindling motor. He was, indeed, driving like Jehu. A cloud of dust bellied behind like a continuous explosion, through which, more and more faintly, twinkled points of light where the sun from over the house behind caught the bright brasswork and polish.

And then, as the last points vanished, she became aware that the noise of the dogs was quite unbearable.

She turned and looked; and there they both were, sitting together with elevated noses, raising a common lament.

"Stop those dogs!" she said sharply. Then she was ashamed of herself.

"Come along, my son," she said. "We must go and learn our lessons."

Chapter II

(1)

Mrs. Bessington was talking gently to herself — inaudibly, yet with her lips moving — as she surveyed the luncheon table half an hour before Nevill was expected. Enid was in her bedroom.

It was a pleasing little dining room, this — the first on the left from the entrance to the flat, with a shallow square bow window from which could be observed, sideways the trees of Cadogan Square. Enid had done most of the furnishing. There were good chintz curtains, slender mahogany furniture, a quantity of little silver things on the lightly-carved mantelpiece, and a general air of coolness and space. A number of good engravings hung on the brown-papered walls; and the round dining table was quite satisfactory. Mrs. Bessington had just stepped in from the sitting room opposite to make certain that the flowers were fresh.

No human being in the world ever knew really what was Mrs. Bessington's scheme of life. Her general manner of existence was, presumably, satisfactory to herself, and not intolerable to Enid. She circled gently through London, Paris, the Riviera, Rome and back, every year, as has been described. In each place she visited the proper things In London she went to see the Academy and several theaters, and dined and lunched out with friends as decently conventional as herself; in her cottage, when she went there, she read the newspapers, and sat a little in the garden, and called upon the Rector's wife; and went to a few afternoon parties. In Paris she drove out each afternoon in the Bois; and occasionally went to the theater in the evening if there was anything about which anyone was talking. In Rome she led the kind of life that has been already described. And in London and Paris and the Riviera and Rome she talked gently all the time.

This, then, was the surface she presented to the world; and her smiling kind face remained unmoved. She wrote a good many letters to her friends, full of small talk; and especially to her nephews, giving them good advice all the year round, and generous tips at Christmas. Probably she kept a little pocketbook of engagements in which these duties were entered. But beneath that surface no human being had pene-

trated. It appeared as if she expressed herself so continuously in this unceasing dribble of talk and letters that there
was no interior reservoir left at all; that she resembled, let us
say, a pond through the center of which a small stream flows
in at one end and out at the other, so that the excavated
space never has time to fill. No one even knew how much
money she had: it was only quite certain that she had
enough, and denied neither herself nor Enid anything that
was proper to the kind of life they led. This flat must have
cost at least three hundred a year; they had an excellent little motor landaulette throughout the season; their cook was
quite good and their wines above reproach.

At this moment, however, Mrs. Bessington was alone in the
flat, except for Enid and the maid in the bedroom at the far
end, and the cook in the kitchen, since Alice, the parlor maid,
and the last member of the establishment, had just been sent
out to see why the cucumber had not arrived. She had
slipped out, just as she was, round the corner; as the cucumber had been promised by twelve, and the little Louis Seize
clock on the mantelpiece had just sounded one. When the
bell, then, tingled sharply, Mrs. Bessington of course thought
it was Alice come back, and that she had forgotten to take
the key; so Mrs. Bessington stepped out to the door of the flat
and opened it; and there was Nevill.

"I know I'm dreadfully early," said Nevill, "but —"

He wished to explain that he had had two mishaps on the
way up — the bursting of some little valve and the puncture
of a tire — that the car and Paul had been left somewhere
near Croydon, that he had taken a taxi on, that he had mentioned the address in Cadogan Walk, as, after leaving Paul,
he had discovered he had no money to pay the taxi with, and
so on. (Of course, he might have told the servants in Elizabeth Street to pay; but that hadn't occurred to him.)

However, it was impossible to get all this out to Mrs.
Bessington, though he tried twice. She drew him into the
drawing room and began to talk about azaleas; and it was a
good ten minutes before he could make her understand that
he wanted seven-and-six. Then, still discussing azaleas, she
got out her netted purse from the drawer of a writing table
and gave him ten shillings in gold. So the taxi driver got a
considerable tip, and said: "Thank you, my lord."

Nevill continually forgot, in spite of all his resolutions, that Mrs. Bessington really did not desire to be talked to, so he tried again, when he came back, to say something about Aunt Anna's messages; but it was useless, so he gave up, and began to think about when Enid would come in. The drawing room was as satisfactory as the dining room; he had never seen either before, but he was quite conscious of its charm, and thought that he saw Enid's personality in it. Those old watercolors, for instance, in brown frames; that Spanish mirror over the fireplace; the delicate tapestry screen — these were of her choosing, he thought.

Meantime Mrs. Bessington talked.

Then quite suddenly there was a rustle outside and a sharp, clear voice spoke to someone outside.

"It's perfectly useless, Peters; you'll just have to go if you can't do as you're told."

Then the handle was turned and Enid came in quickly.

"Nevill!" she said.

Obviously then it was Enid who had spoken; yet he thought he would not have known it. There had been a ring in her voice that he had never heard before — a certain cutting tone. She looked a little flushed, too.

"Yes; I came early. Had a breakdown." He managed to get out his explanations at last. Mrs. Bessington had paid her daughter the compliment of silence upon her entrance.

"It's perfectly charming of you!" she said. "But why not have got them to pay at your house?"

"That didn't occur to me," said Nevill, "until I reached the door."

She smiled delightfully.

"You came just in time for a domestic crisis," she went on smoothly. "Our maid — mother and I share one, you know — our maid is quite hopeless. She's a country girl, and she — oh! Let's leave her."

"No; tell me," said Nevill.

She shook her head.

"Mother'll deal with her. Mother, dear, do go and soothe her. She was crying, and it would be most inconvenient if she left just now."

Mrs. Bessington began to trickle on again about servants as she went out. Nevill felt a shade uneasy.

"Yes; I spoke to her quite plainly," said Enid. "You probably heard me. I'm afraid I was brutal; but you've got to be sometimes. I can't bear it, though."

A very genuine pain showed in her eyes. Nevill made haste to sympathize.

"I think you sounded a bit sharp. But I've no doubt it was necessary."

She turned her calm face on him.

"Absolutely necessary. They don't understand anything else. Now tell me exactly what you've been doing. And how's Aunt Anna?"

(2)

"Why, there's Lord Maresfield!" said Enid suddenly. They were doing the dutiful round in Burlington House — after Nevill had been to change his clothes and come back again — and had been a little silent for the last twenty minutes — silent, because Mrs. Bessington really did not count.

To that lady, a number of pictures in row after row presented a simply inexhaustible treasure in the way of conversational openings. Indeed, they were almost too much for her. If a very greedy squirrel be imagined, confronted suddenly by five hundred nuts, all laid out ready for him to carry away, some faint analogy may be conceived to Mrs. Bessington's situation at the Royal Academy. The names of the artists, the notes in her catalogue, the subjects of the pictures, the faces of occasional acquaintances viewed across the rooms — all these things provided her with material. Now and again she would face round upon Nevill with her back to the picture he was trying to look at, and deliver her reminiscences, joining them on, without a pause, to her previous observations. He was very nearly rude to her once or twice; his head grew weary of assenting with nods; he gave up altogether, after the first ten minutes, any attempt at coherent replies. The ventilation of Burlington House is not of the best; his silk hat felt like a rim of iron round his forehead; he was aware of rising irritation. Enid made no attempt to cope with the situation; she simply moved on, relentlessly, consulting her catalog now and again, looking lovely, cool and dignified, and observing what she wished to observe. She glanced at him once or twice and away again.

When she made the remark chronicled above, Nevill turned, regardless of Mrs. Bessington (who really did not mind at all), to see at whom she was looking. It was a big man, all alone at the other end of the room, his hat rather tilted back, with a big clean-shaven good-humored face. He too turned as Enid spoke and made a little salutation.

Then Mrs. Bessington engaged Nevill again. Then he felt a touch on his arm and turned once more.

"Nevill — may I introduce you to Lord Maresfield? Sir Nevill Fanning — Lord Maresfield."

"Pleased to meet you. Looking at the pictures. What? Sargent's all right, ain't they? Bit stuffy, though. What? How do, Mrs. Bessington? Don't know a soul here, by the way. Except you. Eh?"

Yes, that was the type all right, thought Nevill. Staccato, intelligent, good-humored, capable, robust, certainly a man who would never disappoint one; he would always be characteristic of himself; and one might discover qualities in him, by degrees, which one would never suspect at first. Enid immediately supplied one.

"Lord Maresfield paints perfectly beautifully," she explained. "He's got a studio in Chelsea."

"Splash about a bit, eh? No more. Amuse myself! Idle dog! What? That and polo, y'know. Given it up again, though, now. See you at Ranelagh some time, eh?"

Nevill said he didn't know. (He liked Lord Maresfield.)

"By the way — congratulate you, Miss Enid. What? And you too. Saw it in the *Morning Post*. When's it to be?"

Nevill said they had thought of October.

"Chill October, eh? Well, Mrs. Bessington. Back from Rome. What? Usual round, I suppose?"

Then Nevill became aware that Mrs. Bessington had been talking to him the whole time, unperceived. But she was quite unruffled: she turned the hose tranquilly on to the newcomer, and the four began to drift along. Enid held Nevill back a step or two. Lord Maresfield, in excellent good-humor, was firing staccato shots into Mrs. Bessington's bland mitrailleuse. His genial face, with his hat still tilted back, nodded and spoke in three-quarter profile.

"I like him," said Enid in a low voice. "He's always just the same. We met him in Rome last year. Do get to know him, Nevill."

"I'll do my best. Would he come to the opera on Wednesday, do you think?"

"Ask him."

"My dear girl, I've never seen him before in my life. Never even heard of him. I thought that perhaps you —" She nodded.

"I'll manage it," she said.

"Tell me who he is. Quick. They're off for the tearoom."

He was rather a Bohemian, it seemed, and had drifted about vaguely, in Paris and Rome, in the artists' quarters, painting a little, but not much. He had quarreled with his father years ago, or, rather, as Enid said, it must have been his father who quarreled with him — the kind of quarrel which it does not take two to make. He had come into the title only last summer, had abruptly taken to polo at the age of thirty-two, and had as abruptly given it up again.

"Be nice to him," said Enid. "He's only just finding his way about. He lives in Chelsea when he's in town."

"Married?"

"No."

She managed it quite beautifully when they were all sitting round the little marble-topped table in the tearoom. She introduced in that simple statuesque way of hers which seemed to require no introduction.

"Lord Maresfield," she said, breaking imperturbably in upon her mother's conversation. (Really, it was the only way; one might wait forever for an opening.) "Sir Nevill says he has a box at the opera next Wednesday. Mother and I are going. He was wondering whether you'd care to come. It's *Tannhäuser*, I think."

"Opera? Delighted! Thanks. Very good of you, 'm sure. There last week m'self. *Carmen*. What?"

"Would you dine with us first?" asked Nevill.

"Very good of you, 'm sure. Where? What time? Necessary to know these things. Eh?"

Nevill supplied those details.

"Delighted. Was at Bayreuth last year. Richter and Meistersingers. What?"

(3)

"Nevill, you must stop a moment. I've got something to say—"

"But —"

"Oh! They're all right. Mother's got hold of a good listener. That's exactly what I want to speak about." She was detaining him at the door of the last room on the right, by a hand on his arm.

He felt much better after a cup of tea. That rim on his forehead seemed no longer to be made of hammered iron; it felt almost like the leather lining of a silk hat. He suddenly wanted to kiss the gloved hand. Before them, through the emptying room, drifted the elder lady, a feather on her bonnet quivering as she talked, and the genial ruddy man who was attending to her so nobly.

"Look here, Nevill; it's going to be impossible. I never realized before how trying it was going to be. What can we do about Mother?"

"My dear girl, I don't know what you —"

"Yes, you do; you needn't be polite. She's my mother, you know. (Walk on slowly and be looking at the pictures.) She talks to you simply the whole time, you poor dear! And I can't get a word in. It's all right just for this moment; but all the way here, and till Lord Maresfield came, and again at tea, I couldn't get in a word. What's to be done?"

She looked so distressed that he did not know what to say. She seemed so wholly thoughtful for him.

"But, my darling, I tell you —"

"Yes, of course you're bound to say that. But I can see what you feel. Well, I suppose there's nothing to be done. But can't you get somebody always for her to talk to — like that man? Do try! Whom have you got for tonight? Anybody?"

"Algy Lennox."

"Who's he? Well, it doesn't matter. But I did want to tell you that I minded just as much as you. And do put Algy Lennox, whoever he is, next mother. I do mind, Nevill. I mind dreadfully. You know that, don't you?"

Her face was full of distress. She looked adorable. His faint irritation went up like smoke and vanished.

"My dear, I think your mother's charming. Certainly she talks; but they're waiting for us."

Nevill admired the other man more and more as, with incalculable slowness, they all drifted out and down the stairs. Mrs. Bessington kept on, of course — that goes without saying; but it was entirely indifferent to her as to in whose ear she poured her observations. As he came behind with Enid, he noticed how completely the elder man filled the situation. His head was turned all the way down the stairs towards Mrs. Bessington's bonnet; he fired his little staccato shots, and he even sent one or two behind. At the cloakroom too he was adequate and businesslike.

"Got your tickets — eh? Better give them me — what? Soon manage it. I'm nearest the bar. What a crush — eh? Here, you chap! Hand them out! There you are, Miss Enid — eh? That yours, ain't it? That yours, Sir Nevill? There we are, then!"

He got them their car too, with the same promptness, and helped the ladies in, while Nevill was directing Mrs. Bessington's chauffeur to drop him at his own house and then go on to the flat in Cadogan Walk.

"Wednesday, then? Seven-fifteen sharp, eh? That's all right. Pleased to see you all at my little studio some time. What? Nothing to show, though. Only splash a bit. That's all. Well — right, chauffeur."

He raised his hat and stood smiling.

And then Mrs. Bessington began on his biography.

(4)

Nevill felt a great deal better after a bath.

It had been a considerably wearing afternoon, and he was astonished how relaxed he felt. Neither could he conceal from himself that Mrs. Bessington was responsible for most of it. To be talked to incessantly is perhaps the most tiring mental exercise of all; it is certainly more tiring than talking.

He was touched by Enid's sympathy, and she had done it, too, he thought, in quite the tenderest way; for it is not easy to find fault with one's mother to a third person without at least an appearance of unfiliality. Her suggestion was, of course, admirable in itself; the only difficulty was to carry it out. He supposed he would have to warn Algy Lennox of what his function was to be. A tag from the Latin grammar came to his mind as he lay in his bath and considered these things. *"Fungar vice cotis,"* he repeated softly to himself. "I will perform the function of a whetstone." That was exactly it.

Hartley seemed a very long way away as he dawdled over his dressing. It was almost unthinkable that he had only left this morning; that it was not yet twelve hours ago since he had bathed with Jim, and sat in the woods and, in blue pajamas, carried him down to the house on his shoulders.

For London has an extraordinary power of absorbing instantly the newcomer from the country; of bringing him, by the simultaneous assault that it makes on all the senses at once — sight, hearing, smell, touch, and even taste — into a completely different mental attitude. This time last night he was sitting with Aunt Anna in the pavilion, looking out on to the river; he had been in flannels and without a jacket. Now he had just taken off one set of London clothes and was to put on his white waistcoat. Last night, after dinner, they had sat out till half-past ten on the terrace; tonight he would be in a theater, seeing Selva. He felt completely different already. Yet all that he had done was to lunch with the Bessingtons and to go to the Royal Academy.

As he dressed he thought again about Enid.

She too had seemed different. Down at Hartley she had dawdled about with a parasol and no hat; she had talked gently and tranquilly; she had been, in fact, exactly what he had expected her to be. Up here, however, while completely herself of course, her manner had been ever so slightly different. There was that little sharp sentence she had said to the maid — no doubt entirely deserved: yet he could not quite think of her saying it at Hartley. It was not completely characteristic of her, as he had known her. Then there was her speaking to him about her mother. That too was, of course, only natural; it showed her desire to please him; and she had not said one word that she should not. Yet she had never said it at Hartley, although her mother had talked quite as much there. Oh! But he had forgotten: Aunt Anna had performed the function of a whetstone at Hartley. Yes; that explained it. He smiled a little. Dear Aunt Anna! How she would have loathed this afternoon — the crush, the talking, the rows upon rows of pictures. She was essentially of Hartley.

A tap came at his door, and then Charleson's voice.

"Mr. Lennox, sir; I've shown him into the drawing room."

"Oh!" (Nevill glanced at the clock. It marked five minutes to seven.) "Show him in here."

A brisk young man, very fair-haired, with an assured manner, came in. He had been at Stonyhurst with Nevill, and
they had kept up with one another more or less ever since.

"Sorry, old man. But you said seven, didn't you?"

"No. Quarter-past. Doesn't matter. Sit down somewhere."

Algy seated himself on the bed.

"Don't mind a cigarette in here? Then that's all right. I like
a cigarette just before dinner. Makes you so jolly giddy."

"Algy!"

"Yes?"

"I'm glad you've come early. You've got to be talked to, my
son."

"Go ahead."

Nevill finished tying his tie before speaking. He thought
the face in the glass looked a little dark under the eyes.
"About tonight. You've got to sacrifice yourself, you know.
The Bessingtons are coming — oh! I told you. Well, the old
lady's a terror to talk."

"I'll deal with her."

"That's exactly what you've got to do. But I warn you. She
talks all the time. And she'll talk all through the play too —
if I know her."

"That's all right. I've seen Selva before."

"You needn't say much. Just let her run. That's all she
wants. And say 'Yes' now and then, and so on. But you've got
to attach her."

"It shall be done."

Algy was a cheerful and a loyal youth, and Nevill knew he
could depend on him. Besides, he was the kind of young man
towards whom middle-aged ladies always felt motherly. He
was just about Nevill's age, but looked five years younger, as
well as very innocent and good; and, indeed, his looks did not
greatly belie him.

He finished his cigarette before Nevill was ready, and took
up a small hand mirror from the dressing table.

"Nice bit of work this," he said, examining the chased back.

"Out of the way, old man," said Nevill, who wanted to get
at his watch and chain.

Algy retired a little from the dressing table, and began to
practice tennis strokes — the wrist supple and the forearm
horizontal. There was a crash.

"I've done it, old chap. Lord! I'm sorry."

"Pick up the bits then," said Nevill, "and kindly don't touch anything else."

"I was only trying my stroke," said the boy. "Gad! I'm sorry! It caught the bedpost."

He regarded the handle and back of the glass a little ruefully.

"Then pick up the bits," repeated Nevill.

"And it's so jolly unlucky too," said Algy, going down on his knees. "I say, old man."

"Yes?"

"You must let me have it refitted."

"Kindly put all the bits into the fireplace and . . . and what's left of it on to the table. And don't talk rot."

"But really —"

"You just do as I told you about Mrs. B. and you'll pay for it ten times over. Just touch the bell, will you?"

Nevill straightened himself finally before the glass. Certainly he didn't look very well. But that was just Mrs. Bessington's conversation. He'd be all right after an hour or two with Enid.

"Yessir," said Charleson at the door.

"Oh! Just take that looking-glass handle away, and get it re-fitted some time. Mr. Lennox has just smashed it."

"Yessir. Motor just drawn up, sir."

"Come along, Algy. I want to see if the room's all right. Show them into the morning room, Charleson. Is Macpherson there?"

"Yessir."

(5)

"My word! She'd think it *was* all right," exclaimed Algy.

It was not a very big house; but it was an exceedingly satisfactory one; having been built towards the end of the eighteenth century and left practically unrestored. It was the one single house in Elizabeth Street that had not been rebuilt over and over again; and it still had quite a fair garden at the back.

This room into which the two had just come was paneled in white from ceiling to floor — large cool panels — and in the center of each hung a single good picture. It was arranged more or less as a drawing room, with a big rug by the hearth and chintz sofas round it; and a quantity of fantastic china stood on the high mantelpiece. But a vast kneehole table was set to catch the light from the window, and beyond it opened the double doors on to the flight of steps that ran down into the garden, that formed a pleasant green background of shrubs and lawn and a bank of rhododendrons. From the center of the molded plaster of the ceiling hung an elaborate spider chandelier, filled with wax candles.

But it was the flowers that had made Algy exclaim.

They stood on every possible table and shelf, in silver bowls and slender green glass vases — (they had come up from Hartley that afternoon). They were all white, and their scent filled the room.

"Smells a bit like a funeral, though," said Algy, who spoke his mind undauntedly.

Nevill said nothing. He stood on the hearthrug, with his hands in his pockets, surveying slowly from side to side. Yes, it seemed to him quite satisfactory. Then he perceived that Algy had spoken.

"Eh?" he said.

"Smells like a — like a wedding, old chap," said Algy.

The rustle of dresses was heard outside as the ladies went past to take off their wraps. Nevill had received very precise instructions from Aunt Anna that the morning room — (the only sitting room that faced the street) — was to be provided with looking-glasses and a maid, and so forth. That would leave the three rooms — this drawing room, the library and the dining room — that all looked out on to the garden, and that communicated with another by double doors, entirely free.

These doors were now all set open, and Algy could see straight through to the white-laid dining table, with the candles burning, in spite of the evening light from the garden.

"Glad you've got candles, old man," he said. "I must say I like to see what I'm eating."

Suddenly Nevill smiled at him — a perfectly simple unconscious smile of pleasure. He was not attending to a word Algy was saying; he was thinking how perfectly delicious it was to be here in his own house, to be able to entertain Enid like this, to have all those flowers to greet her. This too was to be her home some day; and therefore when she saw it for the first time, let it be full of welcome.

"Yes?" questioned Algy, puzzled at the smile.

"Nothing, old man," said Nevill. "I was just thinking. By the way, are you free next week? Come in and dine on Tuesday."

"Right," said Algy.

"And Thursday?"

"Can't on Thursday. Going to a crush. And I'm dining there first."

"Where?"

Algy named a house.

"Well, we shall meet there, then. I'm going with the Bessingtons."

Then through the opening door came Charleson, who announced names; and Enid sailed in after her mother.

(6)

By halfway through dinner Nevill was thinking that Algy must be something very like a genius. Mrs. Bessington sat on her host's right, and Enid on his left; Algy faced him, with his back to the windows. Nevill had, too, taken Mrs. Bessington in, and she had conversed as they went through the library. Yet after the moment they had sat down, there had been no more trouble.

Algy instantly played the Academy as his lead, before Mrs. Bessington had done more than glance at the menu, and then the stream had begun.

Along that stream, like bobbing chips of wood, flowed the names of Academicians, solutions of all Mr. John Collier's conundrums, reminiscences on the late Mr. Sidney Cooper's accuracy in painting the hair on the hides of cows, Mr. La Thangue's sun-flecked foregrounds, and the eyes of Mr. Briton le Rivière's collies. Then, when the stream began to run clear again, and Mrs. Bessington was still talking of course, but talking about nothing in particular, Algy had again led off with Selva, whom they were presently to see. Obviously he was about to say he had seen her before; but he was unable to get this out, because Mrs. Bessington began to relate plots of plays in which she had seen Duse and Sarah Bernhardt. Apparently there was no reason why she should ever leave off doing this, because she even compared the rival merits of Italian and English scene-painters — in parentheses; and if one comes down to that, an infinity of subjects suggest themselves. It was enough for Mrs. Bessington that any kind of connection should exist in her monologues —

connections of period, place, merits, association. Each thing "reminded" her of the next, in unfailing sequence.

All this Nevill heard fragmentarily, as he talked in a low voice to Enid — answering her questions about the portraits that hung opposite, suggesting small plans for the future. Once he caught Algy's eye across the orchids between them, and the agonized fortitude of his friend's expression made him hastily look away again. He knew exactly what the other was feeling like. He would have laughed suddenly and loudly if he had looked a moment longer.

But his young friend's genius, no less than his fortitude, was a complete surprise. Mrs. Bessington had not said anything to her host at all, since they sat down. Certainly Algy was the man to dine with them as often as possible. But Nevill thought he must relieve him when the ice came.

Meantime Enid was entirely fascinating.

She was dressed in some kind of filmy blue, with a single line of sapphires round her white throat. It was precisely the right tone, and finished the chord of which her clear brunette complexion supplied the rest. (She had come out of the last shadow of mourning for her father at Easter.) Her hair was dressed in the heavy manner that Nevill loved, with blue flowers in it, and she carried another bunch at her breast. She seemed too even more vitally alive than this afternoon; her face was steady and clear, and her eyes shone. . . .

As soon as the green bomb of ice appeared Nevill turned to the right, after a look at Enid. Enid dropped her eyes demurely.

"I'm simply delighted we're going to see Selva," he said. "I think —"

Mrs. Bessington turned unseeing eyes upon him.

"Well, and it was at Milan, as I was saying, Mr. Lennox, in the year eighty-two —" Nevill was reprieved. With a sigh of delight he turned again to Enid. He was not in the least annoyed. It had happened a hundred times before. For Mrs. Bessington, when she was really under way, appeared to be simply deaf.

(7)

"Whoo! Old man!" said Algy, as Nevill came back from the door after the ladies had gone. He sank back in his seat, and passed a handkerchief across his forehead. He really looked almost faint.

"Have some port," said Nevill, "or a cigarette? There's not time for both. I should suggest port."

"But I say —" began the boy.

"You may break a looking-glass every time you come, if you'll do that again. You were superb."

"She's a terror! I've never had so much information in my life. I feel an experienced man of the world at last. No; a cigarette. Something light."

"How did you do it?"

"It wasn't me. She did it all. I'd four points ready: Academy; Selva; portraits; and the cup in the middle. I spotted that after I'd sat down. But I only got to Selva."

"You'd better have some port, really. You've got to keep it up till eleven, you know."

"Can't do it; can't do it, old man. And about Tuesday —"

"I'm sorry," said Nevill. "But you're engaged. A quarter-past eight."

Algy poured himself out a glass of port after all, meditatively; then he sipped.

"Tastes like oily ink," he said.

"If you will smoke too —" began Nevill.

"I'm drinking it to support me," said Algy. "Not pleasure, I assure you. Pleasure! If I can keep body and soul together, it's as much —"

"You were superb," said Nevill again. (He saw that violent flattery must be supplied.)

"But, my dear man," said Algy, "I know she's going to be your mother-in-law and all that, and I don't want to be offensive. But where does she get it all from? It's . . . it's incredible. You look tired too. Suppose it was the Academy this afternoon. I say -—"

"Yes?"

"I haven't congratulated you yet. Well, I do now."

"Thanks, old man."

He did indeed feel tired. During dinner he had been elated enough, in a quiet sort of way. Even to sit by Enid seemed to him enough, but to talk uninterruptedly to her! It was almost as good as Hartley. Yet now he felt suddenly blank again, as if vitality had been running from him all the time. Perhaps he had been wrong. Perhaps the very presence of Mrs.

Bessington had been enough to drain his energy. He remembered rather a great doctor telling him once that some people
were like that — that the old vampire-tales really had a substratum of truth, and a more considerable substratum than
most people recognized. The doctor had said also that that
kind of temperament had no connection whatever, so far as
he knew, with moral character. Quite nice and good people
were vampirish sometimes.

That was it then. Poor Mrs. Bessington was a vampire! The
pressure on his head had returned a little.

But the dinner had been a success. There was no doubt
about that. Not a detail had missed fire. The room had
looked perfect: the flowers had been perfect: the dinner had
been perfect. He must congratulate Mrs. Ferguson tomorrow
on her admirable management. It really was good, considering she had only come up yesterday.

There was the vibration of a step in the next room; and
then Enid appeared, a vision of loveliness, in her swansdown
cloak and the hood over her head.

"Charleson says the motor is here, Nevill. We must go if
we're to be in time."

Ah! How charming that was! How naturally she had said
it! The house really might be her own. Well, it would be, in
three or four months.

He smiled at her, without answering.

Chapter III

(1)

The house was crammed as they came into their box at twenty minutes past eight.

"This is what Jim calls Sawdust," said Nevill. "We shall have ten minutes of it, after all."

"Sawdust!"

"Yes; don't you know the smell of it in a circus? It's . . . it's a kind of symbol for anticipation. Jim always insists on getting to entertainments about ten minutes before they begin. He likes to sit and smell and watch horses' feet under the flap. I entirely sympathize."

Enid nodded emphatically.

"I quite see," she said. "But it's rather subtle."

"Not in the least too subtle for Jim. . . . My word! What a packed house!"

As he leaned forward and surveyed it from the seat furthest from the stage, with Enid next him, then Algy, and then Mrs. Bessington — (Mrs. Bessington always desired to be as close as possible on every occasion) — he began to perceive that there was another kind of Sawdust too that he was enjoying. It was inexpressibly delightful to be here with Enid — actually sitting next her, drawing her cloak off her shoulders over the back of the chair, making small remarks when he wished to. He would have about three more months Sawdust and then the curtain would go up. And . . . and they would be both on the stage as well as in front. It would be a dream come true for once. . . . He could hear Mrs. Bessington's voice rumbling always to Algy. . . .

"Why, there are the Heckers," said the girl suddenly.

Nevill followed her eyes, and there indeed they were, in the stalls below — both with that extremely finished and adequate appearance which Americans in London always have. Mrs. Hecker's costume caught the eye at once; it was largely orange in color — what there was of it. Mr. Hecker looked as if he had been born in his clothes, and had had them ironed on him every morning and evening ever since, with a continuous replacing of their wasted tissue. Mrs. Hecker was inspecting people slowly through a lorgnette: Mr. Hecker

held the opera glasses ready for her when the curtain should
go up.

Enid's face suddenly dimpled with laughter.

"I wonder what Selva will have to say to her," she said.
"What will the message be to her, right here and now?"

"It's a responsibility for Selva," said Nevill. "If she only
knew. She's an Australian, isn't she?"

"She'll be equal to it," said the girl. "Yes: I believe she is."

"You met her in Rome, didn't you? I mean Selva."

"Yes, at the Heckers'. Don't you remember? You couldn't
come."

"She's perfectly extraordinary, isn't she?"

Enid hesitated.

"I know you'll hate what I'm going to say —"

"Go on."

"Well; men always think so. Of course, I see her power; but
— but I don't think it's of a very high sort. Well; you'll see.
Certainly she holds the house."

"She's got her house, anyhow. That's one thing. What is she
like to talk to?"

"I hardly spoke to her," said the girl indifferently.

Then the orchestra began; and Nevill took up his program.

The program was of that kind that Selva had made famous. First, it cost a shilling; and there were no advertisements at all, beyond the announcement of the plays in which
Selva would appear, with their dates. Most of them were of
the usual kind — *La Dame aux Camélias, La Tosca* — and so
forth. But tonight she was playing *Margaret*, "A Comedy for
Men," written, it seemed, especially for her by an Australian
dramatist.

The program proceeded to give an "interpretation" of the
play, of the kind generally associated with concerts and the
performance of Beethoven's sonatas. It was indescribably
solemn and reverent, like the handling of a fragile piece of
china by a connoisseur. It gave the most precise account not
so much of the play itself as of its "symbolism," and informed
the audience carefully of the emotions which were proper for
them to feel at each point.

"Margaret," herself, it seemed, stood for Womanhood; and
Womanhood for a Tragedy that to the rest of the world was a
Comedy. The writer of the program — probably James Dan-
iells himself, the author of the play — was just tactful

enough; he argued that there were no doubt various opinions
— *quot homines tot sententiae,* — but that on the whole it
must be confessed that Woman even now had not risen to her
proper place in the world; that she tended to become either
the toy or the drudge of man. (At this point he quoted some
lines from *Locksley Hall* and some more from *The Princess.)*
This play, then, was intended to set out the Tragedy of
Womanhood; but the audience were entreated, ironically, to
remember that it was only a Comedy for Men. In the First
Act they would be invited to witness a perfect domestic circle
— the Man, the Woman and the Child — sanctified by Holy
Matrimony. (Here the writer permitted himself a sneer or
two at the Christian religion.) In the Second Act they would
see the old foundations of human instinct emerging; the Man
beginning to assert himself, as he always did; and the
Woman struggling to keep pace with his impossible demands. For "Margaret" was the social inferior of the Man; he
had married her, telling her that she would take his place in
Society, cheating both himself and her. In the Second Act,
therefore, this begins to come out. "Margaret," who loves like
a Woman — idealistically, spiritually, exquisitely — finds
that the Man's love is not like hers. She has begun to lose her
freshness while the Man is merely maturing: she makes one
or two little social mistakes. Well; there is an explanation;
and a reconciliation.

In the Third Act, the exquisite point of the Comedy begins:
for, after another *gaucherie* on Margaret's part — an impul-
sive act founded on generosity of character — the Man begins
to find sport in watching her make an exhibition of herself:
he leads her on to commit social blunders, out of a devilish
kind of cruelty; he laughs over her with his friends. She
knows nothing of this. A friend of her husband's makes
mock-love to her, with the husband's approving delight; she
takes him seriously, and begins to love him in return. Then
— the catastrophe; she confesses to her husband; and is met
by his brutal indifference. It does not matter to him what she
does; she has already ruined him and dragged him down in
the world. The scales fall from her eyes; and she perishes by
her own hand.

Such was the outline of the story. To call the program prig-
gish and pedagogic would be to pay it a considerable compliment.

Nevill wrinkled his nose, as he finished it.

"The man's a bounder," he said under his breath; as the curtain brightened suddenly and the talking stopped.

(2)

At the end of the First Act Nevill leaned back with a sigh of pleasure; and turned to Enid. Talking had burst out in an excited roar suddenly and loudly all over the house, mingled with ecstatic clapping. He turned back again to the curtain as Selva emerged all alone to take the applause; and began to clap, himself, smiling.

Selva was a tall and very nearly gaunt-looking woman, made up to the eyes. In herself she was nothing. She had quantities of brown hair, probably a wig; there was nothing remarkable about her figure; her face, seen now against the brutally bright drop-curtain with the footlights immediately beneath her, was sharp and imperious and evidently middle-aged. But, in the piece, she had been exquisite. She had not merely resembled, she had simply incarnated a young wife, very simple, adorably natural, passionately proud of her husband and child. Nothing particular had happened; persons had been introduced who, to those who had read the program, were significant of what was to follow; the general lines had been sketched. But the overwhelming charm was in the picture of a perfect domestic happiness. Selva's little cry of delight as her husband comes in from hunting; the way her eyes follow him; his obvious love of her, with scarcely a touch of patronage — it was these things that a tremendous genius had transfigured. There was probably not a romantic girl in the theater who had not seen the enacting of her own hopes; there was not a married man who did not feel tenderer towards his wife. The thing had been as light and delicate as a summer morning. The "husband" had been quite adequate; but it was Selva who had been the very heart of all the emotion. She was recalled twice; and Nevill marveled.

"My dear," he said, "I don't know what you mean. Surely that was simply perfect."

Enid smiled a little.

"Oh! I don't deny her power," she said. "Did you see —"

"What?"

"Nothing."

Nevill began to examine the people again.

He felt wonderfully elated; for he was conscious, as everyone is conscious when he is entirely satisfied with a new experience, that that was exactly what he had known all along. He had not put it like that before, certainly, but it was what he had always meant. Hartley — to come down to concrete facts — Hartley would be just like in a year or two: a scene of perfect comradeship and passion and peace. He wondered what it was that Enid meant in saying that although Selva had power it did not seem to her that it was of a very high order.

"I say, old man — Beg pardon, Miss Bessington — I say, What about a cigarette?"

Nevill looked round. He did not in the least want a cigarette. But really Algy deserved it. He glanced at Enid.

"Yes, do," she said. "And you might see what Mr. Hecker wants if you can find him. He's been trying to attract your attention."

"She's great," began Algy, when they got outside.

"She's magnificent —"

"I meant Mrs. Bessington," explained Algy. "I've had her entire married life laid before me. And she wants to know why I'm not married myself. I couldn't hear a word they were saying on the stage. But I suppose it's all right?"

It was not so easy to find Mr. Hecker. The passages were thronged with men; and the clink of glasses grew louder as they advanced. A positive roar of voices greeted them as they pushed open the door of the restaurant Nevill looked round. And then Mr. Hecker was on him.

"Great, isn't she?" he said. "Pleased to see you, Sir Nevill. . . . And you, sir —" (Nevill introduced Mr. Lennox). "My wife wants to know if you can come and meet her at the 'Cecil.' She's coming to us on Saturday afternoon. No matinees on Saturday, you know. Much too select. Tuesdays and Thursdays are her days. . . . Try one of these cigarettes: they're straight from Samos."

He was just the same — alert, trim, self-effacing, and intelligent. He belonged to Mrs. Hecker, wholly; just as if he were her electric brougham. Nevill could not conceive of him as possessing an independent existence.

"I shall be delighted," said Nevill.

"And bring your friends along if they'd care to come. I'll send them a card. Care to come, Mr. Lennox?"

Mr. Lennox said he would care to come very much indeed. Had Mr. Hecker known Madam Selva long? And would he have a drink?

"No, thanks, sir. No drink — Mrs. Hecker — she doesn't like that — between meals; and, upon my word, she's right. Yes: we've known Madam Selva since last fall. Ran across her in N'York. She's great."

When they got back to the box, Enid was leaning back silent; and Mrs. Bessington was reading her program But the latter laid it down resolutely at the sight of Mr. Lennox.

"They want us to go and meet Madame Selva on Monday. He said they'd send a card round. I gave them your address."

Enid looked at him, nodded, but said nothing. Then again the curtain brightened; and the talking sank to a great silence.

When the Second Act ended Nevill's eyes were full of tears. He did not consider himself emotional; but it had been simply poignant. The act had ended, as has been said, with a reconciliation; but it was a reconciliation that could not last: the characters of husband and wife were essentially diverse — not complementary but antagonistic. The end was inevitable.

"I suppose there's no hope at all," he said, smiling. "I mean, I should be better pleased if the play was unconvincing — if I could feel that it didn't really happen so, but that the author made it up."

Enid looked at him.

"I can't feel it like that," she said. "I seem to see through her all the time. It isn't Margaret at all, to me. It's Selva. And — and I don't like Selva."

"Oh! Dear me!" said Nevill.

Enid laid a hand on the edge of the box.

"She's made up quite intolerably," she said.

"But, my dear girl, what else could she do? She must be forty-five!"

"Then she shouldn't play a girl of twenty-two."

Then Algy, with the expression of a drowning man, caught his eye again. . . .

(3)

As Nevill, after the final fall of the curtain, followed the ladies down the thick-carpeted corridor, he was moved down to
the very bottom of his soul.

The tragedy had come swift and inevitable as a hammer
falling rapidly.

The Third Act had begun quietly, as a lull before the storm
breaks. It had opened with a little dinner party that went
well. Margaret, obviously a little anxious, had managed matters satisfactorily; but it was her very anxiety that had pro-
voked her husband's wrath; and this wrath had been precipi-
tated by a little tale told to him by his friend over the wine.
Then it was that he had resolved at least to get his sport out
of her; and the fiendish little plot had been arranged for her
humiliation. In the second scene of the act the man had begun to make mock-love, very deftly and persuasively; and
Margaret, smarting from her husband's attitude, had been
tempted to yield to him.

Then, in the third scene came the catastrophe. She had
told her husband with a horrible simplicity of all that happened — overwhelmed with contrition, yet with a piteous
kind of hope that even this confession would mend matters;
and he had burst into dreadful laughter; telling her to her
face, first, that anything she chose to do would be indifferent
to him, that she had already spoiled his life by her
ill-breeding and her empty indiscretions, and, finally, in a
burst of contempt that he had known all the while of what
was happening, that his friend cared nothing for her, and
that the thing was a mere comedy.

It was then that the climax of Selva's acting had come. Up
to that point she had been the simple girl, striving to become,
for her husband's sake, a woman of the world. Then, in silence, with the stage empty of all figures except hers, the
audience had seen that development of character which
should have taken five years, compressed into ten minutes.
She had grown into a woman fierce and disillusioned; she
had seen her spoiled life, in a vista, and that it was incapable
of mending: then, yet more swiftly the primitive passions had
surged up and she had seen that life with such a man — that
life even without him now — was intolerable. The child had
come in to prolong the agony; and the chord had hung sus-
pended. Without the program it might well have been

thought, at any rate at first, that the child's influence might prevail. Then with a real horror, the audience had perceived that one pose was surcharged on another; that Margaret, deadly quiet and controlled, was soothing the child, merely that he might not be terrified; that her mind was made up and that her intention would be carried out. And the child too suspects there is something wrong: and once more, with an appalling self-control, his mother reassures him. The child is at last taken back to bed; then with a swiftness, at which the audience held its breath, she gets out her husband's revolver, and, without hesitation or faltering, shoots herself through the head. As acted by Selva the story was overwhelmingly convincing. So ended the comedy.

It is astonishing how an emotional stimulus, if only deep enough, stirs up a hundred dormant thoughts which, critically considered, have no kind of connection with the thought which arouses them. So it was with Nevill. Objectively taken, there was nothing whatever in common between the play he had just witnessed and his own life — except, indeed, that the play turned on the relations between husband and wife. Not one of the elements or circumstances which had developed the situations on the stage, was present, so far as he knew, in his own relations with Enid. Yet, for all that, his emotions and passions were all astir, as birds when a gun is fired. Vague ideas of sacrifice and love, and the possibilities of tragedy if the conditions of these were not observed, circled about his soul. (Mrs. Bessington, he understood, was talking to him over her shoulder; he assented smilingly; but he could not catch more than one sentence in three.) He felt he must talk very hard to Enid, indeed. He felt that there was a large number of things that must be discussed; but he could not probably, if questioned, have given any coherent answer as to what these were.

There was the usual uncomfortable pause before they could get their motors. (He was to go home in his own, dropping Algy on the way, and the Bessingtons were to go back in theirs.) Algy volunteered to go and look for them; and Mrs. Bessington, of course, with a vague desire to be helpful, followed him out a few steps under the glass porch, and stood looking about, in the very middle of the steps, hindering everyone. Nevill drew Enid aside behind the fastened-back glass doors. They had that little space to themselves.

"It's astounding," he said. "By the way, will you be able to come and meet her?"

Enid glanced at him.

"You want to, so much?" she said.

"Why, of course I do," said Nevill. "I want to take her to bits and see how it's done. I want to see how she holds her teacup and whether she crosses her feet when she sits down, and — and the whole thing. She was three separate and distinct people this evening, and yet they were all Margaret. My dear — you must see what a wonder she is!"

"I see her power perfectly," said Enid, in a rather high voice, "but I don't think she's Margaret. By the way, it's an impossible play."

"I should have said so if I hadn't seen Selva act it," said Nevill.

She let her eyes rest on him a moment, as if appraising him. It was as she had looked at Frascati once or twice.

"Yes?" said Nevill.

She laughed softly.

"Are all men like you?" she asked. "Do none of you see through that kind of thing?"

Nevill really was a little pricked.

"My dear girl, if you don't see that she's a genius, I — I despair. Oh! Don't be tiresome, please. I assure you she's great."

For an instant he thought she was annoyed. Her eyelids came down a little and her mouth grew grave. Then again she laughed, naturally and easily.

"Well, most people seem to agree with you, certainly," she said.

Then Mrs. Bessington was seen through the glass door, with her lips still moving, to be turning her eyes this way and that. Nevill looked out to the front, and there was Algy at the door of the Bessingtons' motor.

(4)

"Come in and have a drink," said Nevill twenty minutes later, as the motor drew up at the door of the Elizabeth Street house. (Algy had, of course, refused to be set down when the time came, and said that he would walk home.)

"Well, do you know, I think I will," he said, as if he were deciding some important point. "Talking makes me thirsty," he added, as an afterthought. "I mean being talked to. Be-sides, I want to hear what the play was about."

"Now tell me the whole thing," he said, when he was set-tled in a deep chair in the library. "That clean shaven Johnny was her husband, wasn't he?"

Nevill assured him that he was right.

"Well; that's all right then. I got that between times, so to speak. And the other Johnny — I couldn't make him out at all. He was after her, wasn't he?"

"That was the idea," said Nevill; "at least —"

"That's good enough for me, then. Well, I thought her rip-ping —"

"Who — oh! Selva, you mean. Yes; she's all right, isn't she?"

He found it difficult to attend to Algy, so violent was his preoccupation — a preoccupation, curiously enough, with the thought of Enid now, rather than of Selva. For somehow it appeared to him that Enid was just a shade displeased with him, and that this had shown itself, not indeed in anything she had said, but by a kind of faint film over her manner as he had seen the two ladies into their motor, and wished them goodnight. It was very slight — so slight that he was not at all sure whether it were not sheer fancy on his part; and it was this doubt that preoccupied him. For he could not imag-ine, if it were so, what was the matter. Certainly he had praised Selva; but then Selva was a genius; there was only one opinion on that point. Was it conceivable that the girl did not like his going out between the acts, both times, for a ciga-rette with Algy? But she had urged him to — besides — it was incredible, anyhow. Was there a single piece of negli-gence anywhere on his part? He ran his mind back over the evening. . . . He could remember nothing that was at fault. It must be — if there were anything in it — that she did not like his not agreeing with her about Selva. But how could he agree? There was only one opinion.

Then, with one of those inconsequent acts of the will that people make in order to quiet uneasiness, he decided that he was being foolish; and that nothing whatever was the matter with Enid, unless perhaps she were a little tired.

Then he suddenly yawned uncontrollably, and became aware that he was very tired himself.

Algy rose promptly to his feet.

"Goodnight, old man; I'm off. After that, you know —"

"I'm sorry," said Nevill. "No; sit down again. Have another whisky?"

"Couldn't dream of it. No; I'm going. Is that a program? Let's have it, will you? I must mug it up. Never do, you know, to have seen Selva and not to know what the play was about. Goodnight, old man. Thanks very much, and all that. No; don't ring. I'll let myself out."

"See you on Tuesday, then."

"Well, if I actually said so —" said Algy.

Nevill felt entirely disinclined for sleep when the boy had gone, in spite of his cavernous yawn just now. It was the kind of weariness that leads to mere inertia — that holds one in a deep chair, always considering the duty of going to bed, yet hindering one from performing it.

It was a quiet studious-looking room — this in which he sat — in which no one ever studied. The walls were lined with locked bookcases, whose contents, enclosed in brass lattices, were of a discouraging character. Hansard was there — row after row of him — bound in neat leather with white labels: there were such works as Agricultural Dictionaries, volumes of dreary travels, bound pamphlets, some eighteenth century poets, volumes of divinity, portfolios of engravings, tied together with green ribbon bows. On the tops of these bookcases stood plaster casts of Greek philosophers; let into panels over the fireplace was an oil painting of nymphs disporting under very heavy-looking trees.

Yet the room was very pleasant. It had a deep Turkey carpet, a large sensible leather-covered table with solid carved chairs; the mahogany furniture was highly polished; there were fine brocade curtains, drawn back now from the tall windows to let the cool air in. On the table lay a heap of illustrated papers, and the tray with siphons and whisky.

It was very quiet here, too, since it looked on to the garden of the house, and the noise of London was no more than a distant rumble like the sound of waves upon a beach.

Here then Nevill sat and thought, too weary to move.

Presently, in spite of that faint preoccupation which, driven from the foreground of his thoughts, still occupied the background, he began to think of Hartley.

He had been there last night — at this very hour — sitting up in the hall. Aunt Anna had gone to bed nearly an hour

before. He had sat up there, smoking and looking forward to
the next day. All the lights had been turned out except one;
he had turned this out himself and groped his way upstairs
in the dark.

What an enormous while ago it seemed!

And then suddenly he began to long for it — to long for it,
not as it had been last night indeed, but as it had been three
weeks ago — on that first evening, for example, after Enid
had come. It had been exactly perfect: they had played foolish games in the hall — the three of them, and Mrs. Bessington, murmuring sentences from time to time, which occasionally he had answered, had regarded them over her knit-
ting. Of course, it was simply delightful to be up here and
Enid only two streets away. (He was to look in next morning,
by the way, and see if any appointment had been made by
the lawyers.) But London somehow did not seem an ideal
background. It was a shade too feverish; the Academy had
been oddly fatiguing; Selva, though stimulating, had been a
little exhausting too. This very room in which he sat had not
the cool spaciousness of the hall at Hartley. Open windows in
his bedroom, presently, would not be the same as those open
windows that looked out on to the gray moonlit fans of the
cedars on the lawn. . . .

So his thoughts moved on — as if they were very nearly external visions that passed before him, rather than as ideas
generated by himself — as his drowsiness increased.

And then, suddenly, in a great flash, Romance poured back—
that Romance which Selva had illuminated by her genius. . . .

He saw himself again in that splendid comradeship which
had dawned on him for the first time in connection with a
woman, when he had begun to understand Enid. He saw how
ludicrously he had been at fault just now, when he had conceived, even as a doubtful possibility, that she was a little
displeased with him. How could she be? For the understanding was perfect.

Again, then, he saw himself and her, not merely as husband and wife, but as comrades, neither of whom could have
a thought or a desire of which the other was not aware; and
this comradeship was now Romantic in an even higher sense
than he had imagined. For he had seen Passion as well tonight; and in its rosy light every cooler relationship glowed
transfigured — it had been, in that play, a Passion that held

tragedy, and a Passion that, under these particular circumstances, could have no issue but one. Well; but his own had no tragedy in it, because the relationship was perfect. It was not to be the mating of two hopelessly dissimilar characters, but of two who, in the great and fundamental things, were (as he had told Aunt Anna) absolutely one. There could be no tragedy there. . . . What, after all, did externals matter? How could it matter whether they were here or at Hartley; in this cauldron of suppressed and seething life which was named London, or in the cool spaces of Hartley, with the cedars and the hall and the river and the pavilion — that dear home of his, of which Aunt Anna was so graceful a symbol?

Then, in sudden contradiction, he began to think of the most light externals of them all, of Enid's blue filmy gown and the row of sapphires, the blue flowers in her hair, her clear pallor, the glance of her eyes as, now and again, he had met them with his own.

(5)

Mr. Charleson gave quite a start as he came round the screen and saw Nevill lying there in the deep chair. He had made certain, as he said to Mrs. Ferguson next morning, that Sir Nevill had gone to bed and left the lights burning, as young gentlemen will, without ringing the bell. He advanced a step, and coughed discreetly.

There was no movement on that sleeping face. The young man was lying back, his head drooping on one shoulder, his arms dangling down over the sides of the well-padded chair. He looked dead tired.

Mr. Charleson coughed again.
Then he put his hand discreetly on his master's shoulder.
"Beg pardon, Sir Nevill."
"Eh?"
Nevill had sat up suddenly, bewildered with the sudden awaking: he looked blankly at the servant.
"Eh?" he said again.
"Beg pardon, Sir Nevill; but it's gone twelve. And not hearing the bell, I thought —"
"After twelve, is it? I've been asleep." He stood up as he made this brilliant discovery.
"Beg pardon, Sir Nevill, but you look very tired, Sir Nevill," proceeded Charleson, who, while not daring yet to aspire to

Masterson's familiarities, occasionally was a little paternal. "Better go to bed, Sir Nevill."

Nevill stretched elaborately.

"Quite right, Charleson, as usual. By George

Charleson waited.

"I do feel cooked."

"First day in London, Sir Nevill. What time in the morning—"

"I think we might say nine. And breakfast in my room at half-past."

Yes; certainly this bedroom was not like Hartley. In Hartley one could move about freely: there was a wide space between the mirror and the bed, where one could even do exercises before one's bath, if one was in a virtuous and strenuous mood. But here — scarcely. He remembered Algy's confounded clumsiness before dinner. And a looking glass too, of all things.

The rumble of the streets too was far more considerable here even than in the library. Elizabeth Street itself was fairly quiet; but from the thoroughfare which led to Victoria a hundred yards away, life was in full movement. He could hear the run of wheels, the hooting of a motor — all the more distracting since they were not quite continuous.

He undressed slowly, yawning again once or twice, and got into bed. The very sheets felt different. They had not that same sweet country smell that his sheets had had last night.

Then he switched off the light and arranged himself. How dog-tired he did feel, to be sure.

Enid. . . . That was the point. He would see her tomorrow. He would think about her now. . . . Enid. . . .

(6)

Enid was perfect next day. She said she would certainly come and meet Selva again; that Selva, whatever one might think of her acting, was a great personality.

"You weren't angry with me yesterday?" she asked, looking up at him from her low chair, with a touch of pathos that went straight to Nevill's heart. She did look a shade paler than usual.

"Angry! With you! Why —"

He went off into a torrent of expostulation.

"That's all right," she said. "I knew it must be so; but I was foolish. Nevill —"

"Yes?"

"You will tell me, won't you — just as we agreed — when you're — you're not quite pleased with me?"

"Why, my darling —"

"But you will?"

"Of course I will."

She nodded.

"That's all right then."

"And you must keep your side of it too," he said.

"Well, if you really wish it —"

"Of course I do. That's a part of the arrangement. I shouldn't dream —"

"Well, I will then. . . . Oh, dear me!"

"What is it?"

"I feel tired. I — I didn't sleep very well last night. I was anxious. I thought I'd done something —"

Nevill was overwhelmed with shame; particularly when he remembered that he himself had fallen asleep in his chair.

"I'm a brute," he said. "Look here, I must make a confession —"

She smiled up at him.

"Go on, my dear."

"I slept too well; I fell sound asleep in my chair. Charleson woke me up and sent me to bed."

"You poor dear! You did too much. You're not strong, you know. No more headaches?"

"Oh, no! And please remember, I'm quite strong always — as strong as a horse. I am, you know."

She sat still in her low chair, looking at him. Then she lifted her arms a little.

"Give me a kiss," she said. "I heard the bell go. That'll be the lawyer."

Chapter IV

(1)

When Americans set themselves seriously to perform a social duty, there can be no doubt whatever as to their adequateness. And the Heckers were worthy representatives of their country.

They had, of course, a suite of rooms at the "Cecil" — three bedrooms and two large sitting rooms; the bedrooms looked out into the court because that was quieter, and the sitting rooms over the river, because that was more beautiful. But this was not enough for the entertainment of Madam Selva and the few friends they had asked to meet her quite quietly. They would want at least two more rooms. A small band must be stationed in the most remote — as everyone, presumably, would want to talk all the time; tea was to be served at a buffet in the next; Madam Selva was to be enthroned in the third; and the few friends were to await their introduction, and talk loudly and continuously in the fourth. They were to arrive; to be greeted by Mr. Hecker first and encouraged to sit down; then, when their turn came, they were to be conducted to the inner door, within which stood Mrs. Hecker; she in turn would present them to Madam Selva, and, upon her approach with another party or individual, they were to pass through to the tearoom, which had another door opening upon the corridor. Through this they would emerge, and, on passing again the door of the first room, could come round and tell Mr. Hecker how much they had enjoyed it all. If they were very important, Mrs. Hecker too would be summoned to say goodbye, and "Yes, isn't she wonderful?"

How the Heckers succeeded in obtaining the use of these two further rooms, God and the manager of the "Cecil" alone knew. The only outward sign of any unhappy circumstance connected with the achievement was to be seen, by observant visitors, in the gloomy appearance of a Colonial Minister, all that afternoon from four to six, who sat in the public rooms for the first and last time during his visit.

The first evidence of any unusual happening in the "Cecil" was encountered by the Bessingtons and Nevill, upon reaching the lift. Here a superb gentleman in a frockcoat with a flower in his buttonhole and light gray trousers bowed slightly and asked whether they were for Mrs. Hecker s reception. Upon Nevill assenting to this, a rapid sign was made to the lift-boy, and a pair of inmates of the Cecil Hotel, who had been noticed approaching, were informed that the lift would be down again immediately.

Upon emerging on the first floor another gentleman in another frockcoat, with another flower in his buttonhole and another pair of gray trousers, was awaiting them. He bowed slightly from the waist, and asked whether they were for Mrs. Hecker s reception. Upon Nevill again assenting, he conducted them down a short, thickly carpeted corridor, in the direction of a curious noise that grew louder every instant, and revealed itself presently as the sound of many voices all talking at once, at full power (Mrs. Bessington visibly brightened as she heard it; and broke off in the middle of a sentence.) Then an inexpressibly formidable footman leaned his powdered head stiffly forward, as the gentleman in the frockcoat retired, and inquired: "What names, sir?" On receiving an answer he slipped within an open door, beyond which could be discerned the outskirts of a crowd, and announced with absolute and resonant clearness:

"Mrs. Bessington, Miss Bessington, Sir Nevill Fanning."

There was a lull in the talking, as there always is upon such an occasion. And then Mr. Hecker, in a neat morning suit, so perfectly correct that one simply did not realize it until one looked, was there — alert, trim and efficient He did not appear to come there; he was there. And he appeared to have been waiting for them, as for the climax of the whole reception.

"Charmed to see you; this is most kind. . . . Yes, Madam Selva is in the inner room; if you wouldn't mind waiting a few minutes. You'll excuse me, won't you? I see some more friends have just come."

He pressed Nevill's hand with a confidential air; and then again, as they moved forward into the room, they heard the same confidential tones beginning again behind them.

In spite of his very real desire to see Madam Selva, Nevill felt gloom fall upon him like a pall. This was nearly everything he most disliked, and that he hoped it would not be. Indeed, it was the parrot house once more.

It was a large room, admirably seated; there was a vast window seat; there were little rout chairs, ottomans, sofas; there were no tables at all. There were, in fact, so many seats that they were not full, in spite of the crowd; and Nevill found very little difficulty in getting his ladies through to the window. But the noise of voices was incredible. Americans, with all their virtues, do talk loud; and seem to find no discomfort in their neighbors' doing so also. And they were, of course, chiefly Americans here.

"Oh! Look at the flowers!" said Enid, as soon as she sat down.

There were no tables, as has been said; but the Heckers were not to be done out of their flowers for all that. The big old mirror over the mantelpiece was framed in pink orchids; and in the center of the mirror hung a great S, surmounted by a crown.

"But what's the crown for?" she said.

"Oh! General glory and honor," said Nevill. "Democratic ideas, you know — Yes, Mrs. Bessington?"

While Mrs. Bessington began to describe to him the only time that she had herself stayed at the "Cecil" he began to look round him and find his bearings; for he felt that with all the good will in the world he could not stay here forever. There was a tall, curtained door on his right, in the middle of the long wall opposite the mantelpiece; and this, presently, he perceived to be the shrine, so to speak. Even while he looked, he saw the hatted head of Mrs. Hecker peep from it for an instant, and simultaneously two persons unknown to him advance and disappear. It was plain that Madam Selva was in the next room.

"I beg your pardon," he said, conscious that Mrs. Bessington had stopped talking. But it was Enid who answered him.

"There's Mr. Lennox," she said.

Algy was, indeed, advancing towards them, behind an obviously American financier, who, in a white waistcoat, was regarding the company with a pleased smile. Algy looked a little weary.

"Well, here we are," he said. He saluted his friends politely.

"I have spotted it," he went on in a confidential tone. "We go in, in lots; and there's tea beyond the — the throne room. Lord, I want tea!"

"Now, if they'd had tea in here —" began Enid.

"That'd never do," said Algy. "Don't you see, Miss Bessington, that tea in the last room is the only thing that'd get people out from Madam Selva? We'd get clogged otherwise, in
there. These Americans know how to manage us all, I must
say. By George! Look at those orchids!"

By the time that their turn began to draw near, and Mr.
Hecker — still apparently bilocating all the while at the two
doors, greeting his friends at one, and handing the next lot
that were due for Madam Selva through the other — began
to eye them once or twice as if to put them on the alert,
Nevill's gloom was profound.

A crowd such as this had always a depressing effect upon
him. The thing seemed so exquisitely annoying and futile
and unenjoyable. Here were, perhaps, forty people — each of
whom, individually, was no doubt charming; each of whom
might be quite interesting taken alone — all talking at once
about things that really interested neither the talker nor the
talked-to. He heard, in moments when he could catch con-
secutive sentences, the weather, Madam Selva, the Hotel
Cecil, the view over the river, the orchids, Madam Selva,
New York, the transatlantic lines, the crush in the Strand,
Paris, Madam Selva, briskly discussed, in such a manner and
at such vivacious speed that nothing could possibly be said
about any of them that could be of any interest at all. There
was no coin on the table, so to speak: there was nothing but
counters. And all this was being done, by tightly-dressed persons, in a room which, in spite of the awnings outside and
the fans in the passage, was getting warmer and warmer. He
was concluding very deliberately that, much as he had
wished to meet Madam Selva, the price was too heavy, when
Enid turned to him again.

"Nevill, I'm sorry; but I really can't bear this much more."

Certainly she looked a little tired. There was a tiny line between her eyes that he had never noticed before; and her eyelids drooped.

"I know," he said. "But what in the world —"
"Now, Mrs. Bessington, if your party will come this way —"
And there again, miraculously, was Mr. Hecker, as efficient
as ever, enticing them towards the door.

(2)

As Nevill, with Algy just behind, followed his ladies in and greeted Mrs. Hecker, he was agreeably surprised to find himself almost in the dark. The shutters were half-closed; a great bank of roses stood in the draft from the window, and their fragrance filled the room.

As he shook hands with Mrs. Hecker, who had managed, apparently by one simultaneous act, to lead the ladies forward and towards a figure seated in a great chair, murmuring their names, and also to be back again with the two men, he saw that she, too, was even more bright and adequate than her husband.

She looked entirely cool, though she must have been darting to and fro like this for at least an hour, on her feet all the while; and completely interested in these two men, though she must have shaken hands with at least forty or fifty before. As she murmured to them, Nevill observed her dress. Her bosom and arms were covered with light lace; she was in white; her hat was a dream. She resembled a highly etherealized country hostess who might, five minutes before, have strolled in from the garden.

"It is really most good of you to have come, Sir Nevill. And you, Mr. Lennox, though I think this is the first time I have had the pleasure of meeting you. Yes. Madam Selva, I may say, is an old friend of ours. We met her in Rome again this spring. We made her acquaintance in the States last year. She likes little, simple gatherings like this, she is kind enough to say — just a few friends, and a few words of talk: no more. You will find tea in there, presently, Sir Nevill. Lord Maresfield passed through just now."

And so on.

Nevill began to understand the procedure.

That white figure, with the huge hat, seated in the big chair, was Madam Selva. Opposite her, apparently carelessly placed, yet in reality with the greatest deliberation, were two other chairs, and no more. In these Enid and her mother were now seated. (He could hear a clear, rather deep voice talking slowly.) Presently, he perceived, Enid and her mother would be moved on; and Algy and he would be advanced. They must not stay too long; they must say a few words to the goddess, and then take their leave. Then there would be tea.

As he perceived this, Mrs. Hecker, with a graceful murmur, slipped from them; and he saw Enid stand up. Then the chairs were empty; the two ladies were passing out at the other door, and himself and Algy were advancing, drawn by Mrs. Hecker's tact, as by a conductor's wand.

When he was fairly seated, and Mrs. Hecker vanished again — (already he could hear her low murmur beginning to the next lot) — he found himself looking at the great actress.

Again she was made up to the eyes; her face looked even chalky in this half-light; her mouth had a kind of delicate grimness; her eyebrows were black.

She was saying that she was glad to meet Sir Nevill Fanning; and even as she said this very trite remark, he was aware of her personality.

Genius is an amazing thing; and there can only be one opinion as to Selva's genius. Even in this darkened room, with the clamor of tongues sounding on one side, the clack of tea things and the faint sound of a string-band on the other, it was entirely impossible to be unaware that this woman was remarkable. She was, externally, scarcely more than a phantom; she was not beautiful, except in her wonderful long hands, blazing with jewels; she was in the dark; her very skin was engloved in cosmetics: a very penetrating perfume came from her; she was saying, for the fiftieth time this afternoon, that she was pleased to see the two people who sat in the two chairs; and she would say it again, probably, to thirty or forty more. Yet; there it was!

He was saying presently that he had had the privilege of seeing her in *Margaret*.

"Ah! Yes," she said, in her deep voice. "That is a play I like. I think that you English —"

Algy burst in. He was obviously exploding with a tremulous kind of excitement.

"It's tremendous!" he said, "tremendous! I beg your pardon—"

She had turned her whitened face on him, and he had realized his interruption.

"I was saying," she said, "that you English need that lesson, I think. Your women have no chance. Now in America, as well as in Australia where I have come from, it is different. Perhaps you do not agree?"

It was really royal, this. It was not at all original; yet it seemed to matter when she said it. It seemed highly gracious of her to ask one's opinion at all, and vitally important as to what one answered.

"I'm afraid —" began Nevill.

"I see you do not agree. Well, well; I must think it over from the English point of view."

"I am so very sorry, Sir Nevill," said a tactful voice, "but there are some more people just come, and —"

It was over. He rose; he took her hand for a moment, and she smiled at him very kindly. Then he was passing through into the tea room, and Algy trod intently upon his heel.

(3)

"Well, and that was all," said Enid, with faint asperity. The ladies, with that confident decision that men lack, had secured a small round table for four in the window, ordered tea, and arranged the chairs. The table was covered with an embroidered damask cloth; there was a silver vase in the center again filled with orchids. As she spoke, a footman approached with the refreshments, slipping deftly through the groups between him and the buffet.

Then, before Nevill could answer, Lord Maresfield came up and greeted them in his genial staccato fashion.

"Bit of a crush, eh? See the goddess! — What? How do, Algy?"

Nevill made a reach for a chair.

"That's all right. Get it myself, eh? Had five words with her. — What?"

"About that," said Enid. "I said I had seen her in *Margaret*."

"Lord! So did I," said Nevill.

"Ah! I scored there. Said I'd seen her in *La Tosca*." ("Another cup, waiter, eh?")

"And she said," continued Nevill, "that it was all to teach us Englishmen how to treat our wives."

He grinned at Enid; but Enid did not seem amused. (Mrs. Bessington had already begun on Lord Maresfield, and that nobleman therefore was out of it.)

"I suppose she said the same to everybody."

"Did she to you, too?" asked Nevill.

"Certainly; and that women had no chance; whereas in America and Australia —"

Nevill laughed aloud.

"Word for word the same," he said. "But, you know, it was worth it."

"Worth it? What do you mean?"

"Why, it really was something to speak to her even. It's no good, you know; she really is a personality."

Enid was pouring out tea, and made no answer.

"She snubbed me all right, didn't she?" put in Algy. "I —"

"Well, you interrupted her in her piece."

"Yes, but, by Gad, she needn't have taken me up like that."

"She was rude to you, Mr. Lennox?" asked Enid sweetly.

"Well —"

"He interrupted her in the middle of a sentence," explained Nevill.

"She needn't have been rude, though," remarked Enid.

Nevill set down his cup with brisk decisiveness.

"Enid, you're really tiresome," he said. "She's a genius. Look here, Maresfield — Oh! I beg your pardon, Mrs. Bessington; I didn't see you were —"

But Lord Maresfield sprang at the opening like a bird at an open cage door.

"Eh! What? What? What's the trouble?"

"Miss Bessington's being tiresome. She will not see that Selva's a genius. Here's Algy, who interrupted her in the middle of a sentence — you know his way. Well; she snubbed him, very properly, and he took a back seat. And here's Miss Bessington saying she was rude, and that there's nothing in her —"

"I said nothing of the sort," remarked Enid, with a flushed face. "I said distinctly —"

Now Nevill honestly did not see that she was in the least annoyed. He felt cheerful, and even expansive, at having passed the ordeal of the two rooms. He waved a hand; and she stopped dead. He did not notice even that at the time.

"Look here, Maresfield. Isn't she a genius? Well; and how in the world can you expect a woman like that, who's on a kind of throne, to stand a chap like Algy barging in? I don't care in the slightest what anybody thinks. I'm delighted to have met her. Aren't you, too? She's tremendous. I felt it in that two minutes, every bit as much as in the play. She's just great. Isn't it so? Now, Enid!"

There fell a dead silence. Enid looked at him quite deliberately. Then she dropped her eyes.

"Have another cup, Lord Maresfield," she said.

(4)

"Just come in for a minute," said Enid quietly, as the motor drew up at the door of the flats in Cadogan Lane. "I won't keep you."

Nevill made a sign of assent. He said nothing.

It had been an extraordinarily unpleasant little situation after Enid's complete ignoring of Nevill at tea. For a moment no one had spoken; and then, for perhaps the first time in her life, Mrs. Bessington's conversation had been welcomed. Apparently she had realized nothing of what was in the air. She had begun in a low, rapid voice to talk about Wall Street, inspired, probably, by the appearance of the American financier in the white waistcoat, who once more was looking round with a pleased smile. Lord Maresfield had joined in with staccato assents, and began three or four sentences which he was unable to finish. Algy had slipped away, making a remark about some more sugar-cakes, with a selection of which he presently returned. Nevill, after an amazed silence, had joined himself, too, on to Mrs. Bessington's subject. Enid, very self-controlled and natural, had continued to dispense tea, and had presently begun to talk quietly to Algy.

Lord Maresfield, a few minutes later, had taken his leave, followed by Algy; and, immediately after, Enid had said that she supposed they ought to be going, and Nevill was coming with them, wasn't he? He had assented; they had gone downstairs together; he had obtained their motor and got in after them. But they had all been silent going home.

Enid led the way upstairs, and when the door was opened, turned to her mother.

"I want to speak to Nevill, Mother," she said. "Shall we go into the drawing room?"

Mrs. Bessington murmured something about taking off her things and hurried away. The girl led the way into the drawing room without looking behind her, and sat down. Nevill followed, shut the door, and went across to the hearth.

He was completely bewildered. He saw there was something very wrong; he was aware of a sense of strong grievance at the way the girl was treating him, but he could not conceive what it was, exactly, that he had done. He was con-

scious of nothing deliberate. Had he possibly been brusque?
Oh! What on earth was the matter?"

"Nevill, dear," said the girl.

He looked up, reassured by her tone. Her eyes were cast
down; she was playing with the fringe of her parasol.

"Yes?"

"You remember our agreement, don't you? You really
meant it?"

"Why, of course I did," he burst out, more reassured than
ever. "Have I done wrong? Tell me, instantly, please; and . . .
and I'll eat dirt."

But she did not quite respond.

"Well, you must be really a little more careful in public.
You were not quite courteous to me, you know —"

"Not courteous!" he exclaimed, more amazed than ever.

"Let me finish, please. First of all, you contradicted me
quite flatly before — before the others. Then you said that I
couldn't see anything in Selva. That was not true."

"Heavens! Let me count ten —"

She smiled, ever so faintly, lifting her eyes to his; and then
dropping them again.

"I didn't quite like your tone, you know. And there's something else."

"Go on, please — finish me!"

Her manner changed a little. She leaned forward, and her
tone was less cold.

"Nevill, dear," she said, "you don't really like Selva, do you?
She's really quite common, you know. I cannot understand
men. She was one plaster of paint; her eyes were darkened;
her dress was outrageous; her manner — Nevill, how can you
think she's great?"

He grinned cheerfully. The crisis was passed.

"Let's deal with the first, first," he said. "And may I sit
down, please?"

He moved towards her, but she made no sign. He went to a
chair instead.

"First," he said, "you've told me that I wasn't courteous to
you. Well, first of all I apologize abjectly for my — my ill-bred
manner. It was quite unpardonable." (Her eyes looked at him
again, with the dawn of surprise in them.) "I was just careless, I suppose. But now, in justice I must say that it never
entered my head that I was being rude, or even careless. I

had not, as far as I am aware, the very faintest shadow of irritation or impatience or anything else in my mind. — No; let me have my say out, please. — That was so; but I do not in the least excuse my — my brusqueness or rudeness. I am very sorry. I beg your pardon. Please forgive me. I'll try not to do it again."

He raised his face to her, brimming with humor and cheerfulness. But, to his surprise, there was no humor in her face; she was quite grave: she inclined her head a little as if to accept his apology in complete seriousness.

Well, he must make another attempt.

"And for the second point," he said. "I concede to you all that you said about Selva's appearance — the paint, the darkening of the eyes. And I bow to you with regard to her dress; though I must say I can't conceive what you mean. But I was not talking about that sort of thing. I was talking about her genius. And that, with all humility, I still maintain. Why, my dear girl —"

He stopped abruptly. She had looked at him again, with such an expression that again with utter bewilderment he perceived that he was on the wrong line.

"Oh, dear me! What have I done now?" he cried.

"Ah! You don't understand —"she said in a low voice. She rose swiftly; he rose with her, really perturbed. She went across to the window and stood there, a slender, graceful silhouette against the brightness: she began to drum gently with her fingers against the pane with her back turned to him.

It was very silent here in this room, looking out on to the little gardens at the rear of the flats. A piano sounded faintly from somewhere in the big buildings about them, but so distant that it formed no more than a melodious background.

Nevill could not conceive what was the matter. It appeared to him that he had blundered frightfully somewhere; but he had no notion in what direction. Had he been clumsy, or stupid? What was it? He was not yet irritated — no more than a blue bottle is irritated for the first instant in which he finds himself hampered by the delicate invisible threads of a newly-spun web. Still less was he in the least alarmed. He supposed she would explain presently.

She turned round; and, as he looked at her face against the light, there seemed to pass across his eyes just a shred of the film that had darkened them ten days ago as he came out from the bathing pool in the early morning. Simultaneously he was aware that the pressure on the top of his head was there again, though it was not in the least severe.

She began to talk rapidly.

"My dear," she said, "I don't want to be disagreeable; but you really are disappointing me a little. I can't conceive how you can think as you do of a woman like that! I should have thought you'd have seen in an instant what a — what a wretched creature she is! I don't deny her power — of a sort: I've said it again and again. But it's not genius — it's *not* —"

She was growing emphatic.

"Would you mind sitting down?" said Nevill quietly. "I can't see you against the light."

She moved away and sat down, without apparently having heard him; and went on. He could see her better now, and her face looked to him quite different; it looked anxious and overwrought: there was none of that fine serenity that he loved so much.

He listened; but she repeated herself. She seemed anxious that he should say that the actress had no genius. He grew more and more puzzled.

"Let me interrupt a minute," he said. "Is it that you want me to say she isn't a great actress? Well, I can't. I think she is. Ask anyone else you like —"

She came in passionately.

"How can she be a genius? She — she looks horrible. I can't bear to hear you —"

Nevill stood up. He thought it began to look like hysteria.

"My darling, I simply will not discuss Selva any more just now. You're overwrought; and I don't wonder. I've dragged you about too much. Enid, dear —"

He came across to her as she sat there; he knelt down and took her hands in his.

"My darling, I'm a beast and a brute. You must for give me, and make the best of me. Just tell me when I displease you in any way; and — and I'll do my best to amend There! We won't talk any more now. You must rest before dinner; we dine at seven, you know. — Oh! My dear love!"

He bent and kissed her hands. She remained passive.

(5)

He felt heavy and dispirited as he came out five minutes later into the street. He had still plenty of time before he had to go and dress — (they were all to go to the theater again tonight) — and he thought that a turn in the Park would do him good.

There are few places so opulently beautiful as Hyde Park on a summer evening, when the flowerbeds are so many flaming fires; when from the heavy trees comes the cooing of the woodpigeons; when the perfect curved lawns have just been mown once more, and the smell of cut grass is in the air; when the rhododendrons are out; when there are a few well-mounted riders in the Row; when the carriages and motors go by for their last airing before the twilight closes in; when all this is seen, smelt and heard under the sunshine of a cloudless June evening.

He turned up by the Achilles statue under the trees, and took off his hat as he walked. Already his head felt better, and there was hardly a line of dimness left before his eyes. He was thankful he had not betrayed it just now. It would have distressed Enid terribly.

It had come to him as a real relief when he had thought that Enid was a little overwrought. Up to this afternoon he had known but one side of her — that serene, tranquil mood in which she hated crowds, loved the country and had understood so perfectly his own attitude to all these things. So she had been in Rome, at Frascati, and at Hartley. Now he had seen another side which he had never suspected. . . . Well, it would make her all the more lovable, no doubt, when he understood it better.

As he went up by the side of the water — fervently praying that he might meet no one whom he knew — a number of other little things came back to his mind, each of which, at the time, he had dismissed as irrelevant, but which now, it appeared, had some kind of link one with another, and the explanation of which he began, he thought, to see.

The first which he could remember was her gentle fault-finding with him at Hartley. No doubt she had been right in her facts — Masterson was a little familiar sometimes; and Aunt Anna certainly had just a shade of masterfulness — but in spite of their truth, he had been a little surprised at their being mentioned at all. Then there had been the little affair

of Father Richardson. Again that was a small matter, and
she confessed that Nevill's own idea had been right; yet certainly she had been rather abrupt with the poor man, who,
after all, had behaved very nicely to her. Then there was the
trifle — (he had scarcely thought of it again till now) — concerned with the rather sharp words she had spoken to her
maid. Well, he hadn't been intended to hear those. Yet he
had heard them: there they were! Finally there had been the
affair this afternoon.

It appeared to him now that these little things were rather
significant; not, indeed, of anything serious at all, but just of
a tiny fact, that Enid, too, was human and had her nerves
like other people. She was human; but she was none the less
lovable — perhaps even she was more lovable. He knew what
nerves were himself. Well, he must remember in future.

Then, one by one, a number of other little things floated up
— things of which he had thought absolutely nothing at the
time, and which, even now, were probably sheer fancies on
his own part.

There was first her attitude towards her mother. Ah! He
remembered now the sharp little things he had heard the girl
say to her as he came downstairs one day at Hartley. Well,
that fitted in. Again, Mrs. Bessington, at the dinner he had
given on his first night in London, had been remarkably lenient towards him in the way of conversation. He had thought
it to have been Algy's tact at first. But then, she had been
really very lenient ever since. Was it conceivable that Enid
had — well — given a hint to her mother not to talk so much
— a hint? And would a mere hint have stemmed that flowing
tide? . . .

Again, he had wondered that Enid seemed to have so few
friends. At first he had not thought much of it; he had supposed merely that he had not come across them: in fact, he
would scarcely have had the chance. Yet, here he had been
ten days in London, and though he had seen various cards in
the flat, and had been to a reception or two, the usual friends
were singularly lacking. Yet Enid was young and charming
and sociable. . . . Perhaps it was Mrs. Bessington's conversation? Certainly she had recognized people at the opera, and
they her. And there were Lord Maresfield and the Heckers
and so on. But where were the rest? Certainly he did not
know much about girls and their ways; they were not in his

line; he had lived hitherto at Hartley whenever he could. But he had thought, somehow, that they always had plenty of friends: Enid, too, must have met hundreds of women, traveling as she did. Yet again, perhaps it was this very traveling that had hindered intimacies — that, and her dislike of crowds and her love of solitude.

Well, here these facts were — each of them quite minute, quite explicable taken singly; yet together they seemed to point to a strain in her he had not previously recognized — a strain that had shown itself just now in her odd behavior about Selva, her "disappointment" that he had not been able to share her view — her — well, it almost seemed like a curious kind of jealous hypercriticism.

He stayed halfway up the walk that ran between the Row and the water; it must be nearly time for him to turn back.

A small boy, with very fat legs, was bent over a little schooner-rigged ship, with an air of very mature seriousness; something was wrong with the rigging. Nevill thought of Jim, and wondered what he was doing.

. . . (Yes; he must just remember that Enid had nerves; he had been clumsy this afternoon; it had all been his fault.) . . .

The small boy set the ship firmly back on the edge of the ripple, as if he were planting it. It immediately rocked over on to the tiny beach.

. . . (And that he must not draw ludicrous deductions from insufficient evidence. He must treat her frankly and courageously, and not inflict his distressing kind of humor on her when she was just a shade on edge.) . . .

The ship was being pulled about again vehemently; its owner's face was set in a frown, and his lips were pursed with energy.

"What a pity!" said Nevill. "The bowsprit's come out."

The boy looked up at him sharply, and appeared satisfied.

"Can't I help?" said Nevill.

The boy moved towards him without embarrassment.

"It goes in there, you see," he said seriously. "Do you think you could get it in again?"

It was extraordinarily like Jim — that unconventional and unquestioning confidence. Dear Jim!

"Yes, I see," he said. "Just hold my stick, will you?"

Chapter V

(1)

Aunt Anna sat in the pavilion waiting for her letters. But, uncharacteristically, she was doing nothing at all. A couple of papers, brought by the local grocer, rested unopened on the round table. She herself sat in the window seat, with her feet up, leaning back against a couple of cushions. Her hands lay in her lap; her gray eyes wandered vaguely out upon the river below the windows and the park beyond.

It was a hot breathless noon. Across all the green spaces not a creature appeared. The cattle were under the beeches on one side, and the deer under the elms on the other: now and again, a faint movement in the shadow showed a head tossed against the swarming flies. The very water itself seemed depressed and flat, as if all the sting and effervescence were drawn out of it by the steady blaze of light that showed three feet behind the dark running streamers of weed and the pebbly patches of bottom. The birds were still. A single pigeon cooed far away, and suddenly left off, as if the effort were too great. Through the door on the left she could see across the lawn, where a single butterfly flickered against the green, the great house, drowsing, with all its eyes half-closed by the lids of the sun blinds. She had even had the awnings put up outside the pavilion windows.

Yet, though the day was one of peace and sleepiness, she was neither peaceful nor sleepy. There was a curious undefined sense of apprehensiveness in her whole being; it had increased steadily and slowly through the last day or two. At first she had put it down, with her usual good sense, to nerves over-strained by the succession of hot days; and then to her own peculiar position and Nevill's absence under these circumstances. But her attempts at reassurance were not successful; and she had begun to perceive (as imaginative and rather superstitious people will perceive) small significant happenings about her that appeared full of omen. She knew perfectly well that she was superstitious, and that she had no right to be so. She had sternly put away these fancies; but they had returned. Just now she had relaxed her efforts, and was reviewing the little list.

She became absurdly superstitious at such times. For example, if she were desiring some event very keenly, she
would "take omens," as she said, almost continuously. If, two
flies crawling on the floor in a patch of sunlight, the one that
looked the browner reached the shadow first, then the event
would happen: if the other, then it would not. If, when the
Angelus bell rang, she could say the Salutation twice before
the last of the nine strokes, then she would succeed in some
little undertaking; if she could not, she would fail. Once or
twice she had spoken of this habit of mind. Once she had de-
fended it with a kind of humorous agnosticism to Nevill.

"We live under a very large number of laws," she had said,
"about which we know nothing at all. And all these laws are
interconnected like the strands of a net. Why shouldn't there
be some real relation between them? Why shouldn't two flies
crawling on the floor be a real symbol of something that's
happening somewhere else? Besides, I tell you, it *does* come
true. I don't mean every omen is infallible, but that a great
number of them do show a general tendency."

"I'm surprised at you, Aunt Anna," Nevill had solemnly answered. "Just you tell Father Richardson and see what he
says."

"I shouldn't dream of it," she said defiantly. "It isn't a sin."

"Yes, it is; it's in the Catechism."

"Bosh!" said Aunt Anna. "Besides I'd always sooner believe
too much than too little. I heard a priest say the other day
that Superstition was a by-product of Faith."

"No, he didn't: he said it was a waste-product. Because I
was with you. I remember it perfectly."

"Well, it's a product, anyhow," said Aunt Anna. "And you
shouldn't waste anything. It's all useful, if you know how to
use it. Like a pig's bristles."

(2)

She was thinking of this now; because all her omens were
being taken on the subject of Nevill, and it was these that
she was reviewing. (Really her defense of omen-taking had
something to be said for it.)

There was first the apprehensiveness in general.

Nevill had been gone exactly eleven days, because this was
Monday, and he had gone on the Thursday week before.
Well; the apprehensiveness had begun on Saturday. She had

awakened with it; at any rate she had been conscious of it as she had hurried back from Mass to see if there were any news from him. But there was none. She had heard only two days before, and it was not likely that he would write again so soon. Neither had there been any letter on Sunday, nor, so far, on Monday. His last (Thursday's) letter had been one bubbling joy. He had written about Lord Maresfield, among other things, and had said that they were all going to the opera together that evening and that they were to meet on Saturday Madam Selva at the Hotel Cecil (he had in an earlier letter described the play they had been to on his first night in London; and the Academy). He had also said that the lawyers had things in hand; and had, of course, raved about Enid.

There had been, therefore, no justification at all for her apprehensiveness. Everything was going perfectly well. She would certainly have heard if there had been any law-difficulty. Algy Lennox was there too, and Nevill was apparently seeing a good deal of him. That was all excellent: Algy, in spite of his tiresomeness about tennis, was a sane and pleasant companion. Nevill had dined out, too, once or twice, as well as with the Bessingtons. He was going to Ranelagh. He seemed as prosperous as possible.

Yet there the apprehensiveness had been; and here it was still. She had taken a perfect torrent of omens all the rest of Saturday and Sunday; she had even caught herself betting (so to speak) at Low Mass as to whether the server would get back from the credence table before he began the *Suscipiat*. If he did, then things would go well with Nevill. If not, not. He had not; he had begun on the second step on his way home. And nearly all the other omens had gone wrong too. A stag had come out from the shade on Sunday afternoon, exactly when she finally settled that he must not. Jim had cried aloud "Mummy!" when she was expecting him to come, but had not finished counting the hundred which she had set as the point before which he must not call "Mummy" if things were to go well with Nevill. Yes; the apprehensiveness and superstition were certainly in full blast.

She was not quite sure as to what she meant by "things going well with Nevill." She had assimilated Mr. Morpeth's cheerful optimism sufficiently to accept the fact that if Nevill must marry Enid he must marry Enid. But she was not quite certain yet that he must marry her. "Things going well" represented, then, a rather vague ideal: to be frank, it meant to Aunt Anna that God's will should really be done and that it should make for Nevill's happiness — it was no more defined than that, when she tried to fix it.

But these voluntary omens were not the worst. The weight on her mind seemed to rise, rather, from a number of little external things that happened, quite apart from her deliberate volition.

First; her tremors had come on her once again, in the presence of the corniced door at the top of the stairs. She had come in from late Mass yesterday by the front door instead of through the gardens, because she had wanted to see whether it were blistering, as Masterson had told her. And, as she entered, in the broad sunlight, a minute or two after noon — under the most prosaic and least suggestive of circumstances — she had been completely certain that there was someone waiting for her there. There was a tall porter's chair, beyond the table, with its back to her, and, so assured was she that someone was there — perhaps Mr. Morpeth, or a friend from a neighbor's house — that she walked quickly round to the hearth. The chair was empty; and she looked round, a little puzzled, only realizing then that her thought had been unjustified, yet wondering whether perhaps her visitor were not elsewhere. She had raised her eyes to the gallery; and, as they fell upon the door, she understood that her absurd fear of it had come on her again.

This would never do. She rang the bell.

"Masterson," she said, "I want the key of the West Bedroom. Would you ask Mrs. Templemore whether she has it?"

She had not been in the bedroom for several months. It had been cleaned and looked after, she supposed, as usual. She waited until Masterson came back with it; and then a thought struck her. Certainly she must face the room; but — but the facing of it alone in the dark (for the shutters were closed and the curtains, she supposed, drawn) was a little too much for her resolution.

"Just go up and undo the shutters, will you?"

The butler went up first and unlocked the door; she heard his feet on the polished boards, and followed him. As she came to the threshold, a great bar clanged within, and he was pulling back one side of the shutter as she entered.

"I think I'll have both," she said.

While he finished opening that window and was dealing with the next, she stood irresolute, looking about her. The great bed rose like a monstrous catafalque, with the curtains drawn so as to enclose it all round. The tables and sofa and chairs (she saw) were all as she remembered them; the washing-place was empty of towels and linen, and a sponging-tin stood in one corner.

"Thanks," she said, "that's all. I'll bring the key down when I come. Close the door, please." (She felt she must add this. Really she must face the thing properly.)

It was just a big, solemn, old-fashioned bedroom. There was a good, though worn, carpet on the floor; the furniture was mahogany and chintz — covered chiefly with dust-sheets; there was a door beside the bed, on the far side, that communicated with the bathroom, beyond which, again, was Nevill's room. She saw the key was in the door on this side.

She felt tremulous, but determined. She told herself she had been silly not to have been here before; it was simply its associations that haunted her. It was here that the end of the tragedy had come — there, beyond those enshrouding curtains. On the side nearest the gallery Nevill had sat, holding his father's hand; it was to that side that the fierce, defiant, bandaged head, with blazing sunken eyes, had leaned to whisper; it was on that side that it had fallen at last, deathly still — and no longer defiant.

Well; she must pull the curtains, and look into the bed.

She went towards it resolutely. If she hesitated, her nerves might snap. She took hold of the curtains nearer the bathroom door and drew them back; and for one sickening instant, her heart stood still. For there appeared to be lying within the bed a stiff sheeted figure. . . .

Then, with set teeth, she tore back the sheet, and disclosed a rolled mattress. . . .

She came out through the bathroom; and there were the familiar signs of occupation — the big wooden bowl of yellow soap, the stiff bath-brush, the exercise-machine hanging on the wall, even a pair of grass-slippers. She went on through Nevill's room. The bed was stripped — which looked dreary — but all else was as it should be, except that there were no mysterious garments and dressing gowns hanging on the tall-hung pegs.

Well; there it was. There had been nothing there; there could be nothing. Yet she did not feel in the least reassured. As she stood in the hall again, exactly the same sense of a burdensome and sinister presence lay on her; and the door was ominous. She had not exorcised her ghost. It was a relief when Jim came bursting in from the garden with the collies. . . .

The second unpleasant little happening was even more unreasonably disconcerting. It was connected with Jim himself.

She had taken him to afternoon Benediction at four o'clock on the same day; and as they came out their path to the gardens lay beside the Fanning grave, where old Sir Nevill had been carried down from the bedroom she had visited that morning. Never before, so far as she remembered, had Jim referred to this place, after he had first been told what it was, and the inscription on the top of the flat altar-tomb within the railings been read to him. This time, however, he stopped dead.

"Mummy," he said.

"Yes?"

"That's where Uncle Nevill is buried, isn't it?"

"Yes; they're all buried there," she said. "Come on, my boy: don't loiter."

"Oh!" said Jim, still not moving, and regarding the tomb with solemn eyes. "And I suppose Cousin Nevill will be buried there too?"

A faint sickness laid its hand on her heart. Yet it was just the kind of thing that Jim did suddenly say, without any context at all.

"Yes, my dear," she said softly. "And so will you, perhaps; and I too."

"Oh! . . . Is it a big room down there?"

She felt a violent desire to tell him to hold his tongue and come away. But it would scarcely be decent in a Catholic mother to avoid such things, when her son questioned her. As he put his inquiry she remembered the "room," as he called it — as she had seen it when it had been opened to receive first her husband's body and then his brother's — a narrow dark chamber, with niches on either side.

"No, my dear; it's not a big room. It's quite little. But it's much better to think about their souls."

"Oh! I know all about that," said Jim, with a touch of contempt. "I want to know about their bodies. Do they very
soon—"

"Jim! I'm not going to go on. — Well; the bodies go back to
the dust again; but their souls are quite somewhere else."

"Yes; I know, Mummy. But I want to know whether the
bodies —"

"There's Mr. Morpeth," she said. "Run and ask him to come
and speak to me."

Well; again that was all. But why in the world on that day
of all days, when she had been into the West Bedroom,
should Jim be so greedy of knowledge as to the processes of
the grave?

Here, then, in the pavilion, on this Monday morning, she
sat and meditated. Jim was out riding with the dogs, and
wouldn't be back till lunch. She meditated upon her apprehensiveness and her omens; she told herself several times
not to be foolish and morbid; she longed for the letters.

Then at last they came. And, once more, it was Masterson
who brought them.

"Letter from Sir Nevill, ma'am," he said, just as he had
said before. And she, too, just as before, tore open the envelope first of all, and glanced through it.

"He doesn't say he's altered his plans, Masterson," she
said, scarcely even thinking it strange, this time, that a servant should be so intimate. She understood better now how
the old man loved his master.

"And Father Richardson's here, ma'am. Could he speak to
you, he says."

(3)

While Father Richardson talked of some small parochial
matters, her mind was still working. She was perfectly certain that, humanly speaking, he would not understand one
thing about her tremors; but, after all, he was a priest as
well. She still hesitated, however, up to the very moment
when he stood up to go: and then took her decision swiftly.

"Can you spare a few minutes, Father?" she said. "I want to
consult you about something."

The priest sat down again.

"I expect you'll think it very foolish of me," she said, "but —
but I'm in what they call a 'state of mind'." (She smiled

rather piteously.) "I've got no sort of reason for it. But I feel anxious. And I don't even know what I'm anxious about."

"Oh, just nerves," said the priest reassuringly and sensibly.

"Yes, that's what I say to myself, Father; but it doesn't comfort me. It's about my nephew, of course. I keep on imagining things."

"What kind of things?" asked Father Richardson, prudently.

"That's just what I don't know — oh! — That he's going to have some misfortune, I suppose; or get ill or die, or be disappointed. Everything seems to point that way, and —"; she stopped suddenly.

"I don't understand quite," said the priest. "I should have thought that his engagement and — and his state of health — were all most satisfactory. Of course, it's a pity Miss Bessington is not a Catholic; but I have the dispensation all right; and I'm sure that she's a most exceptional —"

"Oh! It's not that a bit," she said. "I don't mean in that kind of way — I don't know what I mean."

Father Richardson said most politely and sympathetically that really he did not, either.

"Well; don't you know that sort of feeling one has that everything is going wrong? It's like a cloud; it hangs over everything, and depresses one horribly. And one can't put it away."

Father Richardson assured her again that he did not know what she meant, unless she referred — he put it quite gently — well — unless she referred to indigestion.

Then she saw that it was hopeless. It seemed to her odd that a priest should be so very materialistic about everything. She thanked her own instincts that she had not referred to omens.

"Well; I daresay you're right," she said, with an effort. "Thanks very much, Father. I — I expect you're quite right."

There was a footstep on the gravel, and again Masterson stood on the steps of the pavilion.

"Beg pardon, ma'am. Mr. Morpeth's here."

"Oh — yes — ask him to come out."

The butler retired.

"There was nothing else, Mrs. Fanning?" asked the priest, with an air of having completely justified his role of spiritual physician.

"No; nothing else, Father. I expect it's better not to speak of those things, isn't it? Good morning, Father. Thank you so much. Sir Nevill will be down before the end of next week, I expect. But I'll let you know for certain, as soon as I can, whether he'll be here for the concert."

Father Richardson thanked her and bade her good morning He felt quite pleased at having been consulted, and at having dealt so adequately and reassuringly with her questions. What queer, fanciful people women were!

By the time that Mr. Morpeth's solid form was seen advancing across the lawn, she had taken up Nevill's letter again. (Again the others were unopened.) And, once more, she determined to speak to this layman frankly.

Even she, who had begun to know him so well, had been astonished at the perfect composure with which he had taken his daughter's death. She might have expected that for a day or two, or even a week, he would have kept up his resolution; but it was more than a month now since the girl had been buried; she herself had spoken with him again and again; she had sat in his garden one afternoon, and he had talked of his daughter exactly as if she were just on a short visit away from home: never yet had he shown even an effort not to falter or to give way.

He took off his hat gravely and replaced it again, as he came up the steps. Then again he took it off as he sat down and drew out his handkerchief.

"I just called about the concert," he said. "Father Richardson has sent me no notice of it. I think he thinks I should not come to it, so soon after my daughter's death. Most kind and tactful of him! But I do not feel in the least like that myself. I only wondered what the people would think if I came. Will you kindly advise me, Mrs. Fanning? I would not shock them for the world."

"I — I think they might not quite understand it," she said.

He inclined his head gravely.

"Thank you. That is sufficient."

He fumbled a moment in the pocket of his waistcoat. Then he drew out a small, flat object and laid it on the table.

"Then will you do me one more kindness?" he said. "There is a sovereign in that paper. Would you kindly purchase four tickets on my behalf, and distribute them to whomsoever you please?"

"That is kind of you. I will do it most gladly."

"Thank you," he said.

Then he took up his hat as if to go.

"No; stay, Mr. Morpeth. And I want to consult you about something."

He replaced his hat on the table.

(4)

She began very nearly as she had begun to the priest.

"I'm in what they call a 'state of mind'," she said. "May I tell you all about it?"

He inclined his head.

Then she told him frankly and fully, first that she was in a mood of apprehensiveness about Nevill, and that she had no kind of reason for it.

"Here's his letter," she said; "that's just come. Read it, please."

He took it, drew out his glasses, wiped them on his handkerchief and began to read. (He looked exactly like a businessman studying a document.) As he finished, she broke in again.

"You see it's quite satisfactory, as far as it goes. He tells me about meeting Madam Selva and what she said; and about the crush at the 'Cecil'; and how he went a walk in the Park and met a small boy rather like Jim and tried to help him to mend his ship; and how the ship wouldn't be mended: and then about his going to the Cathedral on Sunday, and how, although the choir sang wonderfully, he couldn't bear the music; and then about Enid, too. It's all natural enough, and quite in his own way, though it doesn't seem to me quite as cheerful as his last. But that's not the point."

"No?" he said, questioningly.

"No; I was unhappy long before the letter came. I've been like it ever since Saturday. And then there are the omens —"

She stopped, wondering whether even to Mr. Morpeth she could speak of her foolishness; but, to her surprise, he showed none himself. He nodded gently when he had taken off his glasses and begun to wipe them again.

"I suppose you notice how things happen," he said, "like birds flying, or a shadow over the sun, and think they're signs?"

"How do you know?" she asked, amazed.

"Because I used to do it myself," he said, "until I learned how useless it was."

"You think it all nonsense, then? Just as I do? — at least, just as I know it is, really?"

"Not all nonsense," he said imperturbably. "I am entirely convinced, from simple observation, that there is some connection between — well, between different things that seem to have no connection. That there are laws that are true and active in all realms at once; and that sensitive or intuitive people can sometimes perceive them. Oh! No, Mrs. Fanning, I don't think it's all nonsense, at all."

"But why did you call it useless?"

"Well," he said, leaning back a little, "because if the thing is to happen it will happen. And, besides that, I do not think it quite — well — quite Christian in spirit. We should have more confidence in God. 'Take no thought' said our Savior — I forget the Catholic version, but it means that we should not fret and be anxious about the future. I should leave that kind of thing alone, Mrs. Fanning."

She was silent a moment.

"May I tell you two more things?" she asked.

"Why, certainly."

She told him then about the West Bedroom and Jim's curiosity as to the grave. He listened without moving.

"I put more trust in your own feelings," he said. "It is your intuition that interprets such events, anyhow. You would have thought nothing of them if you had not been already anxious."

She confessed that this was true.

"I daresay your intuition is quite right," he continued gently. "Many people have that gift — some more, some less. It is like — well, you won't be offended; but it is like a peacock who knows, even before the barometer, that rain is coming."

She smiled with an effort; but she felt a little sick.

"You mean you think I am probably right — in foreseeing misfortune?"

"Well; do not let us call it misfortune — we cannot possibly tell. Let us say that it is pain to one you love that is coming. . . . I think myself it is coming," he added, meditatively.

This time she had to make an effort even to speak.

"You think so? . . . To Nevill? . . . Why?"

He continued gently polishing his glasses, which he had held still for the last two or three minutes. Then he began to speak. She did not interrupt him till he had finished. His voice was quite quiet, as if he mused aloud.

"Well," he said, "if you will watch people carefully, you will practically always find that the type to which your nephew belongs — of which, in every way, he is so excellent an example — the type of happy optimist, who disregards suffering instead of really facing it, always has to suffer, and considerably more than other people. God Almighty, if I may say so, has made them almost violently happy — out of all proportion, so to say. Well, they cannot be left like that, or they would be one-sided. Well, they are prepared for suffering in a very marked manner: they are naturally buoyant; they can ignore, and therefore avoid pain; or they can bear it, in moderation, in virtue of their pride. Now that will not do at all, if they are to be conformed to the image of Christ. Therefore they must suffer; and suffer rightly."

He paused a moment. Then he continued:

"I have observed Sir Nevill; and — I need not say — I have learned to love him. And I see in him every sign that he will have to suffer — sharply. If he did not, I should be afraid for him. Now I know really nothing of the young lady to whom he is engaged. I have seen her twice only: once in the churchyard, and once I had the privilege of speaking to her when she was out with Sir Nevill in the park."

(Aunt Anna looked at him sharply; but she did not speak.)

"Well; I think it very likely that part of his pain must come through her. I may be very wrong about that, but I must confess that I formed an opinion of her. I have a terrible habit of doing so. I often try to correct it. And — and I think that she will be one occasion of suffering to him, whether now or later I do not know. But that is not all —"

He paused again. Ah! This was the very point to Aunt Anna. She, too, had tried to think that all her apprehensiveness came from her knowledge of Enid — it might even be her jealousy of Enid. But this last day or two had taught her that this, at any rate, was not all. There was something even larger approaching — a cloud, greater than any man's hand, was coming up; and its shadow had fallen on the corniced door above the gallery. . . . But still she said nothing.

"That is not all. You will think me fanciful perhaps; but there is a shadow on this house, Mrs. Fanning. It fell on my own house first. I knew that it was there, too. It fell on my dear daughter — ah! A week before God took her to Himself. When Sir Nevill looked in at my window — when he was so good as to come across and bring me the news, I knew what he had come to say. But it was on his face too.

"Now, some men might call this a curse. Well, we may call it that if we will; so long as we remember that a curse is but the shadow of a blessing — that He Himself was made a Curse for us, who is our Blessing. That is all that the shadow is, Mrs. Fanning; it is the shadow of our Father's Hand."

There was dead silence as he ended, and fell again to polishing his glasses. The noon lay hot and still on park, and stream, and house. Far away, again, the woodpigeon began his broken cooing: it was not till he ended that Aunt Anna drew a long, shivering breath.

"Ah! Not that!" she whispered. "Not on Nevill!"

He looked at her compassionately.

"Listen again," he said. "I think we spoke here once of the sins of the fathers being visited on the children. That is not a curse, Mrs. Fanning, as the word is ordinarily used. It is not a vindictive law; it is a law of mercy; that the love which should unite parents to children may do what love alone can do, and that is to turn suffering into joy and pain into atonement. It is when the punishment is not borne here — as if God Himself despaired — it is then that the horror comes.

"Now I know nothing of Sir Nevill's father except what you have told me. I do not listen to gossip —"

She broke in:

"He — he was horrible."

"He was unlovable, let us say. Well, cannot he now be rendered lovable? I know no way except by pain. Would it not be a noble thing if his son could suffer for him, and be himself transformed into — well, into a Christopher? You and I know what Purgatory is — well —"

"I can't bear it!" she cried.

"And you, too, have your part. You are bearing it now; and you will bear it better still if you will choose to understand. That is exactly what love means. You suffer because you love. If you did not love you would not suffer. Then go on; and suffer and love."

She broke suddenly into weeping.

(5)

She sat there again that evening after dinner, when Jim had gone to bed, and the stars were out. The breathless day had passed to breathless night. She sat here, at the open window, without even a shawl over her shoulders; there was not a breath to stir the thin silk curtains that hung over the wide-flung lattices. The house was dark, except for the oblong of light that was the door above the curved steps.

She felt weary in soul and body: but all resentment and resistance were gone. There was no joy yet; only passivity and expectancy. She was as one who has fought against a mortal sickness and has passed beyond fighting; and yet death will not come.

Every word she had heard from her old friend had met with the response of her understanding, although with the savage protest of her heart. She knew that it would be as he said; it was not Enid now that troubled her; there was not even a spark of jealousy left. Enid? Why, yes; no doubt she would be the forerunner of pain, the leader of the grim little procession that must trample over the heart of the lad she loved so much. But there was more than all that. Enid was not great enough to cast such a shadow as that which lay over all that she cared for.

But even her heart now had ceased to protest. It lay there, within her, inert and quiet; in pain, of course; but in pain that could no longer crush, since that on which it lay was already broken.

She had been right, then, from the beginning. Her misery in this dear pavilion, when his first letter had come from Rome, had been true enough in its instinct. Her deepening misery since Saturday had been its corroboration. Yet why had it come so swiftly? Was it that the shadow, too, was darkening as swiftly? Then when would the blackness fall?

Then suddenly she remembered, in an abrupt break of thought, that Nevill had said nothing as to having seen any doctor; and her heart leaped again in a broken kind of hope that there was nothing but some physical illness that impended and that this might yet be stayed off by prudence.

She would write to Nevill tomorrow, and tell him that he must go at once, if he loved her. And then again her heart sank down. A shadow such as this was not just a matter that could be banished by a doctor's consulting room and a few drugs. She would not banish it so, even if she could.

She would not banish it so, even if she could. . . .

Yes, she had thought that; and as she reflected on her thought she perceived that even already she had begun, scarcely knowing it herself, to realize what had been said to her; to understand that Pain was not the greatest of evils; that it might be even not an evil at all, but a good; that a curse, if truly the shadow of a blessing, might be that very blessing that could come no otherwise than in a somber dress.

The lawn was soaked in dew as she walked across it on her way back to the house, half an hour later; yet she did not know it till the chill struck straight through her thin silk stockings.

"Why; it's wet!" she murmured; and went on.

There had begun to rise in her, still incalculably fragile, still to be quenched out again by the faintest breath of personal desire, a thin flickering flame that warmed ever so slightly the cold misery of her heart. She had begun to see that there was a capability of joy in pain — no more than that; that if to love was to suffer, then also that to suffer rightly was to love. And love, after all, was the only joy.

Jim was awake when she came softly into his room with a shaded light. He turned his big eyes upon her, unwinkingly.

"Mummy?" he said.

"Yes, my darling? Why aren't you asleep?"

Jim passed over such an irrelevant question with the disdain of indifference.

"Mummy; did you mind what I asked you yesterday?"

For a moment she forgot.

"Why — what about?"

"About — about Uncle Nevill's grave."

She paused. Then she spoke deliberately:

"No, my dear. At least I did; but I don't now."

As she came out into the gallery again she turned to the right instead of the left; and then stood considering. The house was quite quiet now; the servants were far away; and her maid not yet come up. Yet she had no fear. She was trying to remember whether she had taken out the key of the door between the bathroom and the west room; and locked it after her.

Then she remembered that she had not.

She went straight through into Nevill's room, still carrying the shaded light she used for visiting Jim in bed, through the bathroom and into the place she had once dreaded so much. The bed stood still like a catafalque, with its curtains drawn once more; but she was not afraid.

She stood there, as if listening.

Then she spoke; as if she asked a question, and did not fear the answer.

"Yes?" she said.

Chapter VI

(1)

It's not going to leave off," said Nevill despairingly, drumming with his fingers on the window-pane, and looking out upon the little gardens below the flat. The rain was rain was falling heavily, like rods, from a dreary sky.

He had lunched with the Bessingtons before going down to Ranelagh, as had been arranged, with Lord Maresfield, who was to call for them at half-past two and be taken down in Nevill's car. But the rain had set in with thunder about eleven; and it had rained steadily ever since. It did not seem probable that there would be polo this afternoon.

"Don't be so dismal, please," said Enid from her chair.

They had had a delightful lunch. Mrs. Bessington had managed her conversation quite tolerably; had made an excuse to go away as soon as coffee had come in; and had not returned. Nevill understood that she was making preparations of a private and intimate nature, probably domestic.

Enid had been as charming as ever since Saturday. She appeared entirely to have forgotten the very small misunderstanding they had somehow stumbled into; and it was now Wednesday. But it was Nevill now who felt himself at fault; he felt clumsy and awkward and rather gross, and he could not think why; he had never been particularly aware of these shortcomings before: he supposed it was that he had never before been on these intimate and tender terms with a woman. He had begun, too, more than ever now, to think that it really must have been himself who was to blame for the incident of last Saturday: he had been imperceptive, he told himself; he had jarred erred, somehow, on the fine femininity of the girl: and, above all, he had been a great deal too quick, during his little lonely walk in the park, to put the blame upon her and to see significance in what was insignificant. He had done her an injustice; he must take care to do her more than justice now, to make up.

"I'm sorry," he said, with a genial frankness. "I know I'm dismal. I hate being put off. What are you looking at?"

She held up a magazine, and then laid it aside. Again he felt clumsy: he had interrupted her.

"No, go on reading," he said. "I'll look at the rain. Perhaps it'll stop if I look hard enough — like a watched pot, you know."

He turned again to the window and began to ruminate.

Now, down at Hartley he would go and play tennis with a marker on such a day as this. Here there was really nothing whatever to do. Of course, there was a court at Prince's; but Enid wouldn't care to go merely to watch him. Besides, the court would certainly be taken. He was a discontented brute, he told himself. Yet he really did not know what to suggest; he would have been simply delighted to sit here with Enid, or to go to any form of entertainment that she wished; honestly he asked nothing better. He loved to watch her, to talk of nothing in particular, merely to be with her. But he felt she wanted something else; and he did not know what this was. He could not have believed, six months ago, that any human woman could so engage his attention, could so identify herself with him that he judged of things from her view rather than from his own. He did not say any more "What should I like?" but "What should we like?"; in fact, it was very nearly, if not quite, "What would she like?"

The telephone bell tingled in the little hall outside, and he turned round. Enid had not taken up the magazine again, and seemed ruminating too. Again he felt himself a brute: she had laid aside the magazine in order to be talked to, and he had not spoken. But she smiled naturally at him.

"Do go and see, there's a good boy!"

He went obediently out.

"It's Maresfield," he said, when he came back. "He says he's certain there'll be no polo; what? — and that the thing had better be off, eh?"

She smiled; but he felt he had been a little untactful in imitating her friend.

"Yes, I suppose so," she said. "Just tell him so, won't you; and then we'll see what's to be done."

An idea had come to him; and he proposed it as soon as he returned.

"What about the Zoo?" he asked. "I haven't been there since I took Jim. Let's go and be ridiculous."

Her forehead wrinkled slightly.

"Oh! Do you think, in the rain?"

What an ass he was! Of course — the rain!

"Well, I give up. What a desolate hole London is!"

He sat down; for about the fifth time since lunch seeing that he had said what he should not; since he was in London simply because she was there. Again she smiled; but he felt he had wounded her again. How extraordinarily clumsy he was! Yet he used not to feel so with her; he had been even less careful than he was now trying to be, and yet somehow he had not said so many unfortunate things as he was saying now, in spite of his anxiety.

Then he yawned.

She looked at him; and then humor broke out all over her face.

"You're being quite impossible," she said. "First you don't talk; then you imitate that poor, dear man; then you say London's a desolate hole; and then you yawn in my face. Nevill, wake up!"

She said it so genially that the shadow went from his mind. (It was not till a little later that it occurred to him how rapidly she had narrated his blunders.)

"I know," he said. "But what's to be done?"

"What about a matinée?"

"My dear girl — anything in the world you like; but —"

"I quite understand. Yes; we have been a good deal. Well; it's your turn."

"Let's get into a car and drive and drive; and then come home again to tea. We've got that beastly crush this evening, you know."

She stood up.

"Nevill; that's perfect! You'll drive, won't you; and — yes, that's perfect."

(2)

In ten minutes she was back again muffled up in a suitable manner. He put the difficulty that had occurred to him as soon as she had left the room.

"But what about your mother?" he said.

"Oh; Mother won't come," she said lightly. "I saw her just now. Come on, Nevill. This is going to be lovely."

The car was already there, hooded against the rain; and Paul was waiting in the hall of the flat.

"We aren't going to Ranelagh," said Nevill. "You'll have to go inside, Paul. Miss Bessington will sit with me."

Ah! This thought had indeed been an inspiration. This was exactly what he wanted. He really had had more than enough of the inside of theaters, and galleries, and houses. It was that that was the matter with him, and that had put him slightly on edge. It was the open air and room to breathe, and a sense of space that he needed, and that she needed too.

"Now this is really nice," she said, as he finished tucking her in on the side nearest to himself, and as Paul went round in front to wind up the machine. "We'll just drive and drive, and come back to tea, as you said. Nevill, you're a genius! And I've never sat by you before, while you drove. Where shall we go?"

He proposed a route. They would start to the north, go as far as the time allowed, wheel westwards, and come back by Roehampton and Barnes and Hammersmith.

"That'll be lovely," she said contentedly.

Oh; but this was delicious to Nevill! There they sat, these two, in the world and simultaneously entirely out of it. That world streamed past them; first the crowded streets, then a scrap of open ground, then streets again; and at last would come the open country; they could observe and talk, shut in here, not only from the rain and the desolation outside, but from that pressing, talking world that had so crushed upon the nerves of them both. It was as if Frascati itself, or the seat by the horse's monument at Hartley, were translated into other terms. She was close beside him, that extraordinarily sweet presence; her face turned a little towards him, nestling in its hood; he saw it now and again when he could take his eyes off the road; but he was aware of it all the time. Moreover, their talking could be of the right sort: each could speak when inclined; or be silent — that very essential secret of comradeship. It was all exactly right.

"Oh! Take care of that old man!" she said suddenly, as they whisked up by the side of the Park railings.

He was a first-rate example of the type abhorred of motorists' souls; he came out suddenly, thirty yards ahead looking the wrong way; he set himself, with an open umbrella over his shoulder, with his back to them, irresolute, watching the opposite stream of vehicles, with a view, it appeared, to crossing.

Nevill set his teeth and turned the wheel a little, first sounding his horn; but the old gentleman paid no attention.

Five seconds later the car whisked by the old gentleman, sounding its horn suddenly again as it came opposite him, so soon as it was quite clear that he was perfectly safe. Enid caught an anguished face of terror.

"That'll teach him," said Nevill. "Those are the real road-hogs, after all."

Enid laughed softly.

"You're a little hard on him," she said.

"Not at all. We really have some right to the road, you know."

"You do drive splendidly," she said, as Nevill, after an anxious second or two at the Marble Arch, nipped in front of a heavy dray, whose driver was obviously trying to incommode him.

"And that's another lesson," said Nevill. "What philanthropists we are!"

So they talked, easily, with silences; until, after leaving Edgware when the open country was certain, he turned to her.

"Now talk to me gently," he said, "and I'll put in comments."

"About what?"

"About anything in the world that you like."

She was silent for perhaps fifty yards.

"Well, I'll tell you what I want," she said. — "Oh, Nevill! This is delicious!"

"Go on," he said. And his own heart warmed at her words. Then she began; and talked slowly and meditatively, with pauses.

"First of all," she said, "I want to live at Hartley forever and ever. That's essential. Then I hardly ever want any guests: I want to feel that it's all mine — and yours of course. I want to be able to walk about the garden without being interrupted. . . . In summer I want all the windows opened wide all the time; and in winter I want all the curtains drawn, and the shutters shut, just before it gets quite dark. I *think* I want to go abroad about once in two years; at least, I think we ought to, or we may just possibly get stuffy."

"In spite of the open windows?"

"In spite of the open windows," she repeated gravely. "And I think in the other years we ought to come up to . . . to the desolate hole called London, for about a month — not more — for the same reason. Yes, I know that's very sensible and improving of me; but I can't help it.

"About guests. . . . Yes; I do want guests, one at a time, first a man and then a woman, and so on, alternately. I'll ask the women and you shall ask the men. But not too many."

"No married people?"

"No," she said firmly. "And each of us is responsible for his own guest, and must look after him. You can go down and bathe, or whatever it is, with your man; and . . . and I can sit out in the pavilion and talk Life and Being with my woman — or . . . or drive in a little pony carriage with a fat pony. Nevill, I must have a fat pony; and then I can go and call on the clergyman's wife now and then."

"There'll be no difficulty about that, I should think. And we must have Aunt Anna, you know."

"Why, of course; that's understood."

"And your mother."

"Of course again," said Enid.

There was a very short pause before she began again.

"I shall wear nice clothes at Hartley. I think that's important. Nevill, have you got to do many county things?"

"Oh! Now and then."

"Yes, I suppose so. And I suppose I must, too. What a pity! How very much nicer it would be not to do any of them. . . . Nevill."

"Yes?"

"Does Father Richardson really interrupt much?"

"My dear, he's got to be there, you know. Or someone else."

"I suppose so. . . . Oh, dear me!"

"What's the matter?"

"How heavenly it would be if we really could do exactly as we wanted! . . . without any conventions at all. What do you want?"

"I want exactly what you do."

"But how nice of you . . . ! And there's really no chance at all of getting rid of Father Richardson?"

"It's like this," said Nevill. "Hartley is a Catholic place. It's been so always. There's always been a chapel there, which serves as a parish church. And where there's a chapel, there must be a chaplain. I suppose I could build a church in the village, instead; but it would be frightfully inconvenient for everybody else; and I can't think what people would say!"

"Does that matter?"

"I think it does, rather. You see, Hartley — the house itself — has always been a center."

"I see," said Enid.

"Go on about other things," said Nevill. "We'll talk about Father Richardson later. Perhaps we could manage something."

So she went on, after another inconsiderable pause, describing in a delightful and inconsequent way, as if they were the dreams of a child, all the things that she wanted to do; and Nevill's heart again warmed and kindled to hear how she wanted a small walled garden down by the bridge, where she could sit entirely alone, to which she and Nevill alone had the key — and as an afterthought, the gardener too, when Nevill reminded her of the necessity — and a room at the top of the house, to which she alone had the key. Nevill might have another room like it, if he wished, under parallel conditions.

For he found in her again, as she talked, exactly the same mood and aspect in which he had first learned to love her — that strange and arresting love of solitude which he, too, secretly understood! That particular kind of attitude to the world of which they had spoken at Frascati, with the Campagna spread beneath them and the white line of Rome on the hazy horizon. He really had had some bad moments since Saturday, when he had actually almost believed that she was not quite what he had thought her — a belief which he had veiled to himself by saying that she had "nerves" — moments when she seemed, not indeed like other people after all (for evidently she was unique), but to possess characteristics of other people which he had not imagined her to possess. But those moments were gone now, once and for all; and the balance was restored. He knew now that he had been right at first; that all the comradeship was there, just as he had thought; that she was not only the woman that he loved, but (what does not always follow) the woman that he understood. So peace came back; and he was as happy as ever.

(3)

The rain had stopped; and it was after four o'clock — for she looked at her wristwatch as they left Roehampton Lane — when they approached the steep bridge that passes over the railway line immediately above Barnes Station.

Nevill drove superbly; there had been no more philanthropic lessons bestowed gratis upon the passers-by. Everyone had behaved well, and the car best of all. He had settled down long ago into that instinctive rhythmical mood of the driver who knows his car and his own powers, who acts from that trained subconscious attention which must be formed into a habit before a man is perfectly competent.

As they swung up the steep ascent of the bridge — so steep that a pedestrian coming up the other side is bound to be invisible to the driver of a low car until the two almost meet — Nevill became aware of a toppling motor omnibus in front, just beyond the crown of the bridge, going the same way as himself. He turned the wheel a little to the right, so as to be able to pass it if the road should prove to be empty when he had topped the rise.

Exactly as he swept up to it, a perambulator, pushed by a small girl, with a baby in it, became suddenly visible just over the top.

Nevill had the car entirely under control; but he had very nearly the full power on to take him up the steep; and his hand fortunately was already in place to shut it off. He did so, automatically, and put down the brakes.

All would have been perfectly right if the girl with the perambulator had remained where she was, or crossed over. He would have kept his line slightly to the left and behind the omnibus in one case; or held straight on, in the other. Nothing could have happened. But she did precisely the one thing that made some kind of an accident inevitable. She pushed the perambulator in a panic behind the omnibus; she let go of the handles; and she herself remained where she was.

Nevill had one fraction of a second to decide what he would do. If he kept to the left he would strike the perambulator; if he kept to the right he would probably, but not certainly, strike the girl. He kept to the right; there was simply not time for the brakes entirely to check the car; and with a horrible tightening of his heart he saw that, although the girl sprang away with a scream, she was still in front of the car. Then she fell, whether actually struck or not by the off wheel of the motor, he was unable to be sure.

The car stopped.

There fell on Nevill, for one second, a complete paralysis. He knew that he had done the only possible thing; that he was within the speed limit; that the car was under control; that he had not been guilty of even the slightest rashness. But it was his first accident; and there lay the child, screaming.

Then Paul was out, and running past. Then, as he turned without a word to Enid, she, too, flung off the rugs herself without a word, and sprang out. Nevill backed his car a little, turned, slid by the derelict perambulator, and came to rest clear of the bridge. Then, still sickened at heart, yet knowing that at least there could be no question of loss of life, and scarcely even of injury, he too climbed out of his seat and walked back.

There seemed singularly few people about — owing, probably, to the recent rain. The omnibus had gone on its way; though he had seen figures on the top of it turn and look back. A couple of women, at a distance, turned and stared, horrified; a boy ran up, excited and pleased. A man on the common below seemed to be gazing up with interest. And that was all, except for the little group on the crown of the bridge.

As he came up to them he saw that the girl was already lifted to her feet and had ceased screaming. Paul was hurriedly brushing her down as well as he could: Enid was holding her round the shoulders. The girl's face was a mask of gradually fading terror and resentment; but it was perfectly plain that she could not be really hurt.

When he looked at Enid's face, as if to seek for reassurance, he was astonished at the vivid agony in it. She was as white as paper, and her eyes were large and anguished.

"She's not hurt, is she?" he asked as naturally as he could.

Enid made no answer; she was still staring at the girl, gripping her tightly.

"Come," said Nevill, almost sharply, "let's see the damage. Did it hit you, my dear?"

The child made no answer.

"Perambulator, Paul," said Nevill, jerking his head in its direction. "Wheel it behind the car. Come along, my dear, to the car; and let's see what's the matter."

It was becoming plainer every moment that no harm was done at all. The girl was standing quite at her ease, embarrassed far more by Enid's embrace than by anything else. Of course, it had been a shock to everybody, most of all, perhaps, to the child. However, there was no reason why there should be a scene. Besides, they were all in the narrow of the bridge.

"Enid," said Nevill, still a little abrupt of course, "just bring her along to the car."

He put his hand on the child's shoulder.

"Leave her! Leave her!" gasped Enid.

"Don't be upset," said Nevill. "There's no harm done at all. Don't give way, my darling."

Again he put his hand on the child's shoulder. She was still speechless.

"Leave her!" gasped Enid once more.

Nevill turned in despair; and, to his relief, saw a policeman advancing up the road.

"Thank God!" murmured Nevill.

He shortly explained the circumstances. That was his car; that was his chauffeur. His own name was Sir Nevill Fanning. There had very nearly been an accident; the child had fallen down. The policeman was quite sensible and civil. He nodded once or twice: then he turned to the child.

"Are you hurt, my dear?"

The child shook her head dolefully. The blue uniform seemed to have restored some degree of intelligence to her mind.

"Come along to the gentleman's car," he said.

"Let go, Enid," said Nevill.

Enid turned wild eyes upon him. Nevill went up to unloose her hands; it seemed to him that Enid was really not quite herself.

"Come!" he said. "We'll soon see what's the matter,"

Enid let go unwillingly; but her face was drawn and set. She said nothing.

There was nothing whatever the matter with the girl. She had just been touched by the wheel on the knees; but her stockings were not even torn. The policeman elicited from her where she lived — not a half-mile away.

"I'll take her along home," said Nevill. "Enid, my dear; you jump inside with her and the baby. Paul and I will sit in front."

The policeman said he would take the perambulator home. Nevill grinned secretly at the vision which his imagination presented of this.

"Very good," he said. "We'll wait till you come. You've got my number, no doubt."

"There'll be no difficulty, sir," said the policeman. "No harm done."

When Nevill turned again to see that all three were established inside, he saw that they had grouped themselves oddly. The child-nurse, rather pallid now, held the baby; and Enid, on her knees on the floor of the car, supported the girl's feet on her lap.

"My dear! What are you doing? There's no kind of necessity for that."

Enid shook her head fiercely. Nevill had a spasm of impatience.

"My darling; don't be ridiculous! She isn't hurt in the slightest."

So extraordinarily savage was the face turned on him that he recoiled; yet a strange feeling came upon him that Enid was not quite genuine. He felt very odd and confused. He made to close the door; then he hesitated; then he closed it, leaving them. He could talk out anything that needed it afterwards.

(4)

"My dear girl! Whatever's the matter?" said Nevill, quarter of an hour later.

Everything had been perfectly satisfactory. They had found the girl's mother at home — a sensible woman who said that she had particularly told her daughter never to take the perambulator over the bridge; that no harm had been done at all; and that she hoped it would do the girl good. (So, for the third time that day Nevill had been a philanthropist.) He glanced at Enid to see if she was amused; but was met by a set face and unanswering eyes.

The policeman had followed a few minutes later, with the perambulator before, and a small procession of round-eyed

boys behind; and there, too, everything had been satisfactory
— even so the policeman; for Nevill gave him half a crown,
privily. Yet all this while Enid had stood stony-faced, refusing to sit down; and speaking only when the woman spoke to
her, in a very low voice.

Then Nevill had told Paul to drive; and himself got in after
Enid into the closed car.

She said nothing in answer to his question.

He tried to take her hand; but she drew it away.

"Look here, my darling. Have I done anything?"

"Don't speak to me," she hissed.

He drew back.

"You aren't treating me fairly, my darling. I seem to have
offended you. Remember our bargain. Tell me what I've done;
and I'll beg your pardon."

She turned and eyed him; and if ever he saw hostility in
any face, it was in hers. For a moment she did not speak.
Then she suddenly began; and, as she talked, a kind of sickness grew on the other. It was as if the girl was possessed.

"Very well," she said. "I will tell you. It is the last straw. I
have tried and tried: and it is useless. What have you done?
Well, you have treated me brutally; but this is the last straw.
. . . That you should tell me, publicly, not to be ridiculous;
that you should try to tear me away by force when I was trying to help a poor child whom you had knocked down: that
you should make me a laughingstock — and before that
woman too. . . . But that's only the last of the list. . . . You
have treated me disgracefully. . . . Shall I go through it all? . .
. Well; I will."

Then indeed she began.

She went right back to Hartley. It was there, it seemed,
that he had begun to be careless and offensive. There was an
occasion, it seemed, when he had made her stand while he
sat. (Of this, he had neither then or at any other time the
faintest recollection.) Then, it appeared, he had spoken to her
rudely about Father Richardson; he had told her not to be so
familiar; and then later, not to be so discourteous. Then he
had allowed Masterson to be rude to her; and had laughed at
her with Aunt Anna. Her whole stay at Hartley, it appeared,
had been one series of insults received.

Then she passed on to London.

The insults, it seemed, had begun at the Academy. He had allowed her to go on alone, while he talked to her mother and her mother only; he had shown his dislike of Lord Maresfield; oh! In little movements and glances: he had not said anything outright; but she was not a fool; she could understand him well enough. After dinner that same night, he had kept her and her mother waiting while he smoked with his friend.
. . .

Then the Selva affair came up. First he had been brutal in the way he had flatly contradicted her as to Selva's capabilities He had told her she didn't understand what genius was. He had preferred to lean over the box and stare at that horrible painted woman, sooner than talk to her. Mr. Lennox, even, had had better manners. Then he had gone out after both acts in order to smoke again, instead of doing his duty — she thought he might at least have recognized his duty, if nothing else. Then he had gone and arranged behind her back that she too, and her mother, in spite of what he knew as to her feelings, should go and meet Selva — a woman who was unfit for decent society. He had dragged them there, against their will; he had stayed talking to Selva, leaving herself and her mother alone.

She had borne with these things; and had said nothing at the time, hoping that it was mere carelessness. That was why she had not protested then and there.

Then when she had tried, very gently, to show him what he was doing, he had had the grace to pretend to apologize; but had, really, repeated his offense.

"Didn't you apologize? Can you deny that?"

He bowed his head. He said nothing. (A horrible and grotesque memory came to his mind of how a certain cock at Frascati had once turned savagely on his hens when he himself was unhappy.)

"And now you won't even be civil enough to answer."

Then she swept on.

Tiny incidents he had forgotten — during the last three days which he had thought so happy — were dragged out and flung at him; but they all culminated in today. He had mocked at her friend Lord Maresfield; he had said London was dreary — "a desolate hole" — that to her, while he sat with her! He had stood, sulky, at the window and said nothing, even though she had laid down what she was reading, to talk to him. Then he had yawned in her face. (Nevill was too sick even to be tempted to smile.)

Then, finally, had come the motor drive. He had behaved like a roadhog. He had torn past the helpless old man in the Park; he had tried to get the better of a drayman; he had knocked down a child. And then — then once more came the crowning insult. She had tried to make up by sympathy for what he had done; and he had tried to tear her hands away from the child; he had told her not to make an exhibition of herself, publicly; he had laughed at her fears. He had tried to exchange glances with her in the very house of the poor woman whose child had been knocked down.

"It's the last straw. I can't bear it any more. I've borne enough. Be good enough not to speak to me."

(5)

He sat through it in silence. There was nothing to say. With three or four exceptions the substance of the tale was true enough for him to recognize it. There was scarcely more than a point or two in her torrent of charges that was objectively false.

He sat silent; because after her first three or four sentences he had seen the hopelessness. If she could say so much she could say anything; and no answer was possible.

But what held him, toward the end, in something very like horror, was the shocking change in her whole character from that which he had previously believed it to be: it was as if a mask had been torn suddenly away, and a frightful face disclosed. He had thought her very nearly sublime — unlike others, spiritual, aloof, unique. He had thought her markedly self-controlled, of an exquisiteness transcendent of that which breeding could give; tolerant, charitable, even great. He had loved this presentment that he had seen — loved it as he had never loved any living being before, to his knowledge: he had thought that she understood him perfectly; he had hoped humbly and simply that he was learning to understand her.

Yet now, in an instant, a terrifying kind of coarseness disclosed itself; she snarled at him; she framed, as well as she could, sentences and phrases with the object of giving as much pain as possible; she tortured things and words into sinister intentions that had never even crossed his mind. He was as one who goes to kiss his wife and is met by a devil's changeling. He had had no conception — not merely that one whom he loved could be so horribly transformed — but that human nature itself was capable of it.

Towards the end, some kind of coherence came back to his mind; and, as if without volition on his part, the thread of fiery beads, of which he had caught just a glimpse as he walked in the Park last Saturday — Good God! Four days before, only — that thread began to run past again. He began to see that there had been that element in her all through — the fierce, rending, tearing tiger that loved to wound and mar, that rejoiced in pain. There was the other side of her still; he did not even now wholly forget that; the serene, tender, comprehending girl whose heart leaped so swiftly to meet his; but that disguise of hers — if it were no more than that — was a floating phantom that moved from him as he looked, leaving him with this fiend that seemed at present the unveiled reality.

He grew quieter yet, interiorly, as he saw these things; his whole physical self felt sick and exhausted; but yet the deadly peace increased, as she severed, with her two-edged tongue, fiber after fiber that bound him to herself; it was a deadly peace; he knew that well enough — the peace of a seared and white-ashed countryside over which a devouring flame has gone.

(6)

She did not end till they were sliding up past the Albert Memorial.

. . . "Be good enough not to speak to me." Those were her last words. . . . "Be good enough not to speak to me."

They were in Cadogan Lane by now. It was up at that further end, visible beyond Paul's head, that they had passed out so happily a couple of hours ago. They had turned up through the square, he remembered, and so on, towards the Park.

These were the houses which he had seen when he had walked up in the rain before lunch; he remembered looking at them, and wondering vaguely who lived in them, as he had let down his umbrella.

Yes; and this was the door of the flat where Paul was drawing up so skillfully. Up those stairs was the door of the flat. .

. . The car had stopped now. That was the porter he could see within the glass panels.

Oh! He must get out now; he was nearest that side; and he must hold the door and help her out. The rain had stopped. There was no need to open an umbrella. . . .

Yes; he would just push back the glass door on this side, while the porter held the other, that she might pass through. . . .

She was gone through now. Yes: he had better go home. . . .

. . . "Home, Paul."

Chapter VII

Aunt Anna knew the instant that she saw the coated and capped figure coming across the lawn to her, that the first stage had been reached. She said nothing at all as she held out her hands at the foot of the pavilion stairs, down which she had come so soon as she had recognized him. He said nothing as he took them. Still holding one of his hands, she led him back whence she had just come.

He was in his driving coat still, though the day once more was hot and stifling, and his big cap was pulled forward. His face was quite quiet; but his eyes looked a little uncertain; they blinked three or four times as he stared, first at her, and then past her at the park beyond drowsing in the strong sunshine. She thanked God that Jim was still out.

"Well, it is all over," he said presently, without introduction or greeting. "She told me what she thought of me last night — yesterday afternoon, I mean. So I have come back to Hartley, you see."

He spoke slowly and deliberately, like a dreamer. His voice shook ever so slightly in his last sentence.

"Yes; you have come back to Hartley, my dear," she said.

Then she saw Masterson come down the steps from the house, and hesitate.

"I'll just go and speak to Masterson," she said. "You'll wait here till I come back?"

"Masterson," she said, "Sir Nevill has had a shock. Don't ask him any questions as to his luggage. I expect he hasn't brought any."

"No," said the butler, staring straight at her. His face was all set with anxiety.

"If it is to be sent for, I'll let you know this afternoon. I'll tell you anything I can, as soon as I know myself."

(She spoke as to a friend who shared her sorrow. The old man's face twitched violently. Then he wheeled and went back up the steps.)

When she entered the pavilion again Nevill had not moved. He sat still in the low chair, looking out through the window; his eyes turned to meet hers, and then wandered back again to the sunlit park. On the window seat on which she had been sitting, lay a book or two she had been reading; a rosary of red stones and silver, and half a dozen unopened envelopes. Her post had been just brought to her, and the man gone again, when she had seen Nevill coming.

"My dear, take off your coat and cap."

He sat forward a little and unbuttoned the double-breasted coat; she took hold of it behind, but he shook his head, and himself slipped it off, and then his cap, laying them on the floor. He was in the same gray suit in which he had gone away. He seemed a little shrunken and small. Then he leaned back again; and she sat on the window seat.

"I don't think there's anything more to say," he said, in that same toneless voice. "She told me what she thought of me, when we were out driving. I went home — back to Elizabeth Street, I mean; and later on I sent a message round to her mother. Her mother came after dinner; but — but it didn't help much. She said that Enid wouldn't speak to her. And then she said some more things; but they weren't any use. So I've come back to Hartley. . . . Where's Jim?"

"Jim's out riding."

"That's all right," said Nevill. "With the collies, I suppose?"

"Yes; with the collies."

There fell a silence again. Somewhere within Aunt Anna's soul something seemed spinning like a wheel, so fast that no revolutions could be perceived; but there was there an intense and indescribably swift movement — or it was like a single note, sustained at a pitch so high as to be inaudible; or a color so bright as to be invisible. This movement in her was so keen that it appeared to absorb into itself all lesser emotions and impulses; leaving her reason cool and capable. It was with this upper part of her perceptions that she saw that she must be very quiet and unemotional and sensible. He must not sit there forever; yet she must not disturb him yet.

"Would you like lunch out here?" she said.

He did not seem to hear; and she repeated her question.

"Oh! Yes," he said.

"I'll go in and tell them presently."

Again he did not answer.

"We'll just sit here quietly," she went on, still tranquil and steady, "and you can talk or not, just as you like. If you'll smoke a cigarette, I'll have one too."

He drew out his case and held it out. She took one; and lit it from a box of matches on the table. He held his case mechanically when she gave it back; and did not take a cigarette out for himself till she held the burning match silently before him. Then he lit it, and leaned back again.

"You brought Charleson with you?"

"I don't know. Yes; I think he was behind."

"And you drove yourself?"

"Yes. I couldn't see very well. It was dusty. I think I've got some dust in my eyes."

Here was an opportunity. She got off the seat and went and kneeled down at his side, laying her cigarette on the floor; (it tasted like brown paper and hay); and took out her handkerchief. He looked at her.

"Lean right forward," she said, "and I'll take the dust out."

He leaned forward obediently. She put one hand on the top of his head to steady herself, and with the handkerchief ready in the other, searched those eyes that mechanically rolled this way and that for her search. There was one horrible thrill, when she thought that she would break down altogether, as she felt the texture of his hair under her hand, and held her own face so close to that dear face and eyes of his — the eyes as simple and miserable as those of a child in pain; she even felt his breath on her mouth. . . . She delicately wiped the corner of each eye.

"There, I think it's out," she said, sitting back on her heels.

Then she went back to the window seat.

A quarter of an hour later she met Masterson in the hall.

"Come into the dining room," she said.

He followed her in, and shut the door.

"First of all," she said, "we will lunch in the pavilion. Tell them downstairs. Bring it all out on a tray together — everything, you understand. If there is a hot sweet, don't bring it. But bring everything on the tray all ready. And bring it yourself, please. Master Jim must lunch upstairs, and not come out till I send for him. Arrange that, please.

"Next: tell Charleson and Paul, so soon as they have dined, that they must go straight back to Elizabeth Street. Charleson is to pack all Sir Nevill's things and bring them back with him before dressing-time this evening. While he is doing that, Paul is to go round to Mrs. Bessington's flat: he'll know that; and leave this note on her. It's possible that Mrs. Bessington may wish to come back in the car. If so, she will give him the answer herself, if she is in: if she is not he must find out where she is and go after her. He is to bring her down here this evening, if she wishes to come. I don't know in the least whether she will stay the night or not, if she does come. Just tell them downstairs to be ready.

"And — Masterson — just tell them all that Sir Nevill is in great trouble; and that they're not to gossip. But I don't think they will. They must notice nothing. Don't say a word to him even yourself — will you, Masterson? He is in great trouble. The marriage is broken off. That is all I know myself."

(2)

Half an hour after lunch, trembling a little, she suggested his going to his room and lying down. To her astonishment he consented; saying that he had rather a headache. He stumbled once or twice as he went down the pavilion steps, and up again into the house. He seemed dazed into a dreadful kind of childish simplicity. He had eaten and drunk just a little, without comments or refusals. She saw him into his room, and promised to look in later.

She had learned practically nothing more than he had told her at first; he had repeated three or four times that Enid "had told him what she thought of him"; that he was "selfish and brutal." Aunt Anna steadied herself by a violent effort only, when she understood this. She made no comments except the simplest.

"She doesn't know you, really," she had said quietly. She restrained herself with considerable difficulty from commenting upon Enid.

What, however, bewildered her most of all, was her hopeless attempt to understand what kind of person Enid must really be. She had, as has been seen, suspected her of a few rather undesirable qualities; and even this suspicion she had discounted, because of her knowledge of her own jealousies; but she could not honestly say to herself that she had noticed any symptoms whatever of that astounding cruelty which Nevill's little story revealed. At any rate, Enid was not an adventuress. She had been engaged to a man of a quite considerable wealth and position; and had flung him over, savagely and violently, without the faintest excuse. For Aunt Anna to hear that Nevill had been called selfish and brutal was for her to know that the girl who so described him must, practically, be mad.

But what motive could she have? What occasion could have produced such a fantastic lie? What misunderstanding could be so complete? Or was there no motive at all? Was it merely a ferocious and wild irresponsibility?

She sent for Jim as she passed downstairs again on her way to the garden. He must be prepared in some kind of way for the situation which must reign in the house for the present. When he came out, looking a little scared — for Masterson had been rather emphatic with him — she made him climb up on the window seat behind her.

"Jim, my dear; I want to talk to you as if you were grownup."

"Yes, Mummy," said Jim, making himself perfectly comfortable with a cushion.

"Cousin Nevill has come back again suddenly. You remember that when he went away, Miss Bessington had promised to marry him? Well; Miss Bessington is not going to marry him, after all."

"Oh!" said Jim, wriggling a little on his cushion.

"Well: Cousin Nevill is very sad and unhappy about it. Because, you see, he was very fond of Miss Bessington (You mustn't call her Cousin Enid any more, by the way.)"

"I didn't want to, at first," observed Jim.

"Well; what I want to say is this — that you mustn't talk at all to Cousin Nevill, when you see him, about what he's been doing in London. And you mustn't look at him as if you wanted to know what was the matter; and, of course, you mustn't ask him. Because all that might make him more unhappy. Do you see?"

Jim nodded solemnly.

"Just try to think of Cousin Nevill as he was before — before Miss Bessington and her mother came here at all — as he was, even before he went away to Rome."

"Oh — Mummy."

"Yes, my boy."

"Why was Cousin Nevill so fond of Miss Bessington?"

She set her teeth for an instant.

"I don't know," she said in a low voice. . . . "Well, do you understand? I'm talking to you just as I would talk to a grownup person; because I think you will. And if Mrs. Bessington comes down this evening, and you see her, either tonight or tomor-row, just be quite polite; but don't talk to her or ask her ques-tions at all."

Jim nodded again. His eyes were round and meditative. These were great matters.

"And there's one other thing I want you to do for me. I want you to go to the stables and order Marcus to be saddled again. Then come back to me here, and I'll give you a note. I want you to mount in the stables and ride over to Mr. Morpeth and give him the note. Then you can do as you like till tea. I want you to have tea upstairs again, unless I send for you."

(3)

By six o'clock Mr. Morpeth had long been gone again; and she sat, alone once more, waiting for the next event, whatever that might be. The car was not yet come back.

She had slipped upstairs two or three times and peeped into Nevill's room; and every time he had been lying quite still with his eyes closed, and his cheek resting on his hand. Once he had opened his eyes, in a vague, dazed kind of way; and she had slipped out again noiselessly. She had not even sent tea upstairs.

The old man had said very little about Enid, when she had told him all she knew. He seemed quite uninterested in the personal cause of all this pain; the thing that was "their job" (he had said) was Nevill.

"But have you any theory at all?" she asked.

"It may be any one of three or four things," he said. "It is of no use to theorize. I should suppose she is just an Egoist, with a particular temperament. But that is not the point."

He had described "the point" then, more carefully. It con-sisted entirely in Nevill's attitude. Three things, he said, may be done when real pain is encountered. It may be resisted; or it may be allowed to crush; or it may be accepted. The violent man does the first; the weak man, the second; and in both cases it leads to catastrophe.

"But I think our friend will accept it," he said. "He can do nothing at present, except realize it. But I think he will accept it when he understands. Or else I do not see why God has permitted it."

He had said, then, very little. He had not been dogmatic in any way. Yet his very presence brought a bracing kind of reas-

surance. He seemed so absolutely certain that all was in order; that there was nothing whatever to be astonished at, still
less to fear.

"He will not break down; he will not kill himself; he will not
fling himself into any other extreme. Of all that I am confident. You must brace him, Mrs. Fanning; not try to console
him. You must not soften him in any way at all. You have
been crying?"

"Just a little," she said, "before you came. Not before him."

"You must not; before him."

And so, at last, he had gone, leaving her steadied and courageous.

It was as the clock was striking six that she looked out
through the pavilion door, and saw Mrs. Bessington following
Masterson out upon the lawn.

It was almost appalling to Aunt Anna to see how wholly
herself this woman seemed. She was in the very same black
hot-looking mantle in which she had gone away; she moved
with the same busy kind of step, neither retarded nor acceler-
ated by the knowledge she bore; she smiled in the same rather
hard and wooden kind of way. And, as she greeted Aunt Anna,
she began as usual, her rapid, unconnected comments on the
warmth of the day, and the kindness of Mrs. Fanning in sending the motor for her.

"But I must be getting back this evening," she said. "There
is a most excellent train, that stops only three times between
here and London, that leaves at five minutes after eight. We
came down in very good time."

Aunt Anna could bear it no longer.

"Mrs. Bessington," she said, "you'll forgive me for interrupting you —"

"Oh, my dear —!"

"No; please let me say right out what I want. Then I want to
hear what you think of it all. When I —"

"I am sure —"

"Please let me say right out what I have in my mind," said
Aunt Anna, in so exceedingly an emphatic tone that the other
stopped, and, so to speak, folded up her mouth. And it was
then for the first time that Anna saw through the shal-
low-looking gray eyes that regarded her, a look of extreme and
poignant interest.

Then Aunt Anna began.

She took about five minutes to say what she had to say. She had asked Mrs. Bessington to come down immediately, because she wished really to get at the facts; and because Nevill would say nothing. She knew that Miss Bessington had spoken to him in such a manner that he had, apparently, taken it for granted that the engagement was at an end. Well, Nevill's happiness was of the greatest possible moment to herself. She might say that there was practically nothing for which she cared more. She had asked down Mrs. Bessington, therefore, first in order to learn the facts at once — that there might, for instance, be no doubt about the matter if the engagement were finally at an end; next, if it were not, to know that instead; thirdly, in order, if Nevill wished it, that he might have an opportunity of seeing her. (She eyed, rather anxiously, the house door, from time to time: she had deliberately given orders that Mrs. Bessington was to be shown straight out here, without concealment; but she intended, if she saw Nevill coming out, to go and meet him, and tell him who was come.)

"It is entirely unconventional and very impertinent of me to have asked you down like this," she ended. "But I know you will forgive me. I stand very nearly to him as a mother might. It struck me as the only thing that I could think of to do. Will you very kindly tell me what you think?"

She looked her full in the face; and then she began to understand. . . .

(4)

It seemed to Aunt Anna, as Mrs. Bessington talked, that she was watching (so to say) an extraordinarily fine portrait being painted with the trembling, uncertain strokes of a completely incompetent artist. Yet the artist was infinitely pathetic too: for, for the first time, Aunt Anna perceived, beneath the senseless trickle of words and the set conventional face, not only a humanity which she had never suspected, but a humanity that was in anguish and had, with a stoical kind of courage, succeeded hitherto in hiding its pain under this flat and dreary exterior. Again and again, as the middle-aged woman talked — interrupting herself, wandering away into parentheses that never closed, describing details minutely, and omitting principles — the other was drawn off in a kind of wonder from the repellent vision of Enid revealed by her mother, to the poignant vision of the mother as tormented by

Enid. For the first time in her life Anna stood face to face with a figure of sorrow that was almost grotesquely dull, with a soul that was suffering intolerable pain under a flat and foolish mask.

When the woman had finished — when, rather, she had tailed off into wholly inconsequent repetitions and comments, Anna understood as she had never thought to understand.

That beautiful girl, then, was a practically insane egoist. She had been so the whole of her life long. Obviously she had been spoiled as a child; her father had done the most of it; and her mother had yielded. She cared, really, for absolutely no one except herself; one or two almost incredible little stories were related as to the way she had treated her friends. For now she had no friends at all: her beauty and her charm drew people to her again and again; and, for a week, or a month, or even six months, such friendships had developed. Always, however, sooner or later, she behaved exactly as she had behaved to Nevill; once before she had been engaged to be married, and had broken it off in almost a precisely similar manner. Yet she always considered herself the innocent party; she always professed herself disappointed in her friends; she had begun, for the last year or two, to withdraw herself in a kind of despair from people's company, since she appeared, honestly, to be under the impression that it was these alienated friends who had behaved badly to herself. But, above all, it was in her behavior to her mother that the egoism showed itself most cruelly of all. She insisted on going these rounds; she insisted on living in what she considered a "suitable" manner; — on having rooms in these hotels; on expensive isolation; on continual traveling. Yet, in private, she behaved to her mother with unrelenting cruelty: she continually told her not to talk so much; she reproached her; she sulked for days together in silence; she used her tongue like a whip. Yet, in public, she bore herself with dignity and serenity, and even with a superficial kind of affection. Nerves, no doubt, were responsible for such outbursts as that which Nevill had experienced; but the outbursts did no more than reveal that insanely selfish character which, beneath her calm and her apparent detachment, brooded always within her.

Such, then, was the portrait indicated rather than executed by the woman in the black mantle and bonnet — the portrait that grew upon the air before Anna's eyes, and solved her last difficulties. For every line brought conviction — the jealousy she had suspected in her, the little flickers of abruptness, the sense of which she was aware that this was the very last girl in the world for Nevill, the broken little story which he himself had told — these things all fell into place and joined on with the lines of the character which the girl's mother herself now filled up.

"I could keep it to myself no longer, Mrs. Fanning," said the poor lady, trembling a little, with a large tear in the corner of each eye. "I feel you have a right to know. God forgive me if I am hard upon my own daughter! God knows how I have tried to think otherwise; but, as I have said, she behaves like that both to me and to others; ever since she was a little dot. She is very selfish — I am afraid there is no doubt about that, and thinks of no one but herself; and then she begins to find fault with first one and then another, until there is no one left." (Mrs. Bessington was repeating herself gallantly, without the least misgiving.) "And it has always been so from the first. She used to be the same with her father, too, who — who, well he had made his own way in the world, you know; and she did not like the way he used to pronounce words sometimes; and used to say so to him when we were alone together. But now I must bear with it as well as I can; because I am her mother; and I have never yet said a word to anyone except yourself. But as soon as your note came, and I could see what terrible harm she had done once more, I just slipped on my things and came away; and left a note saying that I was called away: she has shut herself up in her room ever since yesterday; and has never touched a morsel of food; but I did hope that this time would be the last, and that she had at last found in Sir Nevill the very man for her; and I am sure I do not know what we shall do next; or whether she will speak to me again for a while; for she is sure to say that it was all my fault for talking as much; and whatever will you think of me, Mrs. Fanning, for talking like that about my own —"

The two tears rolled suddenly from her eyes, and fell on the black silk mantle. Aunt Anna sprang up and kissed her.

(5)

At half-past seven Aunt Anna stood at the door, watching the back of the carriage that took her guest off to the station.

Mrs. Bessington's conversation, at the early dinner that was served for her in the morning room at seven o'clock, had been a very masterpiece.

Without the smallest softening again of that cast iron exterior of conventionality, she had discoursed with amazing courage of the Academy exhibition, and Selva's acting, the comparative merits of English and Italian scene-painters, the dust on the roads, and her country cottage to which (she remarked unblenchingly in Masterson's presence) she supposed that Enid and herself would soon be going. In its way, it was the most gallant exhibition that Anna had ever witnessed. A quarter of an hour ago in the garden, the mask had been laid aside; and she had seen a woman whose heart must have been very nearly broken by the most unromantic and sordid pain that any woman can suffer — a pain that went on ceaselessly — the continual contempt and cruel hostility of her own daughter. . . . And now, here again sat the original Mrs. Bessington, as Masterson came in and out, with her features composed again into their smiling cast, and not one spark of feeling visible in her eyes: dining well and amply before returning to London to take up the torment again.

Meanwhile Anna had considered, in gusts of thought, what she must do when the other was gone.

She had again peeped into Nevill's room and he was still lying on his bed, apparently asleep. But what must be done when the guest was gone? She had decided not to tell him that she was here till afterwards. There was no purpose to be served: the thing was finished. Not for any consideration in the world, even had such a thing been possible, would Anna have lifted a finger to mend the breach. She thanked God, only, that the matter had been ended, at however dreadful a cost, before it was irremediable.

Here, then, she stood now, with the western sun in her eyes, watching the brougham's back diminish in the distance, as, with Jim and the collies, so short a while ago, she had seen Nevill's car go down the drive. (Masterson had gone back into the house, and she was alone.)

She appeared to herself to be in a strange kind of lull. Just as the poor soul there in the brougham was driving away to face so gallantly one kind of pain, so she, when she turned again into the house behind her, must face another. There seemed a lot of pain everywhere; and all so purposeless. It seemed a miserable sort of affair. That so much unhappiness could be caused by one person! . . .

Then, as she stared at nothing—for the brougham was gone —she began to realize that her attitude towards pain was not as it used to be — not even as so short a while ago as a few weeks. It was no longer to be feared, as once she had feared it, especially that subtle and exquisite kind that arises from watching that of another. There was not that thrill of terror which she would have felt a while ago, as she contemplated in her imagination what she must now witness in Nevill — that dreadful helpless simplicity as of a child. She had no idea of what would happen next — of how she would find him: he must have slept now for at least three or four hours: obviously he had not slept at all last night. Above all, what would he be a few days hence when the lashes his soul had received had passed from numbness to pain once more? . . .

She turned as a step sounded behind her.

"I beg your pardon, ma'am," said the discreet voice of Charleson, "but Sir Nevill seemed unwell when I took up his hot water for dressing."

(6)

At ten o'clock that night, Nevill turned to her and opened his eyes. Then he sat up, rubbing them.

"Why; that's much better," he said. "Was that ten which struck?"

She had been with him for the last two hours.

She had found him nearly speechless with pain, when she had run up with Charleson. His face was ground down into the pillow; he was still in the suit in which he arrived. He had turned, when she had spoken to him, and said something about "horses galloping"; and she had thought him delirious, until he had said that it was just one of his abominable head- aches. The little village doctor had arrived ten minutes later; and had ordered him to bed.

While Charleson was with him, she and the doctor had talked in the morning room; and she had told him that Sir Nevill had had a very heavy shock, in London — (she did not at present specify more than this) — and had probably not slept at all the night before. The doctor had nodded wisely, and talked about over strained nerves. He had also asked her what the specialist had said a few months before, whom

Nevill, at his advice, had gone up to consult. Anna said that she scarcely knew; that Sir Nevill was very secretive about such matters and hated to have his health spoken of; but that she understood he had given the young man some medicine and told him first to avoid worry, and next to come again. Again the doctor had nodded two or three times, and demanded to see the prescription. Anna fetched this from her own room and showed it him. He had said nothing. Then, when the doctor had seen him again, and departed, she had gone back, and sat with the young man in silence, watching him, with Charleson sitting within call in the bathroom next door. She had given him his medicine once or twice and his soup when it came up; but nothing else had happened. She had heard the tick of the big hall clock behind; and the chimes from the stable. That was all. Nevill kept his face turned from her.

Certainly, he looked more like himself now. His eyes were bright and restless; but the peculiar filmy look they had had this afternoon was gone again.

"Yes; that was ten," she said. "Your headache's gone?"

"Well; very nearly. Oh! Yes. Very nearly indeed — and I can see again all right. That was Mrs. Bessington, wasn't it — with you in the pavilion?"

She did not show her surprise.

"Yes. I sent for her."

"I saw her from the window," said the young man, lying back again on his pillows — "Why, you aren't dressed for dinner, Aunt Anna!"

"I shall have something presently," she said.

"And you've been with me all this time. What a beast I am! . . . Aunt Anna."

"Yes?"

"I don't want to hear a single word of what she said. She's a good woman — but —"

She waited.

"It's finished. I know that. I didn't understand, you see. But—"

Again he hesitated; and again she waited. She must just be perfectly steady: she knew that. What was that which Mr. Morpeth had said about not "softening him"? She must show no emotionalism.

"Well; what I wanted to say was this. Do you think I've been such a — such an offensive brute as all that — as she told me?"

She clenched her teeth once, just to make certain that the muscles of her throat were under control. There seemed a strange contracted kind of pain in them.

"No, my dear; you've not been an offensive brute at all. You've been all that is considerate and good. She doesn't understand; that is all."

"You really think that?"

"I am quite certain of it."

His eyes wandered vaguely round the room. The marks of his suffering were very plain in his face, even under that carefully shaded light.

"Well; I'm glad you think that. I didn't mean to be, anyhow. By the way —"

"Yes?"

"I want to move into the West Bedroom, when it's convenient. I don't mean tonight; but in a day or two."

In spite of her resolution her heart sickened. But she crushed it down. She had conquered herself in that matter. Was she not to allow him to conquer too?

"Very well, my dear. The house is yours, you know."

He smiled; and then grew grave again.

"Oh! No: it is ours: really ours once more. It must remain ours, now."

"My dear; you've talked enough. Do you think you can go to sleep now, if I leave you?"

"Oh! I daresay. Jim all right?"

"Jim's very much all right. He's been out nearly all day."

"That's first-rate. We must bathe together again."

"My dear boy: you must go to sleep. Shall I call Charleson?"

"Yes: you may as well, if you don't mind. . . . Then we'll begin again, and try to do better. Won't we, Aunt Anna?"

This time she could not speak. She stood up, leaned forward, and kissed him gently on his forehead, as her custom was. Certainly he was doing as Mr. Morpeth had thought he would.

"Goodnight, Aunt Anna."

"Goodnight, my boy."

End of Part II

Part III

Chapter I

(1)

A lgy, that's a beastly fluke," remarked Nevill.

"Not at all! I tried for it; what more could I do?"

"Well, that's thirty all — isn't it, marker?"

"Yes, Sir Nevill," said a voice from the little sentry box by the net. They changed over.

It was a high dropping shot off the wall into the *dedans* gallery. If it had not come precisely at that angle, it would have been a very poor "chase"; and Algy's play as a whole did not justify the belief that he could make such a stroke once in twenty times. However, he had certainly done it that time.

Tennis — the genuine game, not the bastard played on a lawn — is perhaps the most bewildering game, to the uninitiated spectator, that has ever been invented. So thought Aunt Anna on this September morning, as she had thought, indeed, very many times before on other mornings. Of nine out of every ten fine strokes, she understood nothing. There were things called "chases," she knew — which had something to do with the ball striking the ground for the second time; one changed over as soon as two had been made; there was a little netted partition called the "winning gallery" low down on one side; mysterious phrases were cried aloud from the sentry box. But she cared nothing for these things; she loved, only, to watch the interplay — the strange mingling of an extraordinarily quick delicacy with an apparently slow deliberation. Above all she loved to watch Nevill when he got excited, on the far side, and sent ball after ball whacking straight at the net behind his opponent's head. She leaned her chin on her hand, and her hand on the rail of the gallery above the *dedans*, and began to watch Nevill receiving services.

On the whole she had been vastly relieved by the passing of the last three months. There had been nothing sensational, no reaction, no moods of despair. The Bessingtons had gone again from the Hartley orbit as emphatically as they had come. Only, Nevill had never referred to them again, or told her one word more than he had told her at the begin-

ning. It was finished, as he had said; and he was beginning
again, as he had promised. The usual notice about "not taking place" had been sent to the papers.

But he was certainly a little quieter and more secretive. He
went out by himself, a good deal, into the woods. (She had
noticed, by the way, that the wooden seat by the marble
monument in the woods had been removed; but she asked no
questions.) He rode with Jim two or three times a week: he
complained no more of his headaches. He had entirely refused, by the way, to go and see the specialist again: but he
had promised definitely to do so if the pain came back. But it
had not come back, it appeared. It seemed as if his last headache had been the end of them; as if the shock, and his heavy
sleep, and his couple of hours of real physical agony had, so
to speak, swept his head clean and purged his humors.

Meanwhile he would have no guests; or at least very few. It
was understood that Aunt Anna might have down a female
friend from time to time; that Mr. Morpeth dined with them
occasionally; that a man, now and again, like Algy, would
come for a weekend. But Nevill refused to go away anywhere
from Hartley; he had refused too, so far as she knew, every
invitation to the north for the shooting; he lived a simple,
ordinary kind of life, and appeared content with it.

It had all puzzled her a little: but she had come to see that
it was probably the best thing he could do; that he was assimilating a new experience; and that such an assimilation
would take time. Her only astonishment was that he did not
seem in the least more religious than he had been before: he
still dutifully heard Mass on Sunday; he abstained on Friday;
he entertained Father Richardson to dinner once a fortnight.
But he showed no sign of looking for any consolation in religion; he was not, in that respect at least, at all the broken-
hearted lover of convention. He had not been to the Sacraments since his return.

(2)

Jim wriggled beside her on the seat.

"That was a good one," he said.

It was a good one. Even she could see that. Nevill, in the
far court, had slashed suddenly and viciously at a fast ball: it
had whacked into the side wall and thence thumped into the
net.

"That's quits!" said Nevill. "That's as good as yours. And I really did try mine!"

Algy made an incoherent retort.

Aunt Anna loved to watch two males such as these, when they got worked up. They were so exceedingly rude and brusque to one another; they jeered so genially. It was so entirely unlike two females. She imagined a few of her women friends playing tennis; at least two or three of them would miss strokes on purpose, in order to please the other; or would give a little caress as they crossed over. They would be so very appreciative of their opponent's efforts, and so distressed at failure. But these two males snapped cheerfully; and one told the other that he was a blinking idiot; or triumphed loudly over the other's discomfiture; and bade him not to spread his great feet all over the balls. Certainly Nevill did not talk like this to anyone except Algy; but to him he was refreshingly frank; and Algy responded gallantly. She really did like Algy.

A resounding whack of a ball on the human frame recalled her from her meditations.

"Sorry, old man," said Algy. "But you shouldn't get in the light."

Nevill turned a venomous face upon his friend; and stopped to rub his thigh; because real tennis balls are hard and solid.

"'Vantage to me," said Algy, determined to miss no point that he could make.

"Who's Lord Maresfield?" asked Jim suddenly. "And why is he coming here?"

She explained that Lord Maresfield was a friend of Cousin Nevill's; and that he was coming because he had been asked. (That was the only way to deal with Jim.)

"How long will he stay?"

"Till Tuesday, I think."

"Oh! Will he ride?"

"Yes; I should think so; but he won't ride with you."

"Oh!" said Jim; and took no further interest.

"Game and set," observed the hidden watcher from the sentry box, dispassionately.

"Well; you've surpassed even yourself in fluking today," said Nevill. "I'll bet you five to one in anything you like that you won't do that again in ten shots."

"That's right, old man. Take it out in temper."

Nevill strolled towards the exit, trailing his heavy racquet. Then he turned to the gallery.

"Come on, Jim, for your lesson; clear out, Algy. . . . Going, Aunt Anna?"

"Yes, my dear. It's just gone twelve. I must go and do my letters."

(3)

Half an hour later Nevill and the boy emerged from the passage that led from the dressing room, into the garden. Algy had disappeared ten minutes before.

"And now shall we go and quest for the Holy Grail again?" asked indefatigable Jim. "There's an hour before lunch."

Nevill looked at him.

"By George, we will," he said. "We haven't done that for — for ages. But we won't mount till we get to the garden gate."

"Will that do?"

"Certainly. I'm not a horse till then. I'm . . . I'm Sir Gawain; and you're Sir Galahad."

"But Sir Gawain didn't find it. He . . . he stayed at a pavilion with — with merry maidens," explained Jim, still a little breathless from tennis, yet quoting gallantly.

Nevill winced, ever so slightly.

"Yes; but you see I shan't be Sir Gawain when I get to the garden gate. I shall be your horse then. And if Sir Galahad found the Grail, I suppose his horse did too."

"But perhaps his horse couldn't see it."

"That's true. . . . Well, this one must, anyhow."

By a kind of fatal instinct, Sir Galahad insisted on going to the monument. The horse made inviting suggestions that a small black pond with mud promontories running into it, all under the beech trees, was a far more likely spot for the attaining of the Vision; but his rider would not hear of it.

"No. The monument was where you talked about it last time. I want the monument, please."

Obviously Sir Galahad entertained views of sitting down on the seat when he got there; for he uttered a cry of dismay when he arrived.

"But where's the seat?"

"It's gone," said the horse, which was an answer, but no explanation. "We'll sit down on the ground instead." . . . (He paused.) "Perhaps we shall see better if we're lower down."

So they sat on the dry powdery soil, and leaned their backs against the marble.

It was a clear September day. The world had had its rain in August as usual; and, once more, as usual, September had brought a mellowed summer back again. The high beech-roof hung motionless to right and left, still green, yet with that tinge that heralds dissolution; as clear yet as indescribable as the purple flush that, on the bare branches of March, promises the renewal of spring. So too with the vista that opened down the valley. At first sight it might have been July; yet, as one looked, it was certain that there was no further reserve of strength. The last word of life had been said; and the end must begin. The trees stood, patient and full-blown, waiting for their sleep once more. The picture was painted, down to the last stroke. Let it be looked at then, in silence, before it is carried away.

"Do you see it anywhere?" asked Jim.

"Oh! — the Grail —" said Nevill, who was meditating about something entirely different. "I think so. Don't you remember that we agreed last time that it's really here all the while?"

"No; I don't," said Jim frankly.

Sentimentality obviously would not do with this child. Nevill braced himself up a little. Besides he really wanted to know what he himself did think.

"Well; I believe it is here, you know. But don't you remember my saying that the thing that the Grail means is here all the time? It's — it's the whole thing, don't you know?"

(He felt he was doing it very feebly: but he really did not quite know what he thought.)

Jim looked at him, with an air of disappointment.

"I don't understand a word you're saying, Cousin Nevill."

"Well; to be honest — I don't understand myself."

Jim sniffed a little. This was really rather tiresome.

"Shall we go on a little?"

"No," said Nevill. "Let's sit here without speaking one word for five minutes, and look hard. Then, if we don't see anything, we'll go on and look somewhere else."

"Very well," said Jim resignedly. (This was a stupid kind of game — almost as stupid as the blind-man game they had played once after bathing.)

It was beginning to appear to Nevill that he was being driven from stronghold to stronghold. About five years ago,

during his last year at Stonyhurst, he had really been rather
religious. . . . He had even consulted his confessor as to
whether it were not just conceivable that he might have a
vocation to the Society of Jesus; and had been considerably
taken aback by that priest's emphatic opinion that he had
nothing of the kind; and that his obvious duty was to live in
the world, to marry, and to establish a Catholic family as
speedily as possible.

From that day his lukewarmness had begun. God did not
want him in any peculiar or intimate manner. Very well
then. This mood had grown swiftly; and, by the time that he
went to Rome, he had begun to rest his center of gravity on
human persons. He still held to his religion in the manner
that has been described; but it appeared to him not interesting.

Then, as if to corroborate his mood, had come Enid; and in
her, he believed, he had found precisely that which he
needed — someone sufficiently like himself to be loved, and
sufficiently sublime to be adored. Well, then, just as everything seemed settling down into perfect adjustment, there
had come an earthquake, and his life, he thought, had tumbled to pieces. He had picked up the bits, so soon as he could
do anything at all, and regarded them carefully. It was hopeless. . . .

Very well then. God had repudiated him — in the only way
in which he had seriously thought of serving Him; and now
Humanity had repudiated him — in the only way in which
he seriously thought he could serve Humanity. Of course in
both realms he still did his conventional duties: he heard
Mass on Sundays, and said his prayers; he was very fond of
Aunt Anna, took pleasure in pleasing Jim, and did his duty
to his tenants. But where was his center of gravity to rest?
He had played tennis; he had walked or ridden in the woods;
he had looked after his estate — all to mark time.

And it was here, sitting for five minutes in silence with
Jim, that he thought he began to see light — to see the Grail;
or if not the Grail, at any rate his Grail. God would not do;
man would not do — not, that is to say, as Objects of Passion.
What would do? Was it conceivable that Nature would do;
and that he would find in it, as poets find, that there is a real
Spirit that can be loved?

He regarded the landscape again, as if he scanned the face of a person.

Surely there must be some Unity in this perfection! Above him towered the beeches, like a dim temple roof; here was the clean floor of earth; there was the wide window that looked across the world. And here — here, above all, was the worshiper: here he himself sat, sound again, so far as he knew, in bodily health; alert with vigor. Why had his health come back so radiantly, if not for this? . . . Jim had said that God was the proper Person who made one happy: he himself, in this very place, had thought it to be Enid. Both alike had sought to enshrine a foreign deity. What if there were a deity here all the while, in a house not made with hands — sweet and virile Spirit that breathed now in the scent of the bracken, that whispered in the rustle of the undergrowth; that pulsated in his own strong limbs and heart? Might he not try here, at least? — plunge himself in this heavenly spirit of earth; and find in it his rest? Besides, there really seemed nothing else.

"Come on, Jim. Time's up."

"Do you see it?" asked Jim rather wearily.

"I think so; but I'm not sure."

"Well; I don't," said Jim.

(4)

The smoking room at Hartley is on the left of the staircase that leads down into the garden. It is a charming room. From the walls look down monstrous heads of stag and pig and buffalo. There is an abundance of little colored prints; there are three large sensible tables, and six large sensible chairs. There is a wide mantelpiece of oak on which stand cigar boxes, matchboxes, pinewood spills in bronze jars; a honey-colored bowl of tobacco; and mounted hoofs of horses. There is a clock set always five minutes in advance of the house time. There is a thick carpet, not too new, and a rug of Siberian wolf before the fireplace; and there is just the gentlest possible aroma in the air, that comforts the carnal senses with an infinite and suggestive delicacy. There are also bookshelves, low enough to be within reach of a man sitting back in a deep chair, filled with the proper kind of volumes, and a complete leather-bound set of Punch.

Here, then, the three men sat, after Aunt Anna had gone to bed. The new guest had been exceedingly easy and pleasant, and it was plain that he was not going to be an interruption. He had professed himself entirely pleased to dawdle; also he would be delighted to shoot on Monday if he were wanted; in fact, he had brought his gun as he had been told. On the other hand, nothing could be more to his taste than to sit about generally. These things he had conveyed in that staccato fashion of his that was more convincing than the most luxuriant eloquence.

So easy, then, was the atmosphere, that Nevill, strolling out into the hall, through the door set open to make a good draft with the windows, and thence strolling on to the top of the steps to look at the moon, finally went down the steps without hesitation to take a turn in the garden. The voices of Maresfield and Algy went on intermittently above.

When the faint crunch of the host's footsteps had died away, Algy glanced at the other man. "Suppose you heard all about his trouble, eh?"

"Saw it in the papers, eh? Jilted him, didn't she? What?"

Algy nodded.

"He's a good chap, Fanning, you know. I was at school with him."

"One of the Papist lot too, eh?"

"That's it. You knew the girl rather well, didn't you?"

"Met her once or twice. Not my sort, you know. I could have told him if he'd asked me. Eh?"

"Why did she chuck him? D'you know?"

"Just a fad. Full of em. Art and literature and that. Knows nothing about it, either. Comes and jaws in my little painting room. Too damned positive about everything. Not my sort. Eh? Had enough of her."

"Oh! That's it, is it?" said Algy, looking interested. "Couldn't make it out, you know. Good chap; nice place; everything, you'd have thought."

Then Lord Maresfield summed up his views of Miss Bessington quite as adequately as her own mother; in about one thousandth part of her words.

"Selfish sort, eh? Thinks about nothing but her own damned self. Gives her mother hell, I should think. What? Not my sort. Like the old lady though. Though she does talk above a bit. Eh?"

He blew meditatively down his pipe; and reached for the tobacco jar.

"Can't make out Fanning, though," resumed Algy. "Hasn't said a word about her, good or bad. And he's not the sort of man you'd begin it with."

"'Mind your own business? Damn your eyes?' Eh?"

"Exactly," said Algy.

Meanwhile the great yellow moon rode high above the cedars; and the air was full of those late summer smells in which only the most pessimistic of persons can detect the real autumn flavor. The garden was one scheme of grays and blacks — gray on the lawns; silver gray on the paths and stonework; black beneath the cedars and where the shrubberies stood with their backs to the great shining shield in the heavens.

He turned by the path to the tennis court and came round, along the very same way by which he had led Enid when the lawns were alight with the sunlit rainfall, to the low wall beyond which ran the swift river. He stopped at the top of the water steps and looked down at the shadowed molten stream that talked to itself as it ran, down past the pavilion, past the bridge where he and Jim had missed the big trout, down to the bathing pool where he and Jim had bathed. As he stood, a couple of thunderous plunges out of sight announced that the trout were excited — perhaps joyful in the moonlight; perhaps, less ethereally, greedy of their meal.

He scarcely knew, when first he came down the steps, why he had come. He was beginning to know now; for there ran through his veins a faint tingle of pleasure at the touch of this naked night of moon and water, at the sweet and chilly breath of hers that he breathed. As he glanced back at the house, hearing some word come through the lighted windows of the smoking room, he thought how stuffy and confined all that seemed. There they were, those two pleasant fellows, jawing away at one another, and breathing hot tobacco smoke — (he threw away the end of his own cigarette into the stream, as he thought of it, and listened for the delicious spit with which water welcomes and quenches fire) — breathing hot tobacco smoke, and refreshing themselves with just one more whisky and soda. It all seemed rather stuffy and rather disconnected. The real thing seemed out here.

He stretched himself and breathed another deep lung-filling draft of night air. . . . How perfectly glorious a swim would be! Why should he not go down there beyond the bridge? . . . and let his whole body drink its fill? . . . It would not take ten minutes. No; he wouldn't want a towel.

(5)

The two men looked up as he came in, a quarter of an hour later.

"Lord! Your hair's all wet," said Algy. "Is it raining?"

"Had a bathe," said Nevill — "while you chaps have been frowsting in here!"

Algy regarded him with concern.

"Bathe?"

Nevill sat down: he desired to say no more. But Algy would not let him alone.

"What did you want to do that for?" he asked.

Nevill felt a little surge of impatience. He had been thinking just now how apart from him these men in the smoking room really were.

"Came into my head," he said shortly. Algy lit a last cigarette.

The lights in the hall were out, all but one high up in the roof, as they went upstairs; and the great dim spaces looked mysterious and cool. Yet even there he felt pressed upon and confined. It was the night outside that seemed to him the reality.

As he came back from seeing that Maresfield was all right in his room, again he paused outside the door of the west room that was now his own. Yes; that was the great hearthrug below, with the chairs grouped confidentially in a big half-circle, where he had talked with Enid. It looked dark and deserted now in the half-light. Well; he had done with all that kind of thing now. With the vivid memory of the night outside, and the caress of the breeze and the water, human relationships appeared feverish and distracting. He seemed apart even from the two men to whom he had just bidden goodnight. He felt at once lonely and exhilarated.

When he got into his room and shut the door, the first thing he did was to set back the loosely closed shutters, and to raise the sash of both the windows still higher. Then, drawn again by the night, he rested there, his arms on the sill, staring out into the dark.

This was the more somber side of the house. A great wide space lay open before him, cut in the foreground by the jutting porch, closed to right and left by the set shrubberies; on the right, over the low wall, trooped the black cypresses of the churchyard. But the lawns, cut by the drive that ran straight westwards, lay in the full moonlight, gray and dew-soaked. . . .

To the eyes of the body it was an empty and rather desolate space; but, to his perceptions, all awakened by the touch of the water in which he had swum just now, fructified by his meditations beside the monument — those meditations in which, it had seemed to him, he had begun to discover that for which his heart craved — it seemed rather a stage all alert for sensation. It satisfied his desire for room and serenity; it met his instincts to push away human beings and clear a space in which his spirit might expand. . . . The thought of people in the house; of his two guests whom he must entertain tomorrow; of Aunt Anna and Jim; of all those servants, so necessary, apparently, if one was to live as was expected of one — all this seemed to him rather oppressive and interrupting. It was something, at any rate, that they were all shut up for the night, while he leaned here and drank in the night air.

There, then, as he leaned on the windowsill, life seemed to be smoothing itself out from its creases and complications. He was as one who, after initiation, has bathed in lustral water, and become illuminated by the god.

He undressed, got between the sheets at last, and lay there with his head on the high pillow looking out dreamily through the wide-flung window at the pale moonlit sky and the low far-away horizon. Long ago he had got over the slight discomfort which the associations of this room had at first given him. His first night or two here, with the four chintz-hung posts about him between which his father had died; the sight, beyond the foot of the bed, of the dressing table and the engraved portrait between the windows, on which those dying eyes had last rested, the solemn shining dark furniture that had witnessed that death — those things, at first, had been to him the occasion of a little superstitious uneasiness: it was, in fact, to overcome that uneasiness that he had insisted on sleeping here.

But it was all gone now.

His body glowed with the reaction from the water; his mind with its memory. How delicious had been that plunge into the mystery of its troubled moonlit surface! As he rose to the surface, he had seen the vapor wraiths go floating by; had seen, as from a new point of view, the black shrubberies on the one side, and the post and rails on the other, whence the bullocks had watched himself and Jim only three or four months ago. How marvelously different the world had been then! It had been morning then, with colors and lights; it was the morning on which he had, later, gone up to London to meet Enid. It was night now, and all colors were gone — sucked back into the infinitely simple grays and blacks from which all colors come and to which they must return. His mind had been active and imaginative then; it was passive and receptive now.

He asked himself whether he were happy; and he did not know the answer. But he was sure that there were possibilities of peace in his new point of view that had been absent from the old. Five years ago he would have looked for God, in such a mood — in those days when he had madly thought to be a Jesuit — and would have tried to center those sensations and experiences round the Divine Personality. Five months ago he would have thought of Enid; would have imagined her as his center, as indeed he had imagined her — the secret and meaning of all that he saw and felt. And now, again, as in the woods this afternoon, it appeared to him that he had sought to enshrine a foreign deity in a temple that was not his — in a temple that had been built by other hands and already held its creator.

So he lay and dreamed; and the glow of his body passed into the sheets and reacted again, soothing and quieting him; and his eyes drooped and opened again upon the solemn oblong of sky and moonlight. He felt superbly well and vigorous. . . .

When he slept at last, the night breeze had risen a little; the blind flapped softly; even the chintz curtains round that bed of death creaked and rustled; and a tassel somewhere tapped and tapped again; as if the room itself lived and was stirring itself to action.

Chapter II

(1)

There was no doubt about it, thought Aunt Anna, as, with Jim, she set out to join the shooters at lunch on the day before Lord Maresfield was to leave — there was no doubt but that the mysterious movement of autumn had begun, the third of the year's great symphonies. Three days ago summer had ended on a full close — the day that Lord Maresfield had come: the woods had stood erect and confident for the last time; it was the day too (she learned next day) on which Nevill had actually bathed, all alone, after dinner. They had talked about it at breakfast next morning. The wind had got up that night; the clouds had come; and when she had gone out to give the collies, and Jim, a run, after the early Mass, the first faint agitation of the new season was in the air.

Today the last shred of doubt was gone — the motif, so to say, was announced; for there was come, over the face of the woods, a definite tint that had not been there last week. The key had changed into the minor. The trees were still opulent and full-leaved, the grass still heavy and luxuriant; the warmth was practically as great as three days ago. Yet the thing was there.

Jim was a shade silent this morning. He had secretly hoped that he would be allowed to start with the shooters after breakfast; and had appeared, gaitered and capped, with an assured air, so soon as the keeper came up with the beaters. Lessons, he had seemed to think, would melt as inevitably as morning mists before the sun, in the glory of the first day after the partridges. He had been undeceived — in spite of Nevill's intercession — and sent back to take off his gaiters. Anna had been a little astonished that Nevill had pleaded for him, out loud, in his presence. But she could not relent. Jim's lessons were beginning to rest rather heavily on her conscience — and more than ever now that Downside was postponed till further notice.

"You must keep close," she said, as they came out through the belt of trees towards the approach to the valley where lunch was to be. "You'll remember, won't you?"

"Oh — I know all about that," said Jim indifferently, trudg-
ing along with his hands in his pockets and an ash plant under his arm in imitation of Mr. Dane, the keeper. He presented a very sturdy and resolute little figure.

It was a very charming view on which presently they
looked, as they came out from the trees and halted. Beneath,
a sharp little valley, enclosed in woods, sloped away into a
broad flatness at the lower end on the right, and rose to a
point at the upper end on the left. It was usually the last
drive before lunch, as the keeper's cottage stood conveniently
at the edge of the woods on the extreme point of the valley;
and the birds had a way of taking refuge here after the
drives in the open country to the right.

From where the two stood the whole strategy was plainly
visible, for they were at a point about halfway up the valley;
they could see the line of beaters moving up from the right,
and the three guns in ambush behind little clumps of may-
trees that dotted the pasture on the left. It was possible even
to make out which was which. Nevill was nearest to them, in
his gray suit, perhaps a hundred yards away, and fifty feet
below their level: Lord Maresfield next, in the middle, in rus-
set-brown, and Algy Lennox beyond, in a delicate green.
They had arrived, too, exactly in time, and would see the
drive from beginning to end. The sun, come out for a little
space from the clouds, stood high behind them, and the valley was full of light — from the green pasture where the guns
stood, across the mustard patch halfway, down to the newly-
cut stubbles and pasture, again, up which the beaters came.

As soon as the birds began to arrive, it was evident that
Nevill was in form. (He had seemed very cheerful at breakfast, and had talked almost in his old way.) For the first
three coveys came straight over him; and each time it was
possible to make out they left two of their number behind.

Each time there was a sudden halt, and a cry from the line
of tiny, doll-like figures that labored slowly upwards; something white waved vigorously; and then Anna could make out
a moving pattern of dots, scarcely changing their relative
positions as they came, slide across the background, black-
ish-looking against the yellow of the mustard, brown again
against the green meadowland. Then, as they approached,
came the shots, in each case from Nevill, one as they approached, and one as they passed on; and the covey was

smaller by two. Jim stood dead silent, trembling a little, drawing his breath sharply as the shots were fired.

"O-o-o-h!" said Jim, after the sixth.

The last covey of that drive, numbering at least a dozen birds, broke from the nearer edge of the mustard as the beaters entered at the other, and dispersed wildly; and, simultaneously a hare burst out of the ground. There were shots in all directions; at least three from Algy and two from Lord Maresfield, as well as another from Nevill. Then the two spectators came out from the edge of the wood to make their way downwards. Anna was glad that Nevill had had so much shooting; and that he had acquitted himself so well. (She often found herself watching him during these days.)

(2)

He was in the highest spirits at lunch; and, flushed with exercise, looked as well as he had ever looked in his life. He came round the corner briskly, from laying aside his gun in an outhouse, into the low wide living room where lunch was laid.

"Algy; you bungled that last drive disgracefully. Where's my hare that I wanted to eat?"

"Your hare's sitting in a ditch. At least, I saw him go in; and he never came out again."

"Did you fire twice at him? I couldn't see."

"Please, the sun was in my eyes, and I couldn't see. And the ball shot; and it was a fast wicket; and I'm not feeling very well."

"Well, I am, thank God! Oh! Aunt Anna. Mutton pies! And don't do it again, Algy. Beer, anybody?"

It was really very picturesque, here in this raftered room. Through the lattices the sun streamed in upon the white-laid table, the aluminum boxes of food, the glass and silver, the great glass jug of beer. The walls were brightly papered between the upright beams; a rack of old guns hung over the high fireplace. A kettle sang on the hob. The men, too, looked healthy and exercised; Jim looked charmingly childish. She herself, if she had known it, with her gray hair and young face, was the most picturesque of them all.

A flush of pleasure swept over Aunt Anna. It was all so very healthy and reassuring. It was only at moments like this, yet at none before so strongly, that she realized that vague burden of anxiety that she always carried at other times. Yet she scarcely knew about what she was anxious. There was no question that he had borne his trouble finely; and that it had left none but the most superficial marks. It was obvious, she thought, that he was better than he had been even six months ago. He had not even an hour's head-ache, so far as she knew, since the night on which she had sat by him. Then what in the world did she feel anxious about? The shadow of which Mr. Morpeth had spoken had surely done its worst. . . .

"Jim," said Nevill, "what have you done with your stick?"

"I have left it outside, Cousin Nevill," explained Jim. "Like your gun." (He bit into a mutton pie.)

"Oh! I see. Did you take the cartridges out?"

Jim disposed of his mouthful solemnly, regarding Nevill as he did so.

"I always take out the cartridges before putting it down anywhere," he said at last.

"That's right, old man."

"There are twenty-three partridges — I mean twelve — I mean eleven and a half braces," observed Jim presently.

"Well done, my boy," said Aunt Anna. Jim's arithmetic was a weak point.

He turned a cold eye on her.

"And three hares. And a bird I don't know the name of."

"That must be one of Algy's," said Nevill.

"It's a black-looking bird with blue —"

"Jay. One of mine. What?" said Maresfield. "Got him in the woods."

"Why did you shoot him?" inquired Jim, anxious for infor-mation.

"Steal eggs, old man. No end. Eh?"

"Why do you always say Eh?"

"That'll do, Jim," remarked his mother.

"Eh — What?" began Maresfield. And then he laughed loudly.

She liked Lord Maresfield thoroughly. But he was a very odd mixture. Yesterday he had sat out all the afternoon mak-ing a perfectly charming sketch of the pavilion on a little wooden panel of which he carried two or three always in his flat traveling paint box. (When it was quite finished, Jim had come out, and inquired what it was meant to be.) And now today he looked a competent sportsman. She perceived that he was distinguished from his type by a streak of art that he had never learned to be ashamed of. He was very pleasant always to Jim, too; and never exchanged glances with grownup people while he answered him. She liked that. She often found Jim a good touchstone. She made up her mind that she would have a little talk to Lord Maresfield before he left.

"We'll do the down last thing," said Nevill presently, feeling for his pipe. "In honor of you, Maresfield."

The other inquired what this might be. Nevill explained that the down was a steep grass slope with roots at the bottom. Driven properly, it furnished the best beat of the day. Driven improperly, nothing happened whatever. They would drive it properly this afternoon; the guns would be stationed in a kind of dry ditch, with a view against the sky.

"They come as thick as peas," he said, "in a good year. We ought to do pretty well this afternoon. Birds aren't too shy, yet."

(3)

It was within an hour of sunset when they began to take their places for the last drive; and the sky was beginning, ever so delicately, to show a premonitory flush.

The afternoon had been delightful. She had never meant to keep Jim out so long; but she simply had not the heart to take him away: she contented herself by a word to him that he must do his lessons better than ever tomorrow morning. Jim had regarded her with a detached kind of air. He was in another world altogether by now.

He was very conscientious, too, in his attentions to the sportsmen; and attached himself by turns to each. She had asked each, privately, to send him back to her if he was troublesome; but his reports were excellent. He remained quite motionless; he spoke in a whisper and not too much; and he collected all the empty cartridge cases at the end of every drive. The pockets of his jacket bulged with them by now. His face wore a rapt expression.

They had really done very well; and the shooting had been excellent. She herself had stood now with one and now with another; and there was not much to choose between them. Above forty brace of birds, besides extras, were laid out at the end of the last drive, before the sportsmen descended to the dry ditch in the hollow.

It was her turn with Lord Maresfield now; and she led him, since he did not know the ground, with infinite precautions, lest the birds should be alarmed, under cover of a rise in the ground, out to the extreme left. Algy would be next, in the middle; and Nevill on the right. The three guns were quite enough: the slopes rose on either side up to copses, sufficiently high to steer all but the most obstinate birds over the hedge of death. When they reached the position, she sat down on a convenient bank.

"There's plenty of time," she said in a low voice. "The beaters will be ten minutes yet. They've got to go right round behind, you know."

He sat down beside her, and took out his pipe and pouch.

"He's on the spot, eh?" he said, without even mentioning Nevill's name. "Told me so, anyhow. Looks like it. What?"

(Nevill had indeed distinguished himself by a very swift right and left at the end of the last drive.)

"Lord Maresfield," she said. "I want to ask you something. Do you know my nephew well?"

"Eh? Well, pretty well, I suppose. Good chap. (Very impertinent of me to say that!) Like him immensely."

"I thought you did. And you've heard about his trouble, I suppose?"

He nodded, without speaking. And, somehow, she liked that, too. Above all, she liked him for not saying that everyone had heard of it.

"I think it was with Miss Bessington that you first met him?"

"That's it," he said. "Academy, wasn't it?"

"I want to know what you think, if you don't mind telling me. I mean whether you think it is a misfortune, or not."

He puffed at his pipe an instant.

"I think it's a very good thing," he said suddenly. "Not suitable, you know. Eh?"

Her heart warmed to hear him.

"Well; I thought so too, you know. And you don't think it's done my nephew any harm? He's not different at all, is he, from when you first got to know him?"

Again he puffed for a moment before answering.

"Daresay it's all my fancy," he said. "But —"

"Yes?"

"Seems a bit more apart, don't you know. More silent, somehow. Eh? At least, I thought so till today. Natural enough, though. But I didn't see very much of him in town, you know."

"And today you think he's better again?" she pursued, disregarding his explanations. Somehow she felt a confidence in this man's opinion, and wanted to know what he thought.

"Why, yes. Talked first-rate at lunch. Eh?"

She sat, silent and relieved. It was not just her fancy, then, that his spirits were beginning to come back. She felt very grateful to Lord Maresfield for agreeing with her. She said so, presently, in a word or two.

Meanwhile, in his corner in the dry ditch over on the left, Nevill, if only they had known it, could emphatically have corroborated the views of his friends. It seemed to him as if this new spirit that had come to him and whispered to him so coherently only three days ago, had more than kept its promises. The air and exercise of this long day, the genial warmth and sunlight, his own success, the pleasantness of the party — all these things combined to make him very content. Over him rose the faintly flushing sky, clear now of clouds; the grasses that fringed his horizon in front, the tops of the copses which he could see on either side against the sky; the general sense of wellbeing — all these appeared, as nature will appear to sympathetic humanity — to adapt themselves exquisitely to his own individual point of view. Again, as he mused over a cigarette, waiting for the beaters, he told himself that he had found his balance once more; that his instincts, the other night, had been right; that a man who is sane and healthy is best at home with his own Great Mother: that God and Man may be very well for the specialists in emotion; but that those who do not aim at being emotional had better leave such things alone — beyond, so to speak, a bowing acquaintance with them. After all, what more could he want? God was too remote; men and women were too near. A man was his own best friend, or at least could make himself so. What more could he want? He had his health again; his position; his wealth; the companionship of Anna and Jim and congenial friends — an excellent thing, this companionship, so long as it was not emotional. And he had found all this out for himself — at a certain considerable price, it is true; but the price was now paid, and the article

was his. Never again would he trust emotion; it had led him
wildly wrong, at least twice. He had thought both God and
Enid other than what they were. Very well; he was initiated
now; he had found his grail: he would drink it sedately and
steadily as it deserved. And if a little cynicism was mixed in
that cup; if, for the future, he found himself just despising
women a little, and finding men clumsy; if he grew a little
materialistic in his philosophy and took more pains about the
perfection of his bodily, rather than of his spiritual health —
well, the sweetest cup was none the worse for a little sour
spicing. . . .

"I think they might be coming soon," said Anna in a low
voice. "Shall I be all right here?"

"That's all right," said the man shortly. He beat out his
pipe softly: opened and snapped to again the breech of his
gun, and slipped to his feet.

The sky had perceptibly deepened in color during the last
ten minutes, revealing what the eye had scarcely taken in
before — a multitude of tiny, fleece-like clouds, ranged, it
seemed, in a great curved vault down towards the west. The
sun was behind the hill on their right; and the slope up
which the position looked was in shadow.

But the ditch was so deep in which Anna sat and her companion stood, that nothing but sky was to be seen over the
brow by which the birds would come; and so wide that it
would be possible to loose the first barrel as they topped the
horizon: the second barrel must be fired behind the line.

As Anna looked along the line westwards, first two caps
were very visible, one of the greenish tint that went with
Algy's clothes, the other of the brown which Jim had been
allowed to choose for himself. Those caps were visible, close
to one another, as if their owners were discussing some high
matter together. (It was beyond all reasonable doubt, all
things considered, that Jim was being allowed to handle his
friend's empty gun.) The rest of them was hidden by a break
in the bank on which they sat. Quite clear and detached,
however, forty yards further on, was the gray figure of
Nevill, seen against a bramble patch on the slope of the hill.
It was the sudden appearance of this figure, gun in hand,
that had caused her to speak. Nevill was obviously alert:
perhaps he had caught some sound or sight coming down the
ground.

The world, however, seemed perfectly quiet, rapt in a sunset calm. (It really seemed a little hard, thought Anna, on the birds — that they should be routed by stick wielding apparitions and sent skimming once more down the long slopes, out of their fragrant coverts, just when a Sabbath peace descended on the earth.) The sky looked like a vault whose lines were strewn by those mackerel clouds. Behind the line, as she turned her head to look, lay the meadows and the beginning of the park proper, clear of the shadow of the hill, bright in the last hour of sunshine.

Two sudden explosions to the right brought her back from beauty to sport. Algy had fired twice; and when she looked, the two caps had parted company. The green, supported by Algy's head and shoulders, stood up clear the brown remained motionless in its original position. As she looked, Nevill too raised his gun and fired once.

Then began for her that confused state of the spectator who watches shooting from the side of a shooter; for the birds began to come immediately overhead. She crouched lower on her seat, so that she should not distract her companion, hearing now and again, as from another world, the reports from further up the line; but with her nerves braced to bear the shots fired in her immediate neighborhood. Covey after covey came over: Nevill indeed had been right in saying that they ought to do pretty well at "the down" this afternoon. They whirred up, suddenly visible, against the sky, twenty yards ahead, to be met by one barrel, and speeded by another, as they sank behind. It was impossible for her to know, except very rarely, how her companion fared. Two or three times only did she catch sight of that strange transformation that takes place when one bird in a covey passes in an instant from the high intensity of life to the passivity of death; and only once did she hear the thud of its body over the bank behind. He seemed satisfied, however; he fired, wheeled, fired again, and reloaded, swiftly and mechanically. Now there came a pause, when he waited; now he tore at his pocket to snatch out another cartridge or two.

It was not till a final pause came, at the end of which he drooped his gun, and relaxed his tense attitude, that she looked again down the line. And there, to her astonishment, Nevill was sitting on the bank, smoking a cigarette, with no glimpse of a gun visible. As she stared, Mr. Dane's ruddy face appeared over the top of the bank.

"Pretty good lot of birds, my lord!" he said. "Hope your lordship had plenty of shooting?"

"First-rate, eh?"

She waited a minute or two, as Lord Maresfield stood on the top of the bank, directing Mr. Dane and one of the beaters as to the line in which his birds had mostly fallen; and for that minute thought no more of Nevill. But when she turned again, her surprise came back.

The gray figure was still seated on the bank; but there was a little group of three about him. Algy and Jim formed two-thirds; and the other was one of the elder beaters. They appeared to be regarding the sitting figure.

She said nothing to her companion; but began to walk towards them. She was not yet exactly uneasy; but she wondered why Nevill was sitting down; why Algy and Jim and the beater were looking at him. That was all.

"Absolutely no good, my dear man," she heard him say as she came near. "Couldn't see a thing."

He looked unusually flushed and upset, she thought; he was drawing almost savagely upon his cigarette.

"What's the matter?" she asked.

"Couldn't see. Chucked it," he said.

She ran her eyes over him, vaguely uneasy.

"How do you mean, my dear?"

And then she saw that the hand that held the cigarette was shaking violently. . . . Surely he couldn't be as angry as all that?

"I couldn't see," he repeated steadily.

Jim was staring on him with solemn eyes of reproachful wonder.

"You hardly fired at all," he said.

"No, old man."

"Are you going blind, Cousin Nevill? Like the game?" She saw a very strange expression pass over his face. At first she thought it to be anger. Then she perceived that, at any rate, it was not all anger.

"Game?" she asked.

Nevill got up. His whole bearing seemed odd and unusual.

"Yes. Someone's having a game with me," he said softly. And his voice shook.

(4)

"Just stay up here," she said, commanding her voice as well as she could. "I'll send tea up to you. The doctor will be here in half an hour. I'll send at once."

The walk back had been very strange and disquieting. She told herself a dozen times that it was liver, that it was the sun in his eyes earlier in the afternoon. But he seemed to follow her very closely along the wood-paths; and he stumbled half a dozen times: then, as she came through the garden gate, she suddenly felt his hand on her arm. (The other two had walked on ahead, as if unconscious that anything was wrong. Yet she knew that it had been deliberate.)

"It's no good," said a voice in her ear, which she would scarcely have recognized. "You must give me your arm, Aunt Anna."

It was not until she had got him upstairs that she attempted to face the thing out. She planted him in a chair where the light would fall on his face; and sat down.

"Now then, my dear," she said. "Just tell me what's the matter. What is it like? And when did it begin?"

He was silent a moment. Underneath the wholesome tan on his face she could see his pallor; and there were unusual lines about his eyes and mouth.

"It's perfectly ridiculous," he said; and she could hear that he, too, had to make an effort to speak naturally. . . . "Well; it began just before the birds began to come over, at the last drive. It was only little lines and — and skeins at first. I fired one shot at the first lot. I've had it before, you know, as bad as that — I — I think it must be liver."

"And you never told me!" she said quietly. "Go on, my dear."

"What was the good? I thought it was liver — or — or a hundred things. . . . And it always went away again."

"Go on, my dear."

"Well; after the first shot it suddenly became worse. I rubbed my eyes; and that did no good. Two more lots passed me. I heard them; but I couldn't see more than streaks. Then I sat down."

"Is it worse since then?"

"Yes."

"Oh! My dear; do tell me."

"Well; I could just make you all out. I couldn't see your faces. I had to follow you very close behind. It grew worse. At the garden gate I knew I couldn't go on."

"How bad is it now?"

"Well; I can make out that it's you, by your dress. But everything else is all whirling and spinning."

It was then that she stood up, and said that he must have tea up here; and that she would send for the doctor.

He sat quite still, without protesting. Yet there was no sign in his eyes themselves that anything was wrong. They seemed to her exactly as usual — the dark iris, the clear white below it. Was it, perhaps, what she had thought it? — the glare of the sun, or a disordered digestion?

"You don't feel anything else?" she asked suddenly.

"My head feels a bit heavy. That's gun-headache, I expect."

"Shall I come up and have tea with you?"

"I'd sooner not," he said instantly. "Besides, there are Maresfield and Algy." And, upon the words, the suspicion came, swift as light, that he wished to be alone to — to face the thing he feared. She trod it fiercely down; she must not give way to her tremors. Neither must she encourage him in his own.

"Well; I'll send up Charleson," she said. "I — I wish you were in your old room."

He said nothing. A great tenderness suddenly welled up in her.

"Never mind, old boy: you'll just be sent to bed early and wake all right. Well; I'll send down to the village at once."

She stooped and kissed him lightly on the forehead; and, from the start he gave, she understood how complete was his blindness. But again he said nothing.

Such was her emphasis in the message she gave to Masterson that before tea in the hall was half-over, she heard the wheels of the car draw up outside; and, simultaneously, Masterson came up from the servants' staircase. He, too, must have been looking and listening.

"That'll be the doctor," she said cheerfully to the two men. "That's the worst of living in a hall; either one has to bolt, or one can't escape. I'll see him in the morning room, Masterson."

She was in there when he came through — an incompetent little man who had at least the grace to know his limitations.

There was never any bother about calling in a consultant. He was a small, clean-shaven man with a diffident manner.

"Good evening, Dr. Mackenzie. Yes; it's about Sir Nevill. I thought I'd better see you in here first, and answer any questions I can. He hates being fussed, you know."

"I understand from the servant that it was his eyes —"

"Yes: I expect it's only liver. But one wants to know. It began quite suddenly, out shooting this afternoon. But he's had it before, he tells me. I thought he'd better stay upstairs till you came."

She described very briefly what Nevill had told her.

"And he has no pain in the eyes at all?"

"None. But he has a little headache. That's only natural after shooting, isn't it?"

"Very likely," said the doctor. "Is he quite blind, at present?"

She winced a little.

"Well; he said he could make out my dress, just now. But it was getting rather dark, you know."

He nodded. "I've brought a few things in a bag," he said.

"Perhaps you'd better see him at once," she said, rising. She touched the bell. "I think I'll ask you to go up without me. He hates a fuss, he always says. And — doctor — I'll be here till you come downstairs again. I should like to know at once, what you think. . . . Take Dr. Mackenzie up to Sir Nevill's room, Masterson."

She sat very still again, when the door had closed behind the two men. Outside in the hall she could hear the two guests talking once more, but she was entirely unable to face them. It would be all right, presently, of course. As soon as the doctor had come down and gone again, she would go out and tell them that there was nothing whatever to be anxious about — that Nevill's liver was badly out of order, and that that was the one and only cause of the trouble. Of course that was the truth. Only she thought she would wait till it had been certified to be so.

This was a homely and pleasant room in which she sat. It was here that she had her own writing table, and added up the books and interviewed servants and wrote her letters when it was too wet or cold for the pavilion. An oil painting of Nevill, at the age of five, in frilled knickerbockers, holding a feeble-looking bat, with very much tumbled hair, and the bridge and bathing pool in the background, hung over her table. She had thought, sometimes, of having Jim painted in the same kind of way.

But the room was a little gloomy at this particular hour of the day, as its windows looked very nearly eastwards; and the shadows were gathering steadily and swiftly in the corners. The sun must be set by now, she thought. . . .

She could not sit still very long; for if she did not keep moving or distracting herself, certain other memories came up which she did not, just now, want to think about. For instance — Nevill had had this affection of the eyes before, and had not told her. Would he not have told her if it had been as unimportant as he pretended? There was that sinister little game of Blind Man — of which she had learned the details from Jim as she went to see that he had changed and was having tea, properly, in the upstairs schoolroom. Surely that was a very odd game to play on a summer's morning after bathing! Besides it had bored Jim considerably. But these were not the worst. Back and back to her mind came her memory of Mr. Morpeth's talk in the pavilion — of the "shadow" of which he had spoken, of his severely disturbing certitude that some experience lay before Nevill which the world might call a "curse." She had thought that the remembrance of this talk of his was fading from her mind during these last three months: things had gone so surprisingly well. Yet it came up now, from that strange under-region of human consciousness where nothing is forgotten or even attenuated; it came up, like some sinister person whom one thinks to have left the house, but who has been in hiding all the while — it came up and looked her full in the face, until she turned her back upon it by an effort of will.

She was standing at the darkening window presently, and looking out upon the garden; humming softly to herself, and framing little unspoken sentences for her own reassurance. He would be "better after a night's sleep." Probably "he had better not come down to dinner." She would "order something light to be taken up to his room." What a "bore" it all was, just when there were guests in the house! How nice the two men had been just now at tea — so easy and unanxious!

Outside, the garden grew darker as she looked; for she felt it was more reassuring to look out-of-doors than in. And still there was no step outside, nor hand laid upon the door. How cross poor Nevill would be, with such a long visit from the doctor! He hated being "pulled about."

A thrush skimmed suddenly out upon the lawn from one of the shrubberies, lighted and skipped three or four yards in long springy hops, and paused. Then he bounced again two or three times and vanished. Then, from the shrubbery whence he had emerged, came the sound of a bird's loud scolding — that fierce sharp twittering, in which the note of fear as well as anger is so evident, uttered only when some danger threatens that will not depart. Then out came another bird — perhaps a missal-thrush; she was not sure — flew, lighted, skipped again and disappeared. She watched the shrubbery, wondering what it was that had disturbed its inmates. Then, as she half-expected, the head of the stable cat — a lean and subtle Tom, who disdained her always in the stable yard — appeared cautiously and looked this way and that. Then he, too, came out, and went at a businesslike jog-trot in the direction of the cedars. She rapped sharply on the window; but he never turned his head; he quickened his pace a little, and also disappeared. How maddening it must be, she thought, just when one had settled for the night on a suitable branch, to be hunted out like that, and to see the face of one's supreme enemy peering up from below. But it was better, at any rate, than being caught in one's sleep.

Still darker grew the garden; and still there was no step outside, nor hand laid upon the door.

The colors now were practically gone; there was no more than the dullest glow from the rows of autumn flowers below the terrace; the cedar ferns were gone gray, and the shadows beneath them were as thick as wool. It was like going blind, surely.

Then, from the grand piano in the hall she heard a few chords struck. That must be Algy: he had played a little to them last night. No; that could not be Algy; it sounded too competent. It must be Lord Maresfield. She didn't know that he played at all. But why that melancholy Russian thing, whose composer's name began with *Rach,* and ended in *inoff?* It was like darkness incarnate — darkness lit by fiery wheels — such as a man saw when he was going blind. . . . But perhaps Masterson had turned on the lights in the hall, by now. For no one could have the heart to play such music in the dark.

Then the music ceased again after a bar or two; and one or two desultory chords sounded again; and then came silence. It must be that the doctor was coming downstairs. Should she turn the lights on before he came? She hesitated. No; it was still light enough to see; and she did not want more than was necessary.

And still there was no step outside; nor hand laid upon the door.

When he came in at last, Mrs. Fanning started up from a chair so suddenly as to make him jump.

She said nothing, but waited. It was so dark that he could not see her face.

"Mrs. Fanning?"

"Yes."

"I am afraid Sir Nevill must go up and see a specialist at once. It is some trouble with the optic nerves, I am sorry to say. It is beyond my province. It is probably some pressure upon the nerves from behind. I think a brain-specialist — for instance, Sir Arthur Handsworth — had best be consulted first. I think it was Mr. Matthieson last time he went to. Sir Nevill complains very much of headache. That is what makes me fear that it is the brain, rather than the eyes themselves. . . . Yes; I am afraid it may be serious. I have not told Sir Nevill what I fear."

Chapter III

(1)

"hy have doctors' waiting rooms always got such thick carpets?" asked Nevill genially, so soon as it was plain to him that the manservant was gone, and that there was no one else in the room beside Algy, who had brought him. By this time he could not see at all, beyond just being able to distinguish the difference between light and darkness — although it was now only Friday; and darkness had first fallen as they finished shooting on Tuesday.

It was still all new enough to be interesting, now that he was quite sure that there was no organic injury to his seeing apparatus; and yet it appeared to him that an almost incalculable time had passed. The first night and morning had been the worst. Aunt Anna had come to him, five minutes after the doctor had left; and had told him his verdict. She had done it quite admirably: she had not been in the least dramatic or over-tender; she had simply begun: "My poor dear!" in an extraordinarily natural tone; and had then told him, still genially, that it was entirely his own fault for not having gone again to a man in London; that Dr. Mackenzie had assured her that there was no organic injury to the eyes, but that the headaches were responsible. The headaches, therefore, must be looked to at once; and he must just be content to be in the dark, in every sense of the word, for a few hours. She had, with Dr. Mackenzie's consent, wired for an oculist and proposed to send the car to London, if Nevill approved, the first thing in the morning, to bring the oculist back. Meantime, she proposed to come and dine with him in his room, and show him how not to put his spoon and fork into his nose and ears. The guests must just take care of themselves.

That, then, had been Scene One. The hours that followed had certainly been very oppressive, particularly as his head had ached again, though not as acutely as before. Waking in the morning was rather bad; as, though he could hear the birds under the eaves, he had been able to make out no more than dim oblongs where the windows ought to be, so soon as Charleson, who had slept in the bathroom, pulled back the curtains at his command and assured him that it was half-past seven. Besides, in spite of himself, he had nourished a hope that somehow or other he would be able to see again, just as usual, after a night's rest. He had one or two spurts of impatience at breakfast in bed, when Aunt Anna had looked in an hour ago, especially when he dropped a spoonful of porridge and milk just inside his pajama jacket. It seemed to him that Charleson was really rather clumsy not to have prevented that. His cigarette, too, was disappointing: it tasted precisely like brown paper.

After breakfast, Algy had come up and sat on the bed — which was annoying; and Maresfield had come in later to say goodbye, carrying a cigar: and he particularly disliked the smell of a cigar in his bedroom. He said to Aunt Anna with some bitterness, afterwards, that it reminded him of a Commercial Traveler.

The oculist had arrived about noon; and when Nevill heard the tread of his feet on the threshold and Aunt Anna's genial, "May we come in?" for a moment, the ironical ill-humor with which he had deliberately tried to hide his interior apprehensiveness, had deserted him.

He felt very helpless and rather frightened; because, really a good deal depended on what this new man said. He had gathered that, generally, from Aunt Anna's remarks: and yet he was not sure how she had conveyed it.

There followed a very uncomfortable quarter of an hour. The oculist first asked him a number of questions; and then proceeded, as Nevill would have said, to "pull him about." He had to sit very upright, with pillows packed behind him, and to open his eyes wide. There followed disconcerting flashes of light; the grip of rather cold, dry fingers about his temples; palms of hands laid on his forehead. Aunt Anna was in the room, too, all the while; and he did not like this: it made him feel rather like a child. There then followed some more questions; and then a little silence.

"Aunt Anna."

"Yes, my dear," came her quiet voice, from a position much closer to him than he had expected.

"I want you to go downstairs, please. I'll send Mr. Braughing down as soon as he's done with me."

Then he was perfectly certain that she and the doctor were exchanging glances: and he felt infuriated. Before he could speak again, she had answered him.

"Very well," she said.

He heard the door close.

"Mrs. Fanning's gone?"

"Yes, Sir Nevill," came the steady voice.

"Well. . . . What's the matter with me?" (His lips and throat felt curiously dry.)

"I really can't quite tell yet, Sir Nevill. I can only assure you that there's no organic injury at all."

"That's good news, is it?"

"The very best. I do not mean for a moment that the thing may not be serious. But what I do mean is that there is no injury to the instrument itself. It is perfectly sound —"

"Then what in the world is the matter? Why can't —"

"One moment, Sir Nevill. I say that there is no injury that I can detect. But it appears to me almost certain that there is some pressure upon the optic nerves — the nerves, you know, that connect the eye with the brain. The wire, if I may say so, is clogged in some way; it is not in itself injured; nor is the retina."

"What's the next thing to do, then?" snapped the young man, a little peevishly. It seemed to him that this man was unnecessarily wordy.

"The next thing is to consult a head-specialist. He will be able to give you a first-rate opinion as to the cause of this pressure, and to advise you how it may be removed. What you have told me about your headaches —"

"I see. Then you've done your job?"

"Well; I have detected that there is no job for me to do. Mrs. Fanning tells me that the doctor here has recommended Sir Arthur Handsworth. You could go to no better man. Dr. Mackenzie is downstairs; I will have a word with him again if I may."

It seemed a very long while before Aunt Anna came back; and she did not seem quite so exultant as Nevill had expected. She was quite quiet and controlled; she said that so far the news was good; but scarcely more. She then said that she was sending a note by the car, straight up to Sir Arthur, asking for an appointment.

"I suppose I'd better go at once," remarked Nevill, with a detached manner.

"My dear, of course you must. We'll all go up together."

It was later in the afternoon, after they had received the answer that Sir Arthur Handsworth would be happy to receive them on Friday morning at twelve o'clock, that Nevill announced to Aunt Anna that she was not to accompany him to the surgeon.

"You mustn't think me brutal," he had said: "but I must have it out alone."

"But, my dear, you won't be able to —"

"I've asked Algy to come up with us, and to go with me on Friday morning. You'll be at Elizabeth Street; and when we come back, we'll all have lunch together; and then, if this man has taken away the pressure on the what's-his-name, we all go to the Zoo. That's much better. Please, Aunt Anna! I really mean it."

After an instant's silence, she had said simply that it should be so.

Here then, on Friday morning, at five minutes to twelve, sat Nevill and Algy in two armchairs in the room that had the thick carpet: and Aunt Anna was waiting for them in Elizabeth Street, where they had arrived in time for dinner last night.

(2)

"It's to deaden the shrieks," said Algy, in answer. Nevill laughed, a short bark. "You're a cheering chap," he said.

Algy felt as much bewildered and out of his element as such a man always must feel under such circumstances, and, equally characteristically of his type, he bore himself most suitably. Without actually expressing it to himself, he felt that any change of manner really might alarm his friend; he felt it to be far better, as indeed it was, to behave as usual.

"Now tell me all about the room," said Nevill. "I hear a clock. Is it black marble? It sounds portly, somehow."

"Well, you're wrong. It's Empire, and extremely good. It is also observing that we are five minutes early. I told you so."

"Go on about the room," said Nevill. "Pictures? Engravings?"

"There's a Burne-Jones over the clock. A Johnny in armor with a horse. There are large engravings on the other walls, with very wide borders. The carpet —"

"I bet it's red."

"Well, you'd lose. It's chiefly black and yellow."

"Chairs mahogany?"

"No; walnut. At least, I think so. You're on the wrong tack, old man. It isn't Early Victorian, you know —"

"Go on. What color's the paper?"

"It looks like Spanish leather; but I bet it isn't."

"What's on the table? *Graphic, Times* —"

"Well; the *Tatler's* on top; and I can see a corner of *Country Life.*"

"What's the view out of the window?"

"Well; I can see a terra cotta sort of house, rather rich. It's at the corner of the street. There's a cat on a balcony. Over the other side there's a little green and white shanty. There's a car —"

"That's enough. By the way, what time's lunch?"

"I think Mrs. Fanning said half-past."

"That's all right. We shall be in loads of time. I suppose this chap won't want to do the job bang off. If he does, I think I shall —"

He stopped short, as, to his strained and listening ears, there vibrated a step outside. Then the door opened softly; and a discreet voice spoke.

"Will you come this way, sir?"

When Algy came back to the comfortable room with the black and yellow Turkey carpet, and the *Tatler,* and the Empire clock, two minutes later, he was trembling a little. Yet he had seen nothing that was not pleasant and reassuring.

He had gripped Nevill by the arm as he rose, and led him after the servant. (He could hear him breathing as they went.) They came out into the comfortable little hall, through which they had passed on their first arrival, and turned to the right. A man, in a coat not yet buttoned, was picking up his hat and gloves from the black oak table by the stairs: plainly he had just come out from the specialist's room: he did not look at all alarmed or upset, and eyed the stiffly walking figure of Nevill with interest. They went on through the hall towards a half-opened door, which the servant pushed wider, himself stepping back to let them go in. As they entered, a tallish man with rather kind narrow gray eyes, in frockcoat and gray trousers, clean-shaven except for little gray whiskers by his ears, was standing by a kneehole table from which, plainly, he had just risen.

He bowed a little, as the door closed almost noiselessly behind them.

"Sir Nevill Fanning?"

Nevill put out his hand rather awkwardly: the other made
haste to take it.

Then Algy steered his friend to a deep-padded armchair,
indicated in silence by the surgeon. The surgeon then nodded
at him, again in silence.

"Well, I'll be going, old man," said Algy. "I'll be in the waiting room."

Nevill too nodded, without speaking; and Algy went out
once more.

What in the world, then, was he frightened at? There had
been absolutely nothing in the room in the least suggestive,
to a layman's eyes at any rate, of anything in the least approaching disease or death or pain. There had been a tall
narrow bookshelf in the little room; there had been a deep
carpet, as in here: the fireplace had been just ordinary, with
bright fire irons, and a little fire. There had been just a curtained doorway at the other end of the room that might, con-
ceivably, lead to some other sort of consulting room. The
presence of the inhabitant of that room, too, had been strong
and kindly. Yet Algy was undoubtedly frightened. He supposed that it was because it was his first visit to such a place.

He had never realized till now how very fond he was of his
friend. Up to now, he had taken him for granted, rather, ever
since school days. He went down every now and then to stay
at Hartley. He had been sincerely grieved over Nevill's catastrophe in the summer; but, until now, he had had no idea
that beneath the genial bantering with which he treated
Nevill, there was anything that could be called deep affection. He would have thought, in fact, that such an emotion
would have been rather weak and sentimental. Yet, having
faced that surgeon, side by side with his friend, he was conscious that his own sentiment, at any rate, was not weak. It
was there, anyhow.

So he sat down again, pulled the *Tatler* towards him; and
only just caught himself in time beginning to bite his nails.

The *Tatler* of September the 28th seemed to him a singularly poor number.

On the front page was a large picture of a very stupid-
looking Royalty, of the greatest possible importance, with a

row of five pearls round a well-polished neck. There was not much comfort there: she at any rate had never sat in a surgeon's waiting room waiting for a verdict on somebody else. On the next page, under the heading *In Town and About* were first two pictures of girls' faces framed as if they were miniatures; and inscriptions underneath. He read one carefully through. The lady was Miss Alexandra Bennett; she was the youngest daughter of some old fool, and was going to be married next Tuesday to the Hon. Carvell Compton, of the Grenadiers, in the Guards' Chapel, Wellington Barracks. That wasn't much good. The marriage couldn't come off, anyhow, if on the previous Friday she had had the inside of her head examined by a kind-looking man in a room with a curtained doorway at the back. The third picture on the page represented the departure of the Dowager Queen of Spain's aunt from Victoria Station. Foolish men stood about the carriage, bare-headed, with a crick in their backs.

He began to turn the pages in despair. The letter press was, of course, out of the question; but he stared meditatively at a number of pictures. There was a champion golfer with his legs terribly twisted, and a cigarette in his mouth; apparently, he had just driven a ball. Dim persons in straw hats, looking like dummies, formed the background. There were two white dogs, resembling crumpled wool-mats, with their tongues hanging out; there was an American actor with a very long stick, and very long legs, photographed in company with an American actress whose name Algy remembered as having been connected with a *cause célèbre*. There were four people in a white motorcar, all looking very ugly, because their faces were screwed up against the sunlight, who bore distinguished names. There were some political skits — one representing Mr. Asquith as a scullery-maid washing up a saucepan with a significant word printed upon it; and another, Mr. Redmond crowing like a very small cock, on a very large dunghill, labeled "Coalition." And so on. Finally came some Elliman's advertisements. Algy tossed it from him in despair.

Then he began to walk up and down the room. Fortunately there was a thick carpet. Oh! Yes, the poor old chap had said that — first thing after the man had gone out. What a time they were in there! He looked at the Empire clock; it marked seven minutes past twelve, only.

By twenty-five minutes past twelve Algy took up *Country Life,* convinced that the worst must have happened; though he could form no conjecture at all as to what the worst might be. It struck him as very odd that there was no one else in the waiting room, until he became even further depressed by the guess that perhaps the oculist and the Hartley doctor had written about the case, and informed Sir Arthur that it would be a long business.

He began, gallantly, at *Country Life;* but suddenly laid it down again; because the "corner of the hall in the seat of Silas Mond, Esq., in the county of Westmoreland" reminded him of another "corner of a hall" in the seat of Sir Nevill Fanning, Bart., in the county of Sussex. He felt as if he had been stung in the middle of his mind.

Then he determined to begin a study of the pictures round the room; and began with "the Johnny in armor." It appeared to him unconvincing; and he moved on to the next. This was of a small girl in a large bonnet; and he wondered why on earth such a repellent and simpering face should have been selected by any artist, for immortality.

He was moving on to the next, when his heart leaped and stood still.

There was the vibration of a step outside. Then a hand was laid on the handle of the door, and he heard a firm voice speaking. It struck him as a good omen. Surely no one could speak so resolutely and loudly if there were any bad news about.

Then the door opened and the surgeon looked in.

"Mr. Lennox?"

He could not speak.

"Sir Nevill has just got his things on. Would you give him your arm to the car; or would you prefer —"

He was out and in the hall without a word. Nevill was coming towards him, led by the sleek and discreet servant. Algy moved the man aside, and himself took his place. He remembered as they approached the hall door to nod to Sir Arthur; but no more.

"Four steps down," he said.

They crossed the pavement. The car was drawn up, and Paul made haste to open the door.

"Mind the step up," said Algy.

He tucked the rug round his friend as Paul went round to the front. Then he could wait no longer.

"Well, old man?"

Nevill hesitated.

"Got to go through with it," he said. "He says, operation as soon as possible. It's pretty bad."

The motor began to throb violently.

(3)

By the time they had reached Elizabeth Street, Algy had succeeded in assimilating the fact. A large number of minor aspects and relations had to be adjusted; and this took a little time. It also made it extremely difficult for him to ask intelligent questions and, still more, to absorb the answers. Briefly, however, he knew the outlines of the matter. Sir Arthur had diagnosed a tumor on the brain that was the cause at once of the headaches and of the temporary blindness. This tumor must at once be removed, if indeed it was operable; for it pressed upon the optic nerves, and would presumably press still more. It would be what was called a "severe operation." Of course it might be found that the tumor could not be removed, if it were in a vital spot. But an exploration at any rate must be made. The process was called "trepanning" or "trephining."

"When?" asked Algy.

"He suggested next Monday for the nursing home, and Tuesday morning for the operation."

When a violent shock has been received, the nerves, mercifully, refuse to respond to anything else for a little while; and Algy, in spite of a consciousness that Aunt Anna would have to be told almost immediately, did not realize at all that this would probably be very unpleasant for Aunt Anna. He just regarded the fact, as a man, after a bad fall from a horse, regards the blood on his hands and clothes. There it was!

As the motor drew up outside the Elizabeth Street house, and the door opened as if their coming had been looked for, Nevill put his hand on the other's arm.

"Just take me through into the drawing room: she'll be waiting there. And then go straight on into the library and shut the door."

"Right," said Algy. (He had not said a word of consolation; and could not.)

When they came in, arm-in-arm, through the drawing
room door, Aunt Anna was standing on the hearthrug. Her
hands were clasped behind her back; and her gray piled head
was flung back, as if in defiance. She looked at them with her
bright eyes; but she said nothing.

"Here we are," said Algy fatuously.

He steered Nevill past Anna, to the chintz chair that stood
with its back to the light, and placed him there.

"Got to go," he said, yet more fatuously. He went past Anna
without looking at her, through the library door and closed it
behind him. He could hear no voices in the room he had left.
He sat down miserably in the window seat, staring out into
the garden.

(4)

By the time Aunt Anna saw them come in, she had arranged, she thought, her attitude in a completely satisfactory
manner. Nevill had breakfasted in bed; and she had gone to
his room afterwards to see him light his cigarette, and to
hold the match. They had talked together, very carefully, on
a completely different level from that on which they were
really thinking: they had kept up a cheery sort of conversation, with even a little banter. Then she had gone out and
resolutely written letters till Nevill came in a little before
eleven conducted by Charleson: she had jumped up and
steered him to a chair; and they had talked again about
when they should go back to Hartley. There had been a few
desperate silences, which each made haste to break. Then at
half-past eleven she had gone to the door to see them start.
Then she had come back to the drawing room and sat down.

The attitude she had arranged during the hour that followed had been that suggested by Mr. Morpeth. Here the
thing was; it was nobody's fault; whatever happened had to
happen. He must not be softened by the wrong kind of tenderness. She must be quiet and businesslike and natural.

Again and again during that hour, with her hands knitted
tight in her lap, she had emphasized all that to herself: yet,
across that interior rigidity, flashes had come and gone, of
which she could not tell the nature — whether they were
gleams of knowledge that a great pain was a great good if it
were rightly met, or lurid streaks of horror that such a thing

should come to Nevill — to Nevill! These she dared not stay to analyze. . . .

Then she reminded herself that perhaps all this tension was entirely unnecessary; perhaps the verdict would be simply that Nevill was overwrought in some way: that he must follow a certain diet perhaps; that he must not get up till midday for a few weeks. She knew, after all, nothing beyond what Mackenzie and Braughing had told her, and they had told her very little. They did not profess to know for certain: they only guessed.

For quite a long time this cheerful optimism worked beautifully. Her temperament and her mood were such that such self-suggestions as these had a great temporary effect. By half-past twelve she was practically certain that there was nothing whatever the matter with Nevill; they would all be laughing over it all at lunch in a few minutes.

Then, when the hall door opened she sprang to her feet: and, by the time that the two had slipped off their things and were coming in at the door, the whole of the tension was back again, and she was ready for anything. She could not speak one word as they entered.

When the door had shut behind Algy, she turned and looked at Nevill. The window was behind him, and it was a little difficult to make out his face: his eyes were closed. Then she saw that he was trying to smile.

"Well; what did he say?" she asked, determined that her voice and words, at least, should not betray her.

Nevill raised his face a little and his eyelids flickered.

"Got to go through with it, my dear," he said (using the same words he had used to Algy. He had settled on them in those few seconds after the doctor had pronounced sentence.) "He isn't quite certain yet; but he thinks it's a tumor. At any rate he's got to find out."

"An operation then?" she said quietly.

"That's it. Next Tuesday."

"Where? Here?"

"No, a nursing home. He telephoned for me at once. They've got a bed all right. Got to go in on Monday."

For one fierce instant her whole emotional system shook her like a storm. A violent impulse seized her, to run to that patient miserable figure, and kiss those dear eyes, and —

and wash them clear again. Fortunately he could not see her face. She bit her lower lip savagely; but she could not speak.

"Aunt Anna."

"Yes?" (Ah! Her voice shook ever so little. That must not happen again.)

"I want you to promise me something; and then I don't want to talk about it any more at all."

She waited.

"Do you hear, Aunt Anna? Come nearer."

"I'd sooner stand. . . . Go on, my dear. What is it?"

"I want you to promise not to talk to any of the doctors behind my back. What they say to you, they must say to me. Do you understand?"

"Yes . . . I promise."

"That's all right then. Because there's something else. They're nearly sure it's a tumor on the brain. It's that which causes the headaches and the blindness. They want to remove that, if they can — I mean Handsworth does. But the point is, Why have I got one? Well, I know all I want to know: and all that anyone must know — I mean you. No one else must know anything at all — about the reason, I mean."

He spoke abruptly and spasmodically; and she could see how strong was the emotion behind.

"Do you hear, Aunt Anna?"

"Yes, my dear. And what is the reason?"

"Do you remember what father said to me before he died?"

She had not expected this, or remembered it; it simply had not entered into her recent meditations at all. It was as if a hand had gripped her heart without warning. She could not speak. Fortunately he did not seem to need any answer, for he went on almost immediately.

"Well; it seems that there was something in it. Handsworth asked me quite plainly about my parents, and so on: asked me outright what my father had died of; what his life had been like, and so on. I told him that my father had lived wildly — drink — everything. And then he seemed to understand —"

Again he paused: and again she could not speak. Back again, like a great darkness, surged the memory of a talk she had had with Mr. Morpeth, and then of another. What Nevill was saying now seemed as prearranged as a play. There seemed not a detail missing. Here was pain indeed; here was the physical suffering, and added to it a further bitterness; here was the old curse that the old man in the country had dared to call — no, had called — the shadow of a blessing. She must hold tight to that; it must be the shadow of a blessing, or she could not bear it. The sins of the fathers — "that was a Law of Mercy, not of wrath:" she must hold to that. "To love means to suffer"; but Love is the only joy: therefore there must be joy in suffering. . . .

Nevill was talking, was he not? What was he saying?

. . . . "Well; he seemed to think that that explained everything. He wanted to tell me details: but I refused: and I forbade him to tell you, or anyone. He promised he would not. I don't want details. Principles are — are all I can deal with. It is enough that I know so much. I'm weak — constitutionally — that was the word he used. That is why this thing has developed. Do you understand, Aunt Anna? . . . Oh! Do say that you understand." (His voice rose nearly to a wail.)

She was half away across the distance between them, driven again by that fierce impulse of love and pity, before she caught herself up. She must be quiet: she must not soften him. But — but how in God's name did he know all this — this mystery of love and atonement? For his words surely bore no other meaning.

She drew herself up then, within an arm's clasp of his patient upturned face. Oh! She must be resolute. Yet his face quivered before her eyes.

"My dear. I understand. Of course I understand. We will not speak of it again."

Then, very gently, as her custom was, she kissed him on the forehead, above his open unseeing eyes. He caught her suddenly in his arms.

Chapter IV

(1)

"Now just describe the whole place," said Nevill, leaning back — "No: I won't have a cigarette, old man. They taste beastly. Go on, Aunt Anna."

She had been on the morning of the next day, at Nevill's request, to see over the nursing home and to bring back a full report. The last twenty-four hours had passed, as time does pass, with a deadly swift kind of slowness, like the moving of wheels that neither jar nor sway. He had lain down after lunch; then she had gone to have tea with him and had read to him afterwards. He had come across from his room after dinner and had sat with her and Algy, too, who was under orders to come in for every principal meal until further notice; and she had played for a while on the big grand piano that was in the drawing room. The next morning after breakfast she had read his letters to him and then gone off to view the battlefield. They had not talked any more at all as to the future or the past; he had really meant what he had said; they formed no plans; they reviewed nothing: they merely waited.

Aunt Anna drew off her gloves: she had come straight in from the hall and through the drawing room, and had found Algy in the library window seat and Nevill in a big chair with his hands before him. The voices stopped talking suddenly as she came in.

"Well; I've seen all over it," she said. "I like it. Yes, I do; and I like the people and the nurses and the whole thing."

"Go on."

"It's in Curzon Passage, as you know; St. Joseph's is just across the way; I went in there for a minute or two afterwards. Well, the drawing room is just like any other drawing room; but you won't see much of that, you poor dear! Miss Brance came in almost at once: she's a Catholic, you know; and most of the nurses are."

"What's she like?"

"She didn't say very much. She's quite gray; she's very small with very delicate features: she was extremely well dressed."

"I like that," put in Nevill. "That's Form. Let's be decently dressed anyhow."

"Well; then she asked whether I wouldn't like to see your room. So we went upstairs and—"

"Did you see the operating-place — the theater, isn't it — as I told you?"

"Yes," said Aunt Anna, steadily. "I saw it on the way up."

"Well?"

"It is a little room on the top of the first flight. It's perfectly white and looks very clean and fresh."

"Tiles on the walls?"

"I think so. The — the bed arrangement is a stretcher covered with sheets and blankets. It faces the window in the middle. There are things to wheel about — plate glass tables; there are disinfectant jars, and so on. There's a kind of small stove to — to disinfect the instruments in. It all looks very empty and clean. It has two doors on to the landing: one is a baize door."

"See the instruments?"

"No. . . . Well; then we went upstairs. Your room's at the top, looking out on to the back. It's quite big. It's very nicely furnished. The bed's in the middle of the room with its head against the wall; and the bell and electric switch are within reach. It has wardrobes and tables and everything. It's extremely nice in every way. Then Miss Brance sent for your nurse."

"Well?"

"I like her particularly. She is a Catholic, by the way, and Irish. She's tall and very quiet, with gray eyes and dark hair. Her uniform is delightful."

"What color?"

"Blue, with a white apron and a white linen cap."

"Will she be there during the operation?"

"Yes: and Miss Brance too. Miss Brance is a fully qualified nurse, by the way."

"And you asked all about the operation, too?"

"Yes." (Her voice trembled a little; but she recovered herself.) "They asked me whether you'd prefer to be put under the anesthetic in your own room, or whether you'd walk down to the theater."

"Yes?"

"I said you'd do exactly which they preferred — as you told me. Well; of course they'd sooner you went down to the theater. They said —"

"Yes?"

"They said some people couldn't stand that. I said I was sure you could."

"Go on."

"Well; it's fixed for half-past nine. The surgeon and the anesthetist will be ready by then. Then the nurse comes to tell you; and you put on a dressing gown and slippers and walk downstairs. Then you climb up on to the bed and they give the chloroform. Then you wake up in your own room. They carry you back before you recover consciousness."

"How long will it take?"

"They can't tell for certain. It depends what they find. It'll probably be between two and three hours."

"Then I shall just be in time for lunch."

"My dear, you won't want any lunch. You won't want anything at all that day: but of course you'll have to have something, whether you want it or not."

"Oh! Shall I!" said Nevill defiantly. "We'll see about that. By the way, shall I be able to see when I wake up? Did you ask about that?"

"They hope so," said Anna. "It depends on what they find."

There was a pause. It had been a considerable effort to relate all this; and she was glad for once that he could not see her face. She could not have done it at all, if it had not been for the day and the night that had passed since sentence had been pronounced. But she had had just enough time to wrench her attitude to his, and to meet it with the mingled silence and frankness with which he was facing it himself.

"Algy," he said presently.

The figure in the window seat turned round. He had been staring very earnestly out into the garden while she had been giving her descriptions.

"Yes, old man."

"Think it sounds all right?

"First-rate."

"You'll be downstairs with Aunt Anna, won't you, on Tuesday?"

'Why, yes," said Algy.

"Aunt Anna, I wish you'd ask Maresfield in to dinner to-morrow. I suppose you'll be going to church, won't you?"

"Of course, I'll ask him. . . . Yes, I had thought of going, unless you wanted me."

"And that reminds me," continued Nevill. "How long do they starve me for, before the affair comes off?"

"Yes: I asked them that too. You won't be starved much. You'll have a light lunch on Monday, soon after you arrive: but not much else. Just a cup of tea about five and some soup later."

"That all?"

"Yes; that's all."

(2)

It is said of condemned criminals that, of the period between sentence and execution, the worst time is not, as might be expected, the night before the execution, but the night immediately after the sentence. Nevill found this, in its measure, to be true of himself. The Friday night had been a considerable burden; for, alone there in the dark, he had been able to face facts with a deliberation that had scarcely been possible during the day. But the result was that by Saturday morning his attitude had been arranged and established. The Saturday night was considerably easier; and the Sunday night easier still.

Maresfield had come and gone; his breezy, abrupt personality had been a distinct stimulus; and Nevill awoke on Monday morning in a state of far less apprehensiveness than he would have thought possible three days before.

The start was made about half-past ten; for his orders were that he must be in the Home by eleven to begin his grim preparations. Medicine had to be taken; the top of his head had to be shaved: he had, all round, to settle in and be made comfortable.

He had a few minutes of loneliness and even of a little horror, as he sat, dressed, in the drawing room before the arrival of Algy, listening to the preparations in his room across the hall, the passing of Charleson's footsteps and Aunt Anna's, the carrying out of bags and the one or two returns that were made for small things that had been overlooked. He felt very helpless — like an intelligent sheep waiting for the coming of the temple attendants. . . .

Then, at last, he heard Aunt Anna come in; and that she did not shut the door behind her.

"Now, my dear," she said. "We're ready."

They did not talk much on the way. Vaguely he tried to follow their route.

"We're at Hyde Park Corner, aren't we?" he said. And then again, "Now to the right, isn't it?" And at last the car stopped.

He felt yet more helpless as he was led indoors. He could hear a rustle as of two or three people as he came in through the door on the right.

"How do you do, Sir Nevill?" came a very gentle voice that, for all its gentleness, had a considerable strength about it.

He put out his hand, smiling with an effort; and felt it taken in the small hand of a woman. She retained it as she led him forward to a chair.

"There," she said. "Now, if you'll allow me I'll leave you for five minutes while I just look upstairs once more. And then, I am afraid, I shall have to take you away."

He murmured something polite; and heard her go out.

"I like her voice," he said. "But I suppose it's like walking along the street, to her. . . . I wonder if she knows —" (He stopped. That line would not do.) "Room smells all right," he said genially.

"Not a bit what I thought it would be," remarked Algy.

"What did you expect?"

"Oh! I don't know. I thought it would be dingy or pious, or something."

Yes; this was certainly the right line, thought poor Anna. Naturalness was the only possible attitude. Yet her whole heart longed to turn Algy out of the room and say — say — she did not know what she wanted to say — something to Nevill. She would not see him again, she knew, for at least forty-eight hours. He must be delivered over to other hands than hers — hands which, however tender or skillful, held knives and basins and bandages. But this naturalness was better; and she herself managed to say something presently about the old mirror over the mantelpiece.

Then, after what seemed an incredibly short interval, the door opened once more, and the dainty little gray-haired lady stood on the threshold.

It was they who had to go first, after all.

"Well; good luck, old man!" said Algy, and shook him warmly by the hand.

"Goodbye, my dear," said Aunt Anna. "We shall both be here tomorrow, you know."

He felt her warm lips linger on his forehead. There was a rustle; there was a sound of footsteps; then the hall door closed heavily. He stood waiting. Then there came the sound of another step.

"Ah! Here is Nurse Deacon," said the gentle voice. "This is your patient, Nurse."

It was a long way upstairs, and the space seemed rather contracted. Miss Brance went before, directing him at the corners; the nurse came behind. At the top of the first flight he stopped; for not only did he remember what Aunt Anna had told him, but he perceived a very distinct and peculiar smell, not unpleasant, but reminding him of a chemist's shop. Smells had come to mean a good deal to him during these last days.

"This is the theater, isn't it?" he said.

"Yes; how did you know?" By the tone he guessed that she smiled.

"My aunt told me. Besides, I can smell it."

Halfway up the next flight a thought struck him.

"Any operations this morning, Miss Brance?"

"Yes. Two."

"Doing well, I hope?"

"Splendidly."

He perceived by her tone that he must not be inquisitive. He wondered why. Surely they weren't afraid for his nerve!

"Here we are," she said at last; and took him by the hand to lead him forward. "Sit down a minute, Sir Nevill, and get your breath. It's a long way upstairs."

This room smelt charmingly of flowers, and of absolutely nothing else. He perceived that he was facing the light; and, from the warmth on one side, he understood that there was a fire on the right. He considered these things while she talked.

"Can you get ready for bed by yourself?" she asked. "Or would you sooner have Nurse to help you — or your manservant?"

"Thanks very much," he said hastily. "I can do it by myself." Then the door shut, and he understood that the nurse was gone.

"May I sit down for a minute or two?" asked the other voice. "There are just one or two things I would like to mention."

"Why, certainly," he said, wondering what in the world they could be.

"The first is about the other patients. You know we have to have a very strict rule here that patients shouldn't know about one another. It would never do. So I know I can ask you, quite simply, not to ask any questions. The nurses have orders in any case not to answer."

(Yes; this lady had plenty of the governing faculty, he perceived. Her voice had not belied her.)

He assented; and said that he quite understood.

"Thank you, Sir Nevill. And the next thing is about yourself. The male patients sometimes have a certain difficulty in their minds about the nurses. I want just to remind you, if I may, that it's all perfectly natural to the nurses to look after patients in every way. It's their ordinary accustomed work. You won't feel any difficulty about it, will you?"

"I'll remember," said Nevill.

"Thank you. The third thing is about a priest. The Fathers at St. Joseph's can always send a priest at any time, day or night. We never, of course, suggest this to Catholic patients. That is not our business. Our business is the body, not the soul. But if you should want a priest to hear your confession tonight, or at any time; or to bring you Holy Communion, you only have to say so. We are quite accustomed to that. And it is the same, of course, for Protestants."

"Thank you very much," said Nevill. "I don't think — just at present —"

"Just so," said the quiet, steady voice. "Then I'll leave you, now, Sir Nevill: so soon as I've shown you where the bed is, and so on. Your man is here, and will come up when you're in bed, unless you'd like him now."

"No: I can manage all right, thank you. I hate to be waited upon, you know."

Again he could tell by her tone that she smiled.

"I'm afraid you'll have to submit here," she said. "Now let me show you."

(3)

When he heard the nurse come in with his soup about eight o'clock that night, he put into words the decision he had at last come to.

"Is that you, Nurse Deacon?"

"Yes, Sir Nevill, with your soup."

"Could I have a priest from St. Joseph's, do you think? To hear my confession? And I should like to have Holy Communion in the morning too."

"I'll send across directly," she said.

He could not have believed that an afternoon and an evening could have made so great a difference in his feelings. The time had passed very tranquilly indeed, broken only by little events, quite unimportant, yet oddly exciting. It had been an event when his lunch had come, a couple of hours after he had been in bed — a lunch well-cooked and alluring, though strangely tasteless, as all food had been ever since his blindness. He had eaten this lunch with the help of Nurse Deacon, who steadied the plates and directed his movements. Then he had slept and dozed alternately till about four. Tea had come up a little later, and, with tea, Miss Brance, who brought the suggestion that Nurse Deacon might, if he cared for it, read aloud to him for an hour. He had declined this; and he did not know why, except that he wanted to think. About seven the barber had come; and, when the barber had gone, he had passed his hand over the shaved top of his head with a strange feeling of excitement. Matters seemed drawing to a crisis. The sheep was decked for the sacrifice indeed.

His first intelligent emotion about himself was that he was not really Nevill Fanning at all; that his consciousness had been tricked somehow into believing in its own continuity; that it was not really he at all who lay here waiting for the morrow, but someone else with whom he had been identified. It seemed incredible that he, who had bathed and ridden and shot and played tennis — he who was so essentially a health-loving, air-loving person — should have been caught so swiftly and chained down here like . . . like an invalid. He ran over his memories three or four times — he fingered the links that had led him here — before his emotion as well as his understanding grasped all the connections.

He did not know at exactly what point he had decided to
receive the Sacraments. He had known perfectly well that as
a Catholic he ought not to hesitate; yet the last time he had
received them had been at Easter in Rome — at Easter when
his life seemed turning to pure gold under the spell of Enid.
Since then it had seemed impossible.

Yet, during these hours of expectancy, matters had begun
to adjust themselves in a manner he would not have believed
possible. Certain elements of thought retired; others advanced; there was a striving and a rearrangement that appeared to be going forward independently of his own volition.
His helplessness of body, it seemed, was but a symbol of an
infinitely deeper helplessness of soul. There was an atmosphere here — a harmony of pain and tenderness, and charity
and terror — as bewildering as a completely new experience.
The nurse whom he could not see appeared as a kind of tan-
gible incarnation of it all. The touch of her hands when she
settled him to eat and drink; the cool linen of her apron
which he caught at once in mistake for the side of the bed;
the smell of the flowers in the invisible room; the sound of
the fire in the grate — there was not a sense that was not
affected, not a sensation that was not eloquent.

There seemed then to emerge in him, drawn out by envi-
ronment, that old frame of things and thoughts that, formed
in him by education, had been overlaid by his later experiences and actions. It was as if his own inner childishness
came up and took charge once more. It appeared to him absurd to allow his own little thoughts and philosophies to
dominate him any longer; he was to stand in peril of his life
tomorrow — he knew that well enough, in spite of all his
presences; then what better thing could he do than prepare
his soul for that encounter? It was not that he was conscious
of any religious emotion, nor even of definite fear; but the
shadows were falling faster every hour. Then it was but reasonable to meet them in the way that was most familiar. By
eight o'clock it seemed obvious to him that he must make his
confession and receive Holy Communion tomorrow.

A little before nine the priest had come. Like all Jesuits he
had the infinite tact of utter simplicity. He said nothing except the plainest things. When Nevill had finished his little
story, he remarked that an experience such as Nevill had
passed through, might be the occasion of the greatest merit,

if it were rightly accepted; he bade him commit himself without reservations into the hands of God; he gave him absolu-
tion; and he told him he would bring Holy Communion to
him at half-past six the next morning.

Again he felt no emotion; rather, he felt the relief of its absence. It was not that he experienced any ineffable peace, or
that he felt particularly more cleansed than he had felt before. Merely he was conscious that he had done the suitable
thing; that in that strange exterior world which was called
religion, he had performed the proper actions.

Then he said the three Hail Marys assigned to him as his
penance; and settled down for the night.

(4)

He awoke, suddenly and completely, about six o'clock, and
after a minute or two of hesitation, touched his bell. For he
awoke to the entire consciousness of where he was, and of
what awaited him.

The night nurse came in, told him what time it was, and
asked if she should bring in the necessaries for Holy Communion. He assented.

At seven o'clock the priest had come and gone, and the
nurse had cleared away the flowers and linen cloths and the
lighted candles. He had seen nothing of this; but he had followed her actions by the little sounds she made. Then she
left him in quiet, telling him to ring if he wanted her; unless
he rang, she said, no one would interrupt him till Nurse Deacon came to him at nine.

Then, once more, he settled down to consider.

His night had been like the night of a traveler. Certainly
he had slept a great deal; he had slept continuously from
three till six. Yet, previously to that, he had no more been
wholly unconscious of what approached so swiftly than the
night traveler is unconscious of the steady roar of the wheels
and the rush of the night outside. But it was not Fear that he
felt; he had never even been remotely tempted by that which
so afflicts many who await such an ordeal — the knowledge
that he could yet refuse it and go out again at his will.
Rather his emotion had been one of contemplation of a fact
that cannot be evaded. Now and again he had heard a clock
strike softly; once in the silent hours he had heard the low
talking of a man's voice on the landing outside, and supposed

that the doctor had been summoned in haste for some other patient. Yet the burden of anticipation lay on him as heavy as lead. . . .

One emotion he had had, however, which he had not anticipated; and that was the thought of Enid. Again and again during the night he had thought of her; her image had grown upon him like a giant, now that in his helplessness he could no longer put it away. It was not that he wanted anything particular from her; not for a moment even now did he desire, however helpless and vague his mind might be, that that Enid whom he now knew, should come to him. But, with a sentimentality of which he had not believed himself capable, he had longed to hear the voice and feel the touch of the Enid whom he had once thought he knew — of the quiet, serene girl who understood him so quickly — the Enid of Frascati and Rome and Hartley — of Hartley at least in the first few hours of her visit there — the Enid of that ideal which he had once formed of her who had so ruthlessly torn away the mask and shown him the cruel reality.

Now, however, even this had passed. . . .

Then he considered the sacred ceremony in which he had just been a partaker; and was quietly amazed at the absence of emotion it had caused. He had received That which, in his deepest being, he believed to be the Body of Christ; he had quieted his thoughts that he might contemplate that fact; yet there had been no reaction of devotion. As in his confession last night, so again this morning, he felt nothing except that he had performed the action proper to his religion. . . . The priest had come and gone; and he lay there reflecting.

At nine o'clock the nurse came in.

"Good morning, Sir Nevill. I hope you slept well."

"Oh yes; pretty well, thanks."

"You'd like your hands and face washed, wouldn't you?"

"Thank you."

This was done: the sponge passed smoothly and gently over his face and ears. Then he laid first one hand and then the other in the warm water. Then these were dried; and he lay still. Then he had listened to the basin being put back. Then the door had shut.

Then, once again, the sense of helplessness and fatality came down on him like a pall. By now, he knew, somewhere in the house below him, waited Aunt Anna and Algy; and, for the first time, a kind of childish fury seized him at the thought of them. Of what use, after all, were all Aunt Anna's prayers and Algy's sympathy? For, somewhere, also, in that very house, his butchers were gathering — the man who would drug and stifle him into insensibility; the man who would open his head with knives and saws and scissors. (There was a horrible little instrument, too, of which he had forced poor Algy to read aloud to him from an encyclopedia — an instrument that faintly resembled an elaborate kind of mechanical corkscrew.) . . . If there were anything in prayer and sympathy, why could not these horrors be prevented? It was all very well for Aunt Anna to be meek and courageous, and Algy to be silent and emotional; but what had they to suffer? They would wait in that pleasant drawing room, while he was being choked and hacked upstairs. . . . He put away, with a kind of savage selfishness, the thought that they, too, were suffering. What, after all, he asked himself, were mental sufferings compared to physical? It was the naked bodily nerve that hurt, in the long run, and not memories and anticipations. . . .

About twenty minutes past nine he was quiet again; and lay there, indeed, like a sheep on the steps of the altar. His whole attention seemed fixed on the faint noises of the house. He heard the hooting of a motor, and wondered whether it were his surgeon who was coming. He heard the faint chink of china; and wondered whether it were a basin being carried down to catch his blood. . . . For one mad instant he desired that there might be some delay; that the surgeon might be called elsewhere. . . . There flashed across his consciousness — come and gone again in an instant — the knowledge that he was yet free to say no, and to demand his release.

The end came far more swiftly and undramatically than he imagined.

The door opened so quietly and ordinarily that it seemed nothing.

Then the quiet, steady voice spoke,

"They are quite ready, Sir Nevill. Will you get up and come downstairs? I will help you into your dressing gown and slippers."

(5)

The faint, drug-like smell smote his nostrils suddenly, as, with outstretched hands and fingers from behind guiding his arm, he shuffled in through the double doors on the first landing. (One of them was baize, he remembered.)

"Good morning, Sir Nevill. Feeling pretty well, I hope?"

It was Handsworth's voice: he remembered that, and put out his hand.

"Good morning. . . . Oh, yes; thanks."

"This is Dr. Martin, who will give you the anesthetic."

Again his hand was taken.

"Good morning, Dr. Martin. I — what am I to do, please?"

"That's all right, Sir Nevill," came Miss Brance's delicate voice from behind. "Just slip off your dressing gown and slippers."

As he was doing this he wondered whether he ought to say anything. He decided not. Standing in his pajamas, barefooted, he felt more helpless than ever.

"What —" he began.

"Now, please: the bed is just in front of you. By the way, you have no false teeth, have you?"

"No."

He groped forward, feeling with his hands, till they encountered a sheet-covered edge. It seemed unusually high, he thought. The light was on his left. Then, with his exploring foot, he felt a step. This altar had steps, then.

Very carefully he climbed up on to the bed; it seemed extremely hard and narrow. At least two pairs of hands guided his movements. He lay straight down on his back, and felt bedclothes laid lightly over him; and it was then for the first time that he was aware that his heart was beating sharply and almost painfully about midway, it seemed, between his throat and his breastbone. There were sounds of soft footsteps about him, and of some article moving lightly on wheels.

"Now, Sir Nevill," began the anesthetist's voice — "yes: your hands just crossed on your breast, please. When I put the mouthpiece on, just breathe as deeply and deliberately as you can — just like a child. Don't pant at all, please — just long, slow breaths."

(Yes; he knew that. He had made up his mind to that. Ah! Why would they not begin? They seemed to him intolerably slow. He longed to escape — and to leave his body here. Then he would come back to it when all was over.)

So suddenly that he started a little, he felt some kind of curved rubber receiver laid gently across his mouth and nostrils. It curved down on to his jaws on both sides. There was no catch or fastening of any kind; yet he felt as if it pinned him down, as might a chain. He conceived the possibility of struggling and throwing it off.

"Now begin to breathe quite gently," said the soft voice. . . . "*Now*." . . .

Ah! There it was. . . . It was not at all a violent or shocking scent; on the contrary, it was just a shade sickly and attenuated. Then he began to count, drawing in his breaths deeply, to the full extent of his lungs. He had fancied, somehow, that four or five breaths would send him off.

There came down on him suddenly a sense of great quiet and expectancy, as if the world stood still; but he disliked this expectancy. He wished to escape; but time appeared to stand still. He wondered if this were unconsciousness beginning, and directed his attention to his body and limbs. No; they were still his: he could feel the texture of the rather coarse linen beneath his clasped hands and above his toes.

That was the seventh breath; the eighth; the ninth. . . . Each was very slow and deep, as had been ordered. Each occupied at least three or four seconds.

At the tenth he thought he would put a test to himself. He began to try to separate his interlaced fingers; they moved, but it was certainly slowly and with difficulty; and they felt slippery. He ceased to try to move them.

As he continued to breathe and to count, again there came down on him the sense of tranquil expectancy. It appeared to him as if in a new kind of way he was the center of attention. There were several pairs of eyes fixed on him, he knew; the anesthetist was watching him with skilled observation, to see that all was as it should be. Handsworth, somewhere behind the head of the bed, he thought, was standing, either in a white coat or with his sleeves turned up, with a glittering instrument, perhaps, already in his fingers. Miss Brance, he had an idea, was standing with her back to the closed doors; and Nurse Deacon, probably, beside the little plate glass table covered with strange articles. Perhaps, too, there were others in this room of whom he had heard nothing. He did not know. Then there were Aunt Anna and Algy downstairs in the drawing room, pretending to read, perhaps — certainly not talking. There were other patients in bed upstairs — some waiting their turn for today or some other day, some having already passed through these strange experiences.

Then, outside there was the London street, and motorcars and policemen and shops. Perhaps somewhere there was Enid; he did not know whether she were in London or not. Then there was Hartley, and Jim, and the hall and the river and the pavilion, and Father Richardson. . . . And, somehow, he himself was the center of all these things; they radiated from him, and looked towards him.

At the seventeenth breath a note began in his head, quite soft and clear, and not unpleasant, a kind of curved note that moved upwards, like a very melodious siren whistle; at the eighteenth it was moving more rapidly, as if the curve grew acute. He counted nineteen. . . .

Chapter V

(1)

There was someone stroking his hand; and that stroking gave him ineffable consolation. It was a regular rhythmical movement from wrist to fingers; and he remained with his eyes closed, enjoying it.

Then he perceived that his left hand was also firmly and tenderly held; and this double support on both sides reassured and bore him up.

Then he became aware of Pain that rested on him, like a hat drawn down to his eyes. It was exterior, not interior; it was not, that is to say, in his consciousness, but, rather, was faced and contemplated by it. The pain was a continuous pulsation, rather like the throb of a motor engine, though far slower — a series of noiseless explosions from a point, like the bursting of a shell; and he perceived that the color of them was a kind of electric blue. As he opened his eyes the pain sensibly decreased; or at least retired a little way off. A voice was talking gently and soothingly; and this, like the stroking of his hand, was an extraordinary consolation, though he did not at present understand one word that it was saying.

The stroking stopped, and there was a stir in the room; he thought that someone had gone out.

"Go on with that, please," he said, moving his fingers a little. "I like that."

The stroking began again.

"Is it all right?"

"Yes; perfectly right. It's all over."

"What time is it?"

"It's just half-past twelve."

"Why, I can see!"

"Yes, of course you can."

He remained without speaking again for a minute or two, turning his eyes about, taking in new impressions, and considering the marvel that he could do so. The pain was there still, just as before, like a person hammering heavily on a closed door and seeking entrance: he felt he could not bother to open and see who was there: he would presently, when he had had time to look about him.

There was a mirror over the fireplace, framed in gilt carved wood, with a kind of little rail at the top of the glass. This was extremely interesting, because, although he knew it was a mirror, it was also the Thames at Westminster; the rail was the bridge, and the glass was the surface of the water, and above there were the houses, lit from within and glowing with the light of sunset upon them. It was extraordinarily beautiful. How curious that it was both a mirror and the Thames. . . . Were other things in the room like that?

On the right there was a tall folding screen; and the top of the white door appeared above it. These were all right; but in front was a kind of tall, carved lamp support, like a very elongated table; there was a vase of flowers on this. But it was not only a table and flowers; it was also the leg of a giant, from the knee to the ankle: the rest of the giant must be above the roof.

He became more and more interested, and looked to the left. The window was on the left, with the blind drawn down; and before it stood another table with a tall, flowering plant. But it was not just a table and a plant; it was also the figure of a Cavalier in a plumed hat with his hand raised, as in defiance. He thought he really must be a little feverish; or was it that his eyes were not quite right after all? It was surely unreasonable and impossible that these things could be themselves and yet also things with which they could not really have even the remotest connection.

"Can I really see all right?" he asked.

"Oh! Yes. Perfectly."

He turned his eyes to see who spoke. He had practically forgotten these people. The woman who had spoken was a little gray-haired delicate-looking person, dressed in white. It was she who was holding his left hand. He liked her face; she looked human and kindly. Then he turned his eyes to the right; and a tall girl, in blue, with a white apron from her throat to below her knees — (which was as far as he could see) — sat there: it was she who was still stroking his hand. She had a clear steady face, dark hair and gray eyes; she was rather of the Enid type. Yes; he liked her too.

"You're Nurse Deacon, aren't you?" he said.

"Yes, Sir Nevill."

"And you're Miss Brance," he began, turning his eyes back. But at that instant the knocking Pain waxed intolerable; and he drew a swift hiss of agony.

"Oh! It hurts!" he moaned, and shut his eyes.

"The syringe again —" he heard whispered across the blazing explosions of blue light. . . .

Presently he felt his left arm being handled, as if someone had pulled up his pajama sleeve and was lightly fingering his forearm. Then there was a tiny touch of a different kind — no more than that. Then, little by little, though the pain did not cease, it grew more remote and even tolerable.

After a period he began to feel restless. He supposed that it was morphia that had been given him; and he was coming to the conclusion that morphia was a very much over-rated drug. It had quieted him in a sort of physical way; but it had not really touched the seat of the trouble. The pain was there, just as before, hammering still, though in a muffled kind of way; but it was practically as bad: and there were no delicious sensations, such as he had always understood resulted from an injection. He felt merely oppressed and restless, not soothed.

This would never do. He drew a long breath and opened his eyes once more. He thought he would talk a little bit, and find out things. Besides, it might distract him.

"Miss Brance."

"Miss Brance has gone downstairs. She'll be back presently."

"Oh! It doesn't matter. Look here, Nurse, was the operation successful?"

"Yes; perfectly," came the quiet voice. "Why, you can see again!"

"Yes: that's all right. Nurse!"

"Yes, Sir Nevill?"

"Doctors gone, I suppose?"

"They've been gone over an hour."

"Oh! I suppose Sir Arthur will be coming back?"

"He'll telephone for news this evening. We've told him you're doing very well. He'll come if you want him, of course."

"Did I use bad language this morning? Don't tell me lies, will you?"

He turned his eyes to see her face as she answered; and saw that she was smiling a little.

"No, Sir Nevill. Indeed you didn't. You only spoke twice —"

"When? . . . What did I say?"

"Once during the operation; and once when the men were carrying you upstairs. You said, 'Oh! My God!'"

"That was really all?"

She nodded.

"Yes."

"Oh! . . . I say, Nurse, you know, that wasn't a prayer. I'm not a bit pious. That was an — an expletive."

He heard her laugh softly. Really she was very human and pleasant.

"Would you like anything to eat or drink, Sir Nevill? Are you thirsty at all? You mustn't talk much, you know."

He questioned himself. Was he thirsty? — No. Hungry? . . . On the contrary food seemed entirely disgusting.

"I wouldn't eat if you gave me a hundred pounds. You can let go of my hand, please."

He drew his hands together as she lifted the sheet for him to do so.

"Now I must talk. I want to know a lot of things."

"Don't you think you can go to sleep a little?"

"No. How can I with this beastly bandage all over my head? Has my — I mean, has Mrs. Fanning gone away? I should like to see her. And Algy."

"I'm afraid you mustn't, Sir Nevill. Besides, they've both gone away. Miss Brance went down half an hour ago to say how well you were doing."

"Oh! Why are the blinds down? I'm not dead, am I?"

"Indeed you're not, Sir Nevill. But the light would bother you. Just lie quite still, if you can, and —"

"Well; and the operation really was successful? It wasn't — wasn't cancer, was it?"

"Nothing of the kind, Sir Nevill. And you're doing very well indeed."

"And it's all over. Really all over. And I shan't have to go down to that — that *beastly* little room any more?"

He spoke vehemently; and the pain in his head grew vehement too.

"Sir Nevill; you really must be more quiet. You don't want me to have to send for Miss Brance? She's at lunch too."

"You'll . . . you'll swear it's not cancer?"

"Of course I will. Now, do you think a little chicken jelly — or soup —?"

He considered this slowly. Soup, of course, was intolerable; but cold chicken-jelly —

"You'll have to have something, you know. You had no breakfast this morning."

"Shall I feel better if I do? I don't feel a bit well, you know. It's not cancer, I think you said? I think perhaps chicken jelly, if it's cold —"

"Of course you'll feel better. Will you lie still if I leave you for two minutes?"

"Yes. All right. And perhaps half a cigarette afterwards. . . . I don't know. Oh! Lord! My head!"

(2)

"Just get the syringe again," whispered a voice at some infinitely later period, across the blinding explosions of pain; "and then get the dressings ready."

He did not know in the least what time it was; and it was far too great an effort to ask. But he opened his tormented eyes, and saw that a shaded electric lamp stood by his bed. Yet still the pain was not actually crushing; he never felt that he really could not bear it any more. Only, it was necessary to keep his attention firmly fixed upon it and his will braced to meet it. The pain and he were two, not one.

He was making, too, other curious discoveries. One was that his nervous system was very much larger than his body; it had thrown out fibers and tentacles throughout the whole bed, so that even the faintest touch on the clothes thrilled through him. Just now one of the women had brushed the end of the bed with her skirt; and he had winced as if he had been struck. Some of the fibers reached even down upon the floor, so that every vibration of a footstep, however soft, ran through him. The center of the system was rather to the left and forward of the top of his head, almost on his temple; and it was to this brooding, incarnate pain that every message came.

He felt the prick of the needle very much more distinctly this time. It was a tiny additional pain. His head appeared to register and acknowledge it promptly.

"I don't think I'll have any more of that," he murmured. "It's no good, you know." Then he closed his eyes again. But the dressing of the wound was a far greater horror. Something in the tone of the voices that spoke to him rendered resistance impossible. He realized that it must be gone through. So he lay still, with his eyes closed, trying to think how pleasant it would be when it was all over, permitting hands to move over his head, feeling a shocking kind of cold at one point that made him shiver, succeeded by a trickling kind of warmth that was followed by a little metallic noise in some vessel. This warmth was faintly comforting — he deliberately kept his eyes closed for fear that that which trickled might be blood and he should see it. Then the bandages closed again on his head: it was horrible while they were being put on; it was reassuring when all was done and his head rested again easily on the pillows.

Then he opened his eyes.

"Thanks very much," he said.

Then he wondered whether he had been behaving well. He couldn't remember having said, "Thank you," before, at all: he wondered whether he had shown himself a shocking coward.

"Miss Brance —"

"You mustn't talk, Sir Nevill. I want you to lie quite still."

He let his eyes wander over her little white figure. She was dressed for dinner, it seemed, in a sort of tea-gown; but had an apron on and linen sleeves drawn over her arms. She looked very familiar and reassuring somehow. It was marvelous that anyone could be dressed for dinner. He looked away from her at a soft sound, and saw that the nurse was wheeling away behind one of the screens a little plate glass table. The table had various things on it.

He decided to pay no attention to Miss Brance's remark.

"Has Sir Arthur Handsworth been again?"

"I am afraid you mustn't talk, Sir Nevill. Just try to lie quite still and go to sleep."

Then the little figure went noiselessly across the dim-lit room and disappeared. He lay, considering.

At some further remote period Miss Brance was by him again. She carried a little instrument in her hand.

"How do you feel now, Sir Nevill?"

"I think I'm better. May I talk a little, please?"

She sat down by his bedside as the nurse rose and went out.

"Well, just a little. But it's nearly ten o'clock, you know. Nurse Deacon will be back to settle you for the night directly; and then the night nurse will come on duty."

"Will she be in the room?"

"No: just on the landing outside. But she'll come immediately if you ring. I want you to have a good sleep."

"I won't have any more morphia, please."

"I've brought something quite different this time.

"What is it?"

"Never mind about that, Sir Nevill. But it's different."

"It's not cancer I've got, is it?" (He felt it was most important to settle this question. It had been on his mind a little; and he meant to have asked Nurse Deacon; but somehow it had been forgotten.)

"Oh! No. Not a trace. You need have no fear whatever of that. Is the pain less?"

"I think it is, a little. But it goes on hammering, you know."

"Well; that'll get better every hour. You've had hardly any proper sleep at all, all today."

"When can I see my aunt?"

"Oh! In a day or two. We shall have to see how you get on. I shall telephone to her tonight as soon as you're settled. We've had a good many inquiries."

"Oh! Who?"

"Well: Lord Maresfield has been once, and telephoned again this evening. Then Mr. Lennox came again this afternoon. Then a Mrs. Bessington called about six."

"What?"

"Mrs. Bessington. She said that Mrs. Fanning had told her. And any amount of flowers have come; but I am afraid you mustn't have them till tomorrow morning."

"I suppose no one else came with — with Mrs. Bessington?"

"No: she came alone."

As Nevill did not move or speak again, the little woman stood up.

"Nurse Deacon is just coming, I think."

When the settling for the night had been finished, Nevill again lay very still.

The process had been really quite interesting. He could not follow all the tactics carried out by the two nurses: he had raised himself a little on their arms; he had lifted his feet, all as he was bidden. His blankets had been raised; a sheet pulled; and then the blankets lowered again. The result of all was that within five minutes he lay between fresh sheets above and below, and new cool pillows. Then the pajama sleeve had been pulled up again; and the prick had followed, more distinct than ever. Finally the two women moved noiselessly about the room, shifting and arranging this and that: a few more coals were put on the fire. Then they had bidden him goodnight. The bell-button and the light-button, with a box of cigarettes, a matchbox, and a covered glass of barley water, all stood within easy reach on the table by his bedside. He had managed, too, with only very slight disgust, half a dozen more spoonfuls of chicken jelly.

He stared at the walls that wavered in the firelight; and the mirror that had been the Thames at Westminster this afternoon.

Mrs. Bessington had been to call this afternoon! He had known well enough, even before he had asked, that she had come alone; he knew now, too, that she must have come without her daughter's knowledge, and that she would not say a word to that daughter of what she had heard. Yet in his weakness and his drug-inspired semi-delirium there was one side of him that strove to pretend that it was not so, and that Enid was at least a little sorry to hear of his new trouble. But it was no more than pretence. Just as he had known this afternoon that the mirror was not really the Thames and that the growing plant was not a Cavalier, so he knew now that Enid was nothing to him — nor he to her — that she had shown herself completely another from that which he had fancied her — even though it gave him a miserably pleasant kind of pain to pretend that she was relenting.

So in his weakness he turned the point in his soul again and again, and the pains of both body and mind began to work. There were other considerations, too, beginning to present themselves.

The nurse looked in noiselessly about midnight, hoping that he might be asleep; but, so soon as she looked, she caught the glimmer of the fire in his black eyes. But he said nothing, and she went out. She looked in again an hour later, and still he was awake. He said he hadn't succeeded in getting to sleep yet.

Between three and four he rang for her.

"It's not the least good," he said. "I can't sleep. Would you just turn up the light and give me a book or two? Oh! Yes: and just cut half a dozen cigarettes in half. I find I can't quite manage a whole one."

(3)

"Now then, Sir Nevill, let's have a look."

It was quite an odd sensation for him, next morning about eleven, to set eyes for the first time upon the man whose voice he knew so well from his first interview with him — the man who had performed the butchery on him only twenty-four hours before.

Sir Arthur Handsworth was not much like Algy's description of him. He was much leaner in body than Nevill had imagined; his eyes were less alert and bright; he was extremely well dressed in a dark gray morning suit.

The process of "having a look" was not pleasant. Nevill had to lie right over on his side, with his face half-buried in the pillow, and feel fingers touching the top of his head in a manner that gave him a sensation of having no skull protection at all. Once or twice during the process, and while the surgeon himself dressed the wound, Nevill caught sight of his long, dry-looking fingers. It was those fingers that had held the corkscrew-like instrument yesterday.

He felt curiously exhausted, not indeed with the pain, since a couple of hours' sleep after seven o'clock this morning had certainly eased it very greatly, but with the effort he had to make to keep his nerves tight and rigid while the examination was made. His nerves felt raw and apprehensive while this went on; and appeared to relax like damp fiddle strings when it was over; and he lay back again on his pillows crowned with clean bandages. He felt a dull kind of resentment against the surgeon.

"Well?" he asked.

"It's perfectly satisfactory," said the other, watching his face with a searching kind of look. "And the pain's better, I hear?"

"Oh! Yes. When shall I be able to go away, do you think?"

"It depends almost entirely on yourself, Sir Nevill. The thing that matters now is the healing of the wound. If you do what you are told, and can keep quiet, I should think you could travel in ten days or a fortnight."

"And the operation was successful?"

"Perfectly," said the other shortly.

Nevill was conscious of a considerable relief. It was true that his nurses had implied as much; but it was more satisfactory to hear of it from the surgeon himself. And immediately his thoughts turned to his own people.

"When may my aunt come and see me, do you think?"

"You want to see her very much?

"If I may."

"Well; you might see her for half an hour this afternoon. She might come and have a cup of tea with you if you liked."

Nevill looked up sharply. He had no idea that it would be allowed so soon. From a very slight air in the surgeon's manner he had thought it would be several days before anyone would be allowed to come.

"Well; that's very good of you. You have seen her, I suppose?"

"I saw her yesterday, after the operation. But she mustn't come unless you really can get some sleep before."

"That'll be all right," said Nevill. "I feel more like it today."

(4)

He awoke that afternoon a little before four, and lay, well-content enough, feeling remarkably light and cheerful. It was as if the sleep had purged his brain of those eyeing shreds of impatience and resentment that had troubled him for the first few hours after his return to consciousness, and that had manifested themselves even once or twice during the surgeon's visit this morning.

Aunt Anna was to come about half-past four; and he was glad to have a little while to arrange, both in thought and word, what he had to say to her. A number of new and rather surprising ideas had come to him during the last twenty-four hours, and particularly during the long night, until he had slept at last in the dawn. He felt even a kind of pleasure in the prospect of the humiliating confession he would have to make. . . .

Then there were various plans he wished to speak to her about — or rather he wished to consult her as to the plans that had best be formed for the carrying out of his future ideas.

For one thing, at any rate, had come to him very insistently — now that he was emerging from his new experience, and looked forward to life once more — that he must really be rather more definite. It was pleasant enough to dawdle at Hartley, and play tennis, and ride with Jim, and hunt and shoot and all the rest of it; but this was not exactly life itself. He must do something; he was not sure whether it would be Parliament, or agriculture; but it must be something. Marriage, of course, might come some day, he prudently reminded himself; not indeed such a marriage as that of which he had once dreamed; but at any rate a decent and Christian matrimony. However, that must take care of itself. Meantime he must look out for some definite line; it was pleasant to think that Aunt Anna and Jim would form the domestic background to this newborn strenuousness.

She came in so quietly and naturally that he was almost taken aback. The nurse who had looked in soon after he awoke, and gone out again saying that she would bring up tea for Mrs. Fanning as soon as she arrived, merely tapped on the door, and then opened it; and Aunt Anna came in.

She came straight up to the bed, smiling, with bright eyes. She looked marvelously young and pretty; it was almost impossible to remember that really her hair was not powdered.

"My dear boy," she said.

She made as if she would kiss him; but, as she reached him, she hesitated. Then she took his hand instead and kissed that.

"Well; here we are, Aunt Anna," said Nevill. "Sit down where I can see you. And for goodness' sake don't touch the bed or I shall scream."

As she sat down, very close to the bed, and facing him, again, the door was pushed open, and Nurse Deacon came in with the tray. There was a soft bustle as Aunt Anna cleared a little table and put it before her.

"You may have tea?" asked Aunt Anna.

"Certainly," said Nevill. "But I think it mustn't be strong."

It was delicious to watch her as she poured it out and noiselessly moved things this way and that, finally putting his cup and a plate of rusks within his reach. He was perfectly able to help himself when once he had been properly arranged.

"Just tell me all the news first," said Nevill.

She drank her cup straight off, and set it down.

"No: I won't have anything to eat," she said. "Well — the news —"

Certainly she seemed a little agitated; but that was only natural, thought Nevill.

"Yes; the news," he said again. "All about what you did yesterday; and Algy and Charleson and everything. I haven't seen Charleson for two days. They won't let him come up, you know."

"Ah! Yes," she said. "Well, I got here about nine yesterday, and had a word or two with Sir Arthur Handsworth. Then they sent down to say you had taken the anesthetic splendidly. Then I heard that the operation was over — and I went into St. Joseph's —"

"But you saw Handsworth, didn't you?"

She appeared to recover herself with a kind of jerk.

"Oh! Yes: I saw him; and he gave me the — the news."

"He told me so this morning," observed Nevill. "Go on."

"In the afternoon we inquired again; and the same at night, about ten. I sent a note round to Mrs. Bessington, you know —"

"Yes: I heard she had come."

"I thought you wouldn't mind. Mr. Lennox dined with me. Then this morning, when I came, I heard that perhaps I should be allowed to see you this afternoon."

She was speaking very quietly and rather rapidly, as if she were controlling herself with great success. Nevill was interested to observe that self-control was necessary for her. It touched him considerably to see that she was, plainly, so much agitated and moved by what was, after all, a comparatively uneventful operation. Of course the whole thing was, itself, an event; but, within those brackets, all had been really very smooth and successful.

"Well; that's all your news?"

"I think so."

He put down his cup and settled himself a little lower in bed.

"I've got a heap to say," he said. "Just give me a cigarette. I can manage a whole one, I think. Thanks. . . . And a match."

She held the match while he lighted up. He drew one or two whiffs; and then began.

"Yes; I've got a heap to say. You won't think me a prig, will you, or sentimental, will you?"

"My dear!"

"Because I really do think it true. Of course it may just be a reaction; but — well; I don't think it is. I've been thinking a lot — Aunt Anna."

"Yes, my dear."

"I've been a smug beast. That's the beginning. Did I ever tell you about the *Pietà* at Frascati?"

"I don't think so."

"Well, she and I saw it together, you know — Enid, I mean."

He saw her catch her lower lip in her teeth for an instant. She looked a little pale, too, he noticed.

"Oh! No," he said, thinking that he understood. "That's all over. It's not about her; at least not much. It began with the *Pietà*. We both said we couldn't bear it."

She nodded. Her face was set in a kind of rigid attention.

"You know what I mean — suffering, and all that. It didn't seem to fit; it seemed morbid, and all that. Well; I don't think that any more, now."

This time she did not even nod: but her whole intense air assented. She seemed waiting for some *dénouement*.

"It began when Enid threw me over," he went on, closing his eyes for a moment or two. "It was . . . was awful. Well; I did the wrong thing. I see that now. I might have run amuck; I see that now. But that wasn't really much temptation. But I did what was very nearly as bad — I deliberately turned my back. I would not suffer. So I turned to other things; and I rode and I played the fool and I bathed with Jim; and I tried to say to myself that I'd be just an animal — a pagan — oh! A decent sort of animal. I honestly don't think I could be the other. And then I found that I couldn't."

He looked up at her again; and her attentiveness seemed even deepened. She was looking at him with an extraordinary kind of strain in her face, as if watching some process of which she knew the end. She did not even shift her eyes when they met his; it was as if she was looking at a picture. It was almost painful so to be stared at. Again he closed his eyes. He was feeling rather exhausted again. He would make haste and finish.

"I couldn't because . . . because God would not allow it. (I am trying to tell you simply, my dear. Don't think me a prig, please.) First of all came the blindness. That set me thinking

— that, and the pain. I did have headaches, you know, besides, that I wouldn't tell you about. Then came what Handsworth said to me. . . . That startled me. About my father, I
mean. . . . And then came the operation. . . . My dear, I'm a
born coward. I . . . I loathed it."

He opened his eyes once more. She was leaning back in her
chair; her elbow was on the tea table, and her hand shaded
her face. Well; it was easier so.

"But I didn't see it all till yesterday — and last night. I
couldn't sleep, you know. I thought and thought. And — I
don't want to whine, you know — but the pain has been sickening. . . . Well; I believe I see the point now. He wouldn't let
me alone. First Enid; and then, when I tried the other, Pain.
. . . I give in, Aunt Anna. I don't want to run away any more.
I — I — well; to put it in five words, I don't hate the *Pietà*
any more. I see the point. It must be there. Bang in the middle of the woods too. It's — it's everywhere, you know.
There's no getting away. So one may as well accept it."

He looked at her again, himself moved very deeply. It had
cost him a good deal to say it. But she, apparently, was even
more affected. He had heard no sound; but she was wheeled
about in her chair, and her face was hidden altogether in
both her hands.

"My dear, I'm sorry. But I've done; that's all. At least,
that's all about that part. You understand, don't you?"

He saw her bow her head in assent. But she didn't show
her face.

"There's one more thing; and then we'll talk about something else. I've been dawdling frightfully, you know. I've done
nothing whatever. Now that simply won't do. And I want you
to tell me what's the best thing, when once I'm back at Hartley.

Then she lifted her face, and he saw a look in it that he had
never seen before. It was expectancy still; but it was more.

"Oh! No; I don't want to do anything sensational, you
know. I'm not going to be fanatical or — or anything like
that. But I must do something. It may be Parliament, or it
may be —"

He stopped dead.

"What's the matter? Why do you look like that?"

Was it the pressure of her hands on her face? Or was it some strange effect of the half-light coming through the thin silk curtains?

She rose as he looked, and slid forward on to her knees. He winced a little as her hands came down on his own right hand that lay outside the coverlet.

"My dear," she said, "I am sure you can do a great deal." (Her voice, too, was strange; it had neither tears nor laughter in it; but there was an extraordinary tone in every word. Her face, too, was tense and *exalté,* yet without even a touch of hysteria.) "You can do a great deal: it is for this that — that all this has happened. Nevill, my dear boy —"

She was holding his hand firmly and tenderly. He said nothing.

"Nevill, my dear; you know what you made me promise? . . . That the doctor should say nothing to me that I didn't say to you. Well, I have his leave: he has commissioned me —"

"Is it cancer?" he whispered sharply.

"No, my dear; it is not cancer. He has told you the truth too: but he has not told you the whole truth. My darling, you won't be afraid. I know that. You have been splendid — splendid. He has done what he could, you know; and now your real work must begin. We are Christians: that is why he has allowed me to tell you so soon. . . ."

Over his whole body he felt the light sweat break out, like ten thousand delicate needle points touching his skin. A solemn deep pulse began to beat at the base of his throat. A light film passed over his eyes; and all that he looked at — her face, the screen by the door, the coverlet on which lay his hand enfolded in hers — all these things appeared to swim a little and then seethe as if in granulation.

"We are Christians, you and I," said Aunt Anna. "There is nothing at all to fear. You had the Sacraments — I know that — before you knew. There is nothing to fear. . . ."

"Tell me."

"You will be able to see till the end, they hope. But they are not sure; though he removed most of the . . . the . . . but he could not remove it all. It must grow again, and —"

"How long?" he whispered.

"Three or four months at the most," whispered Aunt Anna.

(5)

There was no sound at all in the room as she bowed again her face upon her hands, and then, opening them, rested her lips upon his fingers.

Out of the far distance, checked and muffled by the intervening houses, came the moan of a siren; died again; rose again, and was silent. The coals in the grate fell inwards with a soft crash.

When she lifted her eyes again he was lying quite still. He had raised himself a little in bed as he had asked how long; and she had felt him sink back once more as she had answered. Now he was quiet again, with his eyes open and looking out beyond the end of his bed as if he were thinking gently.

She did not speak. She understood something of that strange alchemy of the mind which requires time that a new and unexpected element may be allowed to sink gently down and be assimilated. It was not yet sunk in; he knew what she had said; but he did not yet know that he knew it. He was quite pale; his lips were slightly parted; but there was no reaction of shock or of alarm. He was taking it in gently, as his manner was.

She had formed no plan as to how she was to tell him. She herself had known it, down below there in the drawing room, as soon as she had seen the surgeon's face when he came down from his business. He had told her gently and kindly, just so much (and no more) as she had told Nevill just now.

She had tried to frame some form of words by which she in turn might tell him; and had given it up. She must wait till she saw him. Then she would know. . . .

The surgeon had, at first, utterly forbidden her to tell him for at least a week. She had answered that then she could not face him at all: she had said that Catholics were not like other people; that death was not to them as it was to others.

He had consented at last; for she would not hear the proposal that anyone but herself should tell him. It was from her lips, and hers only, that he must learn it. He had consented at last; or rather had withdrawn his absolute prohibition. But he was emphatic that he did not formally sanction it: and that she must bear the responsibility. . . .

Well; she had done it. And Nevill lay here silent, meditating.

There came a tap at the door. That must be the nurse coming to take her away. At the sound he moved his eyes and looked at her; and somehow the expression in his face was not quite what she had expected.

"Aunt Anna —"

"Yes, my darling."

"Aunt Anna—" he hesitated. "I see what you meant just now — when — when you said that about my work. . . . I'll try. . . . Give me a kiss."

But even the tone of his voice was disconcerting. Had he, then, not quite understood?

Chapter VI

(1)

Masterson was standing, a little before sunset, at the great west door of Hartley, nearly a month later, waiting for the arrival. His nose and mouth twitched a little, as his manner was, in apprehensive thought, and his eyes looked cross, as he stared out at the straight ribbon of road still empty of any vehicle. Behind him the house seemed as empty, and dead quiet. To right and left of him the shrubberies stood like troops of watchers, russet behind, evergreen in front, and the whole arch of sky before and above him glowed with rose and amber.

The household had had time to assimilate the news by now. It had been delivered to them, with an appearance of miserable anger that had ended in choking emotion, by Mr. Masterson himself, three weeks ago, one day after dinner. On that day, at the moment when the six potentates of the servants' hall were accustomed to rise and file out, that they might partake of sweets in what was known as the steward's room, the three of them who were there sat still, all except Masterson, who rose to his feet, holding a letter in his hand.

Mrs. Fanning desires me to read you all this letter," he said, without comment or introduction. Then he had read it, from the heading *Elizabeth Street* down to *Yours truly, Anna Fanning*. He began, as has been said, with an air of wretched anger and sharpness; he ended with a number of curious sounds in his throat. Then the entire household had risen to its feet to speed the solemn line of three potentates who went out in silence.

An air of marked silence had deepened on the house. Even Jim had been subdued; he had said to Masterson one day in the pantry that he supposed it was not proper to ride on Charleson's back just now. (Masterson had agreed, shortly.) He rode out on his pony every day, solemnly: he did his lessons with the governess from the Vicarage at unusual hours; he went to tea three or four times with Mr. Morpeth, and once at the Vicarage itself. He went to Mass on Tuesdays and Thursdays, and knelt all alone in the Hall pew, very grave and observant.

To those who truly love houses for themselves, it is perfectly evident that these have moods as marked as their per-
sonalities. Hartley was mourning; there could be no doubt
about it — mourning in a manner altogether inexplicable on
the grounds that its inhabitants were sorrowful. There was a
silence in it, as of meditation. When Jim forgot himself and
shrieked with the collies on the lawn, the house appeared to
lift its eyelids for an instant and then drop them again. At
night it seemed sleepless; during the day drowsy and
thoughtful. The maids went swiftly and timidly along the
gallery to open and shut the windows, as if fearing to disturb
its deep contemplation; the gardeners looked up at it suddenly, as if it had sighed: but it only looked at them, as if
brooding.

Masterson was not the man to analyze his sensations; but,
as he stood here in the sunset light, he really did not know
how to comport himself interiorly. Exteriorly, of course, all
must be as usual: he must step forward and open the car
door when it came, with that indescribable inclination that
asks for no acknowledgment: he must stand while the travel-
ers went into the house, and then turn to the car to help
Charleson with the rugs and the handbags. (The bigger luggage had arrived by train and wagonette nearly an hour ago.)
He must then go back into the hall, and through it without a
word. But his interior emotions were so mutually exclusive
that he could make nothing of them at all. The master and
mistress were coming back after a month's absence . . . and
the master was coming back to die. Yet he would not be carried in like a dying man — (so much Masterson had learned
from the maids) — he would be fully dressed, he could walk
without support; he looked pulled down, of course, yet conva-
lescent. What, then, were the emotions suitable to such a
bewildering situation? Masterson shook his head slowly.
That was perhaps the inevitable, and the best, symbol. But
his grief was genuine and deep. He was a very loving and
faithful servant.

He suddenly straightened himself as he saw far away on
the straight drive in front a black object approaching.

(2)

The actual arrival was completely devoid of any sensational element.

When the car was drawn up, and Masterson opened the door, Mrs. Fanning, who was sitting nearest to it, smiled and nodded and came out. She turned when she reached the ground, yet not fussily.

"How d'y do, Masterson? All well?" said Nevill as he came past. There was no more than that; Masterson said: "Yes, Sir Nevill"; and the boy went into the house. He was in the gray suit in which he had gone away.

When, three minutes later, the butler went through the hall with the rugs and a bag, Mrs. Fanning called out and said they would have tea, here, at once. Nevill was sitting on the sofa, opening his letters, and his aunt standing by the fire, drawing off her gloves. It would all have been completely natural and ordinary, if only it had been possible for the butler to have said that he hoped Sir Nevill was well. . . . They were still in the same position when he brought in tea. Here, too, for the first time, Masterson saw the appearance of the boy's head. . . .

When the butler had once more gone, Nevill looked up from opening his last letter:

"Where's Jim?" he asked.

"I arranged he should be out to tea with Mr. Morpeth, my dear," said Anna easily. "I thought perhaps you'd find him in the way for the first hour or two."

Nevill smiled, genuinely enough.

"This won't do one little bit, my dear. Remember what we agreed on Monday? We must make no difference at all — none at all. We won't have any more funerals till we've got to."

She glanced up, and down again: and he saw a sharp pain in her eyes.

"And you mustn't look like that," he said tranquilly. . . . "Yes, please, two lumps as usual."

Aunt Anna was finding the situation hard in a completely unexpected way. She had arranged herself, of course, according to Mr. Morpeth's advice, and had determined that no weakness should come from her side: it was to be her part to accept things serenely, not to be sentimental and to support her nephew steadily in the same attitude. But on the second occasion on which she had been allowed to see him in the nursing home, she had found him almost disconcertingly unsentimental himself. He had announced to her that he didn't

want to talk about it any more at all, until it was absolutely
necessary; that he had thought it all out; that he would talk
necessary business later; that he was extraordinarily grateful for all her loving kindness, and . . . and, would she be
good enough to tell him when Charleson would be allowed to
come up and give his clothes an overhauling? Since then he
had talked with a geniality that very nearly amounted to
hardness. It was disconcerting, she thought, when you have
screwed yourself up to a difficult attitude in order to help
someone else, to find that the someone else has already assumed that same attitude with hardly any difficulty at all.
He had discussed with her what he would be allowed to do
when he got back to Hartley; he had told her that Sir Arthur
Handsworth had informed him that the headaches would
recur within a couple of months, and that thence, until the
end, there would have to be a good deal of morphia. . . . He
had begun a few sentences as to the future of Hartley, and
had broken off before finishing them. He had said that he
very much wanted to see Mr. Morpeth as soon as it was convenient, after the return to Hartley. And he had done a little
business with a typist whom he had caused to come in for an
hour each morning, so soon as it was allowed.

He looked almost shockingly natural now, as he slipped his
feet up on the sofa, after finishing his cup of tea, and leaned
back, staring up at the ceiling. Of course he did not look as
he had looked six weeks ago: his tan was gone, and there was
a certain gauntness about his temples and shoulders, as well
as a few hollows and lines in his face. But she had seen him
constantly, and these things were not startling. It appeared,
then, almost shocking that he should look so nearly himself
to one who knew what Aunt Anna knew. . . .

Presently he yawned.

"I'm dog tired," he observed. "Carriage exercise, I suppose.
Aunt Anna —"

"Yes, my dear?"

"There are some things to be fetched from the station tomorrow, and a couple of workmen. Do you mind seeing that
the dogcart and the farm cart go in to meet the ten-
fourteen?"

"Why, yes, my dear, of course. But what —"

"I'm not going to tell you," he said. "Wait till you see. And I
want someone from the village who can build. Who is there?"

She mentioned a local workman.

"Then I want him too, at the same time. . . . No, really, I won't tell you. It's just something I want done in the garden. You'll approve, I think."

His eyes twinkled at her pleasantly. Then he yawned again.

"I want — I want — lots of things. Where's Father Richardson? And I want Jim; and Mr. Morpeth."

"I wrote to him two days ago. He'll be coming tomorrow morning, I expect."

"That's all right then, I'll see him, if I may, as soon as he comes. By the way, Aunt Anna —"

"Yes?"

"Just say something to Masterson, will you? Tell him I mustn't have any scenes — that I want everything to be exactly as usual. As I said, I don't want any funerals at all just yet. There are some things we shall have to talk about, of course; but we'll do them by degrees. I think Father Richardson is the first."

"Do you want to see him?"

"I want," said Nevill quite deliberately, "to tell him in your presence that I'm sorry for the extraordinarily disagreeable way I behaved to him in the pavilion that day in the summer, you know; and that I behaved even more disagreeably about him after he'd gone —"

"But, my dear —"

"Don't be afraid, Aunt Anna, I'm not going to be melodramatic and Sunday-eveningish and have reconciliations and all that. And I'm not going to take back about his not running in here as he likes: that wouldn't be fair on you. But I must just say that, you know, and have done with it. Then I must see Cunningham about the estate. That'll take hours, I suppose. And then I want to have several long conversations with Jim. But I think we'll put that off for the present. I'm making Maresfield one of his trustees, you know, as I told you."

"Yes," she said. "I'm glad. I like him."

"Well," went on Nevill, "how about Father Richardson coming to dinner tonight?"

"But, my dear boy, I thought you were to go to bed early, and —"

"After tonight I will. But I want to have one decent evening first. Let's pretend that I'm not going to die, for once."

She could not speak for a moment. It seemed to her that he was surely callous. Was he going, after all, to die defiantly? But he went on, as if he knew her thoughts:

"My dear; you must let me do it my way. Don't think me a brute. I'm not meaning to be."

(3)

It was with considerable inward apprehensiveness that Father Richardson, in his cassock and long French coat, stood and rang at the front door bell at five minutes before eight that same evening.

He had had exactly the proper kind of letter from Mrs. Fanning, announcing the news, and had written exactly the proper kind of letter back in response. All was perfectly correct. Then he had heard scraps of information from time to time; and had at last heard, only this morning, that they were expected back that afternoon. Then, on his return from the village he had found Mrs. Fanning's note.

He was apprehensive first because he did not know in the least in what state he would find his host, and secondly because he did not know what to say to him. He was perfectly competent in the confessional; that is to say, he would always give the proper answer founded on the soundest principles; but this was not the same thing as to make suitable remarks under social circumstances. It was all the more impossible to decide upon what he should say, owing to his ignorance of how he should find his squire. It was a piece of information, at any rate, to know that Nevill would be at dinner.

But he was not prepared to be greeted by Nevill in the hall. At least he had pictured to himself an invalid's chair. Nevill certainly looked gaunt and thin; and the top of his head looked odd somehow — the priest could not see more than that) — but he was in evening clothes, and actually standing on the hearth as his guest came in. Mrs. Fanning was not there.

"How do you do, Father? So glad you could come in at such short notice. . . . Oh! Here is Aunt Anna."

A rustle sounded overhead.

"We took nearly three hours to come down," he went on. "Can't bear speed just yet, you know. . . . Here's Father Richardson, Aunt Anna."

The two shook hands.

"And look here, Father," proceeded Nevill, still standing with his back to the fire. "Business first; before we go in to dinner. I want just to apologize to you quite simply for my behavior in the pavilion one day, soon after I came back from Rome. You remember, no doubt. Well; I shouldn't have spoken like that. I'm sorry. My aunt was there; so I wanted her to be here too, when I apologized. That's all. I'm sure you forgive me. Let's talk about something else."

The priest was taken completely aback. He had met with frankness from Nevill when he had first come to Hartley: slight constraint had followed gradually, and finally the little scene in the pavilion. From that time there had been courtesy, but nothing else. That frankness should ever again exist in their relations was an inconceivable thought. Certainly the priest could not have done it himself: but, beyond that, he could not imagine anyone else doing it. It will be remembered, possibly, that one of his principles was never to apologize.

"I am sure, Sir Nevill —" he began.

"My dear Father, I know you forgive me. Probably you had forgotten it long ago. In any case let us forget it now. At least, I hope you will try to."

The priest opened his lips; and closed them again. And, simultaneously Masterson threw open the dining room door and announced dinner.

Conversation was exceedingly difficult. So soon as they sat down, and the priest had said grace, he asked dutifully after his host's health.

"Thanks very much, Father. I'm first-rate," said Nevill shortly. "Got to lie up, you know, and take things easily. But I thought I'd have my own way tonight for once. . . . How perfectly charming the place is looking!"

His tone did not encourage any further discussion of his health. They talked of this and that in the beautiful old room, about the round table. Nevill made some remarks about his pheasants. Aunt Anna, whenever a pause came, slipped in a small and appropriate topic; and Father Richardson did his best. But Nevill's health — even after the shocking announcement made by letter to the priest, by Mrs. Fanning, a month ago — never recurred.

Two alternative conclusions began to form themselves in Father Richardson's mind. The first was that the announcement had been gravely exaggerated; that Mrs. Fanning had written excitedly, and from imperfect information, and that the matter was not nearly so serious as had at first been thought; the second, that Nevill was so morbidly terrified of the prospect before him that he would allow no mention of it at all. These two conclusions came up before the priest's mind — now one, now the other — and he could not decide as to which was the more likely. But surely he must find out, he thought; for, plainly, it was his duty to be of service to this spiritual son of his! He did not relish the prospect; but he had that kind of courage which a conscientious and rather timid man can always summon up; and he determined to probe as soon as an opportunity presented itself.

It came immediately after Mrs. Fanning had left the dining room. Nevill came back from closing the door after her; pushed the port across to the priest and sat down without speaking. (Certainly he looked extraordinarily tired; but not worse than the other had seen him before now.) Here then was his chance.

He helped himself to a glass of port.

"Sir Nevill," he said. "May I say something?"

The other looked up quickly and almost sharply.

"Why, certainly, Father."

"Is it possible that Mrs. Fanning's report to me was exaggerated? You seem so much better than I could have imagined from what she said, that I hoped — I hoped —"

Again the young man looked up. But he did not speak.

"— Well; I hoped perhaps that you might really be on the road to recovery."

He did not quite like the expression on his host's face. There was a curious musing look in his eyes that appeared to be considering the other's features. The priest told himself he must be courageous.

"If that is not so," he said, "I was wondering whether perhaps you would not care to have a talk with me? I — I have noticed —"

"Yes, Father; what have you noticed?"

"Well, Sir Nevill. I am your parish priest, you know. And it is my duty —"

"Father, I know that. Please tell me what you have noticed."

There was nothing in the least offensive or peremptory in the young man's tone. But the priest was conscious of a quickening of his pulses. It was really rather like the beginning of that unhappy little scene in the pavilion.

"I have noticed that you have not been to the Sacraments," he said bravely, "since — well, certainly not since last Easter. I suppose you went to Holy Communion then, as every Catholic is bound to do, but —"

Nevill stood up; and the priest stopped short. He was certain a scene was coming. There was an air of tenseness in his host's face he did not like. He looked tactfully down at the tablecloth.

"Father, I must ask your pardon again. I — I am rather irritable, I am afraid, nowadays. You have done quite rightly in speaking to me. Well; I can reassure you. I went to the Sacraments on the day of my operation; and I have been every week since. I propose to go on with that, now that I am home again. Shall we go into the hall and have a cigarette?"

"And — and your health, Sir Nevill? I suppose from what you say —"

"My health? Well: I shall certainly be dead before Easter; probably much earlier. You will pray for me, will you not? I think I hear coffee coming. Shall we have it in the hall?"

"My dear," said Nevill, as he took up his bedroom candlestick, "I very nearly lost my temper again. And I was really entirely wrong this time. I forgot that I was one of his sheep; and only remembered that I was entertaining him. But he's a good little man; and only did his duty."

(4)

A voice answered Masterson and bade him come in, at a quarter to eleven on the following morning.

"Good morning, Masterson. Yes: I'm pretty fair, thanks. Have they come?"

"Yes, Sir Nevill. And I've had all the things taken out to where you told me last night."

"That's all right. Tell them to wait. I shan't be ten minutes. I've shaved and had my bath already."

He looked ghastly this morning, thought the old man. He was lying on his bed in a dressing gown, with his head on the pillows. A breakfast tray still rested on the table by the bedside.

"Very good, Sir Nevill."

"Masterson."

"Yes, Sir Nevill."

"Mrs. Fanning spoke to you no doubt. Well; I want to say something too. It's this. I'm going to die, you know. There's no doubt whatever about that. But I don't want to make a fuss. Just let everyone know that I want things as usual — that I want everything to go on as it always has as long as it can. It isn't that I'm not grateful to everyone. I am. And — and very much to you, Masterson. . . . That's all."

The butler turned without a word, and groped his way back to the door.

Jim and the collies were, of course, making excursions in all directions on the lawn, circling back, as to a center, to where four or five workmen and a large flat article, shrouded in sacking and straw, about four feet in height with a semi-circular top and a flat base, waited at the river wall about thirty yards to the left of the water gate. Mrs. Fanning was in the pavilion, ready to be called as soon as her nephew came out. She had no more idea than anyone else what in the world was forward, nor why the workmen were here, nor what it was that they had brought. A short inspection of the shrouded object told her nothing; and she did not ask.

Now and again, as she sat there, her eyes wandered out over the park, as well as towards the house. She had written to Mr. Morpeth a couple of days ago, as she had told Nevill last night, suggesting he might come and see her as soon as they got back. She wondered whether he might not come this morning. Then, as she turned once more, she saw Nevill coming down the steps, and got up to meet him.

Certainly he looked gaunt and shrunken — even more so than last night. It was seeing him here, she thought, in the morning October sunshine, coming across the familiar lawn which seemed to her a kind of natural background for him, that made her notice it. Jim was already with him, she saw, and Jill was becoming hysterical.

"So here we all are," he said as he saw her coming down the steps. "Yes, you come too, Jim. I want your criticism."

"My what?"

"I want to know what you think of it when you see it."

"See what, Cousin Nevill?"

"It," said Nevill.

The workmen saluted as the three came up. Nevill wore a soft summer hat pulled rather forward to hide his scars. He returned their salute.

"Thirty yards from the water gate and thirty from that tree," he said, pointing. "Oh! I see you've marked the place. That's all right. Why; here's Mr. Morpeth."

That unromantic figure was just coming up from the garden gate that opened on to the park.

"Look here," said Nevill to the men. "You understand the idea, don't you? It's the number three drawing I'll have — the one I sent back marked. I want the bottom edge of the — the relief to rest just on the edge of the wall; and the shallow arch to be built over it."

He gave one or two further directions, and answered a few questions. Then he turned with Anna to meet Mr. Morpeth.

"And you might just unwrap the thing," he said over his shoulder. "I want to see it before you actually put it up. Yes, Jim; you stop and help them. Aunt Anna, you might as well stop too, won't you? I want to talk to Mr. Morpeth alone."

"I'm going into the house directly," she said, "you can have the pavilion to yourselves."

As she sat in the morning room, looking out over the garden, and trying in the intervals to add up accounts, once more she was aware that she was disconcerted.

Somehow the whole matter was not happening in the least as she had rehearsed it in her own mind.

She had had her agony all alone, first in the drawing room of the Nursing Home, when the news had been told to her; then for nearly thirty-six hours, in Elizabeth Street; and this had culminated, and, more or less, ended its acute stage, as she told Nevill that he could not live. From that agony she had viewed and mapped out the prospect before her, and her first little shock was Nevill's manner of receiving the news. She remembered the silence that had followed her announcement, and the sentence or two in which he had told her that he understood. His manner had been unexpectedly composed, and she had thought it to be that perhaps he did not realize it altogether.

But the next time, and the time after that, he had seen her, he had made it even plainer than before that she was not to be of service to him in the way she had hoped. She had thought that he would need helping and encouraging; and he did not seem to need it at all. He had, certainly with complete tenderness, told her that he understood that she cared very much, that he was grateful, and that he could not forget that; but he had also told her, with what seemed rather like heartlessness, that he must do it his own way, and that his own way was not to talk much. Since then he had been as if nothing were the matter. Again she had thought that even now he did not realize what death meant, nor, perhaps, that it was so near him. But he had maintained that attitude resolutely; they had talked scarcely at all of the future: she had been distressed that he had asked for a typist instead of employing herself to do his letters. She felt that somehow she was excluded from his intimacy instead of being, as she had thought it would be, admitted to it even more completely; and it had all been emphasized and driven home by the fact that he had kept up his secretiveness even after reaching Hartley; she did not understand his apology to Father Richardson: she thought it unnecessary and even rather unnatural; she did not like his keeping from her the affair for which the workmen had been engaged in the garden.

She was thinking over these things again, even while she worked at the household books. She finished them at last, and leaned back; and, as she did so, saw the group gathered about the workmen break up, and Mr. Morpeth's solid figure turn towards the house. Nevill, she saw, went back with Jim towards the pavilion. She stood up at once. Mr. Morpeth was coming to see her. Well, she would talk to him frankly. Was it possible, after all, that Nevill was not taking it right? Yet she almost hated herself for the doubt.

(5)

She met the old gentleman in the hall looking, of course, exactly as usual. He made his stiff little inclination and bade her good morning once more.

"Do come in," she said. "I'm so very glad you came."

He followed her in without speaking again; and she set him on the sofa that ran out at right angles from the window. She sat in her writing chair, turned towards him.

"I'm glad you've come," she said again. "You know your letters were no good at all. Why wouldn't you say more?"

He regarded her placidly.

"Because I did not know what to say until I had seen both
Sir Nevill and yourself. And I do not quite know even now
whether I can be of any service."

"But of course you can," she said, with a touch of impatience. "I have been following your advice absolutely. And I
don't think it has answered very well. But perhaps I'm
wrong."

Mr. Morpeth put his hat carefully beside him on the sofa,
his gloves on the top of his hat, and his stick on the floor.
Then he folded his hands. He resembled a stockbroker who
composes himself to listen to a client.

"Will you be good enough to tell me what you think is un-
satisfactory?"

And then, without warning, her emotion rose and gripped
her, in the presence of this man who had been a kind of her-
ald and interpreter of every grief that had come on her during the last six months. Up to now she had followed his advice, she thought, punctiliously; she had driven down every
wave of emotionalism; she had striven to bear herself in
Nevill's presence, and not only there but, largely, even when
she was by herself, with the kind of stoicism that this old
man had recommended. And, amazing as it seemed to her
now, she had (she thought) succeeded.

But the result had been miserable: she felt more oppressed
than ever. Sentimentalism, certainly, might be one evil; but
surely heartlessness was a greater. After the Enid incident
Nevill had seemed, at least for a little while, to turn to her
for comfort: she did not forget how he had said that the house
was "theirs" again. But he had hardened steadily, it seemed;
even the approach of death itself had not softened him as she
wished, or sent him to her for comfort as she had hoped. He
did not want her, after all. The bitterness rose in her like a
swift tide.

She leaned back a little, and gripped the arms of her chair,
looking out of the window as she talked.

"It is all as miserable as it can be," she said in a rapid low
voice. "Certainly it has succeeded in one way. He . . . he
seems to care nothing at all. He will scarcely speak of it, even
now. Perhaps he is stunned. I don't know. But I know that I

am of no use to him; and I thought you promised that I should be. He does things without me. It's all very well to talk of not 'softening' him; but I never dreamed he could be hard like this. . . . And — and I hate myself for thinking it all. He — he is perfectly splendid in one way. But it's unreal: I know it's unreal. How can he keep it up? And even if he can — what's the use? What's the use of anything? Does he really not feel?"

She was beyond tears. It appeared to her that she had driven these down so far into her soul that they could never rise again. She had cried at night, again and again; and morning by morning she had awakened to dry tragedy. But she had not understood till this moment that it was actually with Nevill that she was angry.

"I see," said the old gentleman.

She wheeled on him.

"You do not see," she cried. "You do not see one hundredth part. I wrote to you from London again and again; and you hardly answered me. I don't think you see anything at all — nor feel it. . . . Don't you understand? . . . He cannot live more than three or four months. His pain may begin at any moment. He will not say a word to me. . . . You're not a woman: you don't understand me: you look on us all as machines. . . . Or think we ought to be. It may be all very splendid; but it isn't Christian, or human. And he's just the same. And I never suspected it. . . . Have you been writing to him too, in the same way? He's a different person — simply different —"

She found herself walking up and down to the window and back, without any consciousness of having risen. All the emotional side of her that she thought to have crushed down had risen and taken possession. She felt miserable as never before, even in her agony in London; she felt humiliated and vindictive. As she wheeled at each turn, she glanced at her visitor. He was sitting in the same attitude, with his eyes cast down. And at the third look at him, again her anger and wretchedness broke out.

"The whole thing is spoiled," she said. "And it might have been so — so beautiful. It isn't death that I fear for him now. I had thought that to be the worst of evils. But it's this — this dry heartlessness. He's building a new summer house in the garden; at least, it's something like that. And he's not told me a word about it. He behaves as if nothing was the matter at all. He won't let me do anything. He wouldn't let me come up while he had breakfast this morning. He would only see me once a day in London. He's dying like" . . . (her voice shook violently) — "like a dog."

"Have you spoken to him like this?" came the dry voice from the sofa, yet not unkindly.

She was in her chair again now, without any conscious volition.

"Of course I haven't," she said.

"He has been to the Sacraments," observed the dry voice after a pause.

She was up again, restless and unhappy; and yet, before she had finished, again she was back in her chair.

"Yes; he has been to the Sacraments. I suppose I ought to be glad. But it's all wrong. He's not right, somehow. I don't know what's wrong. He's behaving like a machine, not like a human being. And — and —"

She could not go on. Those tears which she had thought dried forever came welling up from her soul, and burst in a great sob. Her throat was contracted as if gripped from without. The brutal tragedy which she had tried so gallantly to meet, with the hardness that had been advised to her, melted and broke in pathos. In that moment she saw herself and the lad she loved, from without instead of from within: he was dying, and there had risen between herself and him an impalpable hedge of misunderstanding that had sprung from no root that she could discern. They were alienated; and it was the shadow of death that had done it — the very shadow in which all hearts ought to meet and be at one. She threw her face down on her arm and sobbed.

Then she heard the voice beginning, as she grew quieter.

"Mrs. Fanning," it said, "I am going to commit a great indiscretion. I am going to betray a confidence. But that will come presently. May I ask you first of all whether you wish me to speak what is in my mind; or to say the . . . the usual things?"

"Go on," she sobbed. "It's no use."

"I take it that you wish me to speak my mind? Very good. The first thing that I wish to say is that I think you have behaved magnificently. You have done the hardest thing any human being can do. You have acted and spoken contrary to your heart, because you saw it to be right."

She shook her head, as she felt for her handkerchief. But she could not speak.

"That is all the praise I have to give. I am speaking to you now, Mrs. Fanning, as I have never spoken to you before. You wish to know, no doubt, why it seems to you that our plan has failed. As a matter of fact it has not failed, as I shall endeavor to show you presently. But you think it has failed because you are giving way to jealousy again."

It was like a dash of cold water on her soul. She had spoken to him of her jealousy before, when Enid was concerned: but it seemed to her a kind of outrage that he should dare to speak of it now. She sat up, white and trembling. His eyes were still cast down; but he raised them as she stared. She dropped her own. Jealous? How could that be? Of whom was she jealous?

"Just at present," went on the unrelenting voice, "you are hardly thinking of your nephew at all. You are thinking of yourself. You complain that he is hardened. You mean by that, that he turns to God and to the Eternal Verities for comfort instead of to you. You are jealous of God."

(A very curious little ring came into the old man's voice.)

"I will show you presently that that is so. But you might have guessed it. At least, you ought to have assumed it, now that he has come back to the Sacraments. But in your heart you have been thinking of yourself. In words and actions, as I have said, you have been magnificent; since you have acted contrary to your jealousy: but, within you have not really conquered jealousy at all. First you grudged your nephew to a woman who might, for all you knew at first, have been worthy of him in every way; and now you are grudging him to God. You want him for yourself. He is not naturally a stoic nor heartless. You ought to have recognized that. Then how can he appear so? . . . You had not thought of that, had you?"

She was feeling with every word that he spoke, not its truth so much as its inevitability. He did not seem to her so much to be a person saying true things, as a voice revealing the obvious. He appeared entirely dispassionate; she could not even resent what he said. Her own tension had been too great during these past weeks for her to understand the truth for herself. Now it was unrolling before her as if mechanically.

"I said two things just now," he continued. "The first was that I must betray a confidence; and the second that I would prove to you that our plan had not failed. The two are one."

She watched him, as a dreamer looks on his vision, as he drew out of the breast pocket of his gray buttoned coat, a pocketbook, and out of the pocketbook three or four sheets of paper.

"Here are two or three letters Sir Nevill wrote to me from the nursing home. I will read to you a few extracts."

He turned the pages, searching for what he wanted.

"Here is the first —" he said. "Listen, please, Mrs. Fanning.

"'It is quite impossible'," he began to read, "'to describe the change that has come to me. I want to talk to you about that later. But I feel a completely different person. I used to fear death, and hate it. Well, one part of me fears and hates it now; but that part is not myself any more. I suppose it's the physical side only. My self does not fear it at all. I am doing exactly what you wrote to me. I am not talking to my Aunt about it more than I am obliged. She seems to understand perfectly, without that. I suppose it is Pain that has done this in us both. She has been splendid — first about my trouble in the summer, and now about this. I suppose she has known the truth of things all along.'"

(He paused; put away that sheet and turned another — all with an astonishing deliberateness.) "Here again," he said. "'I know I can keep it up now. I feel at present that I could keep it up forever; but I suppose that is not so. But at any rate I can do it for three or four months; and I shan't need to more than that, Handsworth tells me. Of course, I have bad times; when I am terrified; when I want to run to my aunt like a child. But I know I should be ashamed afterwards. Death seems to me now the greatest thing in the whole world. As I said in my other letter, myself knows that perfectly well. I can't form any kind of picture of what happens after death; and I have given up trying. The main outlines of course are all right — Purgatory and so on: but I can't even begin to imagine what it will seem like.'"

(Again he paused and turned a page.)

"'The bad times I spoke of are simply physical. I recognize that now. But I see that they are not my self. They are rather like the bad times I had in the West Bedroom when I first moved in, as you advised. I see one has got to get through them before one can do anything; and that one can only get through them by accepting — and not either resisting or yielding to — the thing that's behind. I am putting it very badly; but I hope you will know what I mean. I must thank you —'"

He stopped.

"And there is one more passage about you, Mrs. Fanning — Ah! Here it is.

"'I can see that my aunt has her bad times too. But she is quite splendid. Yesterday I very nearly gave in. I had had a bad night; and I think she must have had one too. But I remembered what you said, and held tight. I could only do it by playing the fool rather; and I think she must have thought me rather heartless. I am sorry if she does. She manages to keep steady without anything of that sort. Well, I can't always.' I think that's all I need read, Mrs. Fanning."

He folded the sheets and put them carefully away again in his pocketbook. She sat motionless.

"I kept these," he said, "in case they were needed. I thought perhaps they might be, from the tone of your letters. And I brought them with me this morning for the same reason. I need not say that your nephew has no idea in his mind that I could ever betray his confidence. Well; I have done so."

She passed the tip of her tongue over her lips before she tried to speak.

"Nevill wrote that?" she said.

"Sir Nevill wrote that. But that is not all. If you will look out of the window, Mrs. Fanning, you will understand even better."

She rose without a word and looked out. The lawn was not fifty yards across, and she could make out well enough what it was that the workmen had uncovered at last. Nevill, on the terrace, was leaning on his stick, with his back nearly turned to her, and Jim, by his side, was holding his hand. They were both looking at the great arched relief in blue and white that leaned against the wall.

She turned back from the window, and with tearless eyes saw that the old man was smiling.

Chapter VII

Snow began to fall at dusk, just a week after Christmas; and when, on New Year's morning, Anna came out of her room and along the gallery the ceiling overhead was as bright as no mere sunshine could make it, with that clear radiant clearness that the morning light on snow alone can give. The coffered roof ten feet above her was visible in every detail of its blue and gold, and the floor beneath, with its rugs and its chairs and the great shining piano and the gilded pipes of the organ, resembled a Dutch painting, so minute and perfect and homely it all appeared. She went along the gallery, herself extraordinarily pretty and fair-complexioned in that enchanting light, and tapped softly on the door of the West Bedroom. There was no answer; but she was conscious of a vibration from within. Then the door opened softly and Charleson's face looked out. He nodded emphatically without a word, and stood aside to let her go by. Then he closed the door behind her and himself went across into the bathroom so as to be within call.

The room was as unterrible as a death chamber ever can be. It was not quite that yet; but the end could not be far off. The lad's headaches had begun again midway through November; and the doctor had been there every day onwards. Sir Arthur Handsworth had come down twice from London; but had confessed that there was no more to be done. Morphia had been administered from time to time when the patient's pain drove him into delirium; but at all other times he had refused it. A week before Christmas stupor had set in; and, it was thought, blindness. He talked a little from time to time, but had seemed to recognize nobody. Last night, however, he had awakened from unconsciousness, and Anna had had half an hour's talk with him. He had then fallen asleep; and an hour later the news had come to her that he still slept. He had told her, before he slept, that his blindness had come back.

This morning the daylight on the snow outside brightened the room wonderfully, though he would not be able to see it. The white light lay on the high polished furniture, the

frames of the engravings, the folds of the chintz curtains —
and above all, on the face of the dying man and the linen
round his swathed head. He lay high in bed, his shoulders
supported by piles of pillows and his hands hidden beneath
the silk quilt. He had already been shaved and washed; and
the folds and sunken hollows in his cheeks were vivid and
sharp. His eyes were turned on Anna as she came in, and he
smiled as he heard her step.

"That's you?" he said.

His voice was quite distinct and very quiet. It was not horrible in any way.

"Yes, my dear," she said; and sat down by his bedside.

"Give me a kiss if you don't mind."

She rose again, and kissed him very softly on his forehead,
just below the wet bandage. The drug-like smell was very
clear to her as she did so.

"How long have I got?" he asked, as she sat down again.

She did not pretend not to understand.

We must wait till the doctor comes," she said.

"You wired for Algy, as I asked you last night?"

"He'll be here by eleven."

An extraordinary steadiness of will had come down on her
since her last desperate struggle more than two months ago,
when she had turned, in the morning room, on the old man
and poured out on him the last drops of bitterness that her
soul contained. Since that time, when she had learned of her
boy's own attitude to death — how he too had "his bad
times," how he hid them from her, not because he did not
love her, but because he loved her enough to trust her as well
— since the moment when she had looked out of the window
and seen the great Robbia *Pietà* leaning against the wall of
the terrace, and had understood what its erection meant —
since then she had had not even a temptation to resentment.
It appeared to her now that it had not been death itself that
she had feared for him, but its circumstances; and that as
long as she could keep her attention fixed on death itself, its
circumstances could not distract nor trouble her. Since that
revelation she simply had not to struggle at all: it seemed
that she had been lifted clean out of the realm where resentment is possible, where one soul demands attentions

from another, where the small passions rage and fret, and faults are found and grudges cherished. It was like . . . it was like the world, she thought this morning, on which the snow had fallen — a wide white shining realm where roughnesses have ceased to exist, where colors have gone back again, not into the blackness that is their negation, but to the whiteness which is their source and end. The whiteness is deathly cold, but it is not death, it is only silence; it lights, too, the dark roofs and corners of a house within, though it lies heavy on the house without.

She could think, too, broadly and passively now, instead of actively and energetically. She could look back on the past, without even a flush of personal feeling — on Enid and her own jealousies, on Nevill's disturbing detachment, on the long chain of miseries — her omens, her terrors, her apprehensions, on the growing crescendo of Nevill's sickness, his headaches, his sudden blindness, on the horrors of the operation and the drawing room where she had learned the news that he must die, on her dull wretchedness at Hartley again and her flare of anger in the morning room. She saw these now to be but steps of an initiation of which she had never dreamed — an initiation into a secret of which she had thought that she already held the key. She had been told long ago of how serene she seemed — Nevill himself had spoken of it to her when her husband had died: she knew now, in the possession of real serenity, how false the other had been. It had been a trick of temperament — no more than that. But now she could look on this boy's gaunt face against the pillows, at his closed eyes, his wet-bandaged head, on the angles of his shoulders so sharp through his night-clothes, without clenching her teeth. . . . She could watch him and talk to him slowly without even desiring to take his hand: she could picture his dying here before her eyes, without horror. He lay here — she knew that now — in the room that she once feared so much; in the bed where his father had died before him — he lay here, as certainly a part of the enormous Design that enfolded and used them both — as reconcilable with the vast Sacrificial Love that was its secret — as Jim himself playing with the collies on the lawn. The line between good and evil was not the same as the line between pleasure and pain; it was the line rather between the acceptance and the non-acceptance of destiny.

"I don't think there's anything particular to say," said Nevill, after a pause. (He spoke slowly, but quite distinctly, with short silences between his sentences.)

"No, my dear, I don't think there is."

"Handsworth said I should get my senses back before I died, didn't he?"

"Yes. He said it might be so."

"Well. . . . I suppose this is it?"

"It may be so," she said.

"Aunt Anna."

"Yes, my dear."

"You'd better tell Father Richardson to bring the Viaticum . . . while I'm conscious."

"You'd like him to come at once?"

"Directly after Mass, if he will be so kind. . . . And I want to see Jim after breakfast. . . . It isn't eight yet?"

"Not quite."

"You're going to Mass?"

"If you don't want me."

"I'm all right," said Nevill. "Charleson was here just now. . . . The nurse has gone down for breakfast, I suppose?"

"I think so."

"Aunt Anna."

"Yes, my dear."

"I do want to say something after all. . . . I want to be quite sure, you know. . . . You're perfectly happy, aren't you?"

"Yes," she said, quite deliberately. "I'm perfectly happy."

He smiled, still with closed eyes.

"I knew you were. It was ever since the *Pietà* was put up, wasn't it? I'm sorry I didn't tell you about it before; but I had to do it my own way, you know. . . . You'll let it stop there, won't you? . . . I told you about Frascati, didn't I?"

"Yes, my dear."

"Well; it all dates from that, you know. Those are the two points. . . . I began to see that after my operation — as soon as I knew I couldn't live. I saw the point then. Everything fits in perfectly, you know, as soon as you see that. Enid, and everything else."

"My dear, you're too tired —"

"No, I'm not. . . . I want just to say it, bang out. . . . What an ass I was! . . . I wanted to be a Jesuit first, you know. . . . Then I was angry when I was told I mustn't be. . . . Then I tried Enid — instead of God, you know. . . . And then I was routed out of that. . . . And then I tried just being happy alone — Nature . . . all that rot, you know. . . . And then I got ill. . . . I see the point now . . . you do too, don't you? . . . of course you do. . . . So here we are, back again, at the beginning. . . . You do really see, don't you?"

"Yes; I see perfectly," said Aunt Anna.

(2)

Jim went upstairs all alone, very sedate and quiet, as soon as he had had breakfast. He looked back from the top of the stairs, to see if his mother was still looking up at him from the hall. She was; and she nodded reassuringly. He hastily turned away again. He felt a little ashamed of having needed that reassurance.

Then he tapped cautiously on the door of the West Bedroom.

It had been an agitating morning for Jim. So long as Cousin Nevill was really properly ill, nothing much interrupted life. He had, of course, to go very quietly always along the gallery; and the piano was not to be touched at all — not even *God Save the King* with one finger, in F, was to be rendered upon it. Neither were the collies to be brought indoors at all, on any pretext whatever, for fear that Jill might bark. Otherwise, however, matters proceeded as usual, or, at least, as they did when Cousin Nevill was away from home. There had been one rather disconcerting morning when Jim had heard curious sounds issuing from the bedroom door; but he had been commanded to use the back staircase for the rest of that day; in the evening a baize door arrived in a cart and was taken upstairs; and thenceforward life was normal. He was aware, of course, that Cousin Nevill was very ill indeed; but after a week or so this did not greatly affect his imagination.

This morning, however, at breakfast his mother had "looked funny," as he would have expressed it; and she presently told him that he was to go and see Cousin Nevill and say goodbye to him. Jim had inquired whether Cousin Nevill was going to go to Rome again; and his mother had then told him quite plainly once more that Cousin Nevill was going to die.

Jim's views on death were perfectly formed. He knew exactly what happened. The soul went to heaven, after a spell in Purgatory, and the body went into the churchyard. He blinked rather rapidly when he heard that this was going to happen to Cousin Nevill, and played with his toast. He was not sure whether he wanted to cry or not: but crying was discouraged by his mother. And, in any case, for about six weeks he had not seen Cousin Nevill at all; and six weeks is a vast period. He looked up at his mother presently.

"And I shan't see him any more?" he said. "After now, I mean?"

"Not till you die yourself, my dear."

"When shall I die?"

"I have no idea at all," said Anna gravely. "But there's something else too I want to say. Cousin Nevill has been very ill indeed: you know that, don't you? Well, he looks quite different now; he's much thinner and he's wearing a — a sort of white cap on his head. You mustn't touch that white cap — it's wet; and you mustn't be frightened, will you?"

"No, Mummy," said Jim very softly.

"Stop as long as he wants you; and if he doesn't say anything, ask him whether you're to go away. If he doesn't answer, just come away on tip-toe. I shall be in the hall all the time, and Nurse will be in the bathroom. So you won't be afraid, will you?

"No, Mummy."

Here then he stood; and his heart hammered in his breast.

Nothing happened when he tapped; and he tapped again. Then the door shook ever so slightly; then it opened and Nurse Deacon's face looked out. (Jim loved Nurse Deacon entirely; she gave him a rusk sometimes; it was pleasant to meet her face first.) She smiled and stood back: and Jim went in.

He stood on the threshold suddenly petrified. There was a solemnity and there was a curious smell, too, for which he was not prepared. The room looked, too, frightfully white, in the reflected light from outside. Then he saw a face on the pillows, with the white cap over it; and the face did not appear to him to be Cousin Nevill's at all.

"Jim," said a very odd voice, very low.

Ah! That was Cousin Nevill all right then. He had really not been quite sure till he heard that; but it was a whisper which he had heard before, in games. He went forward, with the nurse's hand on his shoulder.

"Good morning, old man? I hope you're quite well. That's you, isn't it?"

"Good morning, Cousin Nevill. . . Er, . . . may I kiss you?"

"Kiss him very gently," said Nurse Deacon's voice.

Jim approached the bed resolutely, and put one knee upon the edge. The nurse's hands held him, that he should not slip. Then Jim administered a careful kiss to Cousin Nevill's left cheek. It felt "funny" to his lips.

"That's all right," said Cousin Nevill. "Now sit down, old man; and don't shake the bed." The big eyes turned to Nurse Deacon and seemed to give some sort of signal. The nurse said nothing, and passed round the foot of the bed. Jim's eyes followed her a little anxiously, as she went through the door into the bathroom on the further side. But she did not absolutely shut the door, as he had feared she might.

"Jim, old man. . . . You're not frightened?"

Jim brought his eyes back again to that rather grim face; and determined that he must not be frightened. He cleared his throat, which appeared to him rather dry.

"No, Cousin Nevill. Not at all, thank you."

"Jim; there are just three things I want to say. Listen, won't you; and tell me if you don't understand."

"All right," said Jim.

"The first is this. . . . Do you remember about the Grail?"

"Yes, Cousin Nevill." (He felt he must be very polite, somehow.)

"Well; you were right and I was wrong. . . . It isn't in the woods; at least not more than anywhere else. We needn't go and look for it. . . . It's anywhere where we are."

Jim's eyes wandered vaguely round the room. He did not understand one word.

"You've got it already," said Cousin Nevill. "Don't lose it, will you?"

"I don't understand at all, Cousin Nevill."

Cousin Nevill did not appear to take this in; for he immediately went on. He simply did not seem to hear. His eyes looked very far-away and bright.

"You don't really find it, till you drink it, you know. You must tilt it right up when the time comes, and drink it all. Then you see it."

Jim cleared his throat rather more loudly. Cousin Nevill seemed to him rather foolish. He raised his voice a little.

"I don't understand, you know," he said.

Cousin Nevill's eyes blinked a little. Then he smiled.

"Poor old man! No, I know you don't. . . . It doesn't matter. . . . Now number two. What's number two? . . . Oh, yes. . . . I'm going to die, you know; and then all this place will belong to you and your mother."

This was more intelligible.

"All of it?" asked Jim.

"Yes: all of it. . . . Every single thing. . . . And when you're twenty-one it'll all be yours. You'll be a good boy, won't you?"

Jim sighed. He had not expected this sort of conversation.

"And you'll always be good to your mother. . . . Won't you?"

"Yes, Cousin Nevill."

(Cousin Nevill was obviously ill and must be humored.)

"You'll be Sir Jim, you know."

This did not seem interesting.

"Shall I?" said Jim.

"Now do you want to say anything to me? Because number three is Goodbye."

Jim considered.

"When are you going to die, Cousin Nevill?"

"Very soon now."

"Oh! . . . When you're dead, may I bring Jill into the house again?"

A glimmer passed over that gaunt face that was like a bad mask of Cousin Nevill; and his lips twitched as if he were trying not to smile.

"Of course, old man. Bring her into the house at once, if your mother'll let you. Tell her it's my house, just now, . . . if she says No. . . . And then see what she says. . . . Anything else, old man?"

"Shall you be buried in the brick room in the churchyard, Cousin Nevill?" inquired Jim, who saw that he was expected to make conversation; and really could not think of anything else.

"Yes, old man. . . . In the brick room. That's right."

"May I go down and look, when it's opened?"

"Better not do that, old man. . . And you'll say a prayer for my soul, won't you?"

"Oh, yes," said Jim indifferently.

There was a pause.

"Well, old man, I think we'd better have number three now. . . . Just press that button. . . . Behind my head." Jim found an interesting sort of handle attached to a string lying on the pillow. He had not seen anything quite like that before, and examined it with interest.

"The white thing, Cousin Nevill?"

"Yes. . . . That's it. Press it right in."

Jim pressed it; and there followed a faint ringing sound from somewhere else. Then the door of the bathroom opened and Nurse Deacon appeared.

"Now, say goodbye, Jim. . . . And give me a kiss."

A curious change had passed over Cousin Nevill's face; his eyebrows seemed flickering up and down, and his mouth was very tight. He was breathing rather quickly, too, through his nose. Nurse Deacon, for once, appeared slightly agitated too: she came round the bed very swiftly.

"Lift him up, please," said Cousin Nevill, in a sharp whisper.

Once more, then, Jim planted a knee on the bedclothes, and administered a kiss. Cousin Nevill's cheek seemed even funnier than before: it was all wet, and rather cold.

"There!" said Nurse Deacon, in rather a quick voice. "Now go and tell your mother I want her at once."

"Goodbye, Cousin Nevill," observed Jim.

"'Bye, old man," came the whisper from the bed.

(3)

At some remote point in time, detached, it appeared, from all previous times and experiences, Nevill became aware that he was in bed, and that his consciousness was still attached to his body. But that, at first, was the utmost extent to which his perception reached. It was as if he were in a little circle; within the circle there was the sensation of touch and even tiny and minute sounds; there was also a faint taste on his lips; but nothing else; and beyond the circle there was nothing at all; there was, at first, even, no memory. He knew nothing except that he was in bed — where, how, or what it was all about, or what time it was, or whether it were day or night — of these things he knew nothing.

Then, like transparent walls, this circle began to glimmer into shadows — at first, only, of memory. He began to remember his last experience — it was of talking to Jim.

Towards the end of that talking a new kind of pain had be-gun in his head; and he remembered that he had told Jim to ring the bell; because he was aware he would presently col-lapse again, and Jim mustn't be frightened. He had been also able to hold on till Jim had kissed him; he had been able even to say Goodbye: then, when he had heard the soft clos-ing of the inner baize door, he had let out his agony in one long moan. The pain had really been intolerable, partly be-cause it was so new and unusual.

Things that had happened after that were vague and con-fused. Aunt Anna had been by him for certain moments; he had smelled a particular fragrance which he associated with her. His arm had been lifted and his hands held; and he re-membered supposing that someone was giving him morphia again. But he had not been able to attend to these things. The blue lights in his head that quivered before him like a permanent lightning-flash shaken from side to side, had oc-cupied him entirely. All this had gone on for a long time; he had heard someone moaning ceaselessly; and it had been quite a while before he had understood that it was himself. Yet once more, as after his operation, he had perceived that Pain was one thing, and himself another; and, by stretching the whole force of his will, he could keep them so. He must not let the Pain come any nearer: he knew that. That had been the last thing that he could remember. And now, here he was back again; and just at present there was no pain — at least, no actual pain. It was like hearing a tune hummed over, only.

After a while not merely memory but present perception began to disclose itself, as the circular wall melted yet fur-ther; and he understood that someone once more was holding his hand — someone on either side. That seemed an inex-pressible comfort. He moved his hands a little to reassure himself that it was really so. Then his right hand was relin-quished, but he twisted it to show that he wanted it to be held again: and another hand came down on it. But, simulta-neously, a damp, faintly stinging thing passed across his forehead, down his face, and into the corners of his mouth. He sucked greedily, and was aware of the taste of lemon. That was delicious. He felt, too, a very faint, soothing breeze all over his face.

Again the circular walls had grown even more transparent, and he perceived, he did not know how, that there were people in the room.

He must ask who was there. . . .

But there was no answer. He wondered whether he really had spoken. He would try again. . . .

This time there came an answer; and he knew it for Aunt Anna's whisper.

"Yes, my darling?"

Ah! That was all right. He was really in communication with people. But hadn't she heard what he had said? He must say it again. . . .

A voice began buzzing in answer. How could he possibly hear if people spoke so fast? They must speak slowly. He would say so. . . .

That was better. . . .

Oh! Algy was there, was he? Then it must be after eleven. He was to have been here by eleven today . . . or was it yesterday? Or last week? Well; he was here. Good old Algy! Who else!

Oh! Masterson was here, was he; and Mrs. Templemore . . . and Charleson . . . and Nurse Deacon. . . . Wait: that's too fast . . . Nurse Deacon . . . and . . . and Aunt Anna. But why wasn't Mr. Morpeth here? He wanted Mr. Morpeth. . . . He would say so. . . .

Oh! Mr. Morpeth had been sent for, had he? That was all right. And Father Richardson? Father Richardson? . . . He had been here, had he? And gone again. But would be back soon.

"Speak more slowly, Aunt Anna, please."

That was better; he could understand it like that.

"Father Richardson — has — been — here — and — has said — all the prayers — for the dying —"

For the dying? Was he dying? Of course he was! What a fool he was to forget that! That was why everyone was here.

Dying!

He fell into an interior musing upon the word; and the walls appeared to grow a little opaque again as he meditated. He could only contemplate one thought at a time — the thoughts that he had rehearsed so often lately. Dying! . . . But Death was something quite different. Dying hurt so cruelly because one was still alive. That was no reason for think-

ing that Death would hurt too. Dying hurt because Death
was not come, not because it was. Well; if Death did not hurt;
if Death ended the pains of dying; what would Death begin?
Obviously it must begin something. . . .

He suddenly began to think of the Grail. (He had talked
about the Grail quite lately to someone — oh! Yes — to Jim.)
Well, drinking the Grail was very bitter. Enid had first really
set his lips to it; and then the physical pain had begun a little later. But when the Grail was empty — when the moment
came that the last drops had been swallowed — what then?
Obviously the first long draft of new air must be sweet. . . .

The Grail!

That was the Cup of Sacrifice, was it not? That was why he
had had to drink it; old Morpeth had told him all about that.
It was for his father, among other things.

So here he was, in the bed in which his father died; and in
the same room. What a fool he had been about this room! The
shadows were only dreadful, so long as one looked at them
from the light: there was no real harm in them when one
stepped forward into their midst. . . .

(Yes; that lemon taste was delicious. And it was very
pleasant to have one's hands held.)

Then he began to wonder whether anyone else were in the
room. He was sure Aunt Anna hadn't finished her list. What
about the doctor? He must ask. . . . No; it was not worth the
trouble. He would think about Death instead.

Then, imperceptibly, the walls closed about him again; but
he did not notice them. He was considering Death. . . .

(4)

Once again at some remote point in time, detached from all
experience, he found that his consciousness was still attached to his body; but it was attached in a new kind of way.
He was aware that somewhere in the universe, as if at an
enormous depth beneath the point where he himself stood
poised, great wheels of blue flame were all crashing and
whirling together. The clamor of them was incredible, harsh
and grinding; but they no longer affected him. There was a
loud rasping sound of breathing too, such as he had heard
when his father died. Then, through the crashing and the
gasping, he heard the thunder of a voice repeating Latin. He
was as a man who, at the edge of a huge chasm, himself at

ease and safety, looks down on the tumult below, where great forces strive together. . . .

Dying, then, was still in process somewhere; and he watched with a kind of pity that dreadful conflict that roared below. It was to him, in some sense, that that Latin was spoken; and he understood its power. . . . Here and there he could catch a phrase. He was being bidden to "go forth" in the name of Powers and Principalities . . . of all those great Existences which, he knew now, waited invisible in that wide expanse that was all about him, poised here above the struggle that raged beneath. . . .

It was down there, then, that all those whom he loved waited about his struggling body. He knew they were there, as a man who has climbed to a great height knows, as he looks back, that there in the valley are the fields and the house that he knows so well. They were all in the surge and the stress still — Aunt Anna, and the servants, and Algy, and the old man — who could not be long after, him, now — there in that plane from which rose up the great words of power that battled with the roar of the pulses in his head, and the blinding shocks of pain, and the fighting for breath — and not with these, only or chiefly, but with the rushing tides of evil and revolt that swayed and tossed — seen by him from up here as a great tumbling torrent or a tossing waste of water looked down upon by a man on a cliff. But he himself was far off and remote. . . .

Where, then, was he?

Then, as he considered this, he, too, began to thrill and vibrate. From beneath rose up thin, imperceptible tides; or, rather, he perceived now for the first time that he was in them still; that he was not yet as wholly apart as he had thought from all acts and volitions and experiences. But they were thin and subtle, as befitted his new condition; and he saw that he could yet act. . . .

Then a great and piercing sorrow surged through him, not indeed at the memory of his sins and rebellions, but at his consciousness of their very essence. It was not that life passed before him as a series or progress of events, but that the quality of it — as he had lived it — had a thin and bitter aroma which he had never suspected. And, as there met him from above that piercing breath of the world to which he went — as clean and sharp and radiant as the light reflected from snow — these two tides mingled in him like a chord of sorrow and love and ecstasy. . . . Every image faded from him; every symbol and memory died; the chasm passed into nothingness; and the Grail was drunk, and colors passed into whiteness; and sounds into the silence of Life; and the Initiation was complete.

The End

Robert Hugh Benson Titles from Universal Values Media

A WINNOWING

Mixing such seemingly incongruous elements as social satire, near-slapstick, and obsession with death, *A Winnowing* flays Edwardian society in terms that bring to mind the comedy of P. G. Wodehouse, and the black humor of Evelyn Waugh.

ISBN 978-1-60210-005-3   224 pp. $20.00

NONE OTHER GODS

This gentle, yet profound satire relates the story of Frank Guiseley, a young man who drops out of college and tries to force God to instruct him personally on what God wants him to do. People of all faiths can appreciate the growing frustration and bafflement Frank experiences until he finally stops trying to make God listen to him, and starts listening to God.

ISBN 978-1-60210-006-0   312 pp. $20.00

THE COWARD

A young man is faced with challenges and manages to fail at every step. He becomes convinced he is an irredeemable coward, and only then begins to find courage. In a damning indictment of close-minded Edwardian society, a supreme act of courage on the young man's part is mistaken for yet one more craven act.

ISBN 978-1-60210-007-7   312 pp. $20.00

AN AVERAGE MAN

Possibly Benson's finest achievement, *An Average Man* rips to shreds the assumptions on which Edwardian upper class society believed civilization itself was built. Worldly success destroys one "average man," while it presents another, afflicted with seemingly endless and crushing defeats, with the opportunity of practicing virtue of a heroic stature.

ISBN 978-1-60210-008-4   340 pp. $20.00

LONELINESS?

Loneliness? examines the life of a woman who sacrifices everything to be accepted by people who can see her only in terms of her singing ability and the roles she plays on the stage, and who is abandoned by them when she can no longer fit into their preconceived ideas. *Loneliness?* may be Benson's least known, yet one of his most insightful — and entertaining — novels

ISBN 978-1-60210-010-7   298 pp. $20.00